SHADOW'S SON

THE BROKEN REALMS CHRONICLE
BOOK TWO

T.J. FISHER

SHADOW'S SON

Published 2025 Broken Realms Publications
Copyright © 2025 T.J. Fisher
Paperback ISBN-13: 979-8-9918967-0-2

For Tolu.
Your friendship is humbling and inspiring.
Thank you.

CONTENTS

1. Settling	1
2. Restored	4
3. Fractionation	10
4. Subjugation	15
5. Yepenzi	19
6. Shaded	24
7. Renewed	33
8. Gariisurii	37
9. Reflection	45
10. Colloquy	49
11. Souk	57
12. Preparatory	62
13. Challenge	68
14. Changes	74
15. d'Kehbezii	78
16. Kaazann	89
17. Delineation	95
18. MiiKette	103
19. Assurances	112
20. Sing for Me	118
21. Ceremony for Ermyjek	125
22. Plan of Action	136
23. A Look	139
24. Particulars	147
25. Shuttered	152
26. Resolve	161
27. Assignment	165
28. Knowing	170
29. Ingress	173
30. Bloodlust	178
31. Nuisance	184
32. Loyalties	189
33. Friendship	197
34. Homecoming	204

35. Reassigned   210
36. Cupun   215
37. Puppets & Master   223
38. Discovered   227
39. Separated, Again   232
40. Black Mass   238
41. Doubt   243
42. Slipping   248
43. Midnight Conclave   252
44. Flight & Fight   258
45. Nomad   268
46. Power Supply   270
    Review   273

    Reference & Pronunciation   275
    Tribes & Beliefs of the Isokanii   293
    Isokanii Language Rules   297
    Acknowledgments   299
    About the Author   301
    Also by T.J. Fisher   303
    Sneak Peek   305
    Irigiim   307
    Castell   313

The Klaroni Cordilla
Ebony Spires
The Forest
Velqona River
The Kingdom of Klynotia
Aria Bells
Lost Lake
Meldari River
Lisica River
Aradyll
Charione River
The Kingdom of Lorea
Loresten Lake
Map of the Broken Realms
Taynos River
Retgrat Peninsula
The S

Temple

Torchid
Letza Mera

Ristern Mera
Byloraan

Night Crystal Quarries

The Shadow Desert

Jearut Oasis

Slate Cliffs

Storm Gulf

Falls

Magician's Cloister

The Tears of Apelgo

Corsair Cay

Tilkt Point

Reana

CHAPTER I

SETTLING

ZERREC

An oily beard glistened in the fenny light of the parted canopy drapes. It wasn't enough illumination to see details, but in the glow of his swirling, dimming essence, Zerrec could make out the fading brown, lightly salted hair that frizzed into an arbitrary rectangle on the pillow below. The same hair crowned an aged face, which looked to have seen too many winters. This would be the oldest body Zerrec had ever bridled, and he doubted he would keep this form for long, preferring younger and slimmer physiques to last him longer. But this body was practical. Using it would serve his purposes.

The inconsistent, ethereal form of his essence floated above the snoring man. Zerrec was weak from traveling. The distance from his physical death in the Forest to the old man's bed chambers had been further than he wanted to traverse in such a vulnerable state; the last part of his journey had forced him to use the whims of the wind to conserve energy. Weeks had passed since he'd been in a physical body, and Zerrec credited his ability to subsist outside of flesh for so long to his centuries of building strength and experience.

He flickered, nearing the end of his vitality.

At least he was where he desired to be, and at the moment, it was all that mattered. Taking over this body would be a delicious sort of justice. Even without a physical form, he could taste the feeling of revenge. It would be delightful to bring Terren low through the proximity of familiarity. Zerrec flickered again. He needed to integrate himself into this new body soon before he lost the ability to siphon a life force and evaporated into nothing.

Strong once again, he mused.

The idea made him undulate through colors with excitement, the brief intensity causing his new host to stir. Zerrec tempered himself, dimming his essence to the flicker of a candle. When his host snored deep once more, he let himself be pulled into the new habitus with the man's next inhale, settling into the back of his host's mind and getting his bearings. Rooted feelings of mistrust and betrayal colored the host's current dreams. That was something to deal with later. Zerrec's immediate focus was on the strength returning to him, though only a trickle. For now, his presence would remain unnoticed until he was ready to take full control, but he could already feel the advantageous aspects of his new host. Despite the age — and this pleasantly surprised him — this was going to be his strongest body yet, so maybe he wouldn't have to abandon it as soon as he thought.

Once his essence was no longer weak, he could begin to wind his way through every fiber of this body, tangling his own soul in and around the one occupying this man. Then, in a swift movement of control, choke out the original host to prevent any fight for dominance. It didn't suit his tastes, taking over the body of someone known to be willful and stubborn, it made imitation more difficult. Reports of this host's cruelty were spread far and wide. Even hermit mountain men like Taam and Sael knew the stories that surrounded this man, of his merciless beheadings and vindictive campaigns to eradicate those with the gift. It would oblige him to play a game of methodic and precise navigation during the transition, but he was Zerrec's best choice to be close to his target enemy and remain inconspicuous.

The thirst to live again was all-consuming, and it would be a test of patience not to usurp his new host before he had complete control.

The simplest of things left him wanting. He didn't need food or drink as an essence, but already the thought of once again partaking of roasted garlic and rosemary chicken, fresh salted tomatoes, and mulled blackberry wine made this host drool in his sleep. Being able to taste such things once again would be a luxury.

But Zerrec also needed to remember to act nothing like himself in order to flawlessly convince Terren and Kiira this was the king they knew. His task for the next few weeks, while he gradually gained strength, was to ingrain specific mannerisms into his consciousness to prepare for accurately portraying Grayten. Any changes he wanted to make needed to be subtle and calculating so as not to draw attention. Unfortunately, he could not observe the king for long before making his gambit. Terren, Kiira, and Liem would pay for the damages they wrought, and when he made his move, it would be swift and without mercy, maybe even in the same way he'd lost his last host — with a sword through the chest.

Zerrec's anger stirred the king.

Patience — yes, that is the key to their undoing. Observation and patience.

With that thought, Zerrec nestled into his new home.

CHAPTER 2

RESTORED

TERREN

"It's time," Liem said.

The words ripped Terren's eyes from the book in his hands to turn a questioning gaze upon the prince before zeroing in on the hand resting on his wife's forehead.

A week had slogged by since Zerrec's defeat, and with Kiira in a forced slumber, if the words just spoken were no lie, then this was a long-awaited moment. Liem had used his limited medicinal knowledge with castings to help her heal faster, the evidence of it showing in a slimmed frame and weighted eyes. Still, knowing the good his brother-in-law's actions did the past week did little to ease the tension of worry knotting Terren's shoulders.

"Do not look at me like that, Terren. Kiira is my twin, I can tell she's ready to wake," Liem snapped.

Terren sighed. A week of close quarters and worrying relentlessly over Kiira had only worsened the tension between Liem and himself. If only he could make the prince understand he didn't dislike him. As it was, their personalities seemed too different to bond. Their conversations since Zerrec's demise were fraught with turmoil, especially after Terren revealed his status as a Shadow Walker and his connection to a Shade Beast. That conversation nearly ended in a duel. He'd hoped that fighting together against an Elder Mage would forge a stronger bond between them, but so far it seemed their relationship as brothers was doomed to dissension. Maybe when Kiira awoke she could act as a buffer, but he didn't count on it.

In the end, none of it mattered. Terren would soon hear Kiira's voice again. He desperately wanted to know what his wife was feeling and to tell her how he was feeling. Since the fight with Zerrec, Kamaria had remained distant and silent. Terren could faintly feel her presence, enough for him to know she was okay, but he missed the easy communication he shared with his Shade Bear, his Yepenzi. All the disquiet fogging his vicinity left him feeling as if he stood on the edge of a cliff, his feet slipping, and with a knife to his throat. Terren straightened. "I trust your connection, Liem, but you said the forced slumber is helping her heal faster. Why wake her now?"

The rigidity in Liem's body eased when he realized Terren would not tell him how they should proceed. "That's true, but her thoughts are restless, and waking her now is not going to do any harm. Besides, my healing knowledge is limited to contusions and minor cuts for use during combat training. As a nature mage, Kiira studied more in healing. She's well rested now and should be able to strengthen the medicinal properties of plants to heal even faster."

"She should not be doing magic while she's still healing," Terren said emphatically.

Liem scowled. "That is for her to decide. For someone who isn't a magician, you have a lot to say about how a magician should use their gift. Kiira knows her limits."

Terren held back bitter words, though they danced along the edge of his tongue. He knew well the bounds of Kiira's limits, having witnessed it during the windstorm, but the prince clearly assumed him imbecilic in matters of magic. If only Liem knew the depth of his knowledge. Living on an island of magicians, even as an ungifted, had taught him much.

Terren snapped the book shut instead of gnashing his teeth at his brother-in-law and moved to his wife's side. "Alright, Liem. You are the expert here." He'd rather be at her head so he was the first person she saw upon opening her eyes, but Liem needed to keep his hands on her temples while he removed the casting. Terren cradled her hand in his, caressing the top with his thumb. Her hands were softer after the weeks of disuse. Callouses still roughened her fingers and palm, but she would gain a few blisters when picking up the bow and staff once again for practice.

Liem gave him an incredulous look but, blessedly, said nothing. With his fingertips pressed lightly to Kiira's temples, the prince took a deep breath before closing his eyes in concentration. Terren kept his focus trained on Kiira, anticipating the moment he could see her beautiful and expressive emerald eyes once more. Tingling danced along his spine at the thought.

Terren clasped her hand tighter as her lashes fluttered, then nothing. Nerves pulled at his gut. Kiira's eyes popped open. She struggled to sit upright, whipping her head to search for danger. Under the casting, she had remained in a state of suspension, relying on the last memory available to her, whatever that was. He'd need to ask. He squeezed her hand again, and Kiira's gaze turned to his. Her fear transformed into elation as she lunged for him, wrapping her arms around his neck in a fierce hug. It nearly choked him, but Terren didn't care, pulling her into his lap to hold her as close as possible. He felt dampness on his skin as she buried her face in his neck. He too, buried his face in her hair of a loosened braid, wild with wisps; unconcerned that it held a week's worth of dirt and dust, tangling his fingers through the curls and knots. In that moment, they shared everything. Relief and joy in equal mixture. Every sound, every sight, every sensation drifted away, including the tightness lodged at the base of his neck. The world was right once again now that his Kiira was back. Squeezing her closer, he whispered, "I missed you."

Eventually, they untangled from their hug. Liem sat across from them, hunched and dejected, and Terren could guess why he looked as such. Though he didn't want to let her go, he let Kiira crawl from his embrace to wrap her brother in a tight hug. Liem was tense at first, but she must have said something because his despondency lifted and he too wrapped her in a bear hug, swallowing most of her in his larger frame. Terren noted the sparkle of tears at the corner of the prince's eyes, though none fell. He lowered his own to give the twins a moment to feel reconnected.

Releasing her brother, Kiira settled back into Terren's lap, making herself small so he could hold her close. He smiled and placed a kiss on the top of her head. She tried to bury herself closer. After several minutes, a dissatisfied grunt floated across the fire. Kiira let out an incredulous huff and wiggled out from beneath Terren's grip to tackle her brother in another hug. Her obvious joy in seeing them both again made Terren smile. It gave him fond memories of Sairah, and he hoped that when he and Kiira returned to Klynotia, his sister would be happy to see him.

Releasing Liem, Kiira announced, "I'm hungry."

Terren looked at Liem, and they both cracked a grin at the bold, uncomplicated declaration. Turning back to Kiira, he said, "If Liem is willing to hunt and begin cooking, I can take you to the stream nearby to bathe."

Kiira grimaced. "That is probably for the best."

Chuckling, Terren pulled Kiira to her feet and led her to a pack with a change of clothing. Kiira pulled several items out before turning to him with her hands full of unfamiliar garments and a confused look on her face. He rubbed the back of his neck and gave her a sheepish smile. It had been unnecessary for him to buy clothing in Kiiroth when he and Liem traveled there for some medicinal herbs. Kiira had packed more than enough clothing for their Lundemai, but after her ordeal with Zerrec, Terren wanted her to have something to make her feel refreshed. While Liem spoke to the apothecary, Terren had ventured to the nearest clothing shop. He'd been tempted to buy a dress just because he thought it would look nice on Kiira, but then noticed the tanner across the street displaying an uncut deep green hide. The moment he touched the soft, richly colored leather, he decided it would make a perfect vest with double-lined pockets at the back to hold her favorite knives. To complement the new leatherwork, Terren had added a cornflower blue tunic and deep brown trousers. He'd been tempted to purchase new boots as well, but didn't think she'd want to break in new shoes after her hardship. Turning back to the clothing, she rifled through the items for a second before leaning over to give him a light kiss on the cheek, dismissing any lingering doubt that he had chosen poorly for her.

"Kiira, what would you like to eat? I've got a couple of rabbit snares set, or I can try to find a deer, if it's not too early," Liem said from across the camp.

"Rabbit is fine, Liem, thank you," Kiira said, offering a smile.

Liem nodded before strolling into the surrounding trees. Clean clothes in hand, Kiira walked with Terren to the stream, her hand enclosed safely in his.

"You didn't need to buy me new clothes, Terren."

"I know, but in a way it helped me not to be so worried about you."

"How so?"

Terren hesitated, not wanting Kiira to view him as weak, but immediately berated the thought. She didn't see him that way at all. "It makes little sense when I speak it, but it gave me hope. I purchased the clothes confident you would wake soon and enjoy them."

"I think that is the sweetest thing I've ever heard."

They continued toward the stream, content enough to be in one another's company. The steady sound of water met their ears, and Kiira asked, "What did I miss while under Liem's casting?"

"Well, Zerrec is dead." Terren did not include that he still wasn't absolutely sure this was true. Something about the pale wisp he saw exiting the body's mouth still bothered him. He planned to tell Kiira, but now didn't seem the best time to do it.

"That is a relief."

"Otherwise we stayed by the fire and only ventured into town for a few supplies. Rather dull, but I am more than happy to have mundane activities after Zerrec." At the water's edge, Terren pulled her close. "I don't think I'm ever going to let you go again," Terren admitted. "It's ridiculous, I know it is, but I don't even want to let you go to bathe."

Kiira nodded against his chest. "I understand. I know it did not take you long to find me, but it felt endless. Zerrec was ... not pleasant."

Terren tightened his grip. "It took too long. If I hadn't needed to travel back to Lorea to seek Liem's help, I might have found you sooner, but I could not have challenged an Elder Mage without him. Just knowing your brother was there to care for you while I confronted Zerrec made my choices easier, because no matter what happened to me, you wouldn't be alone."

Kiira frowned. He wanted to ask why his statement upset her, but imagined her emotions were still raw and needed sorting. Terren noted to ask her later if he saw any unusual expressions from her.

"You did what you could," she said. "Do not hold the burden of it, as I know you likely will. It's not your fault what happened to me. I put myself in that position."

He gave her a quirk of his lips. "Kiira, if I'm not allowed to blame myself, then neither are you. Zerrec was prepared to confront us both in the marketplace. He had two men restraining me, a knife at my throat, and immediately took away your use of magic."

"Still..."

Terren squeezed before letting her go and tipped her chin so he could meet her lips with his. They would continue this conversation at another time. "The stream is just ahead," he said, pointing in the direction. "I'll wait for you here."

"You're not coming with me?"

"If I came with you, Liem would be waiting a long time to eat," Terren said, his gaze twinkling.

Kiira blushed before biting back a smile. "I'll be quick."

CHAPTER 3

FRACTIONATION

KIIRA

Why could he not leave well enough alone? Have we been apart for so long that he's no longer in tune with my feelings? 'Sure, Liem, I would love to abandon my dinner to talk about the horrifying visions implanted in my mind by a madman just so you can feel you helped me.' Kiira let out an extra huff. *'As if his induced slumber wasn't enough.'*

Finding an ancient-looking oak with drooping limbs, Kiira jumped to the lowest branch and climbed. The rough bark felt good beneath her palms; it matched the prickly feeling coursing through her muscles. She wanted to run away. Sparks of restless energy enticed her to give heed to long strides and disappear into the Forest, a small part of her hoping the goddess would bring her to the sanctuary again. The only thing that kept her from doing so was her promise to Terren to never run again. So, instead, she focused the energy into jumping from one stout branch to another. Disappearing into the thick green canopy would isolate her enough so she could fume alone, but keep her close enough to the camp for Terren to find her if he followed.

Kiira felt better as she settled into a comfortable nook in the tree, but she still tapped her foot, stimulated, and with no other exertion options. In the distance, a small yellow dot and a wispy trail of smoke pinpointed the campfire. This high off the ground, the air moved playfully, teasing the broad, healthy leaves of the oak. She took a deep breath, letting it soothe and carry away some of the fury circulating in her nerves. If she hadn't been so focused on the idea of needing to get away, she might have remembered to grab her bow. Shooting arrows always helped to focus her mind and make her feel better. Then again, she didn't have a target, and it never pleased her to put arrows into a strong, healthy tree. The one time she did so on purpose, Kiira immediately stopped and healed the tree with her magic. A sad smile took her as she remembered the day with her mother. They'd gone to the Forest to work on speed and accuracy with the bow from a distance. Everything was fine until Kiira retrieved the fired arrows. Sharp pricks of pain laced her skin as she pulled the embedded projectiles. Like all Nature Mages, she was connected to plants, and that day, to Kiira the tree cried in anguish as if it were a person. Her mother in no way understood the resolve to never fire arrows into a living plant again. How could she? Her mother did not have the gods' gift. Even after she explained her reasoning for protecting a living plant, her parents seemed to whitewash the pain it had caused her. Whether they did so knowingly or unknowingly, it led Kiira to default to keeping tacit about her feelings. Why say anything for it to be discarded so casually?

Kiira replayed the conversation with Liem. Was she bottling her emotions? Did she need to talk about it? Probably, but he pushed too much too soon. She had just been released from a narcoma casting, and an hour later he wanted to rehash what she experienced under Zerrec's thumb. How could anyone expect her to speak aloud so soon about the things haunting her?

Kiira crossed her arms and leaned against the tree with a discarded breath.

Liem is always a little too nosy for his own good.

She'd been free from Zerrec for a week thanks to her husband and brother, yet she could still feel the phantoms of stinging pain racing up her spine, the anvil hammer blows at her limbs. None of it was real since Zerrec used his magic to manipulate the nerve endings, but that didn't stop the hairs on her arms from rising. Kiira rubbed her bare skin as if it would dissipate the haunting sensation of a thousand tiny cuts. She looked at her arm to see a myriad of actual cuts and scrapes from being dragged across the rough stone floor when she couldn't stand. Those itched, and it was definitely not the same sensation.

An owl hooted several trees away, and the memory of the screams of those she loved the most rang in her ears. She pinched her eyes closed, unable to block the bitter sounds of pain and death. Tears trickled down her cheeks.

Terren, Father, Liem, Gemma, Leo, Mother…

Kiira took a moment to let the pain in her chest subside and her breathing return to normal. Zerrec had no boundaries, no remorse. He had twisted her love of them into a special torture. By far, the worst visions implanted in her mind were that of her mother and husband. Her old mentor had forced images of her mother's death to replay in her mind to break her.

"Except this time it was worse," she whispered. Kiira squeezed her eyes shut, letting tears fall, and molded herself into something small. Zerrec had manipulated the images so her mother looked her straight in the eyes, fear glazing them, mouth open in a forever scream of pain as the Oranta closed around her body before swallowing her whole. Kiira watched helplessly as it happened again and again. She knew it wasn't what had happened; she knew it was a magical memory. Still, every second felt real, and every second was a painful reminder of the day. How she had stood frozen in debilitating fear, doing nothing. The crunch of footsteps below interrupted her spiraling thoughts.

"I said I did not want to be bothered," she called down with an irritated sigh.

"Would it really be a bother if I just sit with you? Keep you warm?" Terren asked.

A light breeze sent the leaves of the heavy oaks birling. The air was cooler than when she had first climbed to this height, and she shivered suddenly. Kiira smiled into her knees; she had secretly hoped Terren would come find her. His presence soothed the dark feelings. "I don't think there's enough room up here for both of us," she called, peering down at him.

"Probably, but I have a blanket if you come down here," he said, holding up one of the thick wool blankets she packed to keep warm while in the cordillera.

"I *suppose* that's incentive enough," she said.

Kiira rapidly made her way down the limbs of the tree, landing heavy in the rich loam. She barely stood before Terren had the blanket and his arms wrapped around her shoulders. She didn't realize how much she missed this until now. Peace exuded from him, or maybe it was just being near the man she loved. They settled against the trunk of the tree, and she curled tight against him, resting her head on his chest. Terren encircled her body as much as he could with arms and legs. They soaked in the sounds of the night. Soft *whoo, whoo, whoos* accompanied the *shahh, shahh, shahh* of the canopy.

After a time, she gathered a fistful of rich soil, squeezing it into her palm. Relaxing, Kiira let her magic flow. Stuck in the rocky cave with Zerrec, her magic had suffocated. Solid earth and metals was Liem's magic school, dead things to be manipulated. Her magic thrived when surrounded by open air, fresh water, and endless expanses of green–all things bursting with life. Kiira's chest tingled with excitement as she felt how happy the surrounding plants were, fed by the nutrient-rich earth. Roots expanded in all directions, tangling in and out of one another beneath the dense forest.

Goddess, I needed this.

Kiira sighed, content, and settled more deeply into Terren's embrace. She hadn't felt this whole since her meeting with Windrah.

Terren kissed the top of her head, holding his face there while he said, "I missed you so much. I was frantic to find you."

"I missed you too," she said, though the words felt like an understatement. "I know you found me as fast as you were able."

"Kamaria had a lot to do with it. She was relentless in her search and I owe her much."

"How is she … you know, after she absorbed Zerrec's magic to save us?" Kiira asked.

"Tired still. I have spoken to her infrequently and she remains in the Shade Realm where she is strongest. I believe she will be well enough with time."

"I am so happy you did not lose her. I know it would have devastated you." Kiira bit her lip as she thought about the bond he and Kamaria shared. Despite his professions of love, despite what she knew to be true, there was still a vapor of doubt in her mind about the status she held in their relationship.

She could feel Terren's smile against her hair. "I am too, but losing either of you would have been devastating."

"You would have learned to move on without me," Kiira said.

"Perhaps … but it would have taken a long time." He moved her hair aside to expose her neck. Terren placed gentle kisses as he said, "I think you underestimate how much I love you Kiira."

In that moment, she promised herself to confront her demons of doubt and soon, so they no longer created this self-imposed barrier between them. She smiled and tilted her head to expose more of her neck. Kiira told herself she believed his words, and some buried part of her did. It was a matter of reminding herself when doubt curled black ideas amid her thoughts. Terren was not one to speak of matters lightly, but something enticing whispered she wasn't enough, that she still wasn't the woman he needed.

After several moments passed, Terren said, "We should go back to the fire. I talked to Liem about what happened. I doubt he'll bring up the subject again, and it will be a lot warmer."

"Okay, but stay near me tonight."

"Of course, I could not stay away from you tonight even if you asked it of me."

CHAPTER 4
SUBJUGATION
ZERREC

I can't stand another moment of this wretch.

Zerrec could remain as an essence inside his bridled host indefinitely, but he longed to feel the stretch of muscle again, and genuine air in his lungs and not a proxy's. He craved to manipulate magic again.

Even if I had more time to observe his mannerisms, I refuse to spend another moment inside this man's mind. Besides, I need to move forward with my plans if I am going to be prepared for Terren and Kiira's arrival in Klynotia.

His host lay sprawled on the couch, another drunken stupor rendering him oblivious to the world, his breath sure to be heavy with the scent of beer going stale. Granted, this drunken state was severe thanks to Zerrec's seductive whisper that tonight's ale tasted especially delicious. It took little effort on his part for the allure of one more drink to take hold in the mind of an alcoholic. Still, Zerrec recoiled at the prospect of dealing with the consequences. The hangover was going to be awful. Inebriation did not rank high on his favorite methods of taking control of a body, but he couldn't deny the effectiveness.

He'd chosen this method for subduing Grayten for two reasons. The king was susceptible to consuming large amounts of alcohol, making it an easy vice to capitalize on, and using the intoxicant blurred the edges of the king's surprisingly acute mind so Zerrec's takeover could be faster. His primary concern was resistance. One of the very first things he noticed when hiding in the back of Grayten's mind was the ruler's wariness of any hint of magic being used. That level of cognizance could damage Zerrec in his vulnerable state and prevent him from acquiring the new host. It would take him weeks to recover from a resistant mind, weeks he didn't have. The process of taking over another person was draining to the strength he had stored, and it was painful for the host. So he had forced Grayten into a relaxed disposition to simplify everything. Plus, once he had control of the body, his magic would return, and he could clear the alcohol with a simple casting.

Examining the current status of his new host, Zerrec admitted to maybe pushing the intoxication too far. Grayten was so drunk he barely comprehended his current location. Usually, this process was better in a more secluded area, but the king wasn't known for sleep-walking, and a random disappearance from the castle would be more suspicious than random painful screams.

Although in this instance maybe the sleepwalking could be blamed on the king's level of intoxication.

He pondered it for a moment, but a drunken king attempting to leave the citadel would be heralded by the Nightwatchman and stopped by the guard. Zerrec decided the rumors of screams amongst the staff were easier to control than visual evidence from soldiers.

Besides, the people of Klynotia were about to see a very different king. Once Zerrec had full control of Grayten's mind and body, only nominal amounts of alcohol would pass his lips. He needed to keep his body in peak condition, even improve upon it, if he was going to accomplish all of his goals.

Zerrec readied himself for what was about to happen. The door creaked open.

Kreshkt!

Zerrec forgot the king had called for a concubine to be brought to him. The image of the woman was blurry, but it looked to be the king's current favorite. Not that it mattered. Zerrec endured this aspect of the king's custom for weeks, hiding himself in the darkest corner of Grayten's mind while he enjoyed the pleasures of the flesh. His attempts to separate himself from the unions were never enough, and Zerrec always felt covered in filth afterwards. The concubines were going to be the first thing he would do away with.

"My king? I have come as you asked," the concubine said.

Grayten mumbled something.

Enough of this.

Zerrec began taking over his new host. He let go of his stringent hold on his essence, allowing it to dissipate through Grayten's body.

The old man's chest twitched. An arm spasmed, and then a leg. A grunt escaped as the king curled in pain, clutching his gut. This was the worst part. As Zerrec became one with the muscles, sinew, and bone, he too could feel the pain–the price for taking someone's body and displacing their soul. His body contorted at unnatural angles as he clenched his teeth. More than one molar cracked, and fire radiated up his jaw. He heard a distant sound of a woman's scream, or maybe that was the ringing in his ears. At least his roar of pain echoing through the chamber covered whatever additional noises his body might make as it contorted from one angle to the next.

He never knew how long it took since time was irrelevant during the changeover, but at some point the excruciation eased into a cramp. Searing heat receded from his limbs and localized along his spine into a prickling sensation. Residual pain twitched his muscles. He'd hoped the excessive amount of alcohol would balm some of the pain, but every drop of the intoxicating ale was consumed as if by fire, and now there was just an aching thrum in every limb. Sweat dripped down his temples, and there was a horrible smell wafting up from a dark spot of something on the floor.

As his vision returned, he caught sight of a gaggle of servants blocking most of the light from the door into the chamber.

This is why I usually do this process in isolation.

"Sire, are you alright?" The question came from one of the many pairs of feet he could see through blurry vision.

Was he alright? Zerrec let a massive wave of nausea pass before slowly straightening. This was why he'd always chosen those who were weaker for his past hosts. He could recover faster, but his current pain and what he needed to heal was a small price for the power Zerrec knew he now wielded. A hint of a smile twitched his beard. He had complete control over Grayten's body.

Zerrec began cataloging the things he needed to heal once he felt more like himself. The tension in his jaw eased, and he felt pieces of teeth crumble into his mouth. Several painful weeks of regrowing the teeth with magic would be needed. In the past he'd cracked teeth during a changeover, but crumbling them was new. Then again, he'd never taken over a host as physically strong as Grayten before. His head pulsed with a steady beat, and he pressed the heel of his hand to the throbbing point on his temple. Despite all that, the energy flowing through his muscles was incredible. He could already tell the advantage he had in creating and sustaining bigger castings.

Now Zerrec just needed a little time to build a magic reserve so he could completely push out Grayten's soul. There was a chance, albeit a small one, Grayten could take back over. His spirit was strong, but Zerrec's hundreds of years of knowledge and experience taking over other hosts was no match for this king, who thought so highly of himself.

"Sire?"

Zerrec looked toward the voice he recognized as the king's personal valet. His scraggly beard hid a smug smile.

CHAPTER 5

YEPENZI

TERREN

Terren's eyes popped open. A stirring at the edge of his consciousness alerted him that something was not quite right. Immediately vigilant, Terren lifted his head to peer into the dawn-shadowed trees, waiting for the slightest hint of what lurked at the edges of their camp. Kiira stirred, and though he wanted to pull her closer, the need to protect was stronger. He disentangled himself with smooth movements, crouching low to make sure he remained a small target, and picked up his sword. Wolfcats were the undisputed highest order in the food chain among these trees. They were camped close enough to the nearest town that the Cats hadn't been a problem, but there was always a possibility of an especially hungry one. Terren also didn't discount the possibility of robbers.

Grabbing Kiira's bow and quiver as well, he stepped away from the fire. Just outside the firelight, he looked back to make sure neither of his companions was disturbed. Luckily, he had the best hearing of all of them, so they were both fast asleep. And better not to wake them, Liem was grumpy with little sleep, and Kiira had dealt with far too much in the past weeks to worry about a Wolfcat. He would yell if he needed help.

With an arrow notched and his sword on his belt, Terren crept through the sentinel trees. His eyes darted from one shadowed trunk to the next and up into the boughs. He listened for the slightest change in usual sounds or calls that may be signals. He'd slipped far enough away from the campfire for it to be an ethereal waypoint when Kamaria poked her nose out from a darkened part of the forest. Relief rushed through him. '*Yepenzi,*' Terren said to her mentally, rushing up to her to rest his forehead on her nose and embrace her snout. '*I have been concerned. How are you?*'

'*I have been better, but I shall recover in time. A few more bushes and some flappers and I'll be as refreshed as the forest after the rain,*' she replied.

Terren smiled as he squeezed her snout a little tighter. Leave it to his Bear to feel better after a few bushes of berries and some fresh fish.

'*Kiira is awake, when? How is she?*'

'*Yesterday. She is … recovering. I can tell she is keeping something from me.*'

'*Do you take this well?*'

Terren sighed. '*Yes and no. I want to know all that happened to her while she was a captive of Zerrec. I understand the appeal of ignoring pain. You know I ran from my past for years without speaking about it to anyone. It tore me up inside until I had you. It's a test of my patience to wait until she is ready to speak of her ordeal.*'

Kamaria huffed. '*I sense you are relieved she is at least alive.*'

'*That I am. Enough about me, please tell me what you have been up to this last week. I have missed our connection,*' Terren said as he reclined on her giant paw, using one of her claws to prop his feet, and taking deep breaths of wet earth as he sunk further into Kamaria's warm fur.

Kamaria settled to the ground, popping a few sticks as she did. For a Bear that stood sixteen meters on all fours, she had a way of making minimal amounts of noise. Hesitantly, she said, '*My dame is nearby, so I have spent some time with her.*'

'*Oh? And how was that?*' Terren asked, though he could guess the answer. Even if he knew the answers to all of his questions, it was nice to have his friend close to him once more. His Bear's presence allowed him to breathe easier, and with Kiira safe by the campfire, his family was complete.

'She is as usual.'

'I'm sorry.'

'It is no matter,' Kamaria replied. *'I have chosen to follow in my sire's footsteps. If she disliked it so much, she should have been more selective.'*

He buried his amusement before she could detect it through their link. Despite her indifferent tone, Terren knew the tumultuous relationship Kamaria had with her dame bothered her. He'd never met the She-Bear that bore his friend, but from Kamaria's stories, her mother was a pill to be around, and she judged Kamaria harshly for choosing to bond like her sire. In some ways, his Bear was a lot like her mother, seeing and speaking of the world with candor.

'Do you still plan to travel to your mother's family?' Kamaria asked.

'Yes, but only if Kiira is up for it. She may wish to return to Lorea or Klynotia for the rest of our Lundemai. After what she's been through, I do not want to push her if she would rather return. It would sadden my family, but they would understand once I explained.'

'Okay, Yepenzi,' Kamaria said, laying her head so Terren was surrounded by obsidian fur. The air was stifling and warm. *'I shall wait for your decision.'*

'I love you, my friend.'

'And I you.'

Terren remained with Kamaria, content to sit with her in silence for another thirty minutes before returning to the camp to find Liem poking at the fire with sleep still shrouding his person like morning mists. The prince exuded a sullen demeanor. Terren didn't know if it was from missing the comforts of sleep or if he was still burdened by yesterday.

Settling opposite the prince, he said, "Has she stirred at all?" Liem shook his head, never removing his fixated gaze from the fire. A poke of his stick sent a flicker of dying ash into the air. "Would you like me to take you through the Shade Realm to return you home more quickly?" Terren asked when the silence became awkward.

Liem paled. "No. Definitely not."

"You won't have the same experience as last time, I promise."

"You're right, I won't, because I will not be going back with you via the Shade Realm."

Flatly, Terren said, "You're going to walk back?"

"No. Since you had the foresight to pack plenty of gold, I will be purchasing a horse."

Terren narrowed his eyes at Liem's rude tone. "That gold is for our Lundemai."

Liem gave him a hard stare. "You can spare a few gold coins for a decent horse after dragging me out of my home unexpectedly, without my father's knowledge or approval, and without a mount. You think he liked discovering me missing with nothing more than a brief letter from you stating I was fine and would return soon? What of my friends whom I assured that all would be well?"

Terren raised his palms to end the argument. Liem's points were valid. Buying the prince a horse was the least he could do.

Kiira stirred and pushed herself into an upright position. "Would you two stop bickering. Terren, I know you well enough to know you packed more gold than we need. We can spare some for a horse."

Liem gave him a smug look.

"Wipe the imperiousness from your face, Liem. You should be grateful he came to you for help. I would be in worse condition if he had not humbled himself enough to ask for your assistance." Her brother tried to argue, but she forged ahead. "*Knowing* full well you do not like him and would be thoroughly boiling at the news of my capture."

Liem looked at him, and he lifted his palms, shaking his head. The prince was looking for a reason to fight, and no one could pay him enough to get in the middle of the twins. Terren agreed with Kiira, but he was not about to make the atmosphere around camp unlivable by saying as much.

Seeing Terren wouldn't make himself an easy mark, Liem deflated, properly chastised. "You are ... correct." After a pause he added, "I will admit my main reason for not going back via the Shade Realm is I too want to see some of the world outside Lorean borders before going back to ... expectations."

Kiira softened and nodded. "I understand."

"If Liem is not in need of transportation, are we to continue our journey, Kiira? We can return if you do not wish to go to the Shade Realm," Terren said.

"Of course we will continue!" Kiira smiled at him. "I want to meet your family."

Relief spread through his chest. "Then we will rest one more day and leave in the morning." Standing and stretching, Terren said, "Shall we all go to the town today to look for a horse?"

Kiira snorted. "Definitely. Liem would not know a good horse from a lame one."

"Hey!"

CHAPTER 6

SHADED

KIIRA

"Kiira, are you alright?" Terren asked while turning Tempest to look at her.

She had tried to hide it, but she hadn't been able to keep from biting at her lower lip as apprehension built in her, and apparently Terren had eyes in the back of his head.

Terren lowered his voice. "If you would rather—"

Kiira shook her head fiercely, cutting him off. "I am just going over what happened. How I could have handled the situation differently."

Terren's brow scrunched as if he didn't believe that was the whole truth, but he didn't push for details. "Hindsight always gives clarity. There were things I would have done differently in the confrontation, too, like fighting harder against the men holding me."

Kiira turned her gaze to him. "He would have killed you."

"I told you, Ishaiio, I am not that easy to kill."

She eyed him incredulously. Terren did not know Zerrec like she did. The men who held the knife at his throat had not worried her, but her old mentor's erratic tendencies and mammon of power made him far more dangerous than any mere armed guard. Terren may not be easy to kill, but Shadow Walker or not, his life had been in danger the day she was captured.

"We can camp outside the walls tonight if it will make you feel better," Terren said.

Kiira nodded. "I would prefer to get through the city as quickly as possible. Everything is still so fresh in my mind and"—she shuddered—"after Zerrec's cave I would prefer to remain in the open."

He smiled gently. "I understand." Terren dismounted from Tempest. After removing her saddle, he hobbled her and gave her a pat on the rear. She skipped a bit, off to find a grazing patch of her choosing. "Do you want to hunt or settle the camp?"

"Hunt. Use some muscles sorely abandoned," she said, pulling her bow from the sling on her saddle.

He nodded. "Would you like to spar after our meal? I will take it easy on you." Terren grinned, but it came off more teasing than reassuring.

"Ha!" Kiira said nothing else as she removed Starfire's saddle and hobbled him, but she smiled.

⁂

KIIRA KEPT her eyes glued to Terren's movements as he pushed his way through bodies to access the toll office. She stood to the side of the main road gripping the reins for the horses tighter than necessary, but told herself that nothing was going to happen in the few minutes he was away from her side. She forced herself to let out a long breath and eased the tension from her fingers.

The trek through the city of Forchid took nearly two hours, not counting the stop they made for fresh bread. Terren had hurried through the streets for her sake, knowing she preferred to be out of the city as soon as possible, but the sheer amount of people combined with the city's unique, maze-like design made for a slow trek. Luckily, with their very early start, the sun was just peeking above the walls of the city.

"Why the scowl?" Kiira asked as he returned to her side.

Taking Tempest's reins, he said, "The fee to cross increased, ridiculously. Someone is making a fair bit of pocket change with how many people cross this bridge."

Handing their passage papers to the guard, Terren led them onto the wide stone blocks of the bridge—black as everything else in the city. Kiira bounced on her toes as she peered over the thick guardrail for a better look into the canyon. Unfortunately, she could still only see the other side of the canyon wall, but the air was thick with raw power. People wedged together, shuffling as they fought to enter the narrow portico before the person next to them. She grimaced at the rude behavior, but at least they would be in the open air soon on the wide expanse of the bridge.

Kiira rocked back and forth on tiptoes, attempting to see around the other travelers, but the sunny day washed out the view of anything inside the dark underpass. As they emerged, she blinked first at the sun and immediately gasped at the sheer amount of power boosting her. Racing to the edge, she looked over the tall baluster to see sparks jumping between the canyon walls and the barest hint of the Whispering River thanks to a reflective glint now and then. Turning, she grinned at Terren. This was even better than the glimpse she had weeks ago. "Thank you so much!"

He chuckled. "Of course."

"Am I allowed to use magic here? There is so much raw power."

"I believe small, helpful sorts of castings are permitted."

Kiira tapped her chin thoughtfully. She snapped her fingers, and a miniature cyclone formed and swirled unevenly as it danced across her palm. "This is impractical, but I have always wanted to do this!" Delight raced through her. "Creating cyclones is only something Elder Weather Mages can manage. This would have drained me quickly if we were standing anywhere else." Closing her palm, she wandered over to the edge. "What else is possible?"

Terren smiled at her astonishment. "As much as I would like to linger for you to experiment, it will take us a full day to cross the bridge and reach my uncle."

She smirked. "You know me too well. I shall have to walk and experiment." Kiira took control of Starfire's reins. "How will Kamaria get across?"

"She is already on the other side," Terren said. "Usually she waits for the dead of night and lumbers across, no one the wiser. A lot of Beast do it actually. If people knew how many they would likely live in complete terror, or not live here at all."

"I wonder if that is why the crowd reacted so violently to the image Zerrec conjured? Maybe subconsciously they know Beasts walk the realms?"

He shrugged. "Certainly possible, but I doubt it. Beasts do not wish to be seen anymore than people want to see them."

"Maybe. Another thought for another time." Kiira pulled on the reins a little more and skipped forward. "Let's go! This bridge will not cross itself!"

Terren laughed and followed.

THEY REACHED the far side of the bridge that evening, as expected. But as they drew nearer to the border, her vision blurred and her insides went cold, stunning her. The magic normally coursing through her veins was being yanked out of her. She took dyspneic breaths and clutched at her chest; the Shade Realm was stealing her magic like a starving man snatching food in the market.

Then she blinked, suddenly able to breathe again.

"Kiira, are you alright?" Terren asked as he held her upright after pulling her back to the Sun Realm side of the bridge.

"It's just … gone."

Terren said nothing, but he at least looked sympathetic.

"I mean not completely, but it … I knew the Shade Realm was unkind to magicians"—she took a bolstering breath—"but that feeling is something else entirely."

Objects and people from the Shade Realm always filched bits of her magic when she touched them, most commonly when she interacted with the Isokanii merchants, and on a lesser scale when she touched Terren, but that feeling was nothing compared to what she just experienced. When Zerrec had manacled her, he blocked the magic, but the Shade Realm was siphoning it from her with alarming effectiveness. The sudden loss was a jolt to her senses, leaving her raw and stripped to someone she didn't recognize. She wrapped her arms around her middle.

"We do not have to continue if it's too much." What he didn't say was, "after your experience with Zerrec."

Terren didn't have to say it, but what she felt didn't remind her of her old mentor. What it made her feel was lost.

Who am I without magic?

Distressed nickers from Starfire drew her to him. He pranced, uneasy to cross over the threshold of the realms. She sympathized with her gelding wanting to stay in the Sun Realm. Kiira connected with his mind to calm him, and if she was honest, herself. *'You poor thing. Peace, I understand. Peace, Starfire.'*

Kiira stroked her horse's nose, her eyes dancing back and forth between the shocking difference of colors, deciding if she did indeed want to cross the borderline. In the Sun Realm, colors had perfect clarity. The sky was brilliant blue, the sun white hot, and the bridge stone a scuffed pewter. The colors of the Shade Realm were so different, as if a thin black veil was draped over everything, muting colors into spiritless versions. The sky was a depressing bruise, the sun a hazy morning mist, and the stone had a malicious undertone to the already dark color. She shivered at the feeling of emptiness, as if she were floating in a world not quite completed.

"Kiira?"

She nodded. "Yes, I can do this."

"Not to doubt you, but you should not feel pressured to keep going if it will be uncomfortable," Terren added.

Determined, Kiira set her feet toward the Shade Realm. "I would not be where I am today if I shied away from things that made me uncomfortable."

Gripping Starfire's reins so he didn't bolt, she stepped over the line of inlaid Night Crystals and braced for the poaching of her magic.

Once the roiling in her stomach settled, she took a moment to look around. The temperature was strange. By all rights, it should be warm, burning, since they were almost to a desert. Logically, that is what should happen, but, surprisingly, it was rather cool. Not the type of lingering chill from fall mornings, but an uncomfortable cold like early spring in the Aria Bells. Dots raised all along her arms, and Kiira was glad she had on her cloak.

I will definitely need some time to get used to this.

She wasn't ready to venture further. The shock of such a different world prevented her from moving. They needed to make their way into Byloraan, also known as Ristern Mera, to meet Terren's uncle for the night, but the command to move her feet didn't seem to take effect. She was lucky Terren was so patient.

"Why is everything muted?" Kiira asked, trying to stall for time until she could make her body obey again.

"What do you mean?"

"That must be a stupid question. This is the Shade Realm, why wouldn't things be muted? That makes perfect sense," she said more to herself than to Terren.

"Interesting. You are seeing color but it is muted? The colors are not as vibrant?" Terren asked.

"Yes," Kiira answered, still staring with brow crunched. "It is drastic."

"Everything looks the same to me," Terren said. He pointed through the gate. "The buildings are ashen, your clothing is still a dark brown, and your cloak is the same dark green as always."

Kiira finally looked at him. "Why? How?"

"I have the eyes of my mother's people."

Kiira squinted back toward the way they'd come. "So when you are in the Sun Realm, do things look a different color, like the opposite from what you see here?"

"No." Terren shook his head. "Colors are no different, but now thinking about it, my vision is sharper in the Sun Realm, details are more defined. It has been that way since I was a child. When I first came to the Shade Realm, I noticed a difference, but it never occurred to me it would appear so drastically different to those not born here."

Kiira nodded slowly. "The merchants always told me they wore the cloths over their eyes because the sun would bleach their vision." She smirked. "I now understand how they feel. I feel half-blind."

"I'll have to take your word for it." He paused for a minute before adding, "I wonder if the cloths the merchants use in the Sun Realm will work in reverse for you."

"I suppose it's worth a try," Kiira said.

"We can buy those cloths just inside the gate."

Still uncomfortable with her surroundings, they moved forward slowly. When reaching the exit gate of the bridge, Kiira remained with the horses as Terren stood in line to purchase the cloth from the only merchant allowed to sell it. Even though it was the end of the day, she could see healthy stacks of thin black strips covering his counter. They were definitely the same as what the Isokanii merchants wore during the daylight while in Lorea. Only once the sun was completely below the horizon did they remove the cloth strips to reveal their brilliant blue eyes that seemed to glow despite the flickering light of torches.

Kiira smiled as Terren handed her a strip of cloth, and she pulled it through her fingers. It glided like silk, but something was amiss.

"Would you like me to tie it for you?" Terren asked.

"Yes, please."

She closed her eyes while Terren worked the knot in the back. The Isokanii merchants had told her the strips were a special linen that included the Night Crystals within the cloth. Kiira had asked once how it was made, but the merchants were tight-lipped about it, as they were with almost everything related to their culture. It hadn't stopped her from asking every year.

"How are these made?"

She could feel Terren's smile rather than see it. "Let me guess, the merchants would not tell you?"

"How did you know?"

"Because they seem to think everything in this realm should remain a secret."

"I do not understand. They will tell me about the structure of the tribes, but they will not tell me how these are made? It seems … pretentious."

Terren chuckled. "I think it is well guarded because Night Crystals are so prized in the Sun Realm. I suspect if most people knew they were not as valued here, it would cheapen the market. You know merchants."

"True."

"There. Open your eyes."

Kiira blinked her eyes open. Everything was fuzzy because of the cloth, but she could now see the true colors of the Shade Realm.

"It worked!"

"Excellent."

She let her eyes wander around to the different signs of the shops nearby, and she spotted a few window boxes filled with plants and flowers that added pops of color to the otherwise drab collection of buildings.

"So how are these made?"

"You are asking me to betray the confidence of the merchants?" Terren joked.

"I am your wife, you should not keep secrets from me. Unless it is to surprise me."

"I see," he said, humor lacing his voice. "It is actually not that difficult. When heated to the correct temperature the crystals melt, allowing the workers to pull them into thin strips and they are woven in with the cloth."

"Similar to glass threads?"

"Yes."

Kiira smiled. "Thank you for this, the colors are beautiful. I am thrilled to see more."

"We have a several days' journey to the oasis. There is not much to see in the desert, obviously, but you will love the palace." He placed his hands on her shoulders and whispered, "the hanging gardens will be your favorite."

She grinned at him. "Then what are we waiting for!"

Kiira turned, ready to lead the way, but immediately stopped. She heard Terren's amused chuckle.

He ran a hand across her lower back. "It's this direction to my Uncle Bayyan's home."

"I hope he has plush beds for a pleasant night's rest. I am going to need one thanks to this realm's magic pilfering," she said.

Terren gave her a sympathetic smile and offered his hand. Kiira took it, and with a nod let him lead her even further from comfort.

CHAPTER 7
RENEWED
ZERREC

Groaning, Zerrec pushed upright, squeezing his eyes to burn away the slumber. Light intruded into his sleeping space through a sliver of curtain not quite closed. It seared his vision before he looked away. He hunched his shoulders to stretch but hissed as the muscles in his neck convulsed.

Why is every part of me sore?

With care, he lifted his arms, the movement arduous because his muscles felt like lumps of unworked iron. Zerrec blinked a few times and squinted, hoping to make his eyes focus to better examine what might be causing the pain. He flexed his hands.

Why are my hands so large?

"Sire? How are you feeling today? Shall I fetch you some food?"

Sire? Who is talking to me?

He fumbled with the thick blankets, trying to navigate leaden muscles. His fingers were not dexterous as usual, more like swollen sausages. Zerrec growled in his attempt to escape the trap of bedding. Suddenly, like a spark to a healthy hearth, everything rushed back into place.

I took a new body; he reminded himself.

The heavy weight of his limbs and overall stiffness now made sense. Zerrec sucked in air through closed teeth and clutched at his head. Flashes of memories from his host came in rapid succession, each one sending a stabbing pulse that brought on an eye twitch.

Sairah, Terren … are …

'MY CHILDREN!'

Grayten's mental voice was loud, but not powerful.

A smile crawled across Zerrec's bearded face. Grayten was contained enough until his magic restored to fullness. Then he would suppress the old king's soul into paltry nothingness, just like the others. The roiling pain of yesterday was trivial compared to his newfound status and power. He was the high commander. The morning and evening star to the people of Klynotia.

I am King.

"Sire? Is there anything I can do to assist you this morning?"

Zerrec recognized the voice now. It was the king's personal servant, Bremert. He wiped the smile. Grayten was rather grouchy, and he wanted to fit into the role as seamlessly as possible. He rubbed his chin only to get fingers tangled in the unkempt beard. When he freed his fingers, they glistened with any number of oils. He wiped his hand as best he could, but he definitely needed a bath.

I may have an image to maintain, but I still have standards. This rat's nest is the first thing to go.

Spilling his legs over the side, Zerrec stood gingerly to consider his new proportions. His top-heavy weight was something he needed to get used to. His past hosts were usually lankier in build because they more closely resembled his first body, a piece of his original identity he could never quite shed. Zerrec flexed his hands and wiggled his toes. He had chosen King Grayten out of necessity, but he could feel the advantages of the extra bulk the king maintained because of combat training. This body would fuel his magic even more than he had first imagined. The only downside was the need to maintain it. A matter for deliberation at another time.

Shoving the bed curtain aside, he shouted, "Bremert!"

"Yes, Sire."

Zerrec whipped his head in response. He would need to be wary of the stealth Bremert possessed. He didn't need to accidentally give away clues because he was unaware of someone's presence. "I need a bath, scissors, and a razor brought to the suite."

"As you command. Shall I also bring something to eat?"

Zerrec paused. Was he hungry? A loud groan from his gut answered the question. How long had he been asleep?

"I shall have one of the page boys bring you something right away, Sire."

Zerrec almost said "Thank you" but caught himself. Grayten would say nothing so polite, having clung to the belief that the king's word was law, expecting it to be obeyed flawlessly. Instead, he grunted. Bremert nodded, so it must have been an acceptable response. He would need to unlearn centuries of habits in order to believably portray the king.

Another set of images and memories flooded his mind, and he winced; the amount of information bordered on being too much. The synapses in his mind were working overtime. For as many times as Zerrec had taken over a body throughout the centuries, the sudden bombardment of information was always a shock to him. This time was by far the worst. It's why he usually chose young and nameless villagers or farmers. Their simplistic way of living and fewer years of life meant he did not need to learn as much. The king's many years accumulating vast arrays of knowledge and understanding, however, far outweighed the memories of his past iterations.

Amid endless seconds, Zerrec learned the ins and outs of the court life in Klynotia. It was nuanced and honed by Grayten to be exactly what he wanted, even so Zerrec would bet two golds much was kept hidden from the king by the courtiers. That would be one of the first matters he needed to sniff out. If he was going to craft the perfect revenge against Terren and Kiira, he didn't need his plans undermined because he failed to uncover the machinations of the inner court.

He grimaced as a light knock on the door broke his concentration. The days following a transition were always the worst and made him most irritable. Sights, sounds, and smells were especially grating to his nerves. At least for the next few days, he wouldn't need to act too much to portray Grayten; irritability seemed to be the baseline at which the former king operated.

Unstable as a newborn foal, Zerrec made his way to the table before telling the servant to enter. While food was put out, another six servants quietly entered several times to fill a tub with steaming water. He would finish his meal quickly so the searing bath would not have time to cool. The hot water would be exactly what he needed to feel more like himself again. Just the thought of relaxed muscles and cleanliness renewed the energy sapped from him by getting out of bed. He was one step closer to retribution.

CHAPTER 8
GARIISURII
KIIRA

"Camels are bizarre. The merchants have shown me paintings and described them, but it is very different seeing them in person," Kiira said, circling the animal.

"Hiiraa, biiko chejiira ke!" The hostler rushed over to step between Kiira and the tall beast.

Surprised, Kiira backed into Terren, and he gently wrapped hands over her biceps. He whispered, translating, "My lady, please be careful." Standing tall, he added, "These camels will kick strangers, but they are mostly just temperamental, like most pack animals. Come, ride Omi." Terren maneuvered her with a gentle press against her arms to stand next to the kneeling animal. He gave it a generous rub along its neck as it chewed, working the jaw back and forth, not unlike a cow. Even on its knees, the beast's head was to his chest. "The hostlers say she is the most even tempered."

Kiira, too, petted the content female. "I may have to attempt a drymera as soon as we return to the Sun Realm. I wish I could do one here." She sighed, dismayed. The magic pulled from her by the Shade Realm was as unwanted as an interloper, and she'd only been in this realm for two days. Still, the deeper she ventured, the easier it was to tolerate, and conjectured it was because she was moving further away from the canyon and the Sun Realm. Or maybe she was just becoming numb to the relentless drain, a dull ache settling in her bones. As much as she wanted to meet the Isokanii royal family, a small part of her longed to return home, where she didn't feel so hamstrung. As much as she slept each night, she had so far been unable to shuck the lethargy that had sunk into her ever since crossing the Night Crystal border.

"You are one of the few Sun Realm people to venture this far into the Shade Realm. I am not surprised you have never seen one up close. There are hundreds of paintings of camels in the market of the Oasis. The Isokanii have an attachment to the creatures and like to put them in much of their art. We can purchase one you like."

A pitched scream echoed from the direction of the barn. Kiira whirled, shouted over her shoulder, "I will be right back!" and sprinted toward the building housing her horse.

Slowing in the barn's shade, a wave of cool air hushed her fevered skin. Though her visit to the shaded structure would be brief, she relished any escape from the brutal rays of the sun. How anyone enjoyed living in a desert she couldn't fathom. She preferred humid ocean breezes or thick woodlands to this parching arid heat.

Marching up to Starfire, who was leaning as far out of his stall as possible and trying to pull at the lock just out of his reach, Kiira punched a fist to her hips. "I told you already, you cannot come with us. The sand is too soft for you to walk across." Starfire backed from the door an inch and stamped in irritation. "You will be well taken care of here." This time he flicked his ears in annoyance. Kiira placed a palm on either side of his head. Pulling the smallest thread of magic she could manage, an extravagant feat here, she connected with him and felt the rush of fear and sadness at being left in a strange place.

'Loyal friend, I come back for you. Always. Must stay here now.' Kiira said in his mind, shortening her phrasing as best she could. He always seemed to understand better when she did. A flicker of images flashed behind her eyes at the spirited runs they would take together, except she was missing from his back. His way of saying he would miss her

and did not want her to go. *'I promise, upon my return, we run fast. Stay. Eat hay. Behave.'*

Starfire pushed his nose into her chest. "I love you too, Starfire." She spent another minute giving his cheeks and forehead an ample rub. He leaned over the door, and she wrapped her arms around his neck for one last hug. Kiira stepped away, avoiding his sad eyes. She also gave Tempest a final rub before leaving the barn. Every step away from Starfire burned as much as the beaming sun on her cheeks, but she managed to get all the way to the camels without tears. "Okay, let's go."

"Everything alright?" Terren asked. "You look tired."

Kiira smiled, but it did not reach her eyes. As she mounted the camel Omi, she said, "Starfire is not handling the parting well. I had to connect with his mind briefly to calm him. I think on some level he still remembers me being gone because of Zerrec. He probably understands more about my vanishing than I give him credit for." She clicked her tongue, gripping the saddle and leaning back as the camel rose to its feet.

Terren only nodded, and she was grateful that he didn't pry. He'd described how her disappearance affected Starfire, so at least he understood without more explanation. "Then let's be off. We need to make it to the way station before sundown."

KIIRA SPLASHED her face with the water, and despite its heated temperature, it felt wonderful against her too warm skin. As Terren predicted, they rode from the dry, cracked plains into ever-increasing dunes; the path taking them to a way station just before the last rays of light fell asleep. Already the flicker of stars revealed what was sure to be a breathtaking sight in full dark.

The ride on the camels left her feeling more exhausted than usual. It differed greatly from riding a horse, and it bothered her that she couldn't connect to the animal's mind. The camels were not dumb, taking commands from their hostlers without complaint, but she assumed that, having been born in the Shade Realm, they didn't have a drop of magic in them for her to work with. Not that she needed to exhaust herself for the satisfaction of knowing what camels thought.

She paused, leaning on the rim of the water barrel, to watch the setting sun through the slight break in the tent. Now that it wasn't beating directly on her, Kiira expected it to be cooler, but the Shade Realm stayed at a constant temperature. It was truly disconcerting. The day hadn't been as hot as she expected, but it was still more than a typical day in Lorea. The Shade Realm was so different from everything she had conceptualized. It wasn't hundreds of degrees like her mind said it should be, but the sun was still intense enough to burn her skin. After living here for a couple of years, Terren theorized it was the same sun as the Sun Realm, despite the present veil, so she was still affected by the intensity as if in a true desert. She agreed it was a plausible supposition, but the Shade Realm was the one area of knowledge Zerrec never covered in her studies as a child. Despite his hundreds of years, he never ventured here, or if he did, he never admitted it to her. Presumably because it sucked at his magic and he didn't like the feeling of helplessness.

"Feel better?" Terren asked, pushing aside the heavy material of the tent.

"Mildly. I'm glad this is only a two-day journey, but I wish we could travel at night. It would be more pleasant than wrapped in these layers, sweating, and the sun brutalizing my vision," she said.

"I promise it will be better in the Oasis. Almost every walkway is covered and there are a lot of trees."

Kiira nodded. "Dinner?"

"Just our rations. My uncle is putting together a stew with the dried meat and herbs."

"At this point, anything sounds delicious." With their small party of five, they brought little food to allow for the extra camels to carry more water for refilling the way station.

"Nephew! Niece! Come, come, come dinner is ready," Terren's uncle called from a few shade tents over.

Terren waved an acknowledgement and threaded his fingers

through hers. Before exiting the tent, he pulled her in for a brief but satisfying kiss. Her eyes sparkled.

As they reached the fire, Bayyan said, "Nephew! Niece! Come, come, come!"

Kiira nodded. "You are kind to escort us, Bayyan."

"Ah." He waved his hands with a big smile. "Nothing at all! I have regional business to discuss with the Mafelbno."

"Uncle Bayyan is the Gariisurii"—Terren paused, trying to decide the appropriate Sunarian translation—"the magistrate for the region. My uncles are the magistrates throughout the Shade Realm."

"How many children did your grandfather have?" Kiira asked.

"There are not so many," Bayyan interjected. "Father had taknane."

Kiira raised her brows. Eight seemed like a lot of children, but maybe only to her since most people in Lorea had only four or five at the most. She remembered asking one noblewoman when she was younger why she didn't want more, and her answer was simply she didn't want more. She'd also gotten in trouble for asking such an impertinent question.

He continued, "Some even live in the piirdsutsii and in the ghabaamitsu."

Terren translated. "He means the cordillera and the forests like where Klynotia and Lorea are situated in the Sun Realm."

"Yes, yes, yes. Thank you, nephew. My Sunarian is not always so good," Bayyan replied.

"Really? You are not cut off from them?" Kiira asked.

Terren laughed. "No."

Kiira wrinkled her nose. "I guess that was a silly question. It was the Sun Realm that was destroyed, the Shade Realm was just fractured. It's hard to wrap my mind around it."

"I agree. I have always thought both should have been destroyed when the rending happened," Terren said.

"I assume they all report to the Mafelbno? Or does each region have their own system of government?"

Bayyan answered her this time. "My second oldest brother has taken on the responsibility of the key ruler on the west side of the river. The other brothers go to him first before escalating to the Mafelbno. Jahiim never did like the desert. Ha! So it suits him well, but he still answers to my father."

"I am glad the royal family speaks my native language. I feel like enough of an outcast here," Kiira added.

"Do not be silly! I was so thrilled to hear from the Mafelbno that Terren married, and to our Sun Realm allies." A wide grin split Bayyan's face. Pointing at Terren, he said, "His mother was closest to age with me. We were good friends as children, and I was happy to learn of good outcomes for my family." A frown pulled at the corner of his mouth. "I was furious to learn of my sister's death."

Kiira gave Terren a nervous glance before picking at her food.

Terren snatched her hand just before she pierced a potato and planted a kiss on the back of it. "My family is going to love you. They only have a problem with Grayten. Not me, my sister, or any other Sun Realm native, though you might get some odd glances from those in the marketplace."

Bayyan gave her another toothy grin. "Yes, yes, yes. I have been looking forward to meeting you. The merchants tell me what pleasure it is to barter with the Lorean royal family."

Kiira smiled at the kind words, though the encouragement only softened her worry rather than dissipating it entirely. After a beat, she asked, "How long did it take you to learn Sunarian?"

Bayyan said, "Not as long as some of my siblings. My sister and I had fascination with the merchants as children. We would bother poor Chekkeluu to tell us stories when he returned from the Sun Realm."

"I remember him," Kiira laughed. "I have only ever seen him a handful of times when the merchants are in Lorea because he mostly dealt with my father, but I would play fox in the henhouse with Ojeda and the other children when they visited the capital. Chekkeluu was so stern!"

"Haha! Yes, yes, yes. That is why he did not like us clinging to him asking for stories."

"What is fox in the henhouse?" Terren asked.

Kiira's eyes bloomed. "You never played fox in the henhouse?"

"I was never encouraged to play games growing up," Terren said, embarrassed. Somberly, he added, "After my mother died I … well, then I really was not allowed to play. I spent most of my time looking after and shielding my sister from Grayten."

The mood dampened within their traveling party immediately. Any reminder of Grayten amongst the Isokanii would never go over well. "Well, for fox in the henhouse one person hides and everyone else seeks out the one person. Once you find them, you hide as well, and the last person to find the group is the 'fox'. He or she then must tag as many players as possible before they run away. There was always smugness in not being the 'fox', but if you were unlucky enough to be the 'fox' it was a bragging right for the number of 'hens' you caught."

"That sounds fun! My brothers are so distant in age we did not play with one another. Quii and I spent most of our time drawing," Bayyan said.

Kiira grinned. "It was fun to play in the market. There were usually many children playing, so it made the game a lot of fun."

"You are making me wish I had played it," Terren said.

"Maybe we can someday," she teased, not expecting anything to come of it.

Terren tensed, but she didn't know why. She didn't expect to play inside the Klynotian castle. Kiira needed to change the subject before their conversation spilled in an unwanted direction. Turning to Terren, she asked, "Did you pick up on Isokanii quickly?"

Terren nodded. "Somewhat. Mother would speak to me in her native tongue, so I had a foundation, but I rarely spoke it after she died. If I did it was little phrases here and there to Sairah. Long disused gears in my brain worked hard when I was first here, but after a while it came more naturally and solidified my fluency. I usually communicate with Kamaria in Isokanii to make sure I do not fall out of practice."

"I only know basic communication," Kiira said. "Most of it centered on goods, or to call someone a fox."

A grin split Terren's face. "You never told me you could speak Isokanii. You said the one phrase in the market to the old man, but it's so common I figured you picked it up from the merchants as a stan-dard farewell."

"What phrase is that?" Bayyan asked.

"Mag jou tafii ke ya nagligte gaan." Kiira shrugged. "I guess it's not one of those things I think about until I actually need it. I would have surprised you in the market when I asked for something myself." She grinned back at her husband.

"I will have to teach you more since we are here. This is the perfect opportunity to practice."

"I assumed your family would want to practice Sunarian with me."

Bayyan interjected before Terren could respond. "Ah, that is true. Yes, yes, yes. I am enjoying this practice."

Terren added, "You can speak Isokanii with me so it helps everyone."

"Yes, yes, yes. Now, full bellies help us sleep. Up, up, up early!" Bayyan shooed her and Terren away while busying himself with cleaning dinner.

CHAPTER 9

REFLECTION

ZERREC

His fingers massaged his beard; the aging hairs crooked in different ways. It was a messy thing in serious need of maintenance. He still wasn't sold on keeping it, but the offensiveness of the whiskers had lessened since he'd scrubbed the oil, food, and grime from it in the bath. Fortunately, or unfortunately he couldn't decide, Grayten's poor hygiene made the beard soft and malleable.

I've never maintained a beard before, he thought, stroking it.

Zerrec studied his reflection in the polished bronze, the image almost clear. It surprised him the king never purchased a mirror, or maybe his hatred of magic made him not want one. Either way, he was going to purchase or make a mirror if he planned to maintain a beard. The sporadic length of the whiskers did nothing for his facial features, but it was soft and held the potential to present a refined and distinguished version of himself—with a little effort. His past body selections never gave him this option because he usually chose forms resembling the face he was born with. Tamed, this beard could be suited to a very specific image of authority and power. One he needed to maintain, yet also adjust so public opinion shifted in his favor and away from Prince Terren.

Maybe it's worth the effort to maintain. I'll try it for a week.

Zerrec picked up the scissors. Hopefully, his efforts to clean up the beard did not end disastrously. He could call the king's valet to do it for him, but at the moment was unsympathetic towards the old man's groveling. If he cut the whiskers horribly, magic could easily encourage the hair follicles to grow. So, with care, he lined up the scissors for the first cut, then paused. The outline of the magician's symbol was just beginning to show. The patches of darker skin were the dawn of undeniable evidence of his true identity. This was the fastest he'd ever seen it appear in the many transitions he'd gone through over the centuries.

I wonder if it is because there is more muscle on this body than the others? I will have to take a liking to arm guards and other frivolous clothing if I am to hide my identity for as long as possible. The servants here maintain vigorous suspicion.

Zerrec flexed his hand, studying his inner wrist where the magician's symbol would soon show. That was always the worst part of taking over another body. It required so much energy to form the symbol that he was without magic for a time, and since his magic relied on pulling energy from the ropey fibers of his muscles, his former bodies always took days, if not weeks, for him to have magic again. Of course, he knew it was important to have muscles; he'd always known it, but he cared little about actual power until losing his beloved Loralyn. If he'd been more powerful, he might have saved her from the devastation of the rending, but even knowing muscles were the prime power source for his magic–it was the first lesson his father taught him–he could never quite make himself take over a burly farmhand, preferring to choose bodies that seemed to portray finesse over brute force. The slimmer bodies reminded him of his first self because that was the man his Loralyn fell in love with, a gangly, awkward man who tripped over his own feet. An unconscious way of not forgetting who he had been and why he continued to cheat death so he could preserve memories of his wife. Now, actively seeing the advantages more muscles were giving him, he better understood Prince Liem's obsession with building muscle mass by spending time in the forges and lifting heavy grain sacks. More muscle meant more ropey fibers for him to fuel his magic, strengthening him and giving him more endurance. He would have to be careful not to lose the advantages this body gave him by becoming lax in a training regimen.

He rubbed fingers over the faint magician's symbol on his right wrist. His school of magic was the only group gifted with transferring their essence—their soul—into another body. A handful of magicians from before the war mastered the technique, yet he was the only one alive now with this particular gift because he had the will to live—to keep going. The others all lost their minds, ending their lives early because they could not handle the mental strain that came with this Blood Magic casting.

It's because they had no purpose.

His purpose had changed many times throughout the centuries. First, it was surviving the aftermath of the Mage War, then it turned into bringing back his Loralyn. After scores of failures, he searched for peace at the Nyuten Temple, and nothing ever wholly fulfilled him, but each phase he lived through taught him new strength. It wasn't until his position as the king's advisor in Lorea that he realized his years of knowledge also gave him power. Specifically, the power to change a person's fate other than his own. He looked once more at his reflection, at Grayten's strong brown eyes.

At my strong brown eyes.

Zerrec studied his new look with care. Medium earthen hair grayed at the temples and chin. It hadn't started thinning yet, but knowing the age of this body, that would happen soon if he didn't use his magic to prevent it. Deep smile lines carved the space between his nose and mouth. They must have been made when the king was a younger man, for he didn't once observe a laugh or smile before taking control. Ousting Grayten's soul came with a new history, and this time something felt different. It wasn't just strictly his looks. There was something there he hadn't accessed before.

Power. REAL power.

And not just power magically, but physically. He was king, and that meant he could sway masses with benevolence or strike fear with punishments. Once his magic was fully available to him, Zerrec would have it all. Finally. A pleased smirk twisted his mouth.

'My Power.'

Zerrec shook his head, dispelling the ghostly voice, and held out a fist, rotating it back and forth to study the hard lines of muscles.

Grayten was a terrible king, but I'll give him some credit for being vain.

He needed to search the king's memory of how he maintained the muscles so he could keep the power he currently felt in every fiber of his frame to fuel his magic. The body wasn't perfect, though. Scars, old and new, marred the flesh. They were marks from the many spars he engaged in as a young man. Zerrec jerked his head as if someone had slapped him. No, most of these scars came from self-infliction. But why?

'Punishment.'

The word floated in his mind before being whisked away.

Zerrec narrowed his eyes at the face in the polished bronze. "Why would you punish yourself?" He traced one of the many scars along his arm, waiting for a feeling or an answer. None came, leaving a puzzle for him to solve. He could leave it alone, but he was too curious why Grayten felt it necessary to do such a thing. It would help him understand the former king's personality and better pass as him, at least that was the reasoning he gave himself.

Should I heal them?

These were the marks of a broken king. A king who had lost his purpose. Did Zerrec want the reminder each time he looked at his reflection? They were not, after all, his failings needing punishment. "I'll give it a week, like the beard."

With his contemplation of the old king done, Zerrec set about forging a new likeness, one he would be proud to see. One that was going to give him the revenge he deserved. He closed the handles of the scissors.

A smattering of whiskers floated to the floor, the first of many changes.

CHAPTER 10

COLLOQUY

KIIRA

The morning desert sun already cast a weary heat on the day. Kiira relished one last drink of water from the barrels in the tents before wrapping herself in layers of linen to keep her skin from burning. The material weighed little, but she still felt trapped by it, and would have to wear it for the next four or five hours while they made the final trek across the dunes to the Oasis if she didn't want to look like a ripe tomato tomorrow.

Kiira was about to mount her camel when a grinding drum converted the black dunes into new peaks and valleys. Kamaria appeared in a spray of sand and a joyous roar. All the camels balked, their chorus of groans and pitched screams filling the morning as they tried desperately to run from the triumphant entrance. Two water camels that had just been untied bolted toward their home, the hostlers shouting commands in Isokanii to get them to stop. Yelping, Kiira fell backwards, the loose obsidian sand making it difficult to scramble away. Her camel, Omi, nearly kicked her as it shot out wild legs to follow the herd. Terren yanked the camel's head in the opposite direction to change its focus before it could do any actual damage. She was lucky his quick action even worked; prey animals were dangerous when terrified.

"Kamaria! That was uncalled for," Terren scolded.

The Bear sneezed and shook her head with a grunt.

"I do not care how eager you are to return to the Oasis, you cannot make entrances like that with camels! You may not need camels but we do," he groused, while still trying to calm the desert mounts closest to him.

Kamaria chuffed at him before lumbering in the direction they needed to go. Kiira eyed the massive Bear as she sat, back legs splayed forward, unconcerned, sampling the air while waiting for the party to regroup and begin moving. Logically, Kiira knew the Bear would not hurt her, but ingrained instincts made fear surface easily. Trembling, she accepted the hand Terren offered when he'd sufficiently calmed the camels.

"Kamaria does not look the least bit remorseful," Kiira said, dusting sand from her arms and shoulders.

"She's not, but she knows better and still deserved the chastising. Beasts here are revered, so she thinks she can get away with anything," Terren replied.

"Revered that much?"

"Yes," Terren turned to shout at his Bear, "but it is no excuse for lacking common courtesy!"

Kamaria let out a soft growl in response.

He turned back around with a shake of his head. "Are you okay?"

"I'm fine, really. I just didn't expect to see Kamaria other than from a distance."

"I thought it would be alright if she traveled with us today." He looked unsure for a moment. "I have missed her company and she can travel openly here during the day."

"It's fine … I was just startled." Kiira tried to sound sure, but even she heard the warble in her voice.

Terren looked as if he wanted to question her words, but nodded and moved toward the camels. Thirty minutes into the ride did not dispel the tension she'd felt from him earlier. He must really believe she was holding back and had lied to him.

Kamaria is not a Demon. Kamaria is not a Demon. Kamaria is not a Demon. I need to get over my fear of Shade Beasts.

Taking a deep breath, she said, "Terren, may I address Kamaria?"

He sat straighter in the saddle. "Of course. I will convey her responses."

Kiira chewed her lip for a moment. Raising her voice, she said, "Kamaria, thank you for helping to rescue me."

"You do not need to shout, Kiira. Kamaria has better hearing than all of us put together."

Kiira winced and nodded.

What sounded like a laugh came from the Bear. Terren glowered for a moment at the She-Bear before answering. "You are most welcome, partner of Yepenzi."

Having many mental conversations with Liem, Kiira knew what it looked like. Now she understood how her father felt when she and her brother would have entire conversations without him. It was frustrating and conjured up insecurity, reminding her of the night she first met Kamaria.

"The best way to translate that last word would be ... closest friend," he said.

Based on the way he said it, she thought there was probably a better translation, but he was doing her a favor by changing the meaning. As much as she wanted to know the accurate translation, Kiira did not need to feed the already subtle subordinate feelings swirling in her thoughts. Instead, she appreciated the effort and squashed the need to know.

"Is there anything else you want to say or ask?" Terren said.

She thought for a moment. "How old are you?"

A rumble from Kamaria's chest vibrated the air. The camels danced to the side, attempting to put distance between them and the Bear. Terren translated, "I am not so old. I have been wandering the Shade Realm for three hundred years." After a moment, he continued, "That may seem long for someone who lives for maybe seventy years, but I am young compared to my brethren. My dame is seven hundred years and my sire is eight hundred, but he will pass from this world soon."

"That's right, Terren mentioned you lose your long-life once you choose to bond with someone."

Another rumble. "Yes, and my dame was displeased I chose as such for one my age."

"Your dame is unattached? What is her name?" Kiira asked.

"She does not have an identifier like humans, and has never chosen one, but my sire sometimes referred to her as Tolu."

"And your sire?"

"He is Oye," Terren said for the Bear. Looking to her, not speaking for Kamaria, he offered the chance to meet the sire since he was bonded to Terren's third-eldest uncle.

Kiira swallowed down the immediate fear clenching her throat and turned her gaze to the horizon. "I would of course be honored with such a meeting."

"Kiira." He paused, and she was reluctant to look at him. She came here for him, trying to get to know his family and Kamaria for him; she didn't want to see the underlying hurt beneath his understanding. Terren was practiced at hiding his emotions, but she'd gotten better at reading them. She couldn't ignore him forever, so, carefully, she turned her gaze to his. He continued, "You will not be forced to interact with any of the Shade Beasts. I know this is a difficult subject."

She dipped her head, focusing on the reins of her mount. "I need to let go of my prejudice, Terren. Kamaria and all the other Shade Beasts do not deserve my judgement. I need to let my will dictate my heart this time, not the other way around." After a few moments, Kiira looked to the grand Beast still lumbering beside them across the sands. "Kamaria, what made you choose to bond instead of being free?"

A long pause followed the question, so long that she looked to Terren to see if Kamaria was simply refusing to answer, but he had a look of intense concentration. With hesitation, Terren said, "Kamaria's response was not really with straight-forward words, but she conveyed, because she wished to be part of change. She was not satisfied with pursuing her own desires for all her days like her dame."

Kamaria's response presented a depth of character Kiira didn't expect, and it shifted her perception toward Shade Beasts. Hesitation and fear still ruled, but it helped her to understand what Terren had been telling her about Beasts since they wed. Clearing her throat, she asked, "Kamaria, why did you choose Terren?"

"Because he is strong of heart, and has goals of which I approve," Terren said.

His voice was so deadpan that Kiira laughed. "What? You don't like her blessing?"

He narrowed his eyes at Kamaria. "Her statement is vague enough for me not to be angry, but she knows better than to mention the other thing she did."

"What do you mean?"

Terren moved his camel closer so the interested ears of their fellow travelers would not hear. Keeping his voice low, he said, "Upon our return to Klynotia, I plan to take the throne from Grayten."

Kiira retracted a hiss. When was he going to tell her? She didn't expect everything to come out all at once, but overthrowing Grayten was not an idea that spawned overnight.

"I'm not going to kill him," Terren said, offended at her silence. "Regicide is not the answer. The people would never trust me."

"You think I am silent because you considered killing your father? No, I am silent because you did not think to tell me this sooner!" Kiira replied in a harsh whisper.

Terren raised his brows, and there was a flicker of annoyance in his eyes, but his words remained steady. "When was I supposed to tell you? It was a big enough hurdle just to tell you about Kamaria."

Kiira narrowed her eyes. "This would have been less of a hurdle than Kamaria. People fall in and out of power all the time, Terren. What? You wanted to start with the hardest subject first? I am not happy to just be hearing of this, but we will talk about this later when we have more privacy." She stared at him, making sure he understood the seriousness of the matter. At first there was annoyance, but after a moment his features smoothed and he nodded once before looking away. That was good enough, and for now Kiira decided to finish asking Kamaria questions. "Kamaria, from your perspective, what did the bond with Terren feel like?"

Again, there was a long silence, and she assumed it was because Terren was doing his best to translate emotions and feelings. He answered, but his words were edged, even though they'd changed the subject. "It was not painful physically, but I could feel the pain it caused my partner."

There was real empathy in Kamaria's statement and, again, it was not something she expected from the Bear. "Why does the Beast choose the bond partner and not the other way?"

A soft rumble emitted from Kamaria that almost sounded like a laugh. "You see how large we are, yes? What does a tiny person have the right to choose our fate? We are the ones to lose our long-life and freedom."

Kiira smiled. That response was more like the Kamaria she expected. "What things do you look for in a bond partner?"

"I do not speak for my brethren, it is different for each. Takkai chose Bayyan because he is relational and likes diplomacy.

Kiira glanced up at the large Hawk flying lazy circles above their party. He'd joined them this morning, having waited a day before catching up to their traveling party. "If joining with a person makes it impossible for a Shade Beast to be turned into a Demon, why do not all Shade Beast bond with someone? I can't imagine any of them wanting to be pulled into the Sun Realm and used so horrifically." It was a question she'd wanted an answer to since learning of it from Terren.

There was a stretched silence before Terren gave Kamaria's answer. "You are correct. None of us wish to be used, but being bonded to a human means we lose our long-life, and it is not something all Beasts wish to sacrifice. There are not so many of us in this world and there are not a great many Ermii in the family." Quietly, he added, "Because Kamaria will die when I die, it is one reason she dislikes being parted from me. She feels helpless to protect me."

Kiira scrunched her brow. "But you died in the caves after kissing me." She meant it as a statement, but it came out as a question.

"Yes and no," Terren said. "Kamaria and I were joined and as a Shade Beast, with her natural immunity, she absorbed the magic without it killing her, especially in the form she was in. If Zerrec had run me through with his blade, it would have been different."

"What do you mean in the form she was in?"

"When Kamaria and I bind into one, she loses the physical form you see now and becomes the essence of herself. It's something Shade Beasts can do apart from their partners, and it also helps us join together. When we're one, I cannot be harmed by magic, and it's very difficult to physically kill me … us."

Kiira nodded, not fully understanding but grasping the information enough to suppress any further questions. Terren's response opened an entire book of inquiries, but she would ask them later after giving some thought to what he said. Moving to another subject, she asked, "Kamaria, why are Demons attracted to the use of Sun Realm magic?"

Terren said, "I can answer that for you since it's a sensitive topic for Shade Beast. When they are pulled into the Sun Realm by a magician, Beasts then have a permanent physical form. They are dead to this realm. At that point, magic is really the only thing that can kill them. In that way, it is their kind's greatest weakness. Being pulled into the Sun Realm by a magician is enslavement for the Beast and it means certain death, and because they cannot remain in the Sun Realm without a mage they seek out the one thing that will break their shackles, the death of the mage who summoned them."

"I can see why you hate magicians," Kiira said softly.

"She says 'I like you, but as a whole I do not like them.'"

Kiira laughed. She was beginning to appreciate Kamaria's candid personality. "I am honored I have earned your respect, truly." She lowered her voice. "Especially after the things I said to Terren on the beach."

After a moment Terren said for his Bear, "Your words upset me greatly at the time, but Terren reminded me you spoke from ignorance about our kind and that I should not judge ignorance."

Kiira bristled. She'd never liked the word ignorance, even though it was being applied appropriately. Something about the word just rubbed her the wrong way. She chose not to focus on it and instead moved to her next questions. "How has our marriage affected your relationship with Terren?"

Terren frowned at Kamaria. Kiira glanced at her husband and could see they were having a fierce mental conversation. Finally, he sighed and said, "It still is difficult. Kamaria is very protective of me. Like I am one of her cubs or something." Kamaria growled. "Which is not entirely a bad thing, but it has not made this transition easy."

"I'm sorry," Kiira whispered.

"You have nothing to apologize for," Terren said.

"I know there was nothing to change our fate, but I am sorry you are stuck in a battle of two relationships. That cannot be easy to manage," Kiira said.

It was her turn to earn Terren's displeasure. "Kiira, I told you our relationship"—he gestured to Kamaria—"is more like a long-standing friendship. I love her, of course, but not romantically."

Kiira nodded. "I know." In her peripheral vision, she could see Terren didn't believe her words. She knew the truth, but there were moments she doubted her place in his life, and right now an ember of that doubt was glowing.

Before Terren could interject, a loud screech of joy came from the Hawk above her, and Kamaria echoed the sentiment. The Bear ran across the sands toward what must be the oasis. She looked at Terren to see him smiling. "We are close to the oasis and close enough for Kamaria to communicate with Oye. She is going to meet him and tell him how far we are from arriving. I'm sure there will be a grand celebration for us at the palace."

Kiira returned Terren's smile, happy to leave behind the rolling dunes and find shelter from the sun. A wave of nerves washed through her, causing her stomach to slosh around. Kiira doubted it would settle anytime soon. She was going to be one of the few Sun Born to venture to the Oasis in the hundreds of years since the realms split. This was an occasion; she had yet to decide if it was a wise decision.

CHAPTER II
SOUK
KIIRA

"This is a menagerie," she said, gripping Terren's hand tighter. Someone had just bumped her shoulder, and she nearly lost her grip. As it was, every few seconds, Kiira would briefly lose sight of him as he was swallowed by the herd of people before their linked hands pulled them together once more. It was a complicated gambol, and after two days in direct desert sun, this was tiring.

If Terren heard her comment, he didn't respond and continued to lead her through the throng of people. He was leading her directly down the center of the wide street, the safest place since most congregated to the sides in front of vendor stalls. Large swaths of light-colored ground periodically separated the dense crowd. Not a single person dared touch them, and Kiira almost asked what they were for when a lithe obsidian Fox walked over top of them, using the spots to place its paws. At least someone had the foresight to prevent anyone from getting squished by any of the Beasts roaming freely in the Oasis.

Shouts of merchants rattled her ears as each seller peddled their wares. This was similar to that of the market in Loracia, but this souk felt like someone had done a casting of multiplication. How could anyone concentrate, let alone purchase anything in this place?

Vendors with an endless number of products congested every inch of tables and shelves not designated for something else. Some stalls sold only baskets. Others had colonnades of carpets and rugs. Wooden boxes brimming with beads in a variety of materials, shapes, sizes, and colors. Tables held precarious piles of fat-bottom vessels with elegant thin pour spouts and scrolling handles. Intricately colored glass lamps glowed invitingly from well-shaded corners. Piles of aromatic spices perfumed the air as they were scooped into cloth bags. Delicate, sticky sweets awaited sampling. Fresh figs and dates passed from seller to buyer. An obscene number of chickens clucked inside their cages, blissfully unaware of their fate. Enameled dishes with daedal floral patterns sat waiting for new owners. Tiles used for lining baths reflected bits of sunlight that made it past awnings' shade. Of course, countless fabric stalls added vibrancy to the market.

Kiira made a note to visit one or two before leaving the Shade Realm. She always bought some lengths of fabric from the traveling merchants, but she might as well purchase it from the source while here.

I wonder if Tereyssa would appreciate some fabric to add to her collection?

At least Kiira could enjoy the market for what it truly was instead of the dull tones she would see if not for the black cloth over her eyes. Because of it, she could see the bright colors of clothing each person wore as they shuffled past. Yellow, purple, and green seemed to be a favorite. The same as the pennant used to represent the Isokanii people, but she also saw tints of blue, orange, red, and natural linen. With the sheer number of individuals weaving in and out of the crowd, she imagined–from above–the market looking like a rippling flag. Most women wrapped themselves in loose layers of different colors to create curve enhancing dresses, while the men wore a single oversized robe split to the thigh with loose trousers.

She heard the bleat of an animal and would have halted to stare if Terren hadn't been pulling her through the souk so quickly.

Surely that wasn't a goat someone just used for purchasing?

Kiira twisted as much as she could without tripping, and in her peripherals, sure enough, a kid goat kicked wildly as it passed from buyer to seller. She'd have to ask Terren or someone about it later. Logically, the exchange of animals for goods or services was perfectly viable, but it was definitely never done so openly in Loracia. Now that she was aware of it, she noticed other animals balking or protesting while exchanging hands, pulling at leads and refusing to leave vendor stalls. The constant call of animals didn't compare, though, to the conversations and shouts bouncing between the earthen walls.

Terren continued to guide her through the crowd, but that didn't stop her from whipping her head, following her nose. The smells alone made her imagination run wild with the taste of flame roasted vegetables or the spits of meat packed with rich spices. Kiira spied a vendor as he carved thin portions from a column of layered meat as it rotated in front of a fire. She'd seen nothing like that before, and it became a priority to try some.

She pulled against Terren's hand. Kiira didn't even try to say what she wanted; the souk was far too loud for it, but pointed to the stall with the food. He nodded and mouthed something, but it wasn't loud enough for her to decipher the words before he pulled her through the menagerie once more. It wasn't like Terren to ignore a request without reason, so maybe he knew of a better location. She had to trust him. This whole city was far outside her comfort zone. The busyness was too overwhelming. This was the most people she had ever seen packed into one area. The Yielding Festival always drew a large crowd, but that was nothing compared to this. In all of her dealings with the merchants, she never understood how large the nation of Isokanii people was despite being told stories by Ojeda. Kiira definitely couldn't deny that this was an empire.

"Tell me again why we didn't take a side street. I said I wanted to experience the souk as it should be, but I'm beginning to second guess my choice. We should have followed your uncle along the royal route. This is not fun," Kiira said, pushing away another body. At least Terren had the foresight to warn her of people bumping into her so much; otherwise, she would be inclined to think the majority of Isokanii were rude.

Terren briefly turned to give her a grin before continuing their arduous path through the people. "We are almost to the end. Maybe another five minutes of this and we will be out of the worst of it."

He wasn't wrong. A few minutes more and they were free of the chaos and standing at the beginning of a mostly deserted road. He released her hand, and she immediately wiped it along her thigh to remove the sweat. Kiira had wanted to do that for a while. Her eyes trailed the ascending street as it morphed into a switchback. "Wow, that is steep. Is it built on top of a dune?"

"No, in fact, the land slopes down from here. We're actually going to be walking above the lower palace. A large portion of the water feeding the oasis is covered by the walls to keep it cool, and it also serves as a place for Beasts not fond of desert temperatures—like Kamaria—to escape the heat of the sun."

"Really? This looks like stone."

"It is; mined from the quarries."

Kiira turned to find they were already situated just above the chaos of the souk. From here, she could clearly see there was no space in the souk to even breathe except for the spots designated for Beasts to step. Below her, the movement of people undulated like a desert serpent. It seemed even more ludicrous they had walked that very strip only moments before.

"Seriously, why are there so many people?" Kiira asked.

"There are fewer resources here, and people cannot spread out as much. Luckily, this oasis is large enough to support everyone."

Kiira nodded. "It's still insane."

Terren huffed a small laugh. Pointing to a less busy section of the city, he said, "See there? The principal market has been purposely kept separate from the water collection so it's not a nightmare to get the actual resource people need to live here."

"Clever. How do they get the water there?"

"The oasis is fed by a subterranean river, so it was just a matter of digging wells. Over there is where a majority of people live." He pointed to a spot with tall and short flat-roofed homes stacked on top of one another with lines of colorful linens strung across the top and between them. A glittering blue canal winded lazily down the middle to provide a place for washing clothes and children to play. "A past Mafelbno ordered the ground leveled and the canal dug to reroute a portion of the oasis. You can just see where it disappears underground again."

Kiira squinted. "Oh, yes, I see it. Where does the river come from?"

"I think further west, but the Isokanii believe it is a blessing from Ostiimii. I'd like to venture in that direction some day just to see what's there."

"None of the Isokanii have ever ventured far enough to find out?"

"Why would they? This entire oasis is a blessing from their goddess."

"That doesn't necessarily make people less curious."

"I wish I could tell you. The Mafelbno says it is a blessing and no one questions it. His word is law here."

Kiira frowned.

Curling his fingers through hers, he kissed her knuckles, his lips lingering for a moment as he stared into her eyes. Smirking, he said, "Come, there is a thirty minute walk to the palace, then you can get the bath you've been longing for."

"Oh good. I finally get to stop feeling like dirt is my favorite accessory."

CHAPTER 12

PREPARATORY

TERREN

Terren tracked Kiira's pacing steps, casually leaning against a shadowed corner of the alcove, waiting for the summons to stand before the Mafelbno and Mafayyba. The orange glow from a long-chained lantern that hung at the peak of the vaulted ceiling cast a warm invitation to what would otherwise be a cold and intimidating area. Scroll lines decorating the walls twisted into leaves and budding crocuses. To his left, a solid wood door carved with a geometric pattern kept them isolated until it was time for the introduction. The design of the alcove was inspired by the Janissair Empire across the sea. Not long after the realms split, the Mafelbno ventured across the Reana to make an alliance, and brought back far more than originally intended. The Isokanii gained rich knowledge of new food and design. Those in the forested and mountainous areas held to the more traditional motifs in decorating; still geometric designs but simpler, often single lines of repeating shapes made up of imperfect hand drawn striae and dots.

But Terren's eyes were on his wife, whose agitated circling had started as soon as they'd been left alone and not slowed. He'd told his uncle not to make a fanfare of his return, that it was unnecessary. When Uncle Bayyan insisted, Terren capitulated to something simple to keep Kiira from feeling overwhelmed. He wasn't sure what meeting his family would do for Kiira's nerves after her ordeal with Zerrec. She had moments of steel and fire embedded in her personality that could blaze past any difficult circumstance, and he hoped to see it soon, but so far it seemed the pressure of meeting the Mafelbno and Mafayyba was a bit too much at the moment. He waited until she was close and pulled her into his arms. "Kiira, there is no reason to be nervous."

Her stiff, quick breaths rattled against him. "Yes, but sometimes … my brain does not want to believe the truth." She buried her face in his shoulder. "This is huge. Lorea has always had good dealings with the merchants, and now that we are married, I have the responsibility to represent my kingdom and Sunarian people well."

He rested his cheek on her head. Since rescuing her from Zerrec, Terren held Kiira as much as possible. He wasn't afraid she'd suddenly disappear, but keeping her close comforted him, nonetheless. "I will not downplay the importance of their opinion of you because you are a representative of Lorea, and in a sense all Sun Dwellers, but no matter what they think, it is not going to change how I feel about you. We traveled the length of the Sun Realm together, we have faced our challenges, and I know you intimately." He pulled her tighter to his side and rested his forehead on hers. "Meaning, we're in this together."

"That doesn't make me feel any better," Kiira mumbled. Pulling away from him, she stared at the doors. "I do not imagine blind acceptance on their part. Lorea's relationship with the merchants is still tentative. They trust us enough to barter goods, sure, but they have always been guarded during interactions with my father."

"The merchants are a tribe of their own. They are not my grandparents, not my uncles."

"No, but you cannot tell me there are no similarities in thinking among all Isokanii people. Sun Dwellers are not liked. Tolerated, maybe, but not liked," Kiira rebutted.

Ignoring her protest, Terren said, "Should I tell you the story of the first time I came here? Maybe it will help take your mind off of the introduction."

Kiira sighed and leaned into him. "Sure."

"I came here after living two years on the islands of the Magician's Cloister."

"They let you live among them?"

"Yes, because I helped rescue a group of magicians from pirates."

Kiira leaned back to study him, the disbelief clear in her expression. "Pirates? Really?"

"Yes, I was able to help because I had been part of the crew." Her surprise made him chuckle. "I will tell you the story sometime."

She shook her head—"Pirates"—before making herself comfortable against his shoulder again.

"I initially came to Jearut because I wanted to know more about my mother's people. All I had were vague memories of my mother's stories and songs, so I wanted to discover more about the culture." Terren shifted his stance, and in a quieter voice added, "since I lost her at such a young age."

Kiira nodded, not wanting to speak. She feared he'd close himself off again if she did.

"I hated my mother for years for what she did and thought she deserved her punishment."

"What did she do?"

Terren worked his jaw. "She was an adulteress. Grayten deemed it traitorous enough to be worthy of an execution. Which is why the Isokanii hate him. He beheaded the only princess of the current Mafelbno and Mafayyba." He felt Kiira tense. Rubbing her back, he said, "I came to forgive my mother after learning why she forsook her vows to Grayten."

"Will you tell me?"

"She acted out of mistreatment. I will never condone her actions, ever, but having been a recipient of Grayten's abuse, it painted her in a different light for me. With the wisdom of years and experience, I think the punishment excessively harsh when banishment would have been plenty sufficient."

In a whisper, Kiira said, "That explains your reactions to my going to Leo before we married." She adjusted to look him in the eye. "I am sorry about that Terren. I should have never done such a thing. It was selfish and childish of me."

"I forgive you, and you already apologized for it."

"Not directly."

He kissed her on the forehead and squeezed her close. Clearing his throat, he continued, "My plan was to stay in the oasis and simply observe. I had no intention of making myself known or becoming involved with my family. I was fascinated by the souk and sheer size of the oasis. My presence went unnoticed for many weeks while I explored, until one day Bayyan spotted me talking to a merchant. Pure luck, really. You saw how chaotic the souk could be."

Kiira's breaths had evened out, but he didn't let go of her side. At least his tale was working. "Of course, when I spotted the royal guard trying to corner me I made a run for it." He laughed. "I had no hope of out running them since I was so new to this city I had yet to learn my way around. I ended up blocked by a dead end." He smirked. "I was caged in from both the rooftops and the road. It was the first time in many years I'd been outwitted."

Kiira's creeping smile fell. "This does not sound like it's headed toward a happy ending."

"Well, I am still alive, so it is a happy ending," Terren said.

"That is not reassuring!" She gave a playful smack to his chest.

"Sure it is."

Kiira gave him a soft growl of annoyance.

"After my capture, I was dragged before the Mafelbno, hands bound and weaponless. I thought for sure I was done for. I'd done nothing illegal, so it could only be that they knew I was Grayten's offspring."

"You should stop. This is not helping."

"I'm almost done. The glare coming from my grandfather was menacing, he had one of the most livid faces I've ever seen. At the time I understood very little Isokanii and they were talking so fast I couldn't understand anything, it was terrifying. I honestly didn't know what was going to happen to me. The exchange between the Mafelbno and Bayyan lasted at least twenty minutes, all the while I was bound, on my knees, with spears at my back. Then without preamble, the guards cut my bonds and heaved me to my feet."

Kiira raised her brows.

"I learned later that my uncle stood up for me, telling the Mafelbno I should not be held responsible for the sins of my father, citing the rumors of my disappearance years before as evidence. My grandfather ultimately believed the time apart from Grayten was enough to no longer be influenced by him."

Kiira shuddered. "That's horrifying, and doesn't in the least make me feel better."

"But it did distract you for a bit."

Kiira glowered at him, trying to pull away.

Terren gave her a reassuring smile and tightened his grip on her waist. He planted a kiss on her temple. "I'm well-loved here, Kiira. I am a child of my grandfather's only daughter and am treated as she would have been."

"Now you are, but it started out with you being held at spearpoint! And it only worked out after someone stood up for you! I'm representing my father and all the people the merchants have ever dealt with in the capital, not showing up as a long lost grandson."

"You are going to do amazing in there, and you'll represent your people well. Plus, the Mafelbno and Mafayyba are eager to meet you."

Kiira wrinkled her nose. "Still, I'm sure they would have preferred you to marry an Isokanii woman." She looked at the door again nervously.

"It's true, they did try to match me with a few different women while I was here. Several individually tried to convince me to accept them, but I turned them all down, instead focusing my efforts on becoming a Shadow Walker like my mother before she married Grayten," Terren said.

"You couldn't do both?"

He mulled the question over for a minute. "Getting married didn't fit into my plans at the time."

Kiira turned from the doors to give him a wry expression. "Neither did marrying me."

He answered with a rueful smile. Clasping her hand, he drew close, keeping a steady gaze on her beautiful green eyes. "No, but I'll say this for the rest of our lives: I'm so glad the gods thought differently."

Lowering his lips to hers, Terren gave her a soft kiss. The scrape of the doors broke their embrace, and light flooded the alcove. In an instant, his eyes took in the hall packed with people and Shade Beasts.

So much for keeping it a small affair.

CHAPTER 13

CHALLENGE

KIIRA

The large, aged doors swung in with the slow, imposing effect that accompanied all doors of a grand size. It took Kiira a moment for her eyes to adjust to the flood of natural light covering the hall, a vast change from the dim alcove. Her eyes roamed over the details, momentarily frozen at the vastness of it all.

Columns lining the length of the throne room chaperoned the enormous space well. At least twenty meters high, the pillars could have been encircled by twenty people standing fingertip to fingertip. If Terren's descriptions of the forest in the Shade Realm were true, these columns were the same size as those trees. She squinted, and underneath the colorful silks of purple, yellow, and green, the pillars, which she thought at first were obsidian, were actually rich brown with hints of uneven lines and whorls. Were they indeed harvested trees of the forest? She'd ask about it later.

The massive throne room was as long as it was tall, accommodating several Shade Beasts and people. Extensive swaths of linen, bleached by the sun, criss-crossed in graceful arcs between the columns to shade what would otherwise be a vast open roof. They glowed in the afternoon sun. The silk wrapping the columns reflected the light pouring in, glinting like jewels.

Without the fabric across her eyes, everything looked dull, but wearing the cloth in the presence of Terren's family seemed rude and prominently displayed her greatest weakness, and she felt enough like a beacon of otherness without it. So, she had forgone the useful item. Kiira gripped Terren's arm as he led them into the hall. The weight of a thousand eyes pierced her skin all the way to her nerves, and the silence made it even worse. To keep her mind from ruminating on what ifs, she opened her senses to the hundreds of lush plants and flowers freshening the air. Massive vases—taller than the people— etched with similar graphics as the clothing held a variety of lush trees probably grown in the very gardens Terren was keen to show her. The sweet smell of almond blossom mingling with a hint of pear and lemon came from the ripe quince trees, drooping with fruit.

It's too bad Lorea's climate is not good for the quince tree. I'll have to gorge myself on the fruit while I'm here and bring some back for Father and Liem.

The flora smell refreshed her soul and eased some of the tension pinched between her shoulders. If the Shade Realm weren't constantly pulling the magic from her, Kiira would use it now to coax the almond blooms and quince fruit to produce brighter fragrances. As it was, she could sit in here for hours simply enjoying the smell of the trees.

Terren came to a halt at the base of a grand black marble stair spanning the width between the pillars. Gold and alabaster inlaid in thin lines highlighted the edges leading to the throne of the Mafelbno. Obsidian lion statues carved into a predatory stance flanked the place of honor, and at the back of the throne was another lion mid roar, the open maw ready to engulf the seat. It was intimidating, and she now understood why her husband had been so terrified all those years ago.

The roiling in her stomach would not be leaving anytime soon, especially with the enigmatic stare from a tall Desert Hawk behind the throne. This Beast was smaller than Kamaria, who stood under the easement to their left, observing everything meticulously, but there was little doubt in Kiira's mind that this bird could and would kill with ease. Variegated grey and black feathers swooped back and around one stately, louring obsidian eye. Minute shifts of its head and a rapid blink now and again added to its forbidding presence as the bird took in all the details while prominently displaying its hooked, flesh-tearing beak. The bird's attention was almost worse than the people's since she knew the intelligence of Shade Beasts. Kamaria could have told her brethren any number of things about her partner's new wife, and while they may have come to an understanding, the Bear wasn't necessarily fond of her. Kiira inwardly groaned at that realization. Was she really worried about the opinions of Beasts? Apparently she was. Perfect.

Discretely peering around, she gripped Terren's arm a little tighter. She held in the desire to squirm. Being in front of crowds was a normal part of her life, but she still hated it.

Just ignore them. Umph, goddess, give me strength.

Terren pulled her into a deep, respectful bow as he had her practice during their two-day journey to the oasis—halting her thoughts.

"Rise, son of honored Quii and introduce to us your bride," the Mafelbno said in his native tongue.

Kiira had been speaking with Terren just enough during their short travel to the oasis to kick start her limited vocabulary and grammar knowledge to translate what the Mafelbno—the emperor—said. Terren pulled her up next to him and responded to the adoration given to them in kind. He replied in Isokanii, but had told her beforehand what he would say. "Mafelbno, thank you for receiving us. This is Kiira, daughter of honored Jurica and lauded Herretus of Lorea."

Kiira watched the Mafelbno through lowered lashes, advice given to her from Bayyan, as he rose to make his way down the steps with the Mafayyba at his side. She saw golden-sandaled feet and the hem of a yellow robe stop in front of them, and raised her chin enough to see a massive grin split the Mafelbno's face as he swept Terren into a lung-squeezing hug. Bated anticipation was soothed as every person in the room seemed to let go of a collected breath. She assumed this was not the most traditional greeting, but if the Mafelbno accepted their presence, then she, too, could breathe a little easier.

The Mafayyba gently grabbed Kiira's hand, and she met the gaze of a beautiful dark-brown woman who smiled generously. In blocky

Sunarian, she said, "I am pleased for my grandson. You are welcome always in our halls."

The Mafelbno turned to Kiira. "Yes, my grandson has chosen well."

Kiira's smile froze as she glanced at Terren, but he indicated nothing was out of order. Surely they knew how they had come to be married. Kamaria delivered the news, and she would have said exactly what happened, no doubt about it. Kiira, unsure how to respond, simply nodded at what was meant to be a compliment.

The Mafelbno spoke loudly for everyone to hear, "We celebrate tonight with a feast!"

The room erupted in cheers, whistles, and an odd undulating shout. Rumbles, chuffs, and shifting feathers from the Beast in the room added to the clatter. Kiira's shoulders relaxed, and she even managed a small smile.

A loud clack and the screech of metal scraping against stone silenced the room in an instant.

Something bumped the heels of Kiira's boots, and Kamaria let out a soft, menacing growl. She quickly glanced at the Mafelbno and Mafayyba and saw on their faces a mixture of anger and horror. Twisting, Kiira found a long-bladed dagger, pristine and glittering, laying at her feet. She glanced at Terren, a question on her tongue, but saw him staring at someone behind them with genuine anger in his eyes. It was the same anger she'd seen the night he caught her going to Leo before their wedding. Kiira turned and saw a woman standing in the middle of the great hall, her face twisted with a scornful grin.

The woman spoke in Sunarian. "You"—she pointed at Terren—"reject me to marry this light skinned *injiir maala!*" The woman pointed an accusing finger toward Kiira, and a gasp filled the room.

"Terren, what is going on here?" Kiira whispered.

His eyes never leaving the woman before him, said, "She is challenging you to the d'Kehbezii. It is a traditional challenge if a man cannot decide on a woman to marry." He directed his next statement to the woman before them. "Which is not the case here, Aaliyah."

He had pronounced it EH-luh. It was a beautiful name for someone with such an ugly snarl on her face. Kiira tucked herself a little closer to Terren's side.

"See! She cowers behind you. I would not do such a thing," Aaliyah said. "I would stand proud by your side—to protect you from anything."

Kiira frowned at the comment. She wasn't cowering; she just knew better than to engage in what appeared to be an old lovers' quarrel made public. But she stepped away from him anyway and squared her shoulders. She would not appear weak.

"If I didn't accept your offer two years ago, what makes you think I would now?" Terren asked, his voice tense but even.

Aaliyah flinched before glaring at him. "I do not want your acceptance now and no longer care that you rejected me, I care that you dishonor our family, your mother's heritage, with this *injiir maala*."

"Terren, what do those words mean?" Kiira asked.

"They are not words I want to repeat."

"Just tell me."

He sighed. "She's calling you a useless sunwoman."

Kiira gaped and turned to her aggressor with narrowed eyes. She said to Aaliyah, "I am not useless."

Aaliyah snarled. "Prove me wrong *injiir*."

Kiira glanced at the dagger still glittering at her feet and back at Aaliyah with her nasty mocking grin, every awful thought about her written plainly on her face. Terren loved her, a fact written in stone, and he'd been emphatic that she did not need to seek approval from the Isokanii. Aaliyah's claims, however, poked a sore spot in Kiira's heart. Since Zerrec's easy capture of her, she'd often wondered if she could protect Terren. Despite her husband's reassurances that he was difficult to kill, that day in the market was carved deeply in her memory. His throat had been cut, and without Kamaria he could have died.

She needed to crush the negative chatterbox in her head. She needed to prove to herself and the Isokanii that she had value. It was the only way to move forward. Kiira stooped and picked up the dagger at her feet.

"Kiira! No!" Terren grabbed for her arm, but it was too late.

She twisted the glittery blade.

Nice balance, she thought.

Kiira looked Aaliyah dead in the eye. "I accept your challenge."

CHAPTER 14

CHANGES

ZERREC

"Bremert!" He bellowed for the servant to hear him through the study door. "Bremert!" He shuffled a few parchments around on his desk, revealing the top. He smoothed a palm over the worn oak, appreciating the craftsmanship. The opulence of the king's quarters was a pleasant change of pace. His wasted years in the Aria Bells had provided solitude, but nothing could compare to the smells of warm wood and parchment and the ease of life with servants. Speaking of servants… "Bremert!"

What is taking him so long?

The servant's entrance to his study finally creaked open, allowing the aged man to shuffle inside. "Yes, Your Majesty?"

Zerrec winced as he watched Bremert attempt to erect himself from a stoop and hold in a cough. How had Grayten put up with this man for so long?

'Loyalty.'

He pursed his mouth. There was that "voice" again. At least it answered his question. Zerrec agreed loyalty should be a defining trait in a valet, but preferred they wouldn't have one foot in the grave. "Take a few days leave. I do not need sickness to have a go about the castle."

Especially not a lung disease as nasty as the one I gave you.

"Sire"—he coughed—"I am dedicated only to serving you no matter my needs," Bremert replied.

Zerrec held back a gag. Now he understood what "the voice" meant by loyalty. Bremert was a toady. While he generally enjoyed the deference due him as king, there was a time and place for groveling. Instead, he replied, "I will be fine without you. In fact, you have served me and the castle well, you should retire to enjoy the last of your days and I will find someone else."

"Sire?" The devastation obvious in Bremert's single-word question.

The white-haired, wrinkled, spotted valet had started as a dregs boy in the kitchen and slowly climbed his way to the status of personal assistant to the king. Zerrec had asked a few of the long-time servants about the old josser's rise, and appreciated the endeavor the man had undertaken, but it still did not change his decision. Bremert needed to go. He'd been close to Grayten for too long and would be the first to notice any changes and, worse, question them. It was better to just let the man go with as much dignity as he could. Bremert shook. In fear or not, Zerrec wasn't sure. He held back a sigh.

Right, that was too polite.

"I said leave, Bremert. I no longer want you in my employ."

"Ye … yes, Sire," Bremert said, before bowing deep, a hint of tears in his eyes.

Zerrec's throat tightened as if fingers encircled his neck. Muscles bulged on either side as his eyes widened. He slapped the desk and pulled futilely at the collar of his shirt.

"Sire?" Bremert asked, pausing his slow forward momentum to look back.

Words were bubbling up in his throat unprompted and trying to force their way out all on their own. Zerrec's vision blurred as he clamped his mouth shut, removing any possibility of speech. Finally, he cleared his throat and through a bruised esophagus said, "You may go."

What was that? I've never had that happen.

He rubbed his throat as a pang of regret stabbed at the back of his mind; it took him a moment to recognize it as guilt. Why? He didn't have any feelings of attachment toward the old valet. The words 'but I did' kept flickering in his mind. He rubbed his temple idly while studying a map of the mines throughout Klynotia. Zerrec refused to let Grayten's feelings for the old man test his resolve in letting Bremert go. The man needed to retire ten years ago, and only served as a pharos of the past. That kind of beacon was not something he could allow. Remaining anonymous to the truth was crucial. What he needed was someone altogether unknown to the capital and the citadel. Preferably someone looking for a quick change in status.

'But I did.'

In the many hosts he'd taken over the centuries, Zerrec had never heard direct thoughts before. He expected mood changes, cravings for a certain food, and the influx of the host's memories. Hearing the voice of his host? Never. It couldn't be possible. The entire point was to shove aside the soul inhabiting the body so he could take control of every aspect. It essentially killed the person. Unless this was some unknown side-effect? Zerrec had never heard of such a thing. Then again, he'd lived longer than anyone else with his particular magic. He made a mental note to consider searching through records at the library in Letra Mera if he ever found himself in that part of the realm.

Shaking his head to clear the rabbit-trail thoughts, Zerrec went back to studying the papers strewn about the desk. He drummed his fingers before splaying them flat and tapping on the marker of a remote village. Ideally, his new servant needed to be someone who had lived his entire life only ever knowing poverty. A servant suddenly elevated would be inherently loyal, and that kind of loyalty was vital in controlling his plans. He sneered, crushing the map of the kingdom, as he thought of Terren and Kiira.

I will have my revenge.

He smoothed out the parchment, regaining control of his anger. "Captain!"

The door opened somewhat, and Zerrec heard a, "Sire?"

"Find me a man who has worked the northern mines and lived his life in the mountains. I want someone who is looking for … more,"

Zerrec said. He wanted servants beholden to him, not a sycophant with begrudging senses of duty.

Greed, the grand motivator.

"Sire."

The door clicked shut. He smiled as the tap, tap, tap of boots on stone receded from the study. After ten years of being away from court, living a boorish existence, Zerrec truly had forgotten what it was like to have genuine power. This, though, was just the beginning.

He smiled, just a tip at the corner of his lips.

CHAPTER 15

D'KEHBEZII

TERREN

"Why! Why did you pick up the dagger? Didn't you know what it meant?!" Terren had waited until they were in their room to launch his tirade.

"I did know, but Terren—" Kiira closed her lips as his grandmother appeared in the open doorway.

The Mafayyba nodded to her and Terren.

"I have come to prepare you for the d'Kehbezii. You must leave immediately," she said in a thickly accented Sunarian.

"Ndatenda, Mafayyba," Kiira said, inclining her head.

She turned back to Terren with pleading eyes, begging him to understand—to give her a chance to explain. Keeping his hands clenched at his side, Terren turned his gaze to the floor, unwilling to look at his wife until he could keep his breath steady. Harsh words would do nothing, and he wanted to lash out at her, but as angry as he was in this moment, he didn't want to hurt her needlessly. The d'Kehbezii was dangerous, and she could get seriously injured. How could she put herself in harm's way after he'd just rescued her from it? Did she not know how much her safety meant to him?

Kiira waited a moment longer, the tension between them thick, then dropped her head and shuffled past his grandmother and out of the room. The hair on his neck prickled. He looked up long enough to see his grandmother leveling a piercing gaze upon him. Terren waited for a reprimand or challenge, but she left without a word, taking the stifling air with her. Alone, he breathed normally.

Why would she accept the stupid challenge?

Terren couldn't fathom the reason. His grandfather should have ordered his cousin's challenge moot, yet he had waited to see what Kiira would do. He had kept to tradition rather than have grace for an outsider. The d'Kehbezii was a ritual passed down from the Isokanii gods, giving it preeminent status, but his grandfather still had the authority to forbid the challenge. Terren cared little that it would have made the Mafelbno look weak; it should not have mattered. Kiira was not Isokanii and shouldn't be expected to uphold their rituals.

He punched one of the stone walls weakly and leaned against the cool, smooth surface. There was nothing he could do to stop it, not with so many aunts, uncles, and cousins as witnesses. Terren took some comfort that Kiira wouldn't die; that aspect of the d'Kehbezii had been altered at the end of the Mage War after the realms broke. His biggest worry was embarrassment–not for him, but for her. His cousin Aaliyah was a *morokuumdhozii*. The only reason she still paraded the title of Virgin Warrior was because none of the men she won in battle met whatever unknown standard she had in her mind. If the rumors were true, this would be his cousin's third d'Kehbezii.

Terren watched Aaliyah train a few times during his previous visit, mostly because she made a point to be at the training yard at the same time as him. He'd been, maybe even still was, the object of her attention because he was different. She aspired to be attached to someone who would give her recognition. He was both a half-blood and the son of an Honored child—associating with him would give her the attention she wanted. That's what the d'Kehbezii was really about, he realized. She wanted everyone in the throne room to think this was about honor for their people, but this whole challenge was to groom *her* vanity. He didn't like being dragged into his cousin's game, and worse, that it now was putting Kiira in harm's way.

Kamaria nudged at his mind, and he opened the pathways to allow her to speak.

'You should not be worried about Kiira. You know she is stronger than you give her credit for.'

'That is not the point, Kamaria. She should have just ignored it. I told her not to worry about garnering any favor here.'

'And you're missing the truth in your anger.'

'Care to enlighten me, O' wise Beast.'

'Do not take that tone with me,' Kamaria growled deeply.

Terren sighed and took a soothing breath. He was letting his anger control him. Kamaria didn't deserve it. *'I'm sorry, Yepenzi.'*

Kamaria continued, *'Your anger is not toward Kiira but Aaliyah.'*

'I am pretty sure that I'm upset with my wife.'

'True, but it is born of anger toward your cousin.'

Terren almost denied it. He was angry at Kiira for accepting the challenge, but Aaliyah had issued it recklessly and put her in a difficult situation. Maybe he *should* try to convince his grandfather to cancel the challenge. His cousin was airing old grievances, trying to make a fool of him and his wife.

'Leave it alone, Yepenzi,' Kamaria said, interrupting his thoughts.

'Why? I have a solid argument.'

'You do, but you still should leave it alone.'

'Go on.'

'Put yourself in her position. See the world through her eyes for a moment. She is in a culture she barely understands, representing not only her own people, but you.'

'She doesn't need to represent me and she doesn't need their approval, I've told her as much! She is my wife, isn't that enough?'

'Yepenzi.' She paused long enough to ensure she had his attention. *'You may have told her, but she chose to undertake this challenge anyway. Would you bear the scorn of her people, let HER bear the scorn of her people, just because she told you she loved you anyway?'*

Terren worked his jaw. He wanted to ignore the wisdom of her words, but grudgingly accepted her point.

'I suppose not,' Terren replied, still frustrated. *'She still shouldn't have*

accepted the challenge,' Terren replied, refusing to budge on this point. *'My family, every one of them was fine with her—except Aaliyah.'*

'That is not so, Yepenzi'

'What do you mean?' His anger flared at the idea that anyone would look negatively upon Kiira.

'Many of my brethren have told me of their partner's thoughts. They, of course, would never speak out against the Mafelbno, but it does not mean they like you married to Kiira, to a sun woman. Aaliyah just had the bravery to speak her mind.'

'That was no act of bravery.'

'The word does not matter. What matters is Kiira knew she needed to prove her worth. She wants to show she is not what most Isokanii believe Sunlanders to be,' Kamaria said.

'And how exactly do you know this?'

'I overheard her speaking to your grandmother just now.'

'You were eavesdropping.'

'Of course.' Kamaria replied smugly. *'I am telling you the truth from her perspective and you needed to know so you stop acting like a wounded cub.'*

Terren huffed and closed their connection.

TWO HOURS LATER, Terren was the first in the throne room. The click of his boots was a mournful echo as it bounced off the obsidian pillars. Kiira and Aaliyah would start at the base of the dais to pay their respects to his grandparents, but the fight would move further away from that point. His wife moved a lot in her fighting, something he noticed while training with her at the temple. Not a bad thing, but he would lose view of the duel if he didn't stand in the optimal place. The room would soon burst with people. This was a fight to be penned in the history scrolls. He just hoped they didn't refer to Kiira as only the pale woman, though it would probably depend upon how well she did today.

He acquired a spot a third of the distance from the dais between two pillars. Kamaria soon appeared and settled in behind him.

'Feeling less irritable yet?' his Bear asked.

'Yes. I'm sorry for cutting you off earlier, it was rude.'

Kamaria chuffed at him. *'You will learn your manners as you grow.'* But she stretched a paw forward for him to climb onto, and he seated himself gratefully. It's good his Bear couldn't see him roll his eyes. His attitude earlier wasn't any worse than how she'd treated him at certain times.

From the vantage point of his perch, he noticed the curious glances as spectators entered the room. Now that he paid attention, fragments of gossip touched his sensitive hearing, though most were careful to keep it just out of his range. The anger toward his wife simply because she was not Isokanii, that he'd somehow betrayed the people by choosing her over one of them, or worries over their empire's secrets being betrayed. How had he been so reckless? Had he really been so keen to be here and felt so safe he simply pulled Kiira along blindly? Surely he wouldn't have grown that lax. He would have to examine his intentions later, but at least Terren had his Bear here for solidarity.

'Kamaria, was the gossip like this when you came to announce our arrival?'

'No, but I assume it is because the Mafelbno did not tell anyone. Your marriage was not announced until just before your arrival, so my brethren told me.'

'I understand Sunlanders are not well-loved, but if the people are this riled by our union, why has my grandfather not said anything to counteract the gossip?'

'It is gossip. You expect people to stop talking about it just because the Mafelbno says he accepts Kiira?'

Yes, he thought. But then he sighed. *'No.'*

It was unreasonable, to be sure. The Mafelbno's word was law, but he couldn't control the thoughts of his subjects any more than he could the shifting of sands.

As the time neared for the start of the duel, the room brimmed as others found places in the large hall. Beasts of all manner found spots in the most shadowed corners, as was their habit. Clearly within a matter of hours, word of this historic fight spread. There were more of his relations here than when he and Kiira had entered the throne room for the first time. Terren kept still, but inside he raged, knowing these others had shown only because they wanted to see Aaliyah win.

Uncle Bayyan entered and beelined for him. He gripped his shoulder and nodded once before taking up a place beside him, crossing his arms and sending a challenging glare at the murmuring crowds as Takkai nestled in against Kamaria at his back. At least one of his family and Beast dared to pick his side.

Maybe I rested too much on my mother's laurels if Uncle Bayyan is the only support I have.

A hush whisked around the hall as the Mafelbno entered with the Mafayyba on his arm. Dressed in ceremonial robes and armor, bringing the full weight of their imperial status to the event. Terren frowned. They were making it even more of a spectacle, which felt like a betrayal. If Aaliyah won, he would either have to take Aaliyah as his wife, which he would never do, so that left him to be shunned by the clans for disregarding the results of the d'Kehbezii.

Terren's grandfather started the traditional speech about why the Isokanii practice and uphold the d'Kehbezii, cutting off any other thoughts he had. Whether he liked it, and no matter the outcome, this challenge was happening, and he just wanted this to be over with so he could counteract the repercussions. Kiira was a skilled fighter, but all he knew was that she could handle a recurve bow and the staff. Isokanii were not fond of training with either of those weapons, and he had never seen her truly tested. He would never speak his doubts, but he was worried about the outcome.

A smattering of discourse tiptoed through the crowd until Kiira entered the hall, silencing them abruptly. Terren sucked in a breath, letting his eyes roam over the traditional fighting attire. Her hair was braided in complicated twists with the tail down her back. A silk dress, the material twisted and folded to cover her back to front, hugged her neck before crossing in front of her chest and around her torso to be tied in a loose skirt above her knees. His grandmother had put her in the traditional green of the Isokanii, the same that adorned the imperial halls. Bold. It was possibly a small show of support from the Mafayyba. Maybe he was not as alone as he believed. Maybe she secretly hoped Kiira would win?

His wife gripped her quiver and bow, and her knives were strapped to her thighs. He narrowed his eyes at her choice of weapons. It wasn't uncommon for an archer to carry knives, daggers, or a short sword for close range combat, but he had never seen Kiira fight with them. She wasn't the type to carry a weapon without first knowing how to use it properly, she'd said as much, but could she actually fight with them or just perform basic defense? He'd only ever seen her skin the animals they'd caught during their travels and assumed that was the main reason she carried the knives since she preferred the bow. He should have run her through every skill she had from the start, asked more questions, paid closer attention. Worry and irritation were building in him rapidly, but he held his composure. He did not want people around him to think he was worried. He would be the picture of unwavering support for his wife, regardless of his doubts.

At that moment, Terren decided he would intervene if it looked like Kiira was in trouble. By the rules, neither opponent could kill the other, but that didn't mean she wasn't risking serious damage. Ny had just restored Kiira to him, and he couldn't stomach seeing her in pain again. Any actions he took to disrupt the d'Kehbezii would be frowned upon, maybe even punished, but he wouldn't see her hurt again—especially if he could do something about it.

Aaliyah paraded in next, two impressive knives strapped to each leg, and Terren clenched his fists to keep himself from punching the people on the other side of the column cheering boisterously for his cousin.

After a few more customary words from his grandfather and a reminder of the rules, the match began.

Kiira and Aaliyah did nothing more than circle each other, and already he could feel his heart pinch with the desire to do something.

Restraint, Terren, restraint.

Terren expected his cousin to strike first, letting her temper get the better of her. Her knives were already drawn, set for whatever malicious deed was needed from them.

Kiira, however, was still empty-handed. Why didn't she draw her knives and prepare for Aaliyah's strike? Unless she planned to try and keep her distance and use her bow?

Just as he finished the thought, Kiira, never breaking eye contact with Aaliyah, set her bow gently aside and casually pulled out her twelve-inch bone handled knives. They were a few inches longer than Aaliyah's, and he noted the shock on his cousin's face before it settled into a mask of fury. Terren smiled at the action and even a little at his own stupidity. Kiira had been playing a mental game with his cousin when she casually pulled the knives from the sheaths, shattering the illusion of only one skilled knife fighter in the room, and his cousin's assumptions of an easy victory. Right then, he loved her even more.

Aaliyah's anger triumphed. She ran toward Kiira. Terren prayed to Ny that his cousin's foul mood would allow his wife to have an easier time winning. Kiira waited until Aaliyah was almost upon her and blocked the wild slashes with a fluidity he didn't know she was capable of. Right. Left. Right. Both.

'*She doesn't look to be a beginner,*' Kamaria noted.

'*Agreed,*' Terren replied, so focused on the match, the single word was all he could manage.

His eyes tracked her defense. Kiira blocked an overhand stab, followed by a forearm block to a rib strike. His cousin attempted to kick, but his wife used the opportunity to change from defensive actions to offensive. The blade she blocked from her ribs was pushed out as Kiira stepped into Aaliyah's space, pushing with enough force to knock his cousin off-balance. Wisely, Aaliyah took several steps back.

Both women breathed deeply. Kiira remained vigilant, but also relaxed, allowing her fingers to adjust their grip on the handles. Unhurried, she let Aaliyah again start the attack, but this time, her response to each strike was not just defensive. Kiira didn't just block an overhead swing. She pushed back or brought her other knife up to force Aaliyah into losing focus on her strength attack. Each time one of them made a move, the blades scraped and the ting of steel against steel echoed in the throne room. The longer the two of them traded strikes and counters, the more Kiira took opportunities to make his cousin react in unexpected ways, testing the limits of her fight pattern. It took him a second to realize what was happening.

I am so stupid. She's learning Aaliyah's fighting style. I should have seen it.

Terren blamed his worry about Kiira for not noticing sooner.

'I had no idea she was this good,' Terren said to his Bear.

'Nor did I, but I am quite impressed. She is better than you.'

Terren winced. The comment stung, but he'd admit she was better at fighting with knives. He was absolutely floored by her skill, thankful for the surprise. Still, he had to soothe the thimble of jealousy in him by knowing he was better at throwing knives with more accuracy.

Just then, Kiira launched into her first real offensive maneuver. She stabbed at Aaliyah's left ribs with a follow-up to the gut, both blocked. But instead of disengaging and trying for another stab, Kiira brought the butt of the knife down hard into her opponent's thigh. It gave her just enough time to spin right, past her guard and crush a blade hilt into the back of her opponent's head.

It was risky to move in so close, and Kiira paid the price for it. Before she could spin away again, Aaliyah brought her own blade up and slashed her leg, the blade breaking open silk and skin in a line across the top of her thigh. Kiira cried out and put space between them. Aaliyah, too, backed away, her eyes smarting and blood dripping down her neck.

Pain fisted in the center of Terren's chest. He stood on Kamaria's paw, wanting to jump from his place. Somehow, he stayed. Kiira's leg was bleeding a lot, but not enough to cause alarm. He looked toward the Mafelbno anyway, willing him to call for a respite so his wife could at least bandage her leg, but it seemed his grandfather was leaving this fight entirely in the hands of the challengers.

She gingerly tested the strength of her leg. It held, and she locked back in on her opponent. His eyes flicked between the two women as they got ready to reengage and, to his surprise, Aaliyah looked afraid.

Kiira moved fast, and her first strikes landed before Aaliyah had a solid guard. A few more clumsy blocks kept a couple of injuries at bay, but Kiira was now a whirlwind of motion. Finally, Aaliyah pushed her back hard enough to launch her own attack, but Kiira twisted the blades in her hand just before she blocked the incoming strike. With a little extra twist of her arm, Kiira pulled the blade across the top of Aaliyah's forearm and wrist, cutting to the bone.

It was his cousin's turn to cry out in surprise and pain. A reddened knife fell to the floor with a ringing clatter, smattering drops of blood, Aaliyah's hand hanging useless. Terren rounded his eyes at Kiira's aggression. Or maybe it was the way her aggression seemed more like retaliation. He'd never seen her fight in such a manner, not even when she became frustrated during their sparring with the staff.

Maybe what happened with Zerrec affected her more than she says.

Now with the advantage, Kiira closed in, forcing Aaliyah to give more and more ground, since she could only defend with one hand and blade. His cousin's defenses waned, her countermeasures slowing and wearing into barely anything. Kiira, however, did not relent her viperous strikes, slashing lines of red across her opponent's body, leaving her yellow silks drenched and dripping blood onto the stone floor.

Kamaria's voice interrupted his study of the match. *'The Mafelbno needs to call this soon before Aaliyah loses more blood.'*

'It's hardly a waterfall, Kamaria.'

'That is not what my nose says.'

Now that she'd pointed it out, the smell of blood was becoming overwhelming.

Aaliyah aimed a lowbrow, desperate slash at Kiira's chest, which she easily leaned away from, but not without a wince. This needed to end now, and it was like Kiira heard his thoughts. Suddenly knocking aside Aaliyah's useless hand, she smashed the hilt of the knife into her defensive arm, making her drop her other knife. Before she could react, Kiira stepped a foot behind her back heel and brought her to the ground.

He could hear the whoosh of air as Aaliyah's back hit the floor.

Kiira was immediately on top of her with a knee on her chest to keep her from taking recovering breaths and pressed a glistening red knife to her throat.

Terren relaxed. The d'Kehbezii was over.

CHAPTER 16

KAAZANN

KIIRA

"Yield," she said, pressing her blade into Aaliyah's neck. Aaliyah snarled at her, bucking her hips. Kiira narrowed her eyes and put more weight into her knee until only short, raspy breaths puffed from Aaliyah's lips. "Yield," she repeated, pushing the blade to draw blood, "Or I'll bleed you until you do."

"Yield," Aaliyah managed, though the word clearly pained her in more ways than one.

Kiira leaned closer to whisper, putting all her weight onto her knee, and Aaliyah's eyes rounded as the last remnants of air escaped her lungs in a wheeze. "I will do anything for Terren. The color of my skin doesn't make me less worthy of protecting him. Remember that if you decide to challenge me again."

Grimacing, Kiira stood and gritted her teeth—which she felt all the way to her temple—as she put weight on her left leg.

At least she didn't stab. Anything in the bone would have hurt.

One time, Liem had gotten hurt during training with a stab to the ribs, the point of the sword nicking bone. He described it as the worst pain he'd ever felt. This deep cut into her leg muscles felt like it was going to be a close second to his injury.

Kiira gave Aaliyah one last glare before searching for her husband.

His grandmother made it clear that if she wanted the respect of the Isokanii, she needed to win and also walk to Terren when the fight was over. Kiira didn't understand the custom, something about showing strength despite weakness, the exact opposite of what her mother taught, but she'd do anything to make these people respect her and Terren. Kiira spotted him standing rigid atop one of Kamaria's paws and started limping towards him, blood pouring down her thigh.

Her eyes flicked back and forth as she limped toward Terren. She hadn't noticed before, purposely blinding herself from the periphery as she walked into the throne room, but the sheer amount of people was overwhelming, as was the silence in the room. She thanked Windrah for having been so focused before. Public sparring was not encouraged in Lorea, so the most she'd ever had watching was maybe thirty soldiers around the training ring.

The pain in her leg ratcheted toward excruciating, and it took every ounce of energy she had to focus on Terren and keep walking. His gaze on her broke for the briefest of seconds, flickering behind her, and she heard a faint rustle followed by a scream of rage. Injured as she was, Kiira knew she would not turn in time for a defense, still she dove to her right and raised an arm to block. An elegant, curved obsidian sword caught the blade swinging towards her with a loud clang. She followed the sharp edge to the hilt, seeing her husband standing protectively over her.

He kicked Aaliyah back to the ground and moved between her and his wife. Terren's voice was loud and as icy as his eyes. "You dishonor your position as *morokuumdhozii*." In a quieter voice, but still loud enough for those closest to hear, he added, "Do not ever think to put my wife at risk again, cousin, or it will be my blade that cuts you."

A sea of whispers grew as those closest to them frantically told others what Terren had said. If Kiira's understanding of the d'Kehbezii was correct, it was the woman's job to protect her home, family, and husband at all cost sacrificing herself to ensure he survived to keep a family lineage. To the Isokanii, she was the last line of defense. If so, Terren had just upended his family's cultural expectations by stepping in to protect her.

"Guards! Escort Aaliyah from this place. She is not allowed in my presence for three years for this dishonor," the Mafelbno commanded. The murmuring crowds turned away from Aaliyah as his anger echoed across the stone.

Terren grasped her wrist, helping her to stand.

"You did amazing," Terren said, whispering in her ear. "I wish you had told me you were that skilled at knife fighting. I wouldn't have worried so much."

Kiira smiled even though she was focused on getting her feet under her, her braid falling over her shoulder. "You never asked."

Terren pulled her close to support her. An amused grunt met her ear. "Now I know what Liem meant when he called you cheeky."

She shifted to give mock offense, but in the turn to face him she put too much weight on her injured leg and a searing flame seized the muscle, the pain racing up her thigh and into her hip, blood pumping from the wound. Her leg buckled, and with tears in her eyes, hanging awkwardly from Terren, she gasped, "I'm glad Liem and I block our edges when we spar, this hurts."

Before she could protest, he hoisted her into his arms. "We need to get you to a healer now. Put pressure on that."

She did, but the strength to do anything was quickly leaving her. Terren had only made it a few steps when a loud screech raced along the columns to the very back of the room. The Mafelbno's Beast demanding silence from even the most animated conversation. Terren stopped and faced his grandfather as the edges of Kiira's vision faltered. Why were they stopping again?

Dimly she heard the Mafelbno speak, but none of it made sense.

Kiira mumbled, "I wish I had my magic."

KIIRA BLINKED at the *hello* call of a distant bird and flax-blue morning light. She lifted her head to find arms and legs outstretched like a desert hawk. As her eyes focused on the room, Kiira realized she wasn't in her shared room with Terren. Soft white linen hung in layers around an open air rotunda, and the brush of fabric against the columns was a soothing *swish* as it moved.

She pushed herself up on elbows and noticed a dark brown intricate design covering every part of her hands, feet, and forearms. The ribbed paste cracked as she twisted. Kiira frowned.

What in the realms is this?

"Kiira, you look lovely this morning," the Mafayyba greeted, stepping into her view. "These are my sisters, Siiko, Tendii, and Zahjerra. They are here to help you clean and ready for the day."

"What—" Kiira cleared her throat and tried again, though she was still raspier than usual. "What is happening?"

"Today we celebrate your victory and marriage."

Kiira decided she needed a boosting herbal tea so her mind wouldn't be so sluggish. "What?"

One sister clapped in delight. "Her hair matches the fluff in her brain!"

"Hush, Siiko!"

The Mafayyba sat on the edge of the bed. "You remember yesterday, yes?"

Kiira nodded.

"Terren took you to the healer to clean and bind your injury. After, I insisted there be a wedding. Terren did not wish for one, but I asked indulgence for an old woman."

"I am already married," Kiira said, still trying to sort the pieces into place.

"Yes, but this ceremony will recognize you and Terren with the Isokanii."

Kiira lifted a hand. "Is that what this is for?"

The Mafayyba smiled. "Yes, that is Zkinne. It is a paste to temporarily stain skin. The design is intended to bring good fortune and happy marriage."

She stared at the loops, dots, and swirls. "It is pretty."

"I did it!" Siiko said brightly.

The Mafayyba gave the woman an indulgent smile. "Siiko and

Tendii will help you dress for the baths, Zahjerra and I will meet you there."

"Ndatenda, Mafayyba."

"In private you may call me Bahtii."

Before she could acknowledge Bahtii's words, in a whirlwind, Kiira was pulled from bed by the Mafayyba's sisters, wrapped in a short thin linen robe that left nothing to the imagination, and stood at the sisters' beckoning so they could wipe the paste from her skin using olive oil. They chattered at her the whole time about what the day would bring and how she was going to look so beautiful in her gown. Kiira was glistening with oil as the sisters wrapped her in a purple linen robe and helped her to the baths, one on each side of her to keep her off her injured leg.

The baths were in an extensive open air room, and Kiira froze at the sight of the pool sprawling beneath a curved pergola. A two meter mother-of-pearl-tiled lip was the only space unoccupied by water. What must have been spectacularly bright yellow petals, since they looked dulled to her vision, blanketed the surface of the water, perfectly still as if anticipating a warm wind to disturb them. The heady scent of roses filled the air, and Kiira breathed deep of the wonderful smell.

"Bahtii, this is ... lovely," Kiira said. It was the only word that could describe—barely—what she felt looking at the baths. Maybe she could do something similar once she had settled in Klynotia and had a prosperous garden.

"All for you, my dear. Normally, we do not add petals, but this is how we celebrate all our weddings," Bahtii replied with a grand smile. She was definitely enjoying the moment. "Come, come, we must bathe and then preparations!"

Kiira let herself be pulled toward the water, following the other women's lead as they shed their outer robes and stepped into the surprisingly cool waters. At first, the shock in temperature made the wound in her leg ache, but it soon soothed the laceration, giving her some relief from the throbbing.

"Kiira, like this!" Siiko grinned as she poured the water over her skin, allowing the petals to fall where they wished. "Use the robe to gently rub and remove rest of Zkinne," she instructed.

Kiira did, making sure she reached her feet as well, even though it was laborious. Out of nowhere, a waterfall of cold water splashed over her head, making her shoulders bunch as she squeaked. Strands of hair plastered to her face, and rivulets of water beat against her nose and lips. A gasp escaped when another wave of cool water doused her again. This time she whipped around to see Tendii clutching a large clay basin and giggling. Kiira was quickly learning that Bahtii's sisters had an uninhibited spirit she could not match.

"What? You must wash your hair!" Tendii said, a mischievous smile playing about her mouth.

Smirking, Kiira pushed a decent wall of water in her attacker's direction, and that was all the permission any of them needed. For the next several minutes, Kiira attempted to dodge waves of water the women splashed her way, with very little skill because of her injury, and the Mafayyba and her sisters were proud victors as they exited the pool.

"I have not had such fun since my marriage," Tendii said.

"I agree sister," Zahjerra added, with a smile.

Kiira looked around the circle of sisters as a hushed surprise enlightened each of their eyes, and they all stared at Zahjerra, a woman of few words.

"What?" she asked.

Siiko clutched her sister's arm, and Zahjerra froze like a startled cat. "I'm so happy to see you smile, Zahjerra! I knew the fun part of you was still in there somewhere."

"Get off me, Siiko," Zahjerra groused.

"Come, come, my sisters," Bahtii said, stepping through the circle to interrupt the conversation."This is Kiira's day. No pesky squabbles!"

CHAPTER 17
DELINEATION
ZERREC

"Sire, I found the latest reports of the kingdom as requested. It took some persuasion, but I got every last one," Zulen announced, struggling into the room, attempting to keep the stacks of parchment and scrolls from tipping, but still keeping his wide grin.

Zerrec gave himself a motionless pat on the back as he looked up from the other papers and parchment maps. He'd made the right decision to get rid of Grayten's old servant. This new valet was better than he had hoped. The young man bore a tenacity and eagerness to get ahead; his youth would keep him impercipient of Zerrec's precise goals. He cleaned up well for someone who had worked his entire life in the mines.

Zulen had still been caked in stone dust and the lingering scent of mildew when first presented to him; it took Zerrec little time to see past the exterior and into the cunning gleam of Zulen's brown eyes. Even the few weeks it took to train the cave rat into an appropriate valet was time well spent for a now eager and loyal servant.

Much better than those three idiots I found on Corsair Island.

"Excellent. Set them there, Zulen, I will look in a moment," Zerrec replied.

"Is there anything else that I can get for you, Sire?"

"Nothing." Still sensing the presence in front of the desk, he snapped, "What?"

"I am only waiting to make myself useful at your command, Sire."

"Over-eager puppy," Zerrec grumbled into his beard. Louder, he commanded, "Get out of my study! Make yourself useful elsewhere."

Zulen jumped and scampered away at the rough words. Zerrec rubbed his temples.

That boy is likely to give me a headache one day.

Still, bringing Zulen into his service was the right choice. Shaking his head, he went back to studying the tax ledgers. The numbers just were not adding up. The people were being taxed outrageously, yet the kingdom faltered. Either Grayten was an idiot—which he didn't believe—or he was selfish, and Zerrec was inclined to believe the latter. In the short time he'd been fully in control of the king's body, nothing but the finest clothes, food, and drink were given to him. Well, not the food at first; Zerrec quickly amended the king's standard menu for more variety. His taste buds deserved better than plain venison, boiled potatoes, and over-steamed vegetables. At first he thought not to say anything. It definitely gave insight into the type of king Grayten had been, but there was only so much Zerrec could tolerate before the food proved too boring to continue eating.

If Grayten had luxurious tastes, then he likely poured money into keeping up the appearance of a wealthy kingdom. He reread the stacks of reports more thoroughly.

There.

Hidden under innocuous names with amounts far too high for the item recorded were the numbers Zerrec sought. Now that he knew what to look for, much of the ill-gotten gains was taken in mere fractions of gold. Clever, but it irked Zerrec that the former king was more concerned with other things and maintaining his image than he was in actually running a kingdom. Mostly because he was having to correct the mistake. He needed to speak with the record keeper about these numbers. Was the man lazy and not recording the incoming taxes properly, or was he the reason taxes were raised annually?

Zerrec's eyes paused at the entry for the wedding. He read it through a few times before relaxing into his chair with a whistle. Either Herretus was senile in his age, or Grayten was a solid negotiator. Kiira's bride price was outrageous. The amount would easily keep the castle servants paid for three years without ever touching Klynotia's collected taxes.

Or maybe Herretus is still as tenderhearted as I remember and willingly paid this much to help the people.

The thought made him sneer. Lorea's wealth was no secret, but the king's kindness and generosity made Zerrec itch. He'd once been the recipient of such favor, or so he thought. Herretus had made clear his opinion of him when he denied his marriage to Kiira. Now, at least, he no longer cared for the princess as he once did. He stood to shake away the ants crawling along his skin, needing to think about something else.

Back to the task at hand.

Zerrec shuffled through the ledgers to find the name of the Clerk Master. The signature of a Faramond Osmont was scrawled at the bottom at the end of each accounting. Zerrec rang the bell to summon Zulen. When he appeared, he said, "Have the Clerk Master come to me immediately."

Twenty minutes later, Faramond Osmont stood before the desk in his study, and immediately Zerrec's suspicions were raised. The man looked as if he'd been awoken from a nap and hurried to dress. His rumpled clothes at a quick glance looked plain enough for a man of his station, but on closer examination bulged inconsistently as if he was trying to hide something more than a body created by laziness. His jet hair was as oily as his skin, and he maintained ink-stained fingers. Zerrec played with the edges of the ledger. "Master Osmont, you have been recorder of taxes for the past ten years, yes?"

"Yes, Sire."

"And in that time, you have kept me in proper supply of food, clothing, and drink."

"Yes, Sire."

Zerrec studied him for a moment. He stood and casually circled the desk to stand behind the Clerk Master. Peeking out behind the collar of the linen shirt was a doublet of dull yellow silk, well worn and of a lesser quality. "You have been paid fairly for your service, yes?"

"Yes, Your Majesty."

Liar.

"Your wife and three daughters, they are well taken care of by your financial gains?"

Osmont swallowed. "Yes, Your Majesty, my wife, and daughters are fair and bright, and bring me much … joy."

Zerrec continued his circle until he stood with his prey on the right. Using his magic, he cast to 'hear' the clerk's heart rate. It sounded as if he was running up a flight of stairs. Zerrec wanted to see if that would change. Rubbing a thumb along the tips of his fingers, he asked, "You would do anything for your family? To keep them happy? Provided?"

"Ye … yes, Your Majesty."

Zerrec kept a lingering gaze on the Clerk Master, who, for his part, did admirably to keep eye contact, but every other signal the man gave, besides his fluttering heart rate, said he had something to hide. "I have a question for you, Osmont."

"Certainly, Sire, what would you like to know?"

"Tell me why it seems the allotted amount for the king's finery is more than what is the market cost?"

The Clerk Master swallowed. "The kitchen and clothier staff have stated they are paying for the items at a fair price."

"Truly?" He cocked his head, but kept his focus on the movement of his thumb and fingers. "Then I may need to have a discussion with them about learning how to haggle better prices. Especially in the name of the king."

"Yes, Your Majesty, I have told them as much."

Zerrec retreated behind his desk. He played with the edges of the ledgers, and said, "Tell me the truth, Osmont."

"Sire?"

He flicked his eyes to look at the swindler before settling back in his chair to steeple his fingers. "I dislike having to repeat myself,

Osmont, but I'm in a generous mood today so I am going to say this one more time. Tell me the truth."

Faramond Osmont's heart rate skipped before fluttering again, but the clerk kept his shoulders straight and eyes on him, though a sheen was forming at his hairline. "I am not sure to what you are referring, Sire."

Zerrec sighed. "Zulen!"

The door creaked open. "Yes, Your Majesty?"

"Would you be so kind as to fetch the Master Clerk's family from their home? I would like to have a word with them. They live outside of the citadel to the southwest, if I correctly recall what the steward said earlier."

Osmont blurted, "I have been skimming money from the tax collection and the king's finery for five years now."

"Belay that order, Zulen." The valet bowed in acknowledgment and closed himself once more into the cramped office abutting his.

Zerrec gave his full attention to the clerk now that he'd gotten the truth. "And for five years, you have managed to hide your wealth from the other servants."

Osmont hunched and studied his shoes. "Living outside the citadel makes it easy enough to devise a ruse to keep others from knowing. Only the captain of the tax guard had a hunch, but he never found any evidence."

"I would hardly call one gold from every five skimming, Osmont. Why take such an exorbitant amount? A third this much would have kept you living most comfortably. You've been 'skimming' enough to maintain an army and single-handedly undermined the kingdom's functional income."

Osmont shook his head hurriedly. "It is nothing so treasonous. My wife required a … certain standard of living for her and her daughters."

Zerrec studied every inch of the Clerk Master.

A weak man, then, useless … unless.

"You're rather forthcoming," Zerrec said.

Osmont straightened, but dwindled again. "I accepted the possibility of being caught when I started skimming."

Zerrec relaxed in the chair to grip the edges of the armrests. Here stood an interesting challenge. The Clerk Master's words declared he'd accepted his fate, but everything about his body language—from his bowed head, to hunched shoulders, and averted gaze—told him that this man would choose to live, given the choice. Just to satisfy his curiosity, he asked, "I am assuming you would prefer not to be executed for this treason?"

Osmont flicked his eyes to the king and back down. "Yes, Sire, that would be preferable. I would hate to leave my wife and daughters without," he paused, "provision."

Zerrec nearly snorted. The man may have loved his wife at one point, but any affection for his family had long since evaporated. He probably stayed out of fear or, judging by his unflattering appearance, laziness; viewing his wife and daughters as 'better than nothing.'

Now that he had a confession, he could execute the Clerk Master to win the hearts of the people, but had a feeling that only the castle servants may care if this man lived or died—maybe. Zerrec needed more. Plus, he needed to divert attention from himself with a Grayten-esque act. Already he'd seen curious glances from servants. He could only imitate the former king so much, so he needed to act soon to keep the ruse going. Based on the chronicles of the king, Grayten commonly gave demonstrations to remind the people of his authority, and Zerrec needed to continue the practice. Most of it was showy nonsense, and the citizens bought into it—out of fear—but bought into it, nonetheless.

From time to time during his seclusion, when news had come to his mountain home, he heard reports of executions Grayten performed on mages unlucky enough to be found within his borders. The former king was hell-bent on ensuring no magicians lived in his kingdom, and he made sure everyone knew it. Zerrec would let that particular law wane, since it was born out of jealousy. He would find and execute a magician if necessary, but that was becoming an old turn, and he needed something new to pull at the heartstrings of the people. The point was simple—make people fear him. An easy baseline to achieve, and Zerrec had no qualms about using fear as a motivator. In fact, he preferred it to using his Blood Magic; it was more thrilling to control people while hiding his true nature.

He stood and paced the length of the window, hands clasped behind his back, letting a rainbow of color decorate his otherwise pale face. How could he use this situation to accomplish his task of manipulating the people? Revenge on Kiira and Terren was still a priority, but this was important as well. If he built the frame of his future goals on loose soil, then the possibility of failure existed, and that was unacceptable. He'd also be lying if he didn't admit his new role as Klynotia's king didn't reawaken a lost part of himself from his advisory days in Lorea. He smiled, taking a moment to revel in the power of a king. "I need someone dispensable," he said to the curtains.

Zerrec heard nothing, but he had a feeling Faramond Osmont winced when he spoke. Good, he hoped the clerk believed he'd changed his mind. He turned back to the reports of the tax collections and the Clerk Master. One name reoccurred throughout each report. Captain Denel. A captain of the tax guards would be well known to the people, but also replaceable.

"What was the name of the captain who suspected you, Osmont?"

"Denel, Sire."

Perfect.

He poked through the reports, skimming the information. Within his quick glance, it appeared the captain was a good, honest man, taking only what was required for taxes.

How would Grayten handle this?

He didn't enjoy having to delve into the king's memories. It was often difficult to disentangle his true self from Grayten since he was proving to be a stronger soul than his other past lives, but if ever there was a time to ensure he acted most like the former king, this was it. Zerrec meditated for a moment, smirking when an idea came to mind.

"Osmont."

"Yes, Sire?"

"I will let you live on one condition."

"What is that, Sire?"

"Use the king's guard to have Captain Denel arrested, beaten, and *confess* that he's been skimming money for himself. He will be made the example instead of you, and in return, I will let you keep some of the money you have been taking for yourself, but the majority will be added to the ledger as part of the king's finery. Do we have a deal?"

Zerrec waited as a range of emotions rippled across Osmont's face. The answer was simple: either the charlatan before him wanted to live or he didn't, and he had a strong inkling the clerk would capitalize on the opportunity to live. The only thing that might hold him back would be the disciplinary action Zerrec was requiring.

With hunched shoulders, he said, "I will do as you have asked, Sire."

"Excellent."

CHAPTER 18

MIIKETTE

KIIRA

Bahtii gave her a comforting smile. "They are almost done, Kiira."

She nodded and inched a little in the cushioned seat. Her heavily embroidered dress protested by squishing into a bubble at the minor change. Kiira poked it back down.

"I can see why Terren likes you," Bahtii said, a small chuckle escaping her lips.

"What do you mean?"

"You are the opposite of everything he grew up around. As a child he was surrounded by clouds. Heavy clouds. My daughter would write to me of her life in Klynotia." Bahtii sighed. "It saddened me greatly to see my only daughter succumb to darkness."

Bahtii's eyes turned stormy, and a prickle of unease trailed the fine hairs of Kiira's neck. She could feel the older woman's anger as easily as she felt the skirts beneath her hands. It was a dangerous thing, and she was glad it was not turned against her. She could easily see the Mafayyba being the winner of d'Kehbezii.

"I have known you a short time only and I see the joy in his life," Bahtii continued, her countenance lightening. "For that I thank you.

He and his sister are the only tie I have left of my daughter until I see her again with Lehlo. I only ever wanted happiness for my family."

Kiira smiled briefly before it fell. "Bahtii, may I ask you a personal question?"

"Of course, child."

"Why did the Isokanii not retaliate when Quii was executed?" The question had been burning inside her for some time, and Terren had not been able to answer it. It seemed odd to her for a culture that valued family deeply to not take greater action on behalf of a beloved daughter. Kiira lost count of how many times Quii's name had been fondly mentioned during her stay here.

Bahtii sighed and moved to stand by the window, her head high.

Ever the empress, Kiira mused.

Bahtii surveyed whatever was below for some time before she answered. "We considered it seriously once the news met our ears. It was my eldest son who spoke sense into our grief. He reminded us Klynotia would one day belong to Terren. How could we destroy a kingdom that would be in the hands of our grandson? He did not deserve the consequences of our wrath. Besides, what would we do with a conquered kingdom in the Sun Realm? We did the only thing we could, ban the traders from ever crossing the Klynotian borders, even to pass through."

"The people of Klynotia still obtain your goods through Lorea," Kiira countered.

"Yes, but at what cost?"

Kiira nodded, seeing the full scope of what Bahtii said, though she frowned, because financial ruin could destroy a kingdom as much as any war. Even now, Lorean nobility buying gems from Klynotia helped keep it afloat. Only just. She was not looking forward to correcting Grayten's mistakes once he no longer ruled. Kiira imagined the years of work and restructuring it would take just to make Klynotia a respectable kingdom again.

The Mafayyba whirled. "Enough sadness!" A happy crinkle lined her eyes that bordered on conspiratorial. Pulling Kiira to her feet, Bahtii draped a large piece of embroidered, deep purple silk, almost like a sash, across her shoulder. "My grandson will definitely not be able to keep his eyes off of you tonight! Zahjerra, are you almost done with her hair?"

"Yes, Bahtii."

"Excellent. I will make sure everything is ready for the ceremony and feast!" Bahtii clapped her hands in finality. "Time to make you a princess of our people!"

KIIRA STOOD in front of a polished plate of bronze trying to get a decent look at herself. Having a mirror was normal in Lorea, but the traders could not bring back the reflecting glass from the Sun Realm because they were created with magic. They lost their reflective surface once they crossed the crystal border, turning splotchy and dull gray. Any magician-made item always held residual traces of the casting, and here in the Shade Realm, the little magic remaining in an item was devoured immediately, usually destroying it.

What Kiira could see of herself in the polished bronze reminded her of the wedding in Lorea. She looked just as lovely, but the colors were far from what she thought they should be. Silk in a deep purple, painstakingly embroidered with gold and green thread, gilded every inch of the fabric in swirls and loops. It matched a woven clip of gold atop the middle of her hair with a large teardrop amethyst on her forehead. A sheer purple veil with the same elaborate embroidery as the dress, clipped to the underside of her hair to cover the portion of her curls not pinned. Black kohl lined her eyes and lashes to make her eyes stand out. With the Zkinne on her hands and halfway up her arms, the entire ensemble was dramatic to say the least.

While preparing her for the ceremony, Bahtii's sisters gave her a history lesson on how her current ensemble was a design brought back from the kingdom of Janissair. Before the realms divided, Isokanii wedding attire was simpler, but still just as colorful. The first Mafayyba to reign after the division had fallen in love with the elaborate style of the Janissarian people so much that she adopted it for her own wedding, and it had been used ever since. The reason Kiira's dress had so much embroidery on it was that it had been added to from the first wearer. This was not the original wedding dress from then; that was far too long ago, but this dress held significance. This lush purple silk was first worn over 100 years ago, and had been worn by all the royal females on their wedding day since.

She smoothed a hand over the heavy cloth. The dress was beautiful, but she also felt uncomfortable with the vast swath of sheer fabric exposing her stomach. It made her feel on display, but Bahtii assured her this was normal and no one would think twice about it. Kiira didn't think so, especially since her skin was pale compared to the surrounding people, but she did not want to complain. This moment was special for the empress.

Kiira wasn't sure how she felt about wearing Terren's mother's wedding dress, even if it had been worn by a number of other royal women. She was already wearing the woman's wedding ring. On the one hand, it was an honor to be treated like a daughter, and on the other, it felt almost damning considering what happened to Quii because of Grayten.

The ceremony was a blur as she walked down the aisle for the second time toward marriage. There were many similarities to Lorea, except for the elated music. A rhythmic drum repeated the same refrain over and over as guests clapped and sang and danced, all while the Mafelbno spoke, and they recited vows.

"The Isokanii definitely do not skimp for celebrations." Terren said, squeezing her hand as he helped her limp from the dais.

Now that the ceremony was over and her nerves were not as pronounced, she noticed his attire. A rich green long-sleeved kaftan with elaborate embroidery hung to his knees over matching pants. He wore a hat she heard Bahtii's sisters call a Fila. Together they made an extravagant couple, and Kiira could confidently say that overall weddings in the Sun Realm did not compare to this.

"This is especially extravagant because they are taking a week of celebrations and cramming it into one night. The other feasts usually have just as much food, but different people are invited to each."

"So, we're going to celebrate every tradition done at those feasts all in one night?"

Terren chuckled. "Unlikely. I think most of tonight's festivities will revolve around the traditional wedding feast, but I wouldn't be surprised if there are a few other things added."

"This is almost too much to take in," Kiira said.

"It is overwhelming; I remember my first time attending an Isokanii wedding."

Entering the outdoor gardens, Kiira stopped at the opulence. They stood at the top of a grand stair with vines wrapping in and out of the stair rail, and large vases decorated the steps on each side with palm plants and flowers overflowing the sides. Above them, an impressive wooden arch lush with more vines of wide leaves supported flickering red glass lanterns and a plant that hung like a willow but grew more akin to a necklace of pearls.

The base of the stair ended abruptly at a deep pool of clear water reflecting hundreds of colorful lanterns. Dragonflies hovered over the serene water, occasionally disturbing the mirror of stars and moonlight before flitting away into the darkness. Frogs perched on pads next to big, fragrant white flowers; their song floated on the night air along with the heady scent of the lilies.

A footpath of white marble in the water led to a grassy island with tall and thick palm trees. Long, low tables of the purest gold and silver were surrounded by extravagant plush cushions in every color of the rainbow, the banquet seats taking the free space not occupied by greenery. The gardens were even more opulent than the throne room.

"My grandmother loves the gardens," Terren said, leaning over to whisper. "She did not start them, but it has flourished under her direction. The island is the very center of the Oasis." Terren grabbed both her hands. "Kiira, you're trembling. You have nothing to fear."

"I am not afraid," she whispered. "This is so…" She trailed off, not having the adequate words to describe the emotions zipping through her. She didn't stop the tears of joy from ruining the kohl around her eyes. Since entering the Shade Realm, she constantly felt off balance and limited. Standing here now was a gift, and Kiira felt like she could breathe for the first time in a week. "Is this where the wedding banquets normally take place?"

"No, the three other royal weddings and banquets I attended did not take place in the gardens."

"Does the Mafayyba know I love plants?"

"I did not say anything to her, and Uncle Bayyan would not know to say anything either," Terren said. Confusion flashed in his eyes suddenly and disappeared. His glance at the shadowed areas of the garden, where the faintest hint of large obsidian eyes could be seen, told her what she needed to know.

"Tell Kamaria I said thank you." She smiled toward the Bear, water blurring her vision.

Taking a fortifying breath, she forced stillness into her limbs and dabbed at her eyes. "Maybe with all this beauty around us, the attendees will not be gawking at me."

He pulled her chin to meet his gaze. "If they are gawking it is because you are so lovely." He gave her a light kiss. "Hold your head proud, my Ishaiio, you have more than earned your place to stand among them."

She nodded, allowing the barest of smiles to touch her lips. "I *did* do really well in the d'Kehbezii."

"Beyond amazing."

As soon as they stepped onto the marble path, uproarious cheers flowed. Loud drums played an announcement, and everyone except his grandparents stood to honor their union.

With the riot of colors before, the exceptional spread of food, and the rhythmic music; there was one thing very clear about the Isokanii —they knew how to celebrate. It put the Yielding Festival to shame.

The clatter of golden dishes and exclamations quickly rose in the air. Outside the lantern light, she saw the outlines of Beasts as they were served massive amounts of raw meat so they too could enjoy the festivities.

Kiira scanned the long and low tables laden with food. Each item was arranged artfully, with the dishes vying for the most attractive presentation. Dates, toasted walnuts, flavored rice, stewed tomatoes, spiced yams, marinated cheeses, and mounds of pomegranate seeds. There also seemed to be an absurd amount of charred lemons with onion, and she noticed how the guests would use the dish as a palate cleanser.

Kiira gave Terren her ear as he leaned closer. "There is a specialty dish here representing each of the tribes." He pointed to each so her eyes could follow. "The hummus is from the Barikkaa, and the baklava is from Eshalahee. Since the Eshalahee are the only tribe that trades, they brought those two recipes back from across the sea." He pointed to other dishes of grain salad, smashed beans, fire-grilled vegetables, and fish kebabs made by the Asimesta and Zainadbee. Next, he drew her attention to the rows of spits with conical towers of meat turning at a snail's pace. "The Ramilkretna have perfected the slow roasted meats. The Isokanii originally took the idea from the Janissair as well, but they have definitely made it their own."

"Why did they turn the spits vertically?"

"I'm not sure, but wouldn't be surprised if it was done as an act of showmanship. The tribes are always vying with one another."

Kiira studied the spits for a moment. They were quite an invention, using people or dogs to power the wheel mechanism. She might have to try to buy one from the tribe to take with her. Liem would love to study it. Since stepping foot in the Shade Realm, she had not ceased to be amazed at the ingenuity of people when they didn't have access to magic. It made her appreciate how life was more convenient for it.

Terren pointed to the small bubbling pots, each with its own small fire to keep the contents warm. "The Iamloruu make the best Ewiidu soup, definitely a must try. The Eebaa is a Mandalltii tribe specialty. It's a fermented tuber that's been dried and then rehydrated with water."

"That sounds ... interesting?"

Terren shrugged. "Not my favorite dish, but it's not bad. The last dishes are slow roasted goat, grilled fish, and more mashed beans, made by the Ngozee, Senuresko, and Daswadii."

By the time he was done naming each dish and associating it with the different tribes, Kiira felt almost dizzy from the variety. "I don't know where to start."

"What are you afraid of least?"

She elbowed Terren lightly. "I will try the Ewiidu soup first."

"Excellent choice, my Ishaiio," Terren said before ladling a portion into her bowl.

FILLED with food that rivaled Master Danel's cooking, Kiira relaxed against the plush pillows, nestled next to Terren. The open space held a haze from the excessive use of water smokers, reminding her of the orchards in Lorea and how the morning mists liked to linger. The faint hum of bubbling could be heard each time guests pulled in the flavored tobacco. She hadn't touched the one at their table, but Terren took to the device easily, savoring the apple and pear tobacco. He'd impressed her by making the smoke come out of his mouth in a ring.

Many were still eating, but the entertainment hadn't stopped since the beginning of the feast. The first performers of men and women from the Gahijett tribe, told the story of a centuries old battle, though their movements were highly flourished and exaggerated. It was fascinating to watch. Now, she and Terren followed the fire dancers as they twirled sticks with bright orange tips and danced to the rhythm of the drums. The skill of the acrobats was far beyond her own athleticism. One man sprang from the tables, gaining enough height to do a double-flip before flipping three more times across the grass.

"How does someone even train for this?" Kiira asked, gesturing toward the men and women tumbling like a kaleidoscope before her.

"Most of these dancers begin training as children. They're members of the Gahijett and Jaburshelee tribes," Terren answered.

"No wonder they make such considerable warriors," she replied.

"You're better."

Kiira twisted to give Terren an incredulous look. "I could not do that"—she pointed to the tumblers—"if I wanted to."

He gave her a smug smile. "Aaliyah is from the Gahijett."

Kiira fell back onto the large cushion. "I got lucky, Terren. There was an opening, and I wasn't about to show her mercy, she was not giving me any."

"No, she wasn't," he said, his face darkening.

Kiira laid a hand on his arm. "Everything worked out, let it go."

He sighed. "It is not the way of the Isokanii, Kiira. She knew that."

"Yes, she did, but when do emotions ever speak reason? She wanted you, and I was in her way."

"Even if you had lost it wouldn't have changed anything. The marriage here was not the binding one."

"No, but it would have fueled the simmering unspoken hatred most Isokanii have toward Sun Dwellers. It would have justified her actions if she won," Kiira said.

"Noticed that, did you?" He shifted uncomfortably.

"It's fairly obvious in the way people look at me. Grayten is the cut and I'm the salt in an old wound," Kiira said, hiding a yawn.

He sighed, relaxing his head against hers. "Despite most everyone knowing that the Lorean royalty is different, I cannot disagree." After another yawn from her, he added, "We can leave if you wish. The celebration will continue long into the night."

Kiira's cheeks tinged. "I do not need anyone making assumptions."

Terren laughed loudly enough for the people nearby to give him a curious glance. His eyes danced with genuine humor. Whispering, he said, "That's the point."

"Terren!"

He stood quickly and scooped Kiira into his arms. The guests closest to them started singing a string of words she didn't understand, and cheers rose as Terren strode from the banquet. Kiira buried her head as much as she could in his shoulder. She knew she shouldn't be ashamed, but the feeling still crept along her skin to color her cheeks. It would be a wonder if she could look anyone in the eye for a while.

CHAPTER 19

ASSURANCES

TERREN

"You're awake," he said, setting his book on the table next to the bed. Terren had woken early to a palace bent on keeping secrets from the night before. Probably for the best; and since Kiira was sure to be asleep for a while longer, he capitalized on the silence.

"Those herbs the healer gave us really did their job," Kiira said, inching her way to sitting. She glanced at him before looking at the linen cover and scratching a nail across the fibers. She commented, "You seem tense."

There was no sense in keeping his feelings from her. "Despite my happiness last night at the banquet, I am still angry you participated in the d'Kehbezii. It wasn't necessary."

Kiira raised her brows but continued to pluck at the hem of the sheet. "It was–for me."

An answer he expected, but details always mattered. "Why?"

"I needed to prove I was capable of protecting you. Your family needed to see I wasn't like other sun-dwellers. I sought to be worthy of my position in your life."

Terren squeezed his eyes and took a deep breath. How many times did he need to explain this to her? "You already are worthy."

Kiira nodded. "With you I am, but with everyone else in this realm I am a magician and *not* Isokanii. It taints their perspective. I'm not to be trusted."

"What makes you say that? They do business with you."

She thought for a moment. "It's like being told to fear snakes, but then someone tells you one particular snake is harmless. Maybe you summon the courage to touch this harmless snake when it's held by someone else, but you still do not like snakes and you never will."

It was an interesting analogy, but he had to say, "I get the feeling you're still holding something back. Tell me the deeper reason you agreed to the trial. Please."

"I just wanted to make sure your family saw me as an advantageous alliance. You told me how they reacted to the outcome of your mother's marriage to Grayten," Kiira replied, picking at threads.

Terren studied her for a moment. "I do not believe that's all of it, Kiira. You've not been yourself since Zerrec. Please, be honest with me, I want more than anything to help you."

She sighed, a weighted sound carrying a thousand thoughts, feelings, and burdens. Quietly, she said, "After what I endured with Zerrec..." Kiira paused again, giving great concentration to the threads.

He wanted so badly to encourage talk, but didn't know what to say. Pushing her to communicate trauma she was not ready to speak would only damage any progress he'd made. He hoped she was simply gathering the right words, and that he had made it clear enough in the past she could say whatever she needed to him.

"I took the challenge because I needed to know I could protect you and myself. I did a terrible job of it in the marketplace the day Zerrec took me. Despite my efforts there and in the cavern, he still almost killed you," she said, frowning, sinking lower into the covers.

He wanted to refute her words, but she had a point. Kamaria had been severely weakened trying to save him from Zerrec's magic, and he had been vulnerable. Denying her fear and worry would be foolish of him. Terren adjusted on the bed and dragged Kiira up again to hold her close. He laced his fingers through hers, giving them a gentle kiss.

"Tell me what happened. What did Zerrec do to you in the time Liem and I were searching? Don't let those days be a burden you carry alone, and please do not try to spare my feelings." Kiira squeezed his hand, and the tension in her jaw doubled, likely debating how much to tell him.

She scrunched her brow, and after a few more drawn seconds, she took a shuddering inhale, one that told him she was on the verge of tears. "At first he was considerate. He gave me books to read, paper and writing instruments, and the furniture was comfortable."

"Furniture?"

"Yes, before he took it away … a form of punishment," Kiira answered. "He lavished me with opulence and gifts, but never took away the cuffs preventing my use of magic. Despite the finery and his attention, I still felt cut-off and isolated." She lifted their linked hands to rub a gentle finger over the symbol adorning her wrist. "My gift is so ingrained in who I am I forget it's there, and its absence was a constant ache." She added in a whisper, "I feel much the same now, only it's worse. Instead of being cut-off entirely my magic is being stolen leaving behind mere threads of the power I can wield."

"Did it feel like a hole in the middle of your chest?"

"That is exactly how it felt."

Terren squeezed her hand. He didn't want to say it and overshadow what she said, but that's how he felt when Kamaria left for nearly a month after they married. "Tell me more."

"After the first few days of Zerrec's lavish treatment, and me trying to be as compliant as possible, he came to me as he usually did, but I immediately noticed a change in his demeanor. I had been wary of a change because I remember his mood swings when he mentored me, and it always caused problems between us. Liem told you of our history I assume?"

Terren nodded.

"I tried to reject his advances as gently as I could. In the past, I read his moods well enough to keep him level headed and appeased, but this time he slapped me. In all the years I knew him he never once touched me. It was so abrupt. When I looked in his eyes, I could see there was no hope of me calming him. Something had changed in the ten years he was banished from court."

Terren squeezed her hand as she paused.

"After that moment, everything becomes somewhat of a blur, I tried to block most of it out."

He pulled her onto his lap and wiped a tear from her cheek as she settled in close to his chest.

In a hoarse whisper she added, "Zerrec has power over minds, you know. He made me see things, mostly people dying, my family dying, over and over, and I could never do anything to stop it."

Terren tightened his arms around her. His heart ached.

She continued, "Eventually, I gave up. My spirit couldn't take it anymore. I was ready to die. I'm sorry, I know that's weak of me, but I just wanted it to be over. I was tired. That's when Windrah brought me to her sanctuary. She healed me and gave me words of courage. It wasn't long after when you and Liem showed."

Terren wrapped her in the safety of his arms. "I'm sorry you had to endure that. You are so strong."

She sighed. "Not strong enough. It's what drove me to respond to your cousin's challenge. I had to prove I was capable."

"You are capable, Kiira."

She slapped her good thigh. "That is not the point! I took the trial because I needed to know I could protect you." Slumping, she added quietly, "and myself."

Terren hugged her again. He would hug her as many times as needed. "You did not need to go through the trial to prove any of that, my love. You are more than capable of protecting yourself and me. Zerrec was a surprise, as he intended."

Kiira hunched. "I should not have been so foolish, running after him as I did, blind to everything around me because I was compelled to protect people. I should have known it was an illusion. In my haste, I was reckless and it nearly got both of us killed."

"Zerrec planned his attack well," Terren countered.

"It is no excuse!" Her pitched voice echoed through the sandstone room.

"Kiira, you are not perfect, and that is okay. Stop berating yourself for something that was designed specifically to entrap you."

She worked her lip.

He reached up to tug on one of her curls. "I like you not perfect. I don't want perfect. Ny knows I couldn't keep up with you if that were true. I just want whatever you have to offer."

Kiira reluctantly nodded. "Why are you so annoyingly sweet?"

"Because the gods know I have made enough mistakes in my past for the both of us, and I know the meaning of grace. It was a hard lesson learned."

Vacillant to agree, she said, "When we are back in the Sun Realm, I'm going to find a way to protect you from castings."

"It will not work for me, whatever magic you are thinking of using."

"What?"

"Whatever you are thinking of magically, it will not work for me, remember? I'm a Shadow Walker; my connection to Kamaria negates most magic," Terren replied.

She chewed her lip. "Not amulets though, correct?"

"Yes," he said cautiously. "As long as the amulet is created with a powerful casting, yes, I can use them, but I do not want you to expend energy on something like that. It is not necessary."

"It could keep Zerrec from almost slicing your neck open," Kiira said with venom, whether it was for her old mentor or for her supposed failure he didn't know.

"Kiira," he tilted her chin, "What really is the likelihood of us running into Zerrec again? I was not in as much danger at that moment as you think." Kiira pulled her chin away. He closed his eyes for a second to balance himself. His wife could be incredibly stubborn when she wanted. "I was biding my time. You know fights are mostly about reading your opponent." He pulled her chin again to look at him. "I would not have let him kill me." Kiira searched his eyes, but made no effort to argue, and Terren let the matter go. He was sure this uncertainty would surface again, but he hoped she would find peace in the matter. "We should dress. I want you to meet the blacksmith I worked with while living here, and I hear we are lucky enough to attend an Ermyjek Ceremony."

Kiira sat up. "Really? That is so exciting!"

"Yes, so we should get moving."

"We need to leave immediately?

Terren quirked one side of his mouth, already knowing what she would ask.

"Could we maybe ... being careful of my leg, of course," she said.

Terren leaned down to kiss the side of her neck. "I think we can arrange that."

CHAPTER 20
SING FOR ME
ZERREC

"This man"—Zerrec shoved the bloodied soldier on his left closer to the baluster—"is a traitor to the kingdom. For his crime, Captain Denel will be whipped and demoted." He nodded his head to give the arresting soldiers permission to begin the punishment. A few shouts of approval reached above the noise of questioning murmurs, but by far the loudest sounds were the wails from Denel's family.

Music, he thought.

The citizens of Klynotia were eating up the act, which is what he needed. The soldiers pushed the young captain up a set of stairs onto a platform built to sit above the baluster. He had considered a stage in the courtyard below, but preferred the display this balcony stage created. He wanted all to see the lengths he would go to punish those who went against him.

"No, no, no, no." The young captain's sobs momentarily drowned out the crowd.

Zerrec spotted several looks of sympathy, so he shouted, "Do not feel sorry for this man. Not only has he betrayed his kingdom, but his countrymen."

The cries of pain from Denel with each strike of the whip punctuated his message.

"He's no traitor!"

Zerrec scanned the crowd with narrowed eyes to find the dissenter, but they'd hidden themselves well. Murmurs flitted from one person to the next as they questioned the integrity of the situation. He used his magic to cast a net over the crowd to detect the speaker, but with most heart rates already elevated, the spell's accuracy was compromised. Unless he caught them yelling, identifying the soldier's defender was impossible.

Zerrec turned to the thoroughly whipped soldier. "This traitor, once the proud captain of the tax soldiers, was taking more than designated by the crown. Upon reviewing the tax records, I discovered the error and immediately sought to punish the man responsible for your suffering."

The information was close enough to the truth, making it the best sort of lie to win him the favor of the people. The kingdom's coffers were bursting, and now thanks to his deal with Osmont they would be even healthier, but the people did not need to know. Murmurs turned into louder grumbles.

Now time to reel them in.

"I do not tolerate this kind of turncoat behavior in Klynotia. It is my job as your king to protect, and I have failed all of you." That surprised a few and eased several scowls. Some nods of agreement bobbed among the bodies. "To discover this treachery took me far longer than it should. After some calculations, I can confidently say the kingdom's stores are well enough to allow for recompense." He paused to let that information sink in. "To right the wrong done, there will be no taxes for three months!" A bubble of surprise and agreement reached him on the balcony. Zerrec smiled, enjoying the increasing number of bobbing heads. He raised his arms to gather the praise given. This would buy him the favor he needed since he was only dropping taxes marginally after the grace period expired. Zerrec deepened his voice. "Let this be a lesson to all who serve Klynotia's great kingdom. Treachery will not be tolerated and I will uncover all deception toward the crown. Anyone discovered will be punished"— he pointed to Denel—"accordingly."

The crowd fell silent.

Zerrec kicked the young former captain in his flayed open ribcage, sending him tumbling over the edge. The fall wasn't enough to kill a healthy man, but Denel had been fairly abused before ever stepping foot on the balcony for this show. His screams lasted a moment before the thud of his body signaled his death. A scream broke the silence, and a woman rushed forward. Zerrec stared a moment before turning to give a pointed look at Osmont pressed against the stone of the castle, reminding him he'd narrowly escaped the same fate as Captain Denel. After a moment, he strode back inside. His point had been made, and his place as the King of Klynotia was now cemented.

"I HEAR you have a sister in need of some healing." Zerrec circled the young man, thumb stroking his chin, and elbow resting on his wrist. The boy had a fine layer of dirt all over him, and extra collected under his nails. The ragged clothes desperately needed replacement, the worn patches a testament to how hard he worked to care for his younger sibling. With both parents dead, he saved every coin to pay any physician willing to help keep his sister alive, albeit barely. The boy was malleable, exactly what Zerrec wanted.

My new valet, Zulen, completed his assignment flawlessly. He's becoming a valuable asset.

"Yes, Sire, that is correct."

"What is your name?"

"Mountainsinger, Berro Mountainsinger, Sire."

Zerrec released the hand from his chin to roll his wrist, producing a few coins for show. It pleased him to see the boy lock eyes with the gold, nearly salivating. "And did my valet tell me correctly that you are the bard for a small grouping of mountain villages on the border of my kingdom?" The answer was obvious, considering the boy had a lute, but his questioning held a very specific purpose. It allowed the boy to feel comfortable, and the more he felt at ease, the readier he could be persuaded. Zerrec knew everything he needed about Berro before being introduced to the lad. His valet had known Berro his entire life. Zulen watched his friend struggle for years without parents, and when Zerrec tasked his valet with finding someone, he immediately returned with the young bard in a matter of weeks.

"Yes, Sire, that is true. The owners of the taverns where I play do not pay much for my entertainment, though I have provided entertainment for years, so I also work the mines during the day." Berro hunched his shoulders as his words reminded him how little his efforts provided.

Zerrec leisurely circled the young man, eyeing his ever sinking demeanor. Berro, it seemed, would do anything to help his sister. Desperate times may call for desperate measures, but desperate people will do almost anything, and if it got him what he wanted, Zerrec was happy to provide an open door. "Play something for me."

"Would you like to hear something specific, Sire?" Berro asked, pulling the lute from his back.

Zerrec waved his hand. "No, anything will do."

He backed himself into the shadows so Berro would not focus on his stares; the boy was nervous enough. The bard plucked a few notes to tune the well-loved strings, and when he cleared his throat, a lucent, crisp voice filled the stone room, allowing the reverberation to accompany the song nicely.

Fairly through the hills, my Aria calls
A bell ringing
Her soft white blankets the ground
To keep me ever seeking
Where have my seekers gone?
She asks each crystalline morn'
A bell ringing
Return to me, return to me

My Aria calls
'Ere crystalline morn'

"I DO NOT BELIEVE I have ever heard that one, Berro," Zerrec said.

He blushed. "It is an original, Sire ... my favorite season is winter."

Zerrec acknowledged the confession.

He's better than I expected. He'll definitely do.

"What if I offered you a way to heal your sister, Berro." He let his voice soften to entice the boy. "Would you take it?" Keeping his voice low, free from inflection, encouraged the boy to drop his emotional guard, lulling him toward hope. It took some practice in front of a mirror, but Zerrec learned to use Grayten's voice with considerable skill. This body's deep timbered tone was his favorite voice out of all the somas he'd occupied over the years.

There was every chance for Berro to refuse the offer, and that was fine, but Zerrec had faith in his valet's choice. The young man should cave. After all, who could say no to a king with the power to save a beloved sister? The entire situation lay in his favor. The debate was plain to see on Berro's face. This was a boy very much the opposite of Zulen. He was not afraid of honest work, and Zerrec watched as the young bard examined the offer from every angle. The moment came in a blink, but as expected, Berro capitulated.

His voice trembled, still unsure of his decision, but he said, "I will do anything to save Elanora."

Immediately, Zerrec handed Berro the three gold coins from before, and he said, "Good. Use the money to bring your sister here so the court physician can attend to her."

Not that the court physician could help, from what he'd been told about the girl, but this young bard did not need to know of his magic. Zerrec intended to hide behind the old man's medicinal skills for as long as possible. According to Zulen, the girl clung to life, so Zerrec planned to heal the girl a little at a time to keep the bard loyal. The minor improvements to his sister's health would keep Berro Mountainsinger on a tether.

"Here is a tincture to help strengthen her for the journey," he said, pulling the small bottle from the pocket of his doublet. "Report to me in three weeks."

"Yes, Sire." Berro kept a deep bow as he exited the study.

Zerrec trained his eyes on the young man until the door was shut.

Easiest game of cat and mouse I've ever played.

He smirked. He was about to return to his other work when a knock interrupted. "Enter."

Zulen stepped in. "Sire, I have someone here that wishes to speak with you."

"I am not receiving, Zulen."

"I understand, Sire, but I believe you will want to speak with this woman, if only briefly."

Two weeks ago this would have annoyed him and he would have punished his valet, but Zulen had proven himself with Berro, putting him in a suitable mood. He would see if this visitor was as important as the valet claimed. A dark-skinned woman stepped into the room. A black strip of fabric tied around her neck—in here she didn't need it. Isokanii. She curtsied, though it was clumsy.

"Speak."

"Sire, my name is Aaliyah, and I heard from some … travelers in the north that you were seeking useful information about Prince Terren."

Zerrec narrowed his eyes. He had asked Zulen and the hired mercenaries gathering in the north to discretely spread word, but he never expected one of the Isokanii to show up with information. From viewing Grayten's memories, the people were still upset by the death of their only princess. "What would you know of my son?"

"I am his cousin," she said, a flash of fire glossing her eyes as she straightened her shoulders.

"And you, Isokanii, would so easily talk to me about him? Your people hate me. Are you not breaking the emperor's law by standing here?"

"I have been shamed and banished from my people. Your son did that to me. He was the last in a long line of suitors to spurn me, and I want to show him what he's missing by choosing *her*."

Ah, revenge. Well, that is something I understand well.

Zerrec gave a cordial smile. "Take a seat, Aaliyah, I have a feeling you will be here a while."

CHAPTER 21

CEREMONY FOR ERMYJEK

TERREN

He shielded his eyes against the harsh sun as he waited for Kiira to tie the black cloth around her eyes. She'd described to him what things looked like, but he still found it difficult to imagine colors so dreary, especially in the brilliant sun of the desert. At least they would be inside for most of the day. Terren turned back to see how close she was to finishing. Today, she'd chosen a plain natural linen wrap dress over green patterned voluminous trousers with a deep blue sash and slippers. The only thing not hidden was the intricate Zkinne designs on her hands. He, too, wore the same attire except he chose a blue wrap with natural linen trousers and sash. The commonality of daily garments between men and women of the Isokanii made choosing an outfit each day much easier. Sometimes he wished it were the same in the Sun Realm.

Taking Kiira's hand, he said, "I hope you enjoy the ceremony tonight. It took some convincing to reassure my grandfather you would not repeat any of what you witnessed."

Her brows lifted. "Of course not! I would not betray the trust they've shown me. I never even expected a ceremony while we were here let alone the honor of attending one."

"Your performance in the d'Kehbezii lent toward his agreement."

"How so? Because I refrained from slicing your cousin's neck open?"

Her words had a sly edge to them, and Terren allowed one small grunt of humor. "He believes you fought with honor by accepting the challenge in the first place despite the 'delicacy of Sun Dwellers' as he so bluntly put it," Terren said.

"Delicacy?" She snorted. "I think the Mafelbno is being told ludicrous stories by the Eshalahee. I have never backed away from a challenge."

"Likely." Slinging a bag over his shoulder, Terren pulled her toward a cramped alley between palace buildings. "Come, time for you to meet the grumpiest man to ever live."

"Dymek, good to see you," he yelled over the ring of hammer against steel and braced for the surly reply sure to come.

"Heard you were back. You didn't invite me." The low grumble was nearly inaudible over the roar of the smithy.

Between pings of metal against metal, Terren managed, "You know I did not have a choice in the attendees, but you would have been my guest of honor." He kept his features neutral since Dymek wouldn't appreciate any show of conciliation. The fire-hardened man grunted, the only sign of approval Terren would receive. The blacksmith had been forged by molten metal and glory fires for so long, he'd gone so far as to shield himself from the heat of emotions as well, maybe even to the point of crisping the edges. "I brought my wife," Terren added, hoping to assuage the man. "She wanted to meet you."

Kiira stepped out from behind Terren—she'd been using him as a shield against the heat of the efficacious forge—giving the rough man a small wave and smile.

Dymek briefly glanced in their direction before asking, "Why she want to meet me?"

Terren nodded, encouraging her to reply. Kiira said, "I have been told of your talent, and my brother tinkers with blacksmithing. I have a peripheral interest."

"Humph. Come to put me on display, Terren?"

"Yes, seems only fair after all the years you did it to me." He crossed his arms, pleased with his witty reply. He'd been waiting to use it.

The blacksmith plunged the piece he was working into the nearby barrel of water. The hiss and steam preluded a glare that would have cowed most people. Terren just smiled at the gruff man, completely at ease. Dymek offended most, but after working with him, he could not hide behind the singed outer layers of his personality.

"Payback is it?"

Terren chuckled. "No, but I wouldn't mind you sacrificing an afternoon to break bread with us."

The blacksmith stared at Terren for several drawn out seconds, as if measuring the genuineness of his words. "Fine, but you owe me two days labor before you leave."

Terren grinned. "You have my word."

KHEPRII SHRIEKED, delighted, as Terren stepped through the door. The blacksmith's wife was joyous in opposition to her dour husband. Her long black hair, braided into intricate twists, hung loosely with a bright yellow strip, the same as her dress, to tie it behind her shoulders. A dangerous color for the wife of a blacksmith constantly covered in dirt, sweat, and soot to wear.

"Kheprii, it is good to see you," Terren said. Turning to Kiira, he added, "Kheprii made my miserable days bearable." The cheeky statement elicited yet another huff from Dymek.

"Oh, Terren! Naughty!" She gave him an affectionate slap on the arm.

At that moment, a boy, still unsteady on his legs but willing to use them, burst through the curtain at the back wall. "Amaa, iine ebii."

Kheprii bustled over to the small boy, scooping him into a bracing hug. She turned her bright smile to Terren and Kiira. In Isokanii she said, "This is Bassma. He came as a blessing, thank the gods. I prayed to Lehlo for years and she heard my cries. He is one summer and five moons. "

Dymek briefly stole his wife's attention when she finished talking about their son.

Kiira used the respite in conversation to tap him on the shoulder and whisper, "I did not fully understand."

Terren repeated Kheprii's words, mentioning the miscarriages he remembered Dymek talking about when they worked together. It made the little boy even more special. Kiira frowned.

"What is it?"

"It saddens me because magic has the potential to heal her body making it possible for her to conceive. Almost all Blood Mages have some knowledge of how to heal a woman's body so it doesn't happen repeatedly. Most people in Lorea, even the poorest, seek out healing if it happens more than twice."

Terren nodded solemnly, hearing her heart behind the statement. Sadly, he had to remind her that most magic did not work on Isokanii, not to mention the majority of the people disliked magicians. Kiira nodded, but there was still a wrinkle between her eyes. He was about to add something else when their side conversation ended because Dymek stood abruptly to stomp from the room, leaving a layer of soot in his wake.

"Do not mind him," Kheprii said, apologizing to Kiira. "He does not like when I make him wash."

"Kheprii, Kiira's grasp of the language is still tenuous. The simpler you can keep sentences the better," Terren said, giving his wife's hand a squeeze.

"Oh! Yes, yes, yes! I speak Sunarian."

"That is not necessary, Kheprii," Kiira replied. "I just need conversation to be slower."

Kheprii grinned, proceeding to chatter about life since Terren left, but not before depositing Bassma on the floor with a few simple wooden toys and a plate of food. Apparently, the business was never ending, almost running Dymek ragged with trying to fulfill orders from the Gahijett and Jaburshelee tribes. He was even having to turn away business from many because he could not keep up with it.

"Why does Dymek not seek an apprentice?" Kiira asked.

"Because I do not want some incompetent idiot messing with my designs," Dymek answered, coming back into the room far less sooty than when he left.

Terren grinned, adding, "What Dymek will not tell you is he adopted some of my designs into his own. I should force a percentage out of him." Kiira and Kheprii grinned. He was trying to get under the blacksmith's skin, and she knew it. Across the table, the blacksmith glowered at him while attempting to give gentle attention to his son.

"Terren, do not be so mean. He's always spoken fondly of you, Dymek," Kiira said.

Terren turned a serious eye toward the blacksmith, placing a hand on his chest. "He saw something in me and gave me a chance I never deserved. I learned a lot from him." After a charged silence, he continued with a smirk, "Of course, it never stopped me from giving him constant heartache."

"That's the god's truth," grumbled Dymek.

"Oh, you hush," Kheprii jumped in, serving a platter of bread, olives, and herbed goat cheese. "When Terren was here, I never saw my husband happier."

The conversation descended into the usual back and forth of how each was doing. Kheprii kept most of the conversation going, diving into the holes created at any lull. Terren appreciated the open hospitality since this was the most relaxed he'd seen Kiira since stepping foot in the Oasis.

Before leaving for the evening, Dymek pulled Terren out to his shop. Handing over an oiled cloth, he said, "I had begun making this for you, but you left before I finished."

Gently unwrapping the gift, Terren stilled as shock flowed through him. The knife, a magnificent obsidian blade as long as his forearm, had fine uneven lines of silver running up and down the steel in layers. "Dymek, this is amazing. How did you create this?"

"I used multiple small billets to create a larger billet before hammering it out. Discovered it by accident when I was trying to use up waste pieces," he said. "I managed to produce a few unique patterns, but this one is my favorite. I call it Kiilee's Ladder. The knife is more decorative than anything, since I know you have your favorites."

"It makes a statement, definitely," Terren said, unable to give better words. He balanced the knife on a finger, and despite the blacksmith's declaration that it was mostly decorative, the blade balanced beautifully.

Dymek directed him to a wall of other knives with the same black and silver, but the patterns were all different. "I call this one Ostiimii's Tears."

Terren leaned closer, and sure enough, the pattern looked like little ripples created from raindrops on water. He turned his attention back to the gift, running gentle fingers over the flat of the blade. "Dymek, have you tried to sell any of these?"

"No, they take a long time to make well. I need help."

"You should reach out to the Asimesta clan to see if someone from there is interested in learning. Find a young one that can stay with you until your son is old enough."

The blacksmith pursed his lips.

"Just think about it," Terren said.

Dymek gave a curt nod and trundled back toward the house. Terren wrapped the oilcloth around the knife, studied the forge with one last look—having the feeling he'd never see it again—and followed. This knife would be a treasured gift, always.

"I'll do my best to translate," he said, helping Kiira settle onto a large cushion on the third and highest tier of the colosseum on the back part of the palace grounds. After leaving the blacksmith, they'd had enough time to meander through the gardens, following a path of flowing water with plants marking the barrier on one side. Flowers of every color decorated the greenery. Of course, Kiira was in love. He almost had to pick her up and carry her from the serenity she felt among the plants, even with her magic dimmed.

At least they'd made it to the ceremony, and before they were even comfortable, a servant came through with a tray filled with rock-honey wine, small dried fruits, and nuts. As usual, the moon shone its brightest for the ceremony, and with the clear skies the desert often had, it made the spread before them easy to see.

She waved a hand in his direction. "I'll ask questions later, but what is the general procedure?"

Terren nodded. "Before all of this, my cousin has done three days of fasting. He's had nothing but water mixed with a little rock honey. It allows the body to be weak enough to accept the bond from the Beast, but strong enough to also endure the toll it takes. Which is why this can be dangerous. You have to have a strong will to complete the full ceremony."

"Like the old man in the market? He wasn't able to complete it was he?" Kiira asked.

"Yes, and that reminds me. I spotted him in the souk the first day we were here."

Kiira whipped her head toward him. "What?"

"After you were taken, I spoke to him and he listened to my advice and came home. There are places to help take care of those unable to complete the ceremony. It didn't used to be that way. Before the split of the realms, if you failed you were alone. I did not get a clear look at Dain, but he seemed to be with a group of others like him looking at the wares," Terren said.

"Good."

"Once the ceremony begins, there is an exhaustive amount of oaths presented and agreed to, all of which are memorized even though it is not required to repeat them. Then the summoning begins. None of us completing the ceremony know beforehand what Shade Beast will be attached to us. The Beasts are the ones to choose and it could be any sort of predatory creature." He noticed Kiira's breath hitch. "Will you be okay with this?"

Slowly, she nodded. "I know the difference now, and I'm glad I'm not as ignorant as I used to be, but ... watching someone you love crunched in between the teeth of a vicious animal is not something easily forgotten."

"I understand," he said, laying a hand on her knee. "We do not need to stay."

Kiira shook her head. "No, I want to see this. I want to know what you endured to be bonded with Kamaria."

The indistinct murmur of conversation hushed as a singular figure paraded to the center of the amphitheater. Terren recognized the master of ceremonies from his own time in the center. The massive, elaborate headdress caught the eye, made from the shed feathers of various Beasts that protruded in all directions. His robes changed pattern and color all the way to his sandaled feet. Terren explained to Kiira that the colors represented the different tribes, even though only the royal family bonded with Beast.

"Today, we witness a high honor, given to us by the gods! One of our number has agreed to the challenge of accepting a Beast. With the strength of will, the heart of perseverance, and the mind of dedication you may be witnesses to the birth of a new Stietii Tetsa!

The crowd repeated the last sentence as one, the collective voices filling the open air colosseum.

"Seeker, join me now," the ceremony master said, flinging his arms wide and turning to face the lone man reverently walking toward the center.

"Seeker," he began as he knelt, "It is your duty to protect the people. You will answer the call when needed to protect. You will serve your Beast as it will serve you for the rest of your days. You will be an example to the people. You will protect this realm and all Beasts with your life. Do you agree to fulfill the oath of the sacred call of the Stietii Tetsa?"

"I will," the Seeker responded, his voice clear and strong.

"Let the calling of your partner begin!"

Thoom.

Thoom.

Thoom. Thoom.

The single drum sang into the darkness. Another joined.

Thoom.

Thoom.

Thoom. Thoom.

Then a third.

Thoom.

Thoom.

Thoom. Thoom.

Another, this time frantic. Louder. Faster.

Silence.

The tension in Kiira's shoulders grew with every drumbeat, and she was enthralled by the scene before her. Terren remembered the drums from his own ceremony, his immersion. The loud, frantic beats had made his heart race, and fueled the desire to let his breath run wild. The tension had been so rigid along his spine that all he wanted to do was scream but dared not. He grimaced. The worst was yet to come.

Kiira's head snapped to the right. A twitching nose came and went through the shadows. A measure of fear permeated the colosseum. It was never a positive omen if a Beast came and left, but it was better than them disappearing in the middle of the ceremony, leaving the Seeker pulled between two worlds. Relief exhaled its way along the tiers of seating as another curious nose appeared. A sleek body soon followed, cautious, and slow. A mongoose. Only strict training prepared the Seeker to remain frozen. That was the hardest moment to keep still, and even now, Terren's fingers twitched at the anticipation of what came next. The Beast had to decide, and as long as his cousin remained strong, a successful ceremony looked promising.

The Mongoose continued the perusal of his cousin, even going as far as nosing him. Moving to see the Seeker face to face, the Beast stared at him, making the final decision. Everyone held their breath. Terren included. It didn't matter if he'd experienced this very moment; it still turned his stomach into a pit of snakes.

Finally, the Mongoose crouched, lowering itself as much as possible in front of the Seeker. It's permission to begin the bonding process. His cousin bowed to the Beast to show his agreement, and instantly the drums turned frantic. The Mongoose lost its solidity—the shape still there, but anyone could have walked through it—and crept forward to touch its nose to the heart of the Seeker.

Bit by bit, the Beast disappeared inside his cousin, the enormous shadowy bulk of it pressing forward into his body. His screams were almost unbearable to listen to as they triggered the memory of pain inside Terren. The chanting from the drummers tried to match the wail of the Seeker, but nothing could cover the raw screaming. Terren never remembered screaming during his own ceremony, but afterwards he could not speak in more than a whisper for three days. A final piercing cry came, and Terren winced. He knew that pain. What felt like minutes and hours in the moment actually happened in mere seconds. Bones softening and hardening. Veins swelling and pinching. Nerves firing endlessly. The wails ceased, but pain still etched the Seeker's face. As soon as the Mongoose vanished, his cousin fell, palms slapping the earth. The drums ceased. No sound filled the colosseum, not even the hum of insects. From this distance, he could see his cousin's body move as he gulped for air, and the raspy sound filled the tiered seating as seconds elongated into a minute then two. Stillness reigned as everyone waited. Waited for success. Waited for defeat. Would another Stietii Tetsa be born? Would there be a Pheneojek?

Low, droning rhythmic prayers circled the colosseum. With heroic effort, his cousin put one foot beneath him and then another, standing on newborn legs, but standing as a Stietii Tetsa. Again the drums started, low but growing. Infused with the power of a Beast, his cousin moved like lightning as he darted from one end of the colosseum to the other in a matter of seconds; his acrobatics were heightened to an astounding degree. After a short performance, he came to a stop in the center of the floor.

Terren turned to Kiira, not wanting to miss her reaction as his cousin used his new bond to transform into an enormous Mongoose. Not as large as the Beast itself, but certainly bigger than any human. His wife's mouth dropped open, he doubted she even noticed.

The ceremony ended as the Seeker separated from his new partner, the two now one pair. The partners slowly made their way from the amphitheater to rest, recover, and start the lifetime of friendship that came with such a close bond.

"So what did you think?" Terren asked.

Still dazed from it all, she said softly, "I have a difficult time thinking you went through"—she gestured weakly at the floor—"that."

Terren had no response. How could he adequately describe what it felt like to her? Excruciating? Sure, but somehow even that did not feel like enough of a word.

"What I feel, though, is pride," she amended.

He tilted his head, seeking an explanation.

"You did something not many can do or have achieved, and it makes me appreciate the bond you have with Kamaria even more."

Terren hadn't expected praise, but at the moment an overwhelming amount of love for her buoyed him, seeing the respect she had for his status as a Shadow Walker.

"It does not make me love Shade Beasts, but I can appreciate them," Kiira said.

Terren nodded. He sat with her long after the drummers left their pillows. Long after the tiers cleared of people. Long after the moon fell from its peak. He sat long after Kiira fell asleep in his arms and relived the ceremony that gave him Kamaria.

CHAPTER 22

PLAN OF ACTION

ZERREC

"You know what you are supposed to do?" Zerrec eyed the man, curious about this mercenary from across the sea. He was from the kingdom Janissair, a war-addled country pretending to be united because they claimed a leader. The first Uman was strong enough to strike peace between the clans, his successor was too weak to maintain it, and whispers indicated the current Uman wanted power and prestige—tensions between clans were once again volatile and they were encouraged to send fighters out to gain their wealth. It explained why this mercenary, a man not born of the realms, now stood before him in his voluminous linen pants and cropped vest.

When Zerrec had been an advisor in Lorea, the Uman at the time had been indifferent to clan peace, so the little progress made toward alliances had fizzled into nothing. He remembered Herretus trying on multiple occasions to strike a trade agreement, but each attempt resulted in lost soldiers and ambassadors. After the second attempt, no one volunteered to go.

"Yes, Sire." The mercenary said, struggling to keep a wicked grin from his face.

Zerrec sat at his desk in the light of a few candles, leaving everything else in shadow, hiding the slovenly bookshelves he'd not had time to reorganize. The most he'd managed was to tame the chaotic desk. Taking over this body, one in an established role, prevented him from easing into responsibility. Every day he wondered how Grayten ran the kingdom as well as he did considering the level of dishevelment.

The curtains to his left opened to the courtyard below, a hint of torchlight coloring the glass panes. It was a new moon, and clouds blanketed the night, making it an ideal night to meet with his chosen proxy in secret. This was not a man he needed anyone to know about, not even the soldiers usually guarding his door. He had thought about having Amol meet him in his hidden room below the kitchens, but doing so would risk an encounter with a servant. Here in his study, he could come and go at this hour through a hidden door with no one knowing.

Zerrec steepled his fingers, examining the mercenary. He'd grown accustomed to the nuances of Grayten's body, and he now exuded confidence with smooth, precise movements, no longer coming across as clumsy—or what most people likely presumed as drunk.

The Janissarian's brazenness seemed etched on him. Regardless, that's why Zerrec had chosen him out of all the Janissairian mercenaries to answer his summons. He was placing his faith in Amol to ensure his plans were executed as intended, without qualms or hesitation. Zerrec also hoped that the mercenaries' displayed strength in leadership would prevent loss. His plans for the northern part of the kingdom needed to be made one small chess move at a time. Duke Aubin was a clever man; that much was clear in his correspondences, so the actions Zerrec took needed to be minute in order to survive the long game. He needed to whittle the duke's resources to floundering without implicating himself. Zerrec leaned back in his chair. "If you kill the people, you will not get paid, that is not the point of you being here." Death was not in his plans, yet. If any citizen died because of the mercenaries' actions, every man in the war party would feel his wrath.

"And if soldiers come?"

"You are allowed to make your stance clear, but do not be excessive. You can kill the Duke's men, but if you see soldiers with the royal mark do not touch them." He leaned back into the light to zero in on the mercenary leader with sharp eyes. "If you disobey, my plans will be affected and I will not be pleased." Zerrec briefly constricted the blood flow to the mercenary's heart just enough to make sure the man knew his orders were serious.

The mercenary gasped as his heart beat normally again, and he rubbed his chest, eyeing Zerrec. "The generosity of payment is enough for us to follow orders."

Zerrec smiled. He was giving Amol and his men access to whatever they could haul from the mines for as long as he stationed them in the town, including the use of free labor from the residents. There were more than enough riches in the kingdom's stores—thanks to Grayten and now Osmont—to let the war band have some fun hauling precious stones from the mine. A convenient way to ensure loyalty. When he was done with them, Amol and his war band would return to Janissair with riches beyond measure, and be praised all the more for it. Zerrec wouldn't be surprised if the man before him would be the next Uman after staging a coup.

"Excellent." He tossed a heavy bag of coins and added, "You will be in the company of a bard. He has separate orders from you." He narrowed his eyes and lowered his voice. "If I hear any whispers of abuse toward my bard from any of your men, none of you will live long enough to enjoy the spoils of your work."

"Of course, Sire. He is to be with us the entire time?"

"He may come and go as needed."

"Your orders will be followed to the strictest degree."

"Excellent." Zerrec let his eyes roam over the man one last time. He pointed to the bag of coins. "Find different clothing for you and your men. You'll lose to the harsh mistress of winter otherwise. The mountains are unforgiving."

The mercenary bowed, said, "Yes, Sire," and backed out of the room.

This plan will work. Terren will be at my mercy even if it kills me.

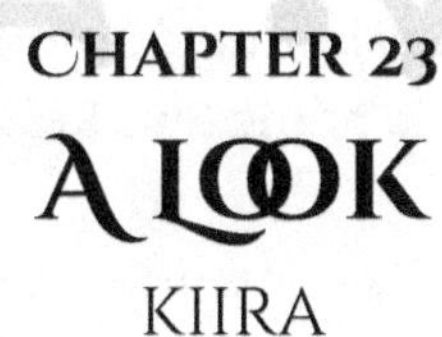

CHAPTER 23
A LOOK
KIIRA

Squinting to better see the dusky horizon, she studied the dull plains of the Shade Realm. A few patches of tilled farmland could be seen from her vantage at Tilkt Point. For as many weeks as she spent in this realm, Kiira could never perfectly imagine the beauty, not when everything looked as if someone had dumped the remains of fireplace ash over everything. Even with the cloth over her eyes, the wefted mute gold of wheat bowing to the strong breeze pushing off the sea seemed half-hearted. At least compared to the Burning Plains. Despite that, this was the last time she would likely set foot in the Shade Realm, so Kiira did her best to memorize the view. She needed to remember paints and paper when they landed in the Lorean port so she could make drymera for the royal libraries. Looking at it now, she would miss this world that was part of Terren. Still, she was glad to leave. Every second felt oppressive, since she could only sense the barest hint of her magic. The Shade Realm was greedy. If it hadn't been for her desire to see as much of the Shade Realm as possible, Kiira would have asked to leave weeks ago.

She closed her eyes, for far beyond her vision lay the rocky and flat mesa home of the Mandalltii Tribe and the Night Crystal Quarries.

The taste of the fresh honey from the large rock bees still tingled across her tastebuds. The peppered rocks where the bees made their home produced an interesting honey with a sharper taste than the honey from the royal gardens. It had also been interesting to learn how the Isokanii mined the treasured Night Crystals. It was so strange that an item of the Shade Realm could absorb and store magic, making her wonder how the crystals of the Sun Realm reacted to magic before its destruction.

A loud crackle turned her attention to the eastern edge of the Glazefire Canyon. Before they ported, she asked Terren if she could stand at the edge of the haphazard and jutting points. It'd been a climb to reach the rim where she could see the magical sparks created by the tension of one realm reacting to the other. Kiira had, of course, seen it along the bridge, but standing at the untamed edge gave her another sense entirely. Even being on the Shade Realm side, she could sense a vast amount of magic swirling between the canyon walls. Did it exist in droves down near the frothing waters? She had never ventured close enough to the canyon from the Sun Realm side to have known such a power existed, but she definitely needed to tell Liem about it. Why this store of magic had never been documented or recorded by past magicians puzzled her. Had no one ever ventured here? It seemed ridiculous, but she never recalled Zerrec talking about it.

The canyon seemed a pittance compared to the memories she'd hold for the rest of her life. She was thankful Terren agreed to bring her here because it was an opportunity her brother would never have, and there was something satisfying about having an experience not shared with her twin. She'd weathered the Shade Realm like no other Sunarian, especially as the first to win and witness sacred Isokanii rituals. Both gave her a new understanding of the realm and its tribal culture. She now understood why she'd offended Terren with her outburst about Beast before the wedding. Her ignorance at the time made her cruel.

"Are you ready, Kiira?" Terren asked, coming up behind to enjoy the moment with her.

She leaned into the affection. "Yes and no. Yes, because I am ready to not feel like a sun-bleached sponge. Having my magic rung from me has been an itch I cannot satisfy, and I want to see vibrant colors again. Yet no, because I have enjoyed myself here. It is so different from Lorea and the Sun Realm."

"We will visit again once Klynotia is stable under our rule. It may take some years, but we'll make it happen. Can you wait that long?"

Kiira gave a long, dramatic sigh and slumped into a deadweight. "I suppose."

Terren chuckled, his warm breath brushing over her ear before he kissed the side of her head. "I love you."

"I love you."

"The ship is loaded except for the horses. Starfire is being temperamental."

"Of course he is. I'll let him go for a hard ride before we board."

Terren guided her to the edge of the cliffs to what the Isokanii call The Skefii, a long, two-hundred-fifty meter slide carved into the side of the cliff that traveled long and straight toward the beach. There was of course a path to walk down, but it would take nearly half an hour to descend, and the slide would take her to the dark sands in under a minute. The smoothed stone was an ingenious way to get things to and from the beach with minimal effort. It saved hours of hard labor since the Isokanii also used the ramp to pull cargo up.

Grabbing a thick mat of woven grass, she settled herself on top, gripping the edges as instructed. Looking toward the end, Kiira felt her stomach drop before she even moved. She'd slid down things before, but nothing this smooth. How fast was she going to go?

"Ready?" Terren asked.

"As I'll ever be."

"See you at the beach!" He said with a firm push against her lower back.

Kiira tipped over the edge, and before her mind could process anything, she felt the forceful wind of speed, her eyes watering and hair flying behind her like a flag. The obsidian cliffs became a blur as the reflective sands came ever closer. Her heart pounded with an exhilaration she'd only known from the back of Starfire.

The steep incline smoothed, and she came to a steady stop. The moment ended, but her grin did not. This was unquestionably something she needed to convince her father to build in Lorea, perhaps from the top of the lighthouse to the beach. It was too bad Klynotia didn't have any cliffs to build such an amazing thrill. Terren, not far behind, came to a stop with a mirroring grin; the unspoken language of pure joy. She handed her mat over to his outstretched hand before turning to seek Starfire.

The manic horse was easy to spot, his nearly white rump standing out as it danced back and forth, carving a deeper and deeper track in the sand. Kiira huffed. Striding toward him, she gave three loud chirping whistles with her fingers. Starfire promptly stilled, but tugged in annoyance at the rope holding him back.

In Isokanii she said, "You may release." Starfire trotted in her direction and butted his head into her chest, nearly knocking her over. "Have you been a terror, my sweet boy?" Kiira asked, stroking his cheek. "Would you like to go for a ride?" The horse's muscles twitched with unrelenting energy. She mounted his bare back and shouted to Terren she would be no more than thirty minutes. Grabbing his mane, she said to Starfire, "Run, Starfire! Run!"

"I'm determined to figure out how to beat you this time," she said, making a few half-hearted strikes with her staff before spinning it away.

"Not sure what makes you think you will," Terren teased. "You couldn't beat me at the temple on solid ground, I doubt you can beat me on a moving ship." He retaliated with several easy strikes of his own.

She narrowed her eyes. Terren had beaten her enough times with the staff for a bruise to color her pride.

I should be able to spot something to give me a tell. There.

A small shift in his hands showed two move sets.

Maybe I am learning to read him better.

She didn't move her hands; he would notice, but sorted through the potential strikes he could use. Kiira tamped down a small thrill of glee at having a chance.

Terren spun the staff, striking to come down on her shoulder. Kiira lifted to block when a force of magic slammed into her awareness. Stronger than when crossing from the Shade Realm back into the Sun Realm. That had been uncomfortable, but this was breathlessness after a fall. She stumbled before hitting the deck. Kiira gasped on hands and knees, her knuckles white trying to grip the smooth planks of the ship. Terren came to her side in an instant.

"Kiira! Kiira, are you alright?"

She didn't need to see him to feel the tension radiating from every muscle. She grasped his arms for support. "Yes," she choked, attempting to stand.

"Let me get you below to lie down."

"No!" Softer she added, "no, take me to the rail"—she pointed weakly—"over there."

Terren's expression said he wanted to refuse, but at least he knew her stubbornness well enough to know she would wobble toward the rail without his help if he denied her. The force of magic eased as she became used to the intensity, and by the time Kiira reached where she pointed out, she stood firm, though kept a tight grip on the rail. Squinting, she could see the faint outline of land. "Is that the Cloister?"

"Yes, it is."

"Wow," the exclamation soft against her lips. She scanned the horizon. "There is so much power coming from the island. I know it is a safe-haven for magicians, but that is incredible."

"It is incredible. The short time I was there was an interesting experience."

"I wish we had time to stop," Kiira said, reaching out a hand to the distant shore. Her heart longed to be among so much power. Zerrec could pack a punch, but this was something else altogether. "I wonder how many Elders live there?"

"Pretty much everyone with a gift is an Elder," Terren said. "The only thing to do on the island is strengthen and hone gifts."

"I am so jealous."

"I will take you one day. We can sail to the Shade Realm and stop there for a time. I made a number of friends."

Kiira rolled her eyes. "Why am I not surprised. How did *you* end up on the Magician's Cloister anyway?"

"Do you remember when I mentioned helping a group of magicians escape slavery?"

She remembered now that he'd said it, but the answer had come so casually she didn't know what to think at first. "Yes, but I distinctly remember you brushing past the topic. Now, I want details."

"I was a crew member aboard the pirate ship *Surveysor* and the magicians captured were destined for slavery in the lands across the sea."

Kiira turned to him, shock now coursing through her. "How could you do such thing?"

"It's not something I am proud of, Kiira. I made amends the only way I could by rescuing the very people I helped capture."

She eased a bit. His past, though some of it was still a mystery, shaped him. Terren was a good man, and good men still had to learn from mistakes. She'd seen it often enough with her father. Kiira desperately wanted to know how and why he had become a pirate, but his body language conveyed that he didn't want to touch the regrettable history. Soothing her thirst for more was knowing she had years to explore Terren's past and get him to open up to her. So, she decided to change the subject to distract herself. "You've been across the sea?"

"Well, yes," Terren said, uneasy. Likely from her change in topic.

"You never told me! What is it like?"

"Janissair is ruthless and brutal, full of mercenaries and traitors," he said, leaning against the rail, his eyes arrested on the expanse before him. "But it is also beautiful." Terren paused for a moment.

"The sea turns from an opaque to a crystalline blue, free of minerals so you can see hundreds of feet to the white sandy floor."

Kiira rested her chin on a fist as she leaned into the rail and imagined a different colored sea.

"That's just the sea. The same waters flow throughout the land in rivers and streams creating lucid lakes surrounded by lush palms. Verdurous plants line sandy cliffs, walkways, and around the ruins of long forgotten buildings. The ones that still stand are a testament to their dedication to create beautiful things."

"Is it as verdant as Lorea?"

Terren nodded. "I prefer Lorea, though. The kingdom may not have vivid yellow hibiscus larger than your hands or mighty pillars, but it has peace. The beauty of something can be easily marred by ugly comportment."

Kiira pursed her lips but nodded. She'd never seen Janissair, as much as she'd dreamed of it. She tried to convince her father to let her be the ambassador for trade agreements, but after the first ambassador's death, Herretus refused to entertain the idea. A small kernel of jealousy knotted in her chest at Terren getting to see it, but his expression showed he was more troubled by his experience than anything else.

Maybe one day, when the country finds peace, I can go.

She wrapped her arms around his shoulders, giving him a kiss through his linen shirt. "Tell me of your escape from the ship with the magicians. It sounds like a fantastic story."

Terren gave a grim smile. "I would not call it that, but it is a story."

"Your Highness," Captain Abiimola of the Merchant Tribe interrupted their conversation. "We will dock in Lorea tomorrow morning."

Terren straightened. "Excellent. Thank you for keeping us ahead of schedule, Captain."

"It is my pleasure, Isikolrii."

"Are you feeling better?" Terren asked, pulling her into a hug.

"Yes, now that we've passed most of the island, the strength of magic is lessening," Kiira said.

"Then, do you think you can still beat me?"

Kiira backed away, smirking. "Oh, definitely." She wandered back toward her staff on the deck. "It may not be today"—she pointed the tip of the staff at him—"but one day you'll lose to me, Terren Mytheries, one day."

Terren gave one abrupt laugh as he picked up his staff with a flourish, ready to face her again.

CHAPTER 24

PARTICULARS

TERREN

Kiira's steps were either fueled by eagerness or anger as she walked down the gangplank. He smiled, concluding it was a bit of both. She'd updated him on Liem's situation as the ship docked, but wasn't sure if the distance from bay to shore would sheath sharp words before coming face-to-face with her twin.

Whatever she planned to say to her brother was put on hold thanks to Skehtra's enthusiasm. The Wolfcat spotted her and pulled free of the laughable tether keeping her in place and pelted in their direction. Kiira braced for the impact and managed to barely keep her feet as Skehtra appeared to attempt to crawl beneath her clothes, an impossible task but the cat still seemed determined to conquer it regardless of her size. They had left behind a tiny cub, and now the Wolfcat reached Kiira's middle. By the time she was done growing, Skehtra would stand eye-level with her mistress. Skehtra ducked her head and rolled into Kiira, successfully pushing his wife to the wooden planks and laying atop her like a rug. Terren waited, holding back a grin. Faint squeals leaked through the mass of silver pelt and muscle as Kiira attempted to shove the Wolfcat away. Terren couldn't hold back his amusement any longer. He laughed, especially as Jemma tried to help, futile as it was. The wood beneath his boots hummed as the cat purred, smug and pleased. Terren did not want to know how Kiira felt taking the brunt of the vibration.

"Skehtra! Let off!" Kiira shouted, and yet the Wolfcat merely laid her head down, stubbornly refusing to move. With a huff, she wrapped her arms around Skehtra's neck.

Terren shook his head. Living with Skehtra was bound to be interesting once they made it to Klynotia. Wolfcats were known in his kingdom, but since they only lived in the Forest Wilds, Klynotians only had sketches and paintings of the large creatures.

The thunk of boots turned his eyes as King Herretus arrived, followed by Liem.

"That cat has been a menace for the last year," Herretus said.

"Well a menace no longer, Sire. She looks to be my problem now."

"Thank the gods for that."

Terren nodded to Liem. "You made it back in one piece."

"I did, thank you again for the horse," Liem said.

"Skehtra, I cannot breathe. Let off!" Kiira must have used her magic because the Wolfcat removed herself with a noise that could only be categorized as a grumble. Finally free and a little disheveled, she joined the group, throwing her arms around her twin. "Liem! I am so happy to see you!"

"I expected you to be upset after you cut me off," Liem replied, squeezing her tight.

"Oh, I'm not happy *with* you, just to *see* you," Kiira said with a massive grin.

Liem groaned.

"Princess, I am pleased to see you doing well," Ariella said.

"None of that, Ariella." Kiira released her twin and looped her arm through the countess' "We are going to be sisters!"

Liem cleared his throat. "Terren, this is Countess Ariella, my betrothed."

Terren noticed the slight discomfort in Liem's demeanor. Why he couldn't predict. He remembered the lady only in passing, as she seemed to be a gentle shadow along the edges of the court. Terren nodded his head. "Congratulations, Countess. Congratulations to you both."

Kiira gave a light punch on the shoulder to her brother, a mischievous twinkle entering her eye. "I am going to give you so much heartache for this. Payback." She whirled with Ariella still attached and meandered down the dock, ignoring the groan from her brother. Their words faded with each step, but their conversation was still clear even over the noise of the lapping water and gull cries. "Congratulations, Ariella. I'm glad my brother prevailed in convincing you to accept his proposal. You will make a fine queen."

"Thank you, Princ—Kiira," Ariella said. "I only hope to do the role justice."

Pulling her closer, she said, "You absolutely will. Our mother would have approved."

Ariella's shoulder's relaxed. "That means so much coming from you."

Herretus cleared his throat with a small pleased smile. "The evening meal has been provided at the inn. Shall we?"

Despite the distance, Kiira still heard. She spoke loudly enough for them all to hear. "Yes, I am starving! Come Ariella, we will discuss your wedding plans. Now, how should Liem dress? In his full military regalia?"

Liem gave another groan. Terren patted him on the shoulder.

"She can be a hurricane, my daughter," Herretus said, fondness edging his words.

Terren laughed. "Kiira has brought much joy to my life, I am grateful for her spirit, and her love."

"It is good they walk ahead, we need to discuss the reports we received from Klynotia," Liem interrupted.

"Liem, I believe this can wait until after we have eaten," Herretus chided. "You have waited months and another hour is not going to drastically change the situation."

"I prefer to not leave Kiira out of the discussion either," Terren added.

Liem sighed. "Fine. We can meet in the king's room after the meal.

I have copies of all the reports to give to you, but you need to know, Terren, the situation is despairing."

"I thought as much," Terren said, heavily bending his shoulders. "Grayten is not … a good king."

"It seems to have only gotten worse in the last few months," Liem said.

Herretus laid a hand on both their shoulders to start them walking toward the inn, but he directed his words to Terren. "We are here to help. Your request to put intelligence officers into Klynotia has proven valuable. However, nothing should be discussed until we all have full bellies."

Liem seemed not to hear him. "The truth is, something strange is going on with the king. We've been given reports of extreme changes in his personality, and he has actually taken an interest in the running of the kingdom now."

Terren furrowed his brow. "That is not the Grayten I know."

"You were only around him for a few months before you got carted off here," Liem said.

Terren caught Herretus glaring at his son, but smirked at Liem's bluntness. "True, but I still kept my ears open as to what was happening in Klynotia the entire time I was gone, and I have a loyal valet within the walls who has been communicating with me this past year, though his mentions of Grayten did not seem so drastically different. I, however, cannot blame him for mostly avoiding the king."

"There have not been overtly obvious changes even to our officers until recently," Herretus added.

Terren nodded thoughtfully. "I am eager to hear more. But as you said, we can discuss more after dinner."

"Good, because I believe we are all hungry and I prefer to not talk business with food before me," Herretus said.

Sitting at the long table, the cozy light of the inn provided a congenial atmosphere. The entire auberge had been cleared just for them. Terren found himself across from Liem. Kiira's voice was low but zealous as she discussed wedding plans with Ariella. He could see the prince was eager to talk about the reports, but Herretus was right;

decisions would be better made after a filling meal. He needed to distract Liem with a different subject to keep the prince from being so moody, and he remembered what Kiira had said. "I was told you are a rather skilled blacksmith. I also enjoy time in front of the forge fire."

Liem looked up from his stew. "Really? Why didn't you tell me?"

Terren almost gave him a deadpan look for asking a question with such an obvious answer, but tempered it at the last second. "One, I was a little preoccupied, as were you, and two, not all Earth Mages are blacksmiths. I didn't know you were interested," Terren countered. But Liem just waved a hand at him, leaning in eagerly.

"So, tell me your favorite blend of metals."

CHAPTER 25

SHUTTERED

KIIRA

Leaning as far over the rail as she dared, she stretched to feel the spray of the sea. It was a fair day, and the fresh air cooled her lungs, pushing away the stuffiness of the cabin and the uncertainty clinging like shadows to their every move. They would dock at the Klynotian royal port this evening, signaling the end of a life she knew and with which she felt comfortable. It had taken less than a week to sail from Lorea to her new home, less than a week for the truth of her life to eventuate, and she felt wholly unprepared to manage it. Some would argue Kiira had a year to prepare for her role in Klynotia. Maybe, but it was easy to side-line thoughts of the future when distracted by the present. Now, all the thoughts she ignored because of the Lundemai had to be confronted, and what she feared the most was the impression she would make on the nobility and the people of this new kingdom. In Lorea she had the freedom to challenge the conventions of behavior ascribed to her station, but Klynotia was different, teetering on an edge, arguably in a poor way. Kiira knew as much and hesitated to accept her new role as crown princess. Infringing on the expectations that came with the title would do little to win the hearts of the people.

And as a mage who must *keep her gift hidden, I've a feeling I'm about to walk a long, lonely road.*

At least she had gotten one last happy memory before leaving Lorea by attending Liem and Ariella's wedding. It had been as beautiful as hers but smaller, and she envied them just a bit for it. Leaving her twin in reliable hands made leaving her home a little easier, since she trusted Ariella to keep Liem in line.

A spray of water wet her face, and she leaned back in surprise. Out of the corner of her eye, Terren stood at the helm, keeping his eyes on the horizon. She frowned and returned to leaning over the rail, allowing her feet to dangle. Since leaving Lorea, a cloud masked her husband's emotions, making him difficult to be near. It reminded her so much of the week leading up to their ceremony. He had turned taciturn, distant, and solemn. This was not a side of Terren she loved, and that it made an appearance during the last part of their Lundemai proved unpleasant to say the least. Kiira was more than ready to get off the ship.

She'd attempted several times to encourage Terren to speak to her about his thoughts on the reports from Liem, but each time he shook his head and said, "Later." The reports by the intelligencers caused concern—it was why her nerves were on edge—but since she could not get Terren to say anything about them, she remained a tangled emotional mess. The last three days on the ship planted small, uncomfortable burs of doubt, frustration, and fear. If he was like this on the ship, it made her wonder how Terren would act once they stepped inside the castle. Surely he would not remain like this. And yet…

"Princess, it is not becoming to lean as such over the rail, showing your backside to everyone on the ship," Jemma scolded, coming up to shield her.

Kiira rolled her eyes before re-situating. As much as the small reminders of propriety annoyed her, the lady's maid was nothing less than a gods-send. "Oh, Jemma, this is my last chance to appreciate open freedom before I am expected to act like the crown princess. You know I am aware of how to act."

Jemma sighed. "Of course you would see it as a burden."

"Quite the opposite," Kiira said, leaning back and crossing her arms. "I know the people of Klynotia have suffered greatly under their king and I want to help facilitate changes. No one, however, aspires to be under constant scrutiny for their actions, and I will be the moment I step off this ship. I expect it from the servants, and I expect it from every noble of the Klynotian court."

"Kiira, may I speak to you for a moment?" Terren asked, his gentle request barely audible over the waves.

Jemma curtsied to them before giving them space. She glanced at her husband but turned around again to keep eyes on the horizon. The flint of light on the crests of water made her happy, something she needed in conversation with her moody husband.

"I wanted to give you a quick understanding of our court customs before we dock."

She narrowed her eyes. "I already know the court customs for Klynotia. Jemma and my mother made sure my education was thorough." She flickered a quick look at him. "Why don't we talk instead about what's really bothering you about the reports Liem gave to us?" She didn't want to be rude, but frustration made her words far more clipped than intended.

"There is nothing to discuss," Terren said, mimicking her posture against the rail.

"Unbelievable." She scoffed, turning to him and leaning a hip against the rail with crossed arms. "I thought we promised to be open and honest? First you hide your plans from me, and now you refuse to utter anything at all. The whole point of me accepting the challenge in Jearut was to prove that I'm capable of handling things. Did that not register with you?"

Terren clenched his jaw, flexing it before closing his eyes and taking a cleansing breath. It was the same thing he had done at the beginning of their marriage—often. It annoyed her that he'd resorted to it now. They'd gone through much during the Lundemai, and they should be united in whatever they were about to face. She was making the same point he did after she used her magic to protect them from the windstorm. Sure, she could be brash and sometimes inept with words, which never helped a tense argument, but his suffocated emotions did nothing for their relationship either.

"Kiira—"

"No, Terren. I do not want to hear it! You insisted our relationship would only work if we shared openly, but you are doing the exact opposite." She waved a hand generically toward the shore. "I know you come out here at night to talk to Kamaria, which is fine, but you should be talking to me, too."

Terren shifted to place his gaze on hers. "It's easy to talk to her, she understands the feeling behind my words."

Kiira's breath halted; his words hurt more than she wanted. It was unnerving to stare into his icy blue depths, and as she held his gaze, rage with a mixture of disbelief boiled in her chest. She tried to be patient, allowing him space and time to process, but this was too much. His face blurred as tears, unbidden, dripped from her eyes. A severe tremble elevated her voice, but she managed, "If you are to claim I am your Ishaiio, then act like it." She shoved away from the rail to leave him to his thoughts. If he wanted to fix things, he could apologize first.

Kiira found her way to the quarterdeck with only the helmsman to keep her company and buried her face in her knees. She was so frustrated at his self-imposed silence and how he defaulted to speaking with Kamaria when he should default to speaking with her. "Windrah, why is this happening? Why can I not fix this?" The sound of the ocean was lost as she felt her mind transported to the goddess' sanctuary.

"Kiira, you are not alone in these feelings," Windrah said, sitting next to her.

"I just thought we were past this," Kiira blubbered.

"Child, this will not be the last disagreement you have with your husband."

"I know, but why is he shutting me out? Even if he said he needed time, that would be better than insufferable silence. I thought he trusted me!"

Windrah pulled Kiira closer. "He does, you know in your heart that is true, but he's afraid of what's to come and learning to navigate this relationship the same as you."

Despite her turmoil, she felt serenity enter her soul as the goddess comforted her. "Afraid that if he tells me his thoughts I cannot handle it?"

"Afraid you will not see him as strong and capable of taking care of you and the situation."

"That is ridiculous," Kiira said.

"Is it? Or is he trying to protect you the only way he knows how to?"

The challenge from Windrah caught her off guard. She thought for a minute. "You're trying to tell me this is the same as when I accepted the challenge in the Shade Realm. I wanted to resolve the problem myself because I felt it was my burden after my failure."

"Yes," the goddess confirmed.

Kiira sighed. "So, he is afraid of failure and the potential negative consequences." The goddess didn't confirm her words, but they felt right. She preferred to prove her ability to be strong through action, and she needed to remember that Terren preferred to reserve action for the very last moment. Information was not easily pried from him because he had spent so many years guarding his thoughts and identity; and in his case, keeping it from Kamaria was difficult. He could cut her off, but doing so for long periods gave him a headache, something she learned while at the temple. Kiira understood, and it lessened her anger, except the future of Klynotia was no longer his sole burden to bear.

"Child, I understand it hurts, but Terren loves you, and he will learn to speak his thoughts—just give him time. After all, it has not yet been a year since your marriage."

Kiira took another deep breath. "Thank you, Windrah."

The goddess pulled her closer into a comforting embrace. "I am here whenever you need me, but I also brought you here to tell you to be on your guard as you enter Klynotia."

"Because of my gift?"

"Not just because of your gift. There are challenges coming to test your resolve. Be strong and courageous, I am with you wherever you go. Remember, a cord of three is stronger than a single strand, you do not have to stand alone. You have many connections that should not be ignored."

Kiira scrunched her brow. What did that mean? Why couldn't she just be given all the pieces so she could prepare accordingly? Instead, Kiira said, "Thank you, Windrah."

The goddess smiled, and the Sanctuary melted away. Kiira lifted her head to see sailors climbing along the masts to furl the sails. They were close to land. She stood to see the royal port of Klynotia not far in the distance. Orders bounced around the deck as the captain prepared to have the oars made ready to steer the large ship to dock.

She spotted Terren keeping his gaze on the horizon, and she looked away when he turned to her. She was not as angry, but Kiira still needed space. To not be a nuisance to the sailors, she remained in her position, watching the synchronized work of the crew as they prepared to make land. It was amazing to watch, and the rhythmic precision was comforting. In little time, the gangplank lowered, and she stepped onto land once again.

Kiira easily recognized Terren's personal servant, the fair-haired Lucen, and she gave the man a serene smile. "Thank you for meeting us, Lucen."

"It is my duty, Princess."

"I am grateful, regardless." She stiffened as she felt Terren come up behind her.

Lucen bowed, and addressing them both, he said, "The carriage is ready to depart as soon as belongings are stowed."

"Excellent, Lucen, thank you," Terren said before striding away.

Kiira watched him briefly before shaking her head in frustration.

"I will do my best to pull him out of his solitude, Princess."

"Thank you. I will be there"—Kiira pointed to a building clearly labeled the Dry Dock Tavern—"when we are ready to depart."

Before leaving, Liem had told her where to find one of the Lorean intelligence officers in Klynotia. The one stationed here received all communique from the northern parts of the kingdom to send back to

Lorea. She would need to contact the other officer stationed near the border on the other side of the Aria Bells via a letter, a tricky matter if she didn't want to be caught.

Stepping into the dim interior, her eyes adjusted to the cozy firelight. Kiira scanned the room for the man Liem described. He was easy to spot, given he had a blatant scar running down the left side of his cheek, but the intelligencer's image blended superbly with the other faces present.

She ordered an ale, both to blend in and to taste something other than the ship's grog. Sitting near the Lorean officer, she said, "It's nice over here by the fire. Beats the wet wind blowing from the South."

The officer glanced in her direction and grunted. "Maybe."

Kiira shifted closer and took a sip of the ale she had purchased. It had a bright citrus taste with an undertone of something more floral, but still in the citrus family, orange blossom maybe? As low as possible, she said, "I was asked to inform you of my arrival."

"Aye, I was expecting ye, Ma'am. The news of the Lorean ship approaching has been everywhere today," the officer responded.

She nodded and took another sip of ale.

"Tread lightly. It seems to only be getting worse." His voice was so low, Kiira had to take a moment for the words to make sense.

"Thank you." Kiira glanced at the door as it swung open. Terren blocked the light, and several men closer to the door grumbled at the draft. Downing the rest of her ale, she hid a gold coin under the mug before stepping away from the table. It would buy the officer several rounds of drinks or help him favor a bribe. She knew he was paid well by the crown, but it didn't hurt to pad the pockets of the people she would rely on for what could be years.

"Who was that?" Terren asked as they made their way to the carriage.

"No one. I was sitting by the fire and he was the closest," Kiira gave a curt reply. She was not ready to back down from her indignation. A tweak in her chest told her she was being petty, but she ignored it.

Terren pulled at her arm, stopping her. "Kiira, I saw the coin."

She gave him a hard stare, but he didn't release her. He had to know the answer already; he just wanted to make her say it for some reason. Kiira pursed her lips and said, "We can talk in the carriage. I want to sleep in a bed that does not rock back and forth." Terren let her go, and she spun to continue eagerly toward the royal carriage. Several whispers accompanied her footsteps. The news of their marriage would have spread wide in a year, and most probably stared out of curiosity of their new princess, but she still didn't like the stares of strangers. Kiira held her breath to keep her shoulders tall. The last thing she needed was for the Klynotian people to think her weak.

"I'm sorry," he said softly as the carriage left the seaport. The carriage rattled along for a while longer before he spoke again. "I am not trying to upset you, I just..." Terren's voice cracked. "You are my Ishaiio, and I trust you with my life Kiira, but the steps I must take to seize the throne from Grayten without crumbling the kingdom must be taken with the utmost care. The smallest mistake could put you in the king's path for persecution. What he did to my sister and to Lucen ... they suffered for my selfishness. Kamaria told me I was being stupid." A wry but sad smile touched his lips. "I never thought I would get relationship advice from a Bear."

Kiira softened. She appreciated the apology, and her affection for Kamaria grew a little more. Switching seats, she settled into his arms and leaned her head against his shoulder. "I can handle Grayten. His sour attitude toward life is nothing to me, plus we've already established I can defend myself." Her attempt at levity fell flat as he squeezed her tighter. "You believe me to be in more danger here than in the Jearut?"

"Yes."

She moved enough to look at him, hoping for more, but that would be all she got. Settling back into the comfort of his arms, she said, "Please do not fear for me. If anything, I am more capable of protecting myself here than in Jearut." She let a small lily-shaped light fill her cupped palm, the orange glow soft in the dim carriage interior. Kiira smiled. It felt good to use the gift given to her. She knew using it in Klynotia was a death sentence, but here in the carriage's safety, she dared to let a little of her light shine.

Terren closed her fingers, snuffing the light, and kissed her knuckles. "You are in danger here as a magician, please do not use your magic if you can help it. There are plenty who are terrified enough of the king to report anything suspicious regardless of your status, including my sister. Trust no one except Lucen, Jemma, and me."

Kiira sighed. "That's going to make befriending your sister difficult."

"I know, but I need to know you are as safe as possible considering the circumstances. It will help me to focus."

"Okay, you have my promise. I will be selective with my magic."

"Thank you." The relief flooding his words made her understand just how tense this situation was making Terren, and a little more of her anger at him evaporated.

CHAPTER 26

RESOLVE

ZERREC

His stomach clenched as Kiira entered the main hall on Terren's arm. He thought all affection for her died with his old body, but seeing her now in a travel worn dress, curly hair frizzed by salty air, it did something in him. He railed against the idea of his feelings still being so strong, but she was even more beautiful than he remembered. When would Kiira not affect him? The woman rejected him without a second thought, and yet the sight of her made him want to forget every vow he'd made since the cavern and taking this new body.

Terren and Kiira stopped close to the dais, and each paid their respects. When they rose, Zerrec looked down at Kiira and for a moment forgot who he was supposed to be portraying. Her bright emerald eyes, so out of place amongst the dark-eyed Klynotians, looked up at him, somehow always expressive no matter how stoic Kiira tried to be.

It's the eyes that won't let me go. They are so much like Loralyn's.

Her eyes drove into his mind, forcing it back further and further until he felt himself sinking into memories he had long ignored.

· · ·

A PHANTOM LUMP of dirt disintegrated just below his ear, small round pieces, and granules slipping beneath his collar and down his back. He smacked his face to his cheek only to find it wet. Too late. The mud striped his cheek. He turned to glare at Loralyn, his neighbor and best friend.

"Hey, Grumpy," she said, emerald eyes teasing. Her braided sunny hair had come loose from working in the gardens all day, and it hung long down her back. She was smeared with a mixture of dry and fresh mud.

"It's bad enough I have to be out here getting my hands dirty, did you also need to make the rest of me dirty, too?"

Loralyn snorted. "You're so prim. At least my Mama is paying you and it got you out of lessons for a day."

"I think I would have rather done the lessons," he mumbled.

Until five months ago, his parents had been terrified he would be a *gioll*. Gifts manifested around five winters for most, but he had only bloomed after eight. At least, his prayers to the gods were finally answered. He didn't want to be the whispered talk of his borough. Zerrec received the same gift as his father, Blood Magic, and the man had started Zerrec's lessons in earnest three months ago. Zerrec wouldn't be surprised if his father even agreed to have him help plant the spring garden so his normally pale skin burned and could be turned into a lesson for his magic that evening. That would make more sense than being given a day off. Most children his age were already skilled, and his father was driving him like a taskmaster to bring him to par. He was not quite at the level that some referred to as Adepts. That term wasn't accepted in his borough, but they'd all heard the rumors of a group of mages wanting to establish a system to measure one's skill and create a hierarchy. Personally, he liked the idea. His father, though, seemed to have a set plan in mind, and that eased his worries.

Loralyn laughed. The bright sound lightened his mood. "You are such a liar! You're happy to be out here in the sun with me." She lobbed another clump of dirt at him, but this time he ducked.

He grinned at her and threw another clump back, nailing Loralyn in the arm. She wasn't wrong, but he wouldn't admit it.

A throat cleared as a shadow darkened his face.

ZERREC BLINKED. It took a moment, but another throat clear from his valet reminded him of who he was now. A king.

Remember why you are here, fool.

His anger at the princess returned. He needed to adjust his thinking if he was to coexist with Kiira until his plans came to fruition. She had rejected him, refusing to live by his side forever, choosing instead a man not fit to run a kingdom nor progress her talent as a magician. Zerrec cleared his own throat, turning to break eye contact. As he lowered himself onto the throne, he allowed all of his memories of Kiira to fade to a hazy grey, replacing them with ideas of how she only served a purpose. He let the last strings of affection tying him to her rot.

Nothing more than a means to an end.

He made himself comfortable on the throne. The entire court waited in anticipation for him to speak, and he would, but they could stay in suspense. If there was one thing Grayten had wielded particularly well during his reign, it was fear. No one would dare make a sound, letting the silence consume every corner of stone. That was fine with him. He needed a few moments to solidify his newly adjusted thoughts about the princess.

Kiira will feel the pain I've known for centuries.

He would kill Terren, taking him so he could watch her crumble in heartbreak after losing someone she loved, and he would delight in every tear, every scream of anger, every sob. Then she would know the true meaning of pain.

Would I be willing to comfort her after such pain? Could I forgive her then? Be her place of refuge?

Zerrec studied the pair. They waited steadily for him to continue.

No, she slighted me in every way. If only I could command her to leave.

Neither Terren nor Kiira looked happy, and her upset could be for any number of reasons. According to Grayten's memory, Kiira seemed to convey a poor first impression of the king, but her nervousness could also be from leaving Lorea. Even he agreed Klynotia was subpar compared to the home they had shared. The princess remained focused on some point behind him. Studying the royal crests of the noble houses? Anything not to look at him. Did she really dislike Grayten that much? All the better for him. He could either exploit the dislike or hide his actions behind the wall of her disinterest.

Zerrec was mildly surprised she wasn't using magic—he would feel it—even the smallest of castings to calm her nerves or enhance her senses.

He shifted on the throne again. There was no time to play nice. He had the prince within reach, and he would send him immediately to the northern mine currently under mercenary control. With Aaliyah's information, he was prepared to best the prince in the first move of a longer game. Terren's Shadow Walker abilities would be easy to surpass with the special castings he'd provided the mercenaries and Berro. Once he knew the prince's reaction to his castings and with the information gathered by his bard, Zerrec would learn all he needed to know. He would catalog every weakness Terren had and then use it to destroy him. He took a deep breath. For now, he needed to throw them off his scent.

'My Son!'

Zerrec gripped the edges of his throne to ignore the voice. Digging through the king's memories of interactions with Terren, he looked for the right tone and body language. He smiled genially, although he made sure his eyes flashed disappointment, and said, "Welcome back, *son.*"

CHAPTER 27

ASSIGNMENT

TERREN

The loud bang of a staff accompanied the declaration of his and Kirra's official titles. The entire Klynotian court watched in stony silence as they entered the throne room. Heads turned like oiled wheels as he and Kiira made their way toward the throne. None bowed as they passed, technically a slight against them both, but he knew the nobles were all too afraid of Grayten to possibly offend him. Hopefully, once he was their king, fear wouldn't rule their hearts. This moment was almost a replica of the first time he came home, not that he expected anything different. A pressure existed in the room that wouldn't abate until this entire parade ended.

Grayten had a purpose for this display, and it had nothing to do with honoring them as heirs to the crown. The only language the king spoke was humiliation, a lesson Terren learned early in life when he was only a gangly squire.

The day Grayten summoned him to the throne room was etched into his memory. He'd been fourteen summers and, despite feeling broken from having just buried the father he'd always wanted, the stern but kind Sir Aldus, Terren did his best to stand tall before the courtiers and the king. His younger self had wondered why he'd been summoned mere hours after his mentor lay six feet under a stone marker. The reason became clear when, without warning, Grayten tossed a sword at Terren. The steel sparked against the stone as it slid across the throne room. Grayten charged at him with a gleaming weapon, and he gave a desperate defense, but Aldus was still using a wooden training sword for teaching, making sure Terren knew his forms instinctively before trusting him with a real sword–even a blunt one. His arms, weak from shoveling, flailed through blocks and parries, but none of it compared to a seasoned man with strength on his side. Grayten had bested Terren that day, and with glinted steel at his throat, said in front of every courtier, "Sir Aldus has failed. You will never be a worthy successor."

The words were seared into his memory as a brand to flesh, and they hurt more than the feel of steel at his throat, his father glowering down at him with hatred and disgust. The king's words then had started him down a violent path to prove he was the opposite of every-thing Grayten believed. Now, he was a better man, but anger still gripped him at the memory. He took slow, steady breaths as the priesthood had taught him and focused on Kiira's hand gripping his forearm. She was nervous, but having her here grounded him, and he was glad for it. Terren refused to give quarter to his emotions. The time was long past for the king to have any sway over his life.

At the base of the dais, they showed their deference to Grayten. Terren kept his gaze on the king as he bowed. There was something different about him; he could see it in his eyes. Hopefully, Liem's reports were not influencing his thoughts. He came out of the bow.

"Welcome back, *son*," Grayten said, putting emphasis on the last word.

Years of keeping a low profile had taught him to sense danger like a second skin. He felt it now as the king glared down at him.

Maybe those reports are valid.

He never disbelieved the stacks of papers Liem handed to him before they left Lorea, but Terren rarely took things at face value, so he'd been cautious upon returning to his kingdom. Now, in the king's presence, he felt a rotten apple roll through his stomach.

Loud enough for all to hear, Grayten said, "Did you enjoy your lack of responsibility for a year?"

Terren, careful to keep his voice mild, said, "It was a pleasure I did not expect, Sire."

One corner of Grayten's lips lifted. Terren's answer was vague enough for the king's reaction to be one of pleasure or irritation. He guessed it to be the latter. "Good. Now that you are back, I need you to leave immediately for Woodlands Deep to investigate bandit raids at one of the kingdom's more profitable mines. The taxes from the mine are being stolen and I will not have Klynotia suffer for it."

"Sire, I am at your service, I will leave three days hence," Terren said.

"No, you will take a company of soldiers and however many knights you deem necessary and leave in the morning."

Terren opened his mouth to argue, but Kiira gripped his wrist, keeping him from saying anything. He wanted to look at her, puzzled as he was by her reaction, but now was not the time for silent communication. "As you wish, Sire."

"Good." Grayten lifted his arms ceremoniously. "Now let the celebration of the prince's return begin!"

THE CALM of his chamber was not so different from the pensive banquet hall. Despite the bright tune from a young man with his lute and few other players, the only person seeming to enjoy the celebratory return banquet was Grayten. He made himself a glutton all while favoring his current choice of concubine. Everyone else murmured, eating what was served and then tactfully excusing themselves. Now, he held Kiira as they lounged on gathered blankets and pillows in front of a low fire, watching the flames lick at wood, keeping the coastal autumn chill at bay.

"Will you make an effort to befriend my sister while I am away?" He asked, tracing soft fingers up and down Kiira's arm, never removing his eyes from the flames.

Kiira replied with a humorless laugh. "You are asking me to stop the winds. She hates me, Terren."

"She does not hate you."

Kiira scoffed, pulling the blanket a little higher.

"You won over Kamaria." Quietly he added, "It would mean a lot to me."

"At least the Bear's anger was understandable. Sairah, I have no clue why she hates me. I have only ever been kind to her."

"It has more to do with me than you. I told you I was her protector for years. I had just promised to never willingly leave her again after barely returning home before the announcement of our marriage, so it probably felt like compounded abandonment. She needs a friend," Terren said.

"Putting me in her path will not do any good. She'll just step around me."

"Maybe not." Terren reached out to stir the fire. After setting the poker down, he added, "But someone needs to extend the hand of friendship first, and it will not be my sister. She's learned to close herself off from everyone."

He sent a silent prayer to Ny for Kiira to agree. He wouldn't push her, but he hoped for agreement. The only friend his sister had was her lady's maid, a mousy but kind woman. He hoped to influence Sairah positively by having her keep company with a strong, confident woman. It might be prying into his sister's life, but he cared about Sairah and he wanted to see her happy. Isolation was not serving her.

Kiira sighed, but it sounded more annoyed than resigned. "Alright, Terren, I will do my best."

"Thank you. That's all I can ask," he said.

He relaxed a little more against the pillows. He would feel easier about leaving Kiira and his sister in the castle with Grayten if he knew they had each other to rely on. "I'll have a second wardrobe brought in here for you."

"Not necessary, I will be fine in my own chambers while you're gone. Besides, I don't want to interfere with whatever masculine artistry is at work here," she gestured vaguely to the bare stone walls and rugged furniture. "And of course you'd have to contend with Skehtra," Kiira finished, turning to put her back to the fire and face Terren.

Terren gave her a wry smile. "I can manage."

She scoffed. "You mean to tell me you would wrestle a three-hundred pound animal every time you wanted to go to sleep? Really, Terren, I should have my own chambers."

"I don't want to be separated from you."

"We have been inseparable for a year."

"Not enough."

Kiira laughed. "You have such a scowl. Let me have my chambers, and I will be in here with you when you are not away."

"Accepted."

"I knew you were reasonable." She gave a quick kiss.

"Not really." Terren took advantage of the opportunity and deepened the kiss, pulling her close and tangling his fingers through her hair. He leaned his forehead against hers. "However, you are right about one thing."

"What's that?" She asked, fighting a grin.

"I really do not want to share any space with the cat." Terren captured her lips before she could form a rebuttal, and as the fire ran out of fuel, they stayed warm beneath the blankets as he enjoyed the pleasures of his wife.

CHAPTER 28

KNOWING

KIIRA

Terren pulled the strap tight to secure the saddle on Tempest. Kiira could see him looking at her from her peripherals as he placed a hand on the horse's twitching neck and watched her stroke the mare's nose. She whispered softly to the gray, using the barest thread of magic so the horse understood the commands to keep her husband safe. Tempest would do so on her own, loyal and brave as she was, but that didn't stop Kiira from giving the commands, nonetheless. The horse nudged her chest in agreement, possibly also looking for a couple of sugar cubes, which she gave to the mare.

"You're sure you will be fine without a guard rotation?" Terren asked. "I do not like you being here alone."

"I am not alone," she said, stepping toward him and encircling his waist. "You've told me the names of the guards should I need to get outside the walls."

Her words didn't seem to comfort him, but Kiira still tried to convey what words didn't. She squeezed him a little tighter, hoping to tell him she was strong and could handle her life here. She hated that his departure came so soon after arriving, and of course she would miss him, but she would be a poor partner and ally if she were incapable of weathering a few weeks without him. Terren had yet to speak about the weight he felt burdened to carry—not that there had been time last night, she blushed and buried her face a little more into his chest—but she hoped he would realize soon enough that he didn't need to conquer a kingdom on his own. Kiira loved him and would do whatever necessary to help expedite his plans to become the king of Klynotia. The little she'd seen of the kingdom thus far revealed these people needed a good and honest king.

He kissed her and leaned his forehead against hers. Whispering, he said, "I need you." He kissed her again. "Be safe, *please.*"

Unwanted tears gathered against her lower lids. She wanted to project strength, not a blubbering mess. To distract herself from the pain of separation, she teased, "I am not as reckless as you seem to think."

Terren backed away and gave her an incredulous look.

"Alright, you have reason to doubt me, but those were all for legitimate reasons!"

"I will miss you," he said, smiling. Leaning down, he pulled her into a long kiss, tangling his fingers in her honey curls as he had the night before.

Kiira leaned into the moment. She was going to miss this. The warmth of his body, his tender touch, the way his eyes danced when he thought she was funny. Her breath hitched; she was failing miserably at projecting strength. Terren ended the kiss to hold her close again. "I will miss you so much," she said, tears spilling.

Terren gave her one last kiss before stepping out of her embrace, but he held her fingers as he turned to his sister. "You will be nice like I asked?" His sister scrunched up her nose. "You have to learn to be civil at some point, Kiira is not going anywhere." His voice held an authority Kiira rarely heard.

Sairah sniffed. "I'm not going to go on picnics with her and gather wildflowers to braid in her hair, but I can be civil."

"Civil enough to break your fast together every day after I leave?" Terren asked.

Sairah narrowed her eyes.

Kiira laid a gentle hand on his arm. "Do not force it. We will have at least"—she looked at Sairah, calculating what she could get from the aloof princess—"five meals together before you return." Then she asked her directly, "Is that agreeable?"

Sairah sucked in a breath at being addressed so forthrightly and turned away to scowl at the ground. Her jaw danced as she considered the proposed number, probably trying to figure out how to decline without upsetting Terren. She did glance at him as if hoping he would lower the number, but he simply raised his brows, waiting for her consent. Kiira didn't understand her reticence. She had only ever been kind to the princess, and five meals was not that many in eight weeks. Plus, she agreed with her husband that his sister needed to learn how to live with others besides her maid. The other woman seemed nice enough, but both of them struck her as lonely.

Finally, Sairah said, "Yes, five seems manageable in the time you are gone."

"Excellent!" He gave Sairah one last hug and Kiira one last kiss before mounting Tempest. He looked at them. "I will be back in eight weeks if nothing happens." He kicked Tempest into a trot, and the loud clatter of hooves echoed across the stone as the company of men joined his departure.

Tears rippled Kiira's vision as she waited until every horse was out of sight. Surprisingly, Sairah stood with her. Her new sister-in-law may not have a fondness for her, but they had one person they loved in common, and she would use that to nudge open the door into her life. When she could no longer hear the hoofbeats of the last line of horses, Kiira sighed as she turned to go. Terren had asked Sairah to break their fast together this morning, but now didn't feel like the right time to force it. "I will be eating in the queen's garden *if* you want to join me."

She felt Sairah's stiffness rather than saw it, but the invitation was the start. Kiira had Jemma, Starfire, and Skehtra to keep her company, but it would be nice to have a sister. They both needed friendship, and she had a feeling her relationship with the princess would take a lengthy time to build, but if she managed it, at least they would not be alone.

CHAPTER 29

INGRESS

TERREN

'*I do not like this,*' Terren said to his Bear.

'*Neither do I, but it is good we are together. I can protect you better.*'

Terren squinted against the clouded sun. The pointed rays cut through despite the grey skies, quite common this close to the mountains. Even on a day like today, Kamaria remained safer blended with him or in the Shade Realm. She could cross over if necessary, but not without an abysmal amount of pain, so he seconded her thoughts. Last night as they camped and ate dinner, he debated joining with Kamaria, especially with the risk of his company finding out. They wouldn't understand, and would likely be spooked by superstition or assume he used magic. He needed their respect; winning the favor of the kingdom's soldiers would make his succession to the throne infinitely smoother. To do that, he needed to protect as many men as possible. Having Kamaria's power coursing through him made that task easier, and luckily, he'd found a secluded place far enough away after the men were asleep to join with his Bear. Now, crouched in the brush scanning the decrepit buildings, he was glad he'd given into his intuition.

An eerie stillness, not unlike a graveyard on a moonless night, pervaded every beam and stone as Terren signaled his men to leave cover and begin entering the town. Ash coated everything thanks to several scalded buildings, now smoldering. He and his men would leave dark, crisp boot prints as they crept along the main road, damp after last night's misty rain.

Terren had stopped at Woodlands Deep when he fled Klynotia as a youth. With it being the last large settlement before leaving the kingdom, the profitable mining town had everything a traveler needed to make it upriver and to the base of the cordillera. Thanks to the recent mercenary rule, this normally thriving town skirted ruin. His natural skepticism told him there were more pieces at play than his eyes suggested, but he would have to puzzle through it later once the mercenaries were defeated.

Joined with Kamaria, his sense of smell was tripled, and Terren knew there were people huddled in their houses, the stench of fear rolling out of every door he passed. Odd. It was late enough in the morning for people to be going about their day. Instead, they cowered inside their homes. Two of the soldiers accompanying him were from here, and the whole way to Woodlands Deep they whispered concerns over the cook fires. He'd hoped for something positive when they arrived, but it seemed he would not be so lucky.

Reports suggested mining was still being done, but none of its profits were going to the kingdom. He'd asked other villages on the way here what they'd heard about Woodlands Deep, but learned nothing veritable, and it unsettled him to form a fighting and defense strategy based on rumors. Grayten had given little information of what transpired here, just that mercenaries had taken over and re-seizing control had been difficult. According to the king, the duke over these lands was doing next to nothing to help these people. The significant number of dead soldiers with his insignia piled outside of town yet to be buried suggested otherwise. The current gossip—what Terren believed to be slander—was that the duke did not see the problem soon enough, *allowing* for this invasion to happen. Terren doubted Grayten's claims, especially now after seeing the reported changes in the king for himself. He was going to reserve his judgment for when he could speak to Duke Aubin in person. The older man was his uncle, and he'd not seen or spoken to him since leaving Klynotia as a youth. Lucen's insight on the peerage said the nobility cared for their people, despite the king's claims, but in most cases were just trying to survive themselves.

'Kamaria, for what do you think someone wants control of a gem mine in Klynotia?'

'The obvious answer is wealth.'

He cautiously made his way along the main thoroughfare. *'I thought of that, but then why not make a stand for the largest mine in the kingdom? If this is a band of mercenaries as reported, it makes more sense for them to take what they want and leave, especially for a mine this remote. Why set up camp? Why here when they probably knew this town would be under peerage protection.'*

Kamaria was silent for a moment. *'Rushing water beneath a calm surface.'*

'Agreed. There is definitely more at play here, and my first thought is to blame Grayten, but that may be my emotions.'

Kamaria snorted. *'You should trust your senses, Yepenzi. I did not like the way Grayten smelled this time.'*

An interesting observation from his Bear. He tried to be discerning in all situations. With Grayten, he'd long given up the idea of the father he remembered as a boy still existing, but he agreed with Kamaria—something about their interactions with him felt wrong.

'This saddens me,' Kamaria interrupted his thought before he could contemplate further.

Looking around at the broken and burned homes tightened his throat. The people of Woodlands Deep would need a lot of help from the crown to rebuild their lives once he alleviated the problem, not that the crown would give it. He'd have to provide the gold from his own personal stores. *'Yes. These people, my people, should not have to live in fear. Someone is responsible for this and I intend to pinpoint who.'*

'Justice is des—I sense magic.'

'I just felt it,' Terren said.

That is when he also caught an unusual scent. It recalled memories of sun-blistered skin and the scent of pipe smoke mixing with the iron zing of blood-stained clothes.

'*Why is this familiar?*' Kamaria asked.

'*Because it is from my memories. This is the same scent from the kingdom of Janissair.*'

'*You have told me about this kingdom. They are full of wealth, yes?*'

'*Yes and no, some tribes are wealthier than others, but all of it is wealth built upon war and ruin. So, the fact they are here does not surprise me. What does surprise me is that a group of Janissair mercenaries came all the way to northern Klynotia.*'

Kamaria contemplated for a second. '*You are questioning why they sailed across Reana to come here for a singular mine. It is too specific.*'

'*Exactly. If you are going to go through that much trouble to cross the sea, why stop here? Why not push for another location after pillaging this one?*'

Kamaria snorted, annoyed. '*Not enough people to keep control and continue to conquer?*'

'*Possibly.*'

"Lucen," he hissed.

His valet stepped up next to him. "Yes, Sir."

"Tell the men to be extra wary. We're about to spring a trap."

"Of course."

As Lucen drifted through the men, Terren tried not to make it too obvious he was looking for the scent direction to pinpoint where the mercenaries held their ground, ready to attack. The men not ordered to skirt the edges of town formed a wedge behind him. He hesitated to take another step into the town in case there was a trap he overlooked, but answers would only be found if he pressed ahead. Terren held his scimitar in a loose grip, scanning the area, waiting for his prey like a hunting owl. Everything seemed in order, but he knew there was a mage present or magic being used. He just had to find—there!

Between a stand of houses, the light twisted, wobbling as Kamaria's immunity to magic worked on it. He crept forward with his sword at the ready, weaving a meandering path toward it, not wanting to give away his intended target.

A burst of light blinded him as the roar of voices gushed from between the houses. Terren felt his limbs move, but not at his direction, Kamaria partially manifesting and using reflexive movements to protect him. He didn't normally like it when she controlled his limbs, but as blinded as he'd been, this was definitely an exception. As his vision slowly adjusted after the blast of light, Terren looked over the four bodies at his feet, covered in red oozing claw marks. Hopefully, the fight would distract his men from seeing them. He would have to take care of these bodies himself before anyone saw how they died.

From his left, a sword swung toward him, and he lifted his Solpur Blade to block. Inanimate as it was, the black sword seemed delighted to be used. Terren moved through the stream of mercenaries, some clashes ending quickly while others took him through the steps of an almost forgotten fighting style. A wave of magic washed over him and dissipated just as quickly.

'*We need to get to the magician now!*' He didn't intend to shout at his Bear, but based on the casting just unleashed, they were dealing with a fairly powerful Mind Mage, and if he was correct, Terren needed to stop him immediately.

CHAPTER 30
BLOODLUST

TERREN

A mercenary stepped in his path. With a yell, he engaged him with an overhead strike. Terren blocked with the blunt edge of his blade and stepped under the attacker's arm to pass and not waste time on useless encounters, but his opponent whirled, forcing him to lift his Solpur Blade and protect his shoulder. Terren kicked him in the knee to knock the man off balance. Using the flat edge, he pushed the mercenary in the ribs, and then flipped it to the blade and opened his torso from hip to chest. The crystal on his blade sparkled, revealing it'd absorbed magic. The now dead man at his feet must have had a minor casting woven into the fibers of his clothes, likely effective in most situations, but his Solpur Blade had eaten through it and was hungry for more.

He refocused on his goal. The mage was still in his spot between the houses. Bunkered between smooth earthen walls and with a handful of armed men for protection. If the leader of this band were smart, those surrounding the mage would be some of the best fighters. From what he could tell at this distance, the mage had not begun another casting yet.

Terren glanced at the state of his men. So far, they seemed to handle the attack well. He couldn't say if the skirmish went in their favor or not yet, but he and his men would quickly lose the advantage if the Mind Mage had the opportunity to complete his next casting. His men were not protected from magic. Thanks to Grayten's classist beliefs, he'd banned all magic years ago, no matter its purpose, meaning the soldiers were utterly helpless against it.

'Terren, stop dallying! Make a decision!'

Kamaria's frustrated command jolted him into movement. He once again stepped toward his goal. A few of his men seemed to realize the same thing he did, and a small group of soldiers clustered around the entrance to the alley trying to get through the guards. This was his opportunity. Only one mercenary guarded the magician, and he'd directed the magician to back away from the main street.

'Kamaria, should we shift?'

'Do not be stupid.'

Of course. Shifting in the middle of this already chaotic scene would cause panic; anything rash could trigger the mage to act sooner, and her size—larger than a normal brown bear—would place them at a disadvantage. He needed to control this situation as much as possible.

Leading to the alley, two mercenaries were engaged with two of his soldiers. He was going to take advantage of their distraction. Luckily, the cloudy day provided plenty of shadows. He melted into the closest shadow and stepped through another at the mercenaries' backs. His actions could not be hidden, and he would need to contrive an explanation for his sudden appearance at the Janissairian's backs, but this put him at a distinct advantage, so he considered the move worth it. Terren pulled a dagger from the hilt strapped to his calf before slipping between the two mercenaries, stabbing the man on his left just below the back of his ribs. The sudden pain allowed the soldier engaged with him to dominate quickly. Seeing his comrade fall distracted the mercenary on his right long enough for him to join his friend in death. Wiping his dagger on the dead man's clothes, he replaced it and said, "You two men. I need you to occupy the protector." He pointed to the last Janissairian standing between him and his target, who had been watching Terren make progress. The mage behind him panicked and fumbled through various small gems. "Pay attention, if he's the last one then he likely has magical protection. If you find you're having trouble defeating him, do not be a hero, step back and I will deal with it."

"Sire, we cannot let you do that."

"You can and you will."

The soldier reluctantly nodded. "Yes, Sire."

He turned back to see the mage had moved further back and was curled against the wall, still fumbling through the various gems. Terren assumed those had held extra power or pre-made castings, but if they did, why hadn't he used them yet? Even something small could turn the tide of a fight. Every mage he'd known had some confidence in his gift, but this one acted like a newborn colt.

'*Something is not adding up here,*' Terren said in his mind to Kamaria.

'*Agreed. This mage has waited far too long to act.*'

The soldiers with him stepped forward to engage the mercenary protector. Using the shadows again to his advantage, Terren opened paths between the realms, bypassing the first fight and stepping directly in front of the magic user, Solpur Blade on guard to absorb any castings. He dropped it a fraction when the young man pulled something from behind him and curled behind the object for protection.

'*Is that ... a lute?*'

'*It appears to be, yes,*' Kamaria said, with just as much confusion.

In all his travels, he'd never seen a mage use an instrument to help with castings—not that they needed anything. All castings from any of the gifts could simply be thought of and it would manifest, though most magicians preferred to make some sort of gesture to help them concentrate, like when Kiira snapped her fingers. Even during his time on the mage's isle, he never witnessed something so laborious for castings. Except, maybe this young mage didn't have any formal training, and strumming his lute was the action that best worked for him. Still.

Terren quickly closed the space between them.

"Please! Do not hurt me!" The young man shouted. "I was just doing as I was told."

He didn't lower his blade, but relaxed enough to appear less threatening. "If you are not a threat to me or my men, set down your … lute, and stand up to face me."

He did as directed. Cradling his hand, the boy—and that's what he was, a boy—stood with stooped shoulders emanating fear. It took significant effort for Terren not to react. Now that he had a better look at him, he doubted the young man was over twenty summers. Kamaria was just as shocked.

"What is your name?" Terren asked.

"Berro."

"Berro, why were you posing as a magician?"

"The mercenaries put these clothes on me, shoved a black crystal in my hand, and said to speak certain words when given the signal."

'A distraction,' Kamaria said. 'But why only one casting? Why this big charade?'

His sensitive ears heard the lessening of steel against steel as shouts of praise came from his men.

"Berro, are there more of you?"

The boy cowered.

"Tell me. Are there *more* of you." Terren didn't shout, but he had a stern edge to his words.

"Yes, sir," Berro answered, hanging his head.

"Where?"

"In the mines and surrounding forest waiting for your guard to come down."

Kreshkt, he thought.

"Please, the mercenaries will kill me! I wasn't supposed to say anything!"

Terren needed to get his men reorganized immediately if they were to have a chance of full victory today. Berro's pleas did not fall on deaf ears. His two soldiers had defeated the mage's protector, whose blood was now seeping into the dirt. "Niell," Terren said.

"Sire."

"Stay with the boy until this is over. He just informed me there are more of them."

"Yes, my prince."

"The prince?" Berro squeaked out.

Terren ignored him, exiting the alley. "Men! To me!"

No sooner had his soldiers gathered than a flood of new mercenaries came toward them. The war cries from the Janissairian men boiled his blood. Terren met the shouts with equal measure and ran without thought into the oncoming fighters. He no longer saw anything, just acted. Blood coated his sword; droplets flecked his skin and clothes. In his mind, Kamaria roared with the same fury. Her anger doubled his speed as he waded through each mercenary with his Solpur Blade. He ducked, spun, shoved, and once, jumped completely over a man to slice him across the back. Terren lost himself to battle rage as his Bear's fervor made him blind to everything but his enemy. These foreigners in his kingdom—these *invaders*—would know pain and fear as the people of Woodlands Deep had, and their punishment for trespassing would be annihilation.

He snarled, slicing the stomach of a man, crimson trailing the sharpened obsidian edge. Snapping to the left, Terren stopped his sword short of cutting air. He turned, breath heaving, ready to fight his next opponent. Only a remnant had escaped the sting of his Solpur Blade, and those were being picked off by his soldiers. Terren blinked.

Every fiber of him tried to deny the evidence of his eyes.

Oh, gods ... oh gods!

His smooth breaths fragmented as he took in the spoor of his carelessness—broken bodies amidst black, cakey ash.

It would be one thing if this emanated from self-defense, but he'd acted without attention. He let the rage of his Beast influence him. Always, he had kept careful control over his mind, so what happened here? How had he welcomed this? This ... this was unforgivable. The tip of his blade gouged the road as Terren lost the strength of his knees.

He'd allowed for the one thing his instructor told him to be wary of when blended. "You are more susceptible to the mind of a Beast when not separated. Be careful to always keep your mind, for when a Beast is angry it cannot think rationally and will act as it did before the bond."

'Yepenzi, I am sorry,' Kamaria said, and he felt her remorse. *'I was only thinking of protection for you and your men.'*

This was not her fault. "Ny, forgive me," he whispered.

"Come, my prince," Lucen pulled at his arm. "Now is not the time for weakness."

"But that is what I am, Lucen, weak," Terren replied, allowing Lucen to pull him to a stand, his blade drawing a line in the ash. "If I hadn't been, this would not have happened."

"Commiserate later, right now, be strong and courageous. Ny is with you always, but right now your men need your leadership."

Terren nodded, numb, but how could he lead others when he felt like he couldn't lead himself?

CHAPTER 31

NUISANCE

ZERREC

"You are positive the magic had no effect on him?"

"Absolutely, Sire," Berro said, his voice low, though he had assured Zerrec he was far enough away from the camp to ensure privacy. All Zerrec could see of the man was his face and the tops of his shoulders; he was holding the projection gemstone too close to his face to see more. "While the other men were blinded by the flash, the prince just moved through the mercenaries as if nothing happened. He was ferocious to say the least, I thought he could have killed me."

"What about the other gems?"

"I used the weaker gems given to me while the soldier they had guarding me had his back turned, the vines and random objects. I did not see all the fighting myself because the soldier placed to guard me wouldn't let me leave the space between the houses, and then I was captured so quickly, but those who saw it said the prince single-handedly killed all of the mercenaries stationed in the town. I did see the line of bodies afterward."

"And none of those slowed him down?"

"From what the other soldiers are saying, no."

Zerrec stroked his beard. It seemed Terren was fairly immune to all magic, confirming what he had guessed after their fight in the cavern. It also annoyed him, since magic was his strongest weapon and defense. He would need to be very selective in how he used his magic in order to best the prince.

And I wasted so much energy on those castings. It took me weeks to rebuild the muscle I lost.

"Thank you, Berro." Zerrec studied him a moment. There was something the boy wasn't saying. "What else?" Berro's face pinched. "You remember our deal, yes? You do as asked and I will do everything in my power to help heal your sister. I am asking for *all* of the details."

Berro nodded. "The prince is far kinder than I believed him to be. The description I received of him does not seem to match what I am seeing."

Clever boy. He knows better than to accuse me directly of giving him a false description.

The sympathy the boy felt for Terren needed to be weeded from his thoughts. "His benign demeanor is nothing but a facade, Berro. I have kept eyes on the prince for years and it is obvious he is strategically playing a long game to steal the throne from me." Zerrec didn't know if that was actually true, but it was a lie the young bard could believe in enough to keep him steadfast. "You are doing well. I need your help. Your sister is making marked improvements, staying awake for most of the day now, and I would hate to dismiss you from my service because you cannot be trusted, and see your sister's health decline due to inadequate care."

"No, Your Majesty, whatever you need."

"Wonderful. Stay with Prince Terren and his men until they return. Keep tabs on everything and report to me what you've seen when you get here." Zerrec cut off the connection to the crystal, allowing Berro to return to the soldiers before his absence became suspicious.

He pulled on his beard. The band of mercenaries lost more men than he predicted, a problem, but the fools had been too brash and arrogant. To secure the help of the Janissairian mercenaries, he'd promised a rather steep sum of gold to the Uman in order to convince his largest tribe to come to Klynotia. Hopefully, it would still be compensation enough after the reported losses. Zerrec didn't want to ruffle any feathers when he requested more men, but Janissairians tended to be bribable.

Clasping his elbows behind his back, he circled the Night Crystal as he processed Berro's report. His heavy fur cloak brushed against his ankles, his boot heels clacking against the stone floor. The damp, musty air of the underground room was pleasant, as was the uninterrupted solitude.

At least I know Aaliyah was not lying to me.

He'd mostly believed her story, but Zerrec never trusted people with ulterior motives, and Terren's cousin definitely had ulterior motives. Terren, it seemed, was indeed immune to most castings, and it was because of his connection with a Shade Beast. Now that Berro had visually confirmed it for him, he understood why Terren had defeated the death kiss he had placed on Kiira. It should have killed him—would have—if his Beast hadn't absorbed the casting.

Strange creatures, Beasts. I've held a grave misconception about them.

From what he knew, Beasts were not affected by magic when it was directed at them, yet magic could pull them from their realm if it was cast by a powerful enough magician. He himself had shifted the gap between the worlds a few times, though it had been at tremendous cost to his strength and reserves. Why would the gods create a creature that could resist almost all magic except the one casting that would kill them? Was it for balance? Order? It all seemed counterintuitive and poorly planned.

"Bah! Now is not the time to contemplate the order of the universe." He swiped at the air in front of him a few times as if his thoughts were a pest. Moving onto the next stage of testing Terren's abilities to better understand how to defeat the prince needed his attention more than answering an endless supply of open-ended questions.

Aaliyah had described the ability of Shadow Walkers to move across vast distances using the Shade Realm as a go between. Apparently, heavenly bodies moved faster in the other realm, so Walkers appeared to move greater distances in the Sun Realm. For not being a

Shadow Walker herself, she had a significant amount of knowledge, knowledge he was still wary of.

Like most Sunlanders, he knew the stories told to children of enormous Beasts roaming the land on new moon nights; their fur and feathers made from shadows, obsidian eyes glimmering in the light of a torch only to disappear when you looked again. There was, however, a memory, faint and misted at the edges from a previous host body that had been obsessed with the tales of the Shadow Walkers. In that memory, he was reading a journal entry of the very thing Aaliyah described. Zerrec tried to recall more, but that host was over two hundred years ago at this point. Still, his knowledge remained theoretical, and he wanted undeniable evidence. He wanted actual calculations for the rate of travel, the size of the shadows used for doorways, and who could open a doorway between the realms—was it the Beast or the Walker? Zerrec especially wanted to know the earliest a Beast could withstand entering the Sun Realm. He needed to be armed with knowledge to give him power, and he liked power. As soon as Terren returned from the north, Zerrec would send him out again, this time with a task that would force him to use those specific abilities.

Zerrec smoothed the neat brown beard he'd become fond of wearing. Subtle streaks of gray made him look refined, distinguished, even, which he used to his advantage. He smiled at his status in life. He'd risen to power faster than in any other of his previous lifetimes. Stupid of him not to take it sooner. Why had he thought moving up in status organically was the way to go? He'd been given instant gratification. Taking over Grayten and being King of Klynotia gave him the power he had craved but never wielded as an advisor in Lorea. Zerrec examined his roughened fingers and the ring bearing the king's seal. This small piece of jewelry represented so much.

Homage. Respect. Fear.

'USURPUR!'

Zerrec ignored the distant voice in his head. For centuries he lived from the overflow of others' greatness. Now? Now everything was for the taking, and he'd done it so easily. People focused on him, shouted praises as he stepped into view, trembled as his words covered them.

This is what he deserved. Sure, he was not known as Zerrec to the masses, but he'd learned long ago how patience could accomplish much. What did matter was that Grayten was obsolete–a relic of the past. Zerrec knew he was Klynotia's future. Only the memory of the old king remained. Everyone and everything in Klynotia was wrapped around his finger, and a new era of leadership was his to shape. One day the whole Sun Realm, from the zenith of Ny's Crown to the lowest speck of sand beneath the waves of Reana, would know the truth of what he had attained, what he had accomplished. One day he would reveal his name, and Zerrec would be spoken with awe and not whispered in fear. His face could change, but his name—set in ink and etched into the timeline of history—would be irrefutable.

CHAPTER 32

LOYALTIES

TERREN

He sat with a group of knights, wordless, as they recounted the day's events. It was the first time he'd been readily invited to join the knights and soldiers around the campfire. On the way to Woodlands Deep, he'd been welcomed to the fires only because he was the prince; now the men welcomed him as a brother. Terren supposed this was better than a pity invite, but he wondered if they only invited him to laud his fighting skills when all he had done was lose control of his senses. The enthusiastic descriptions of how he defeated one mercenary after another rubbed a sore spot in his thoughts.

I just have to remember this day as a victory. I stopped the bloodlust and only killed mercenaries, and only three of my men dine in Apelgo's Hall tonight.

He let go of the tension gathering in his lungs. Terren wished he'd not lost any soldiers in his company, but the flash of light meant to blind the men had fulfilled its purpose long enough for three men to die. He would not call the general attitude of the knights and soldiers gladsome, but he thought they were far too pleased with the outcome, as if to them three men was a worthwhile sacrifice to save a mine and a town. Maybe, but they didn't have to return the bodies and give condolences to their families.

If I focus on the good, I can move past my failure.

At least the magic only turned out to be a boy with trinkets and not a trained magician. Terren stopped himself before he imagined the outcome of such an ordeal, but something about Berro rubbed him the wrong way. The boy claimed he was forced to help the mercenaries, but the gems in his possession now empty of any castings for him to prove his theories—he was told after the battle of the vines and flying objects—seemed too perfectly planned out for the Janissairian mercenaries to just have them primed for use.

"My lord, such a victory today!" The young bard sidled up to him, his lute—an oval-bodied stringed instrument—wrapped around his front. "I shall compose a song of your prowess against the mercenaries and your freeing of the village."

Terren looked over the young man. He believed the boy had been manipulated into helping the mercenaries, but his overly relaxed demeanor felt forced. Terren's years of traveling gave him a sixth sense about people's intentions, and this boy caused shocks to run up his spine and zing at the base of his neck. "That is not necessary, Berro."

"Come, come! Of course it is! I am a rather good lyricist and can pen an excellent song."

"Please, no songs," Terren said, preferring to be left alone.

"But, Sire, it was you who won us the day!" A nearby knight chimed in his support.

"Yes, yes!" Berro agreed. "Tell me, sir knight, your perspective and I will add it to the song!"

"This is not a battle to be remembered," Terren said quietly, keeping his gaze on the fire. "This village is free and that is all that matters."

"But Sire, you not only defeated a magician and freed the village, but you did it with minimal losses." This comment came from a soldier across the fire.

"Oh! Yes, please tell me more. I was forced into the alley and did not leave until the fighting was over. I would love to know everything that happened. It will round out my tale to make it more exciting."

Terren stood. "There is nothing to tell."

"I saw vines wrap around his legs only to watch him rip them free of the ground! Who knew our prince was so strong," a third knight said.

"I saw objects flying at him from all directions and he dodged every one. Uncanny speed our prince has," a fourth jumped in.

Now they're just prevaricating.

"That is quite the tale to be told!" Berro said, nearly vibrating with glee. "This will make a rousing song to be sure."

"Enough! I did what I thought best for the protection of my men and the people, no more no less. No song will be written. That is an order," Terren growled.

"Surely, Sire, there is something to be remembered here? At the very least the way you led the men with valor and honor?" Berro pushed.

Terren stared at the boy long enough to elicit a small squirm before striding away.

Once he was hidden in the shadows, the knights and soldiers slowly came out of their chastised state. He did not intend to snap, but the incessant praise and pandering were not deserved. He didn't remember vines or things flying at him. There wasn't another magician around, so he safely assumed the castings for those things came from the crystals in the possession of Berro. Why did it not settle well with him that the Janissairians had this collection of crystals with random castings to give to the boy? In his limited dealings with the warring people, they preferred magic to be woven into their garments or accessories for a specific purpose rather than just carrying crystals and gems with various castings in them. It's why the larger tribes often paid well for the capture of magicians, so they could enslave them.

"You do not wish to have your deeds noted, my prince?" Lucen asked, joining him on the bent tree root.

"No." Terren gritted his teeth to keep from being rude to his valet. He knew Lucen was attempting to ease his tension, but he just craved being left alone.

"Would it not help establish your authority over this kingdom?"

He huffed. "I do not wish to be remembered for the way I fought, for bloodshed to be synonymous with my name."

"And what do you wish for?"

Terren curled his shoulders and propped his elbows on his knees to stare at the ground. "Is it too much to ask to just be respected?"

"No, but you should know better than anyone that respect is earned, not demanded, and this fight went a long way in doing just that."

Terren nodded. He didn't want to agree, but he understood why his fighting prowess would be praiseworthy. No one wanted to follow a weak leader, but the last thing he needed was for his men to think him strong and then fear him because of it. He refused to be like Grayten.

"How long will you allow the men to rest before returning?"

Good, a topic change.

"Just through tomorrow, I wish to speak to the duke over these lands while the men help the village with some cleanup. I want to know the difficulties from his perspective." Terren wanted no more company tonight. In fact, he needed to open a door to the Shade Realm once all the men were asleep to release Kamaria and spend time with her—if she would even do so. Since the end of the fight, she'd been silent. He could sense her; she hadn't shut him out, but she had likely closed the path allowing him access to her emotions and thoughts. His Bear's silence bothered him. He worried about her and wanted to ensure she could work through what had happened today. Kamaria blamed herself for the outburst the soldiers praised, but it was not her fault, and he needed to make that clear to her.

He stood, intending to melt into the trees. Lucen stood as well, ready to follow. "I just need some time alone." Lucen nodded, faithful despite what Terren did to him. Would he ever feel like he deserved his friendship?

"Shall I pass the plan for tomorrow along to your men?" Lucen asked.

"Yes, please."

"And how many men did you lose?" Terren asked after the duke relayed the finer details of his attempt to retake the village from the Janissairians.

"One hundred fifty, Sire."

Terren frowned at the news. It was a significant number. Most of the northern duchies were small, and Aubin was no exception. He probably had only five hundred ready-trained soldiers at his disposal. If he was caught off guard as he said, and had lost more than a quarter of his forces attempting to reclaim the village, the duke was not as lax as Grayten portrayed him to be.

"Sire, I have always kept these lands safe. My knights and soldiers will defend these lands with everything they have. The mercenaries came with force and the soldiers in the town were killed before they could act. I was not even made aware of the situation until two days later when a young boy came to me. I immediately mounted with my local knights to take back control. It pained all of us when we had to retreat, but I would not sacrifice men needlessly. We were severely outnumbered. When I sought help from the crown, the king promised aid. Your forces are the fulfillment of that promise, though later than I expected," Duke Aubin said.

"How long ago did you send the request?"

"Over a month ago."

Why would Grayten wait so long to send aid to the duchy?

The king Terren knew would never let profits be stolen for so long. He would have sent aid as soon as possible to keep the treasury from dropping even the slightest amount. But Terren's return after the Lundemai seamlessly coincided with the king's sudden interest in sending forces to aid Aubin, as if Grayten had deliberately waited for him to return to Klynotia. It was too big a coincidence to ignore.

"I believe you, Aubin," Terren said. "I know it has been some time since we've spoken, but I have always heard good things about your stewardship."

"Thank you, Sire."

"That being said, with the threat removed I would like you to form a plan to refortify the area so it is not so vulnerable," Terren said.

"My lord, how will I pay for such fortifications? Additional taxes have been levied by … by the crown, and it has forced many sacrifices."

He is talking to me as if I were the king. Ny guide my words. I do not want my uncle to fear me as he fears Grayten.

"When were the additional taxes levied?"

"Almost four months ago."

Terren acknowledged the words but kept his focus out the window.

I really dislike the changes that I am hearing of.

He shifted from one foot to the other while marking the low hills muted in the foggy morning. Soon the sun would fully breakthrough, and a tapestry of green would lead the way to the Aria Bells.

"Where do your loyalties lie, Aubin?" Terren asked.

"With the crown, Sire."

Safe answer, but Terren wanted something more specific. "And with the succession of the crown?" The rustle of fabric suggested the duke had taken a seat. His hesitation forced Terren to turn to judge his body language. The older man concentrated on the folds of his fingers. His brow was not furrowed in thought, but that meant nothing. Many nobles in the Klynotian court knew how to keep a detached expression. It was a survival skill in this kingdom. "Uncle, an answer."

The duke raised his brown, well-creased eyes. "Uncle? That is a title I have not heard in many years."

"It is a title I have not uttered in many years." Terren offered nothing more, but he hoped that acknowledging their relationship would soften Aubin so he could get a genuine answer.

"I have seen ruin come to many in this kingdom that did not deserve such a fate," Aubin said.

"Aye."

Standing, the duke pulled back his shoulders to show every inch of his royal bearing. Terren remained relaxed. He could have done the same, but this was not a contest of wills for him. He knew his place was on the throne of Klynotia, and if his uncle's opinion of him was negative, it would do no good to peacock his way through the conversation. Grayten did enough of that for all the nobles combined.

"Not to be disrespectful, Nephew, but will you be a successor that inspires my loyalty? I know little of you."

Terren narrowed his eyes slightly. They were both walking a thin line, but he posed a fair question. He kept the older man's gaze for a time, formulating his answer. There was much he could say to possibly convince the duke his loyalty would not be unfounded, but loyalty looked different to everyone. Over the years, Terren had seen people loyal because of outright fear, legitimate respect, and cultural norms. The Veripoi chieftain kept his people happy by staying open-minded and interested in others' ideas. The Nyuten priests had loyalty from others because of kindness and service. Aboard the *Surveysor* he learned loyalty so as to avoid a lash to the heels, and the Isokanii tribes followed the Mafelbno no matter the state of agreement. With all those lessons learned, the question of how to inspire loyalty in others still eluded him, but he knew for certain he wanted the people of his kingdom to be ruled with compassion. "I want to see Klynotia prosperous and its people happy, Uncle. I know better than most what it is like to feel the wrath of Grayten, and I do not like to see my people suffer the same. So I will ask you again, do your loyalties lie solely with the crown or can I trust you to support me?"

Aubin studied him for a moment, accessing the truth of Terren's statement. "If that is your aim, Your Royal Highness"—the duke lowered himself to one knee and bowed his head.—"then my loyalties are with you."

Terren walked over to his uncle and, giving him a hand, he pulled him to his feet. Keeping a steady gaze, he said, "Uncle, I do not need your surrender or concession, what I need to know is if you will take a leap of faith and trust me. As I said, I want the best for Klynotia, but things will grow worse before we see peace again. Grayten will not go quietly, and I need reliable men who will support me. Just as you are not your brother, I am not my father. What I can promise is that I have no desire to be him."

Aubin lowered his eyes, studying their clasped forearms. Quietly but firmly, he said, "A leap of faith I will take, then, Terren."

The tone of his voice was exactly what Terren sought.

"And I can trust this conversation will remain between us?"

"Not a breath will be spoken by me."

Terren nodded. "Thank you. I will send the money you need to fortify these lands once I reach the capital."

"How—"

"The how does not matter. I will send enough to ensure you can fortify and rebuild," Terren said, and gripping his uncle's forearm a little tighter added, "just so I am clear, the financial help is not dependent on your loyalty, I just needed to be certain your support of me was not because of it."

Aubin nodded. "Very good."

The duke bowed as Terren left the room. These were the first stones in the foundation of what he prayed would be true loyalty from the man second in line to the throne.

He is the perfect ally to convince others I am worth following. Let's hope he can.

CHAPTER 33

FRIENDSHIP

KIIRA

"I thought I would find you out here," she said, strolling up to the Klynotian princess. Sairah pointedly ignored her attempt at conversation, continuing to paint the mulberry tree. The lone tree drooped, separated from the rest of the garden by a circular path, its leaves yellow in the process of abandoning their summer home. She watched the princess for a while as she oiled various pigments to bring the tree from reality onto a flat surface, and still make it look real. Her control of the colors and brushes flared jealousy in Kiira. She could make drymera, but there was something tremendous about people who had the skills to create beauty with their hands. Stepping around Sairah, Kiira circled the tree and touched the trunk to find it barely clinging to life, and not just because of the season. Maybe when no one was near, she could use her gift to help the tree thrive a little. While strolling back to Sairah, she said, "I have asked to enjoy afternoon tea in the garden. It is such a lovely day and the flowers are giving their last efforts before the cool of fall takes residence. Would you care to take a break and join me?"

"No, and I wish you would stop trying to be a friend," Sairah said with a severe bite. "I have already participated in the five agreed upon meetings, now please just leave me alone."

The so-called meetings had occurred within the first week of Terren's departure, each one of them as short as possible just so the princess would not have to endure her company for long. Kiira settled into the lush grass next to Sairah. Lightly pulling at the verdant blades, she said, "If you do not wish to be my friend would you accept a sister instead? Brothers are fun, but I imagine it is not the same as having a sister."

Sairah slammed her brush onto the easel. She nearly toppled her artwork in her haste to get inside, a stubborn chin leading the way. Kiira would bring everything inside and place it in front of the princess' doors once she finished tea.

"Do not give up, princess," Jemma said, stepping around the corner shrub with a tray of tea and various foods to eat. At least Jemma could sit with her, and the extra food would not be wasted.

"That is not in my nature," she replied, tossing a slice of thin meat at Skehtra, who'd slunk around the corner at Jemma's heels. "For now, you must stay and have tea with me to conspire ways to get Sairah to like me."

Kiira flipped another page in her book. She was curled in a chair by the only window in the castle's sad excuse for a library. Luckily, it faced south, providing her with the perfect lighting, and the chair was warm and comfortable, and the nearby shelves of parchment gave off a pleasing smell of aged leather. This tended to be the least traversed part of the castle, making it a perfect place to think. She tried to focus on the text, but her mind wandered toward the dilemma with Sairah. Kiira studied the ceiling as the afternoon sun highlighted specks of dust as they chose where to settle. A sennight had passed since the day in the garden. In that time, Kiira had graciously given the princess space, only meeting her in passing or at the table of the evening meal, and always offered her a smile. It was an effort to get the tight-lipped princess to open up to her by showing she was not a threat to her peace, though her method was not proving to be a winning strategy.

Kiira sighed, flipping another page. Terren had warned her that Sairah was not prone to talking, preferring the company of her sketchbooks and charcoal. What brief history he could give of his sister recounted what she endured at Grayten's hand. The lengths to which the king went to gain information on Terren's whereabouts made Kiira clench her jaw. No child should suffer abuse at the hands of a parent. It came as no surprise, then, that the princess kept reinforced walls around her heart to feel secure. Kiira barely knew the younger woman, and already she wanted to retaliate against the king on the princess' behalf. Flashes of inspiration to make Grayten's life miserable with minor castings were considered and dismissed once she decided his misery would only wear off on everyone else.

Kiira jumped when the door to the library burst open. Sairah charged in her direction, waving the stack of images in her face.

"What are these?" she demanded.

"They're paintings from one of the best artists in Lorea, a gift," Kiira replied, glancing briefly at the top picture close to her nose; one of the Forest Wilds on a misty morning, a favorite of hers.

The others ruffling near her face were all small paintings on the leftover squares and strips of linen after the artist stretched a canvas on a frame. She'd asked the painter who sold these in the Lorean market once; and he said most of the images were done using leftover oils too mixed or scant for use. He used them to warm up before working on his masterpieces, like she did before sparring or running. It prevented him from being wasteful and still made him some money. The only drawback was Sairah would need to secure the canvas to something, so the linen didn't warp and ruin the painting.

Kiira had written to Ariella not long after Terren left, and she'd done a wonderful job in selecting images that depicted different parts of Lorea. She'd been sent more than she thought would be included and assumed the extras were for her, though the return letter did not specifically say. Kiira had selected a few that did not already decorate her walls and then slipped the others under Sairah's door on her way to the library.

"Why?" Sairah pulled the images away to fist her hips.

Kiira shrugged, turning her eyes down to flip another page in the book. Keeping her tone mild, she said, "I thought you would appreciate them. You are constantly making art of your own."

Silence pooled like the sunlight between them. Sairah obviously wanted more of an explanation, but there was none.

Finally, Sairah said, "This does not mean I like you." Huffing, she barged from the room, punctuating her exit with the slam of the door.

Kiira smirked. The first chunk in Sairah's wall had just been chiseled away, creating a nice little starting point. Now, all she had to do was keep widening the gap.

KIIRA KNOCKED on her sister-in-law's door. Orella opened it and bobbed a curtsy. Sairah rolled her eyes, but allowed Kiira to enter her room. She strolled to the table to lean over the princess' shoulder. Today she sketched a small, long-legged bird with a narrow, pointed beak. "What bird is that? I've not seen that one."

"Really? Maybe because they move further south in the winter. This is a Stilt. They are mostly in the marshy areas closer to the shore." Sairah added a heavy black line to mark a shadow.

"They must go even further south than Lorea, then. There are a fair number of islands between Lorea and Janissair. They must go there."

Sairah shrugged.

Strolling away, Kiira said, "I've arranged to have the midday meal outside the castle grounds. I thought we might venture out to the fields one last time before it gets too cold, I have a feeling the weather will turn in a day or two. Would you join me?" Kiira asked.

"If it will make you finally leave me alone, then yes I will go with you," Sairah said, setting down her drawing pencil.

"Excellent!" Kiira put too much emphasis on the word, but it was to cover her surprise. There was not as much heat in the response as she expected. In the short time her husband was gone, virtually every effort to form a friendship with the princess was met with some sort of hostility. Honestly, if it weren't for Terren, Kiira would have left the younger woman to her devices. She ordinarily had little patience for someone who took a long time deciding, but Windrah must have been listening to her prayers for patience because lately something wouldn't let Sairah sabotage herself into isolation. Perhaps the paintings had done more in her favor than she had realized. "I will meet you at the stables in half an hour."

"I hate horses."

Kiira raised her brows at the new information, almost wailing at the insanity of such a claim, but kept the outburst between her teeth. Jemma would be proud. Instead, she shrugged. "No matter, I will have the Horse Master hook up a cart."

She left before Sairah could find even the slightest reason to object. Happily, she made her way to the kitchens to request more food and snag an apple for Starfire. Kiira, soon after beginning her quest to befriend Sairah, had discovered that many of the servants were very kind, and happy to have her as their new royal. Most kept their natures veiled out of self-preservation, wanting to circumvent the volatile nature of the king. When learning of her intentions with Sairah, they were quick to help with whatever Kiira needed.

"Letta! Good news!" Kiira danced up to the woman, who was busy trussing up a row of pimpled chickens for roasting.

"You got her to agree?" The woman's brows disappeared into her kerchief as her hands moved efficiently over the carcasses.

"Reluctantly, yes, but"—Kiira raised a finger—"she will learn to love me." A mischievous grin lit her face, making the cook chuckle.

"Oh, of that I have no doubt, Your Highness. I had a feeling she'd say yes, so I already had the girls make a double portion."

"You are the best, thank you!"

After pilfering a couple of apples, Kiira left the kitchen in high spirits only to run smack into Grayten. A shiver and a spark ran up her spine as she bumped into him. Why did that sensation feel so familiar? Since entering the castle, something about Grayten had not settled well with her. He was too refined, a far cry from the man she met in Lorea before her wedding. The king she met in Lorea had cleaned himself up so as not to give a terrible impression; the man in front of her now was in control of himself at all times. It confused her because sometimes he would do things she expected, but the actions also seemed ersatz. It terrified her more than she wanted to admit. Kiira did her best to hide her feelings, but it took every effort not to shrink away from his presence. An eerie familiarity lurked in the pit of her stomach whenever she had to be near the king. Despite her heart racing, she held her chin tall.

"What are you doing in the kitchens?" Grayten rumbled.

"I was grabbing apples for my horse," Kiira said.

"Why not send your servant?" He narrowed his eyes.

Why is he always suspicious of everything?

"I like to stretch my legs by doing things myself." The answer was authentic enough.

Grayten stared at her for a moment too long, eyes bouncing between normal and narrowed. "Send a servant next time, that's what they are there for."

Knave! It's no wonder he has to use fear to rule his people.

"Of course, Your Majesty," Kiira said while executing a shallow curtsy. She wrinkled her nose as she clocked his steps down the hall toward the lower parts of the castle.

Why would the king need to visit the dungeons? As far as I know, there are no prisoners here.

Her distrust of Grayten made her more curious. Kiira felt it was her responsibility to look after the kingdom with Terren not here, and if she'd had time she would have followed the king. She shook her head. Probably for the best that she needed to meet Sairah for the picnic. If she were late, the princess would use it as an excuse to decline and retreat. Kiira made a mental note to further explore when she had more information, and she had an amulet to conceal her presence. Purchasing one here in the kingdom would be impossible, and convincing Liem to send one would be nearly so. Making one would drain her quite a bit, but was doable. Maybe while they were outside the walls, she could come up with an excuse to put some distance between her and the princess to conceal her magic and do a casting.

Kiira glanced down at the blue opal on her first finger, her wedding band. No, she didn't want to use magic on something so personal. She touched her necklace. It was the same dark blue opal as her ring, a gift from a courtier. Not the best gemstone to use for holding a casting, but it would do since she didn't have time to return to her rooms for anything else, which reminded her to get moving.

Terren was going to be upset when she told him of her exploits, but something was wrong, and her instincts told her to investigate. If it turned out to be nothing, then at least she would know for certain, and maybe not feel so taut all the time.

CHAPTER 34

HOMECOMING

KIIRA

Soft rain taps accompanied a misty afternoon. The gray light of her room muted as winter attempted to seep through the stone, but a popping fire in the hearth kept it at bay. The dulcet snores of Skehtra as she stretched in front of the fire made the room feel inviting and like home.

In their eight weeks of living in Klynotia, Jemma had procured a variety of Yielding Season plants and flowers native to the area since the castle did not have a greenhouse to grow non-seasonal flora—something Kiira planned to correct very soon. At least her room was alive with blossoms of pink, red, and yellow, but most especially green, making the lifeless atmosphere of the heathered stone brighter. Large clay pots filled with Oleander flanked the doors of the balcony, and next to the fire a Yaupon Holly dotted with bright berries soaked in the warmth. She'd attempted to convince Jemma to bring in a Crepe Myrtle, but was forced to agree that the tree would be more maintenance than enjoyment. Plus, she would have to use her magic to keep a tree like that thriving through the winter inside. That would garner suspicion she didn't need. The smaller plants, though considerable in number, she could keep alive with barely a thought or strain to her magic. It was likely the only thing she could do that would not get her caught as a magician. If anyone questioned the greenery in her suite, Kiira could explain it as having a way with plants. The statement wasn't false; she had a green thumb; her gift simply made it easier.

The days seemed to shorten rapidly now, and Kiira hoped Terren would return soon. He'd been gone longer than he had said he would be, but anything could happen on the road; she just didn't want it to be something bad. In the first couple of weeks her husband was on his errand, she'd attempted to gather the noblewomen for tea, but all the invitations were declined. She thought for certain they would want to genuflect to their future monarch, but she promptly learned no one visited the castle unless they had to, so Kiira focused her efforts solely on Sairah for the time being. Rejection from one person was easier to handle than from a multitude.

But the last time she'd seen and spoken to the princess since the weather soured was on the day they lunched beyond the walls of the citadel, and it was definitely a marker in their relationship. For the better, she hoped. The princess' seclusion now didn't feel so much hostile as a sequestering in her room to huddle close to the fire, as most others were currently doing. That afternoon luncheon had not gone as expected. Sairah had been kind and actually did her part to maintain a conversation instead of leaving Kiira to chatter at her. It surprised her enough that she almost forgot to charge her necklace with the casting she needed to spy on Grayten, which she had yet to use. It was only as the princess walked away from the spread of cold meats, cheeses, and bread to find some late season flowers to pick that Kiira remembered her ulterior goal.

"I do not believe I will ever become accustomed to this weather," Jemma said.

"Are we really going to talk about weather just to fill the silence?"

"There is no need to be snippy, Kiira."

After a beat she replied, "I'm sorry, it is not your fault that I am at odds. I should not have snipped at you."

"What is bothering you?"

Kiira poked her needle through the fabric at the same time a loud pop echoed from a collapsing log. The white bone needle reflected the yellow light of the fire, turning it a creamy orange. Pulling a pale orange thread taut, she pushed it through the fabric again to finish the variegated fill in the bottom left wing of a Monarch butterfly she was embroidering onto the hem of some pale blue fabric. It was to be the first of many butterflies, and once a seamstress turned it into a dress, it would be the perfect attire to welcome the first sunny day of spring.

Maybe I could sew small gems into the design so the butterflies sparkle in the sun. For a little Klynotian flair.

Doing so was not her first instinct, but she felt it her responsibility to take a stand against the drab, austere garments the Klynotians insisted on wearing. Dare she hope that such flaunting of colors and gemstones would inspire the peerage to follow suit? Perhaps not. Even if she didn't add gems, the design would be lovely. Tereyssa would love to see the finished work, and Kiira made a mental note to send a drymera to her. She pulled a few more stitches through the fabric. "I must just be stir crazy."

Jemma nodded. "You have never been one to sit still for long. Even as a child I could barely keep up with you, but I have a feeling there is more you are not telling me. You know you can talk to me. It has always helped in the past."

"I know." Kiira knotted the end of her thread and switched to black before answering. "I think … I feel useless here. Sairah wants nothing to do with me. I have to train in secret if I want to practice anything except my bow, and even that gets me a side-eyed look from the king. The weather here is keeping me cloistered inside. Being around the king makes my skin crawl. I cannot even wear the clothes I want to wear because dresses seem to be the only acceptable garb for women in this kingdom!"

"That is a lot to process at once."

Kiira couldn't tell if Jemma's response was cheeky or not. The comment seemed genuine, but sometimes Jemma had an ornery streak that would blossom at random. She chose to ignore it and continue. "Not to mention my husband has been gone for almost two months with no word of his return or if he was successful because magic is shunned in this backwards-thinking kingdom!"

"Kiira," Jemma admonished.

"What? I am not a danger to anyone!" She slammed the embroidery into her lap.

Jemma gently set her own work down. "No, dear you are not, but you still need to respect the king's orders."

"Or I need to change them."

"How exactly do you plan on accomplishing such a task?"

Kiira slumped in her chair. "I have no idea, Jemma, but I have to think of something. I thought I could handle keeping my magic furtive since I naturally did it in Lorea, but in hindsight I took the freedoms of my kingdom for granted. How can I live the rest of my life feeling like I need to constantly look over my shoulder? At least in Lorea I could use my gift, even if most people were wary of it."

"Most of the people did not know you and Liem had magic."

"True. But there were magic items and amulets traded and sold in the market, so the people were naturally more open to the idea of it. Here, any hint of magic and people scurry like rats back into their holes."

Jemma gave her a look that said, "That was uncalled for", but Kiira refused to apologize. The peerage and the people both acted as if they would be stepped on at any moment. Perhaps the king inspired such a mentality, but fear shouldn't be a baseline for living, and she refused to coddle anyone when they had the power to change the kingdom and chose instead to hide.

Klynotia and Lorea both were only as strong as the weakest worker. She understood the fear, but it was long pastime someone planted seeds of courage and roused them to grow. Kiira wanted to make sure the roots ran deep; she wanted a thriving kingdom that outlasted her and Terren.

Skehtra perked her ears before slinking toward the door. She stared intently, her head cocked to the side while the tip of her tail ticked back and forth. Suddenly she leapt at the door, sinking her claws into the oak, marring an already damaged surface.

"Skehtra!" Kiira leapt from her chair, embroidery tumbling to the floor. "Naughty!"

She shooed the cat away as a light knock sounded.

Pulling the door open, Kiira gasped. "Terren!" Throwing her arms around his neck, she floated from the floor and buried her face in his neck. "I've missed you. Eight weeks was too long."

She could hear the smile in his voice as he said, "And I you." Terren waded inside while she clung to him before setting her down to give her a sweet, gentle kiss. "Mmm. I have missed doing that every day." Skehtra ruined the moment by shoving her head between them and winding in and out of their bodies. Terren rubbed all along the cat's face and behind the ears. "Yes, I missed you, too." Mollified by his attention, Skehtra walked away to settle once again in front of the fire. "Well, she's become quite the chit."

"You have no idea," Kiira said. "I think Jemma spoiled her to the point that the cat acts more like a lady than I do."

"Well one of you had to be a proper lady, and since you didn't seem interested I focused my energies on the cat," Jemma ribbed, putting Kiira's embroidery away.

"Nonsense," Terren said.

Kiira laughed. "She's not wrong, but enough about the cat. How long have you been here? I did not hear the announcement."

"Only an hour."

Kiira raised her brows in question, but Jemma interrupted his reply.

"It's good to see you home safe, my lord. I shall leave you two for the night."

Terren smiled at her. "Jemma, you need not be so formal with me in settings such as this. You can speak to me as you do with Kiira."

The lady's maid gave a small bow. "I shall see to it. Have a good night."

"And to you."

"Night, Jemma. Take Skehtra with you, please," Kiira said while reaching for a hug.

When the door closed, she turned back to Terren with the same questioning gaze as before.

"I had to make my report to the king and bathe."

She nodded. "Well, I have a lot to tell you," she said, pulling him toward the bed, "but I know something that doesn't need a detailed report."

Terren laughed, bringing her into the circle of his arms. "I like details, though." This time he kissed her long and slow, making sure to run his fingers deep into her curls. Kiira leaned into him, enjoying the press of his body.

When both of their breathing was a little quicker, he rested his forehead on hers. "Definitely going to make sure this one has plenty of details."

He kissed her again, carrying them both to the bed and something exquisite.

CHAPTER 35

REASSIGNED

KIIRA

"I hate that he is already sending you on another errand, this one utterly useless! Does Grayten not understand the concept of rest? How are you supposed to be the crown prince he expects if you are not here to take on the responsibility?" Kiira stormed into Terren's suite. The rooms were a sharp contrast to hers, filled as it now was with greenery. His rooms were full of warm, inviting wood paneling, all aged to varying degrees, yet little else of interest filled the space. Not that he'd been given any time to decorate, forced as he was to go from one place to the next.

Terren pulled knives from a velvet lined drawer along with a sharpening stone and oil. Lucen would arrive soon with the saddlebags. He wouldn't be leaving for at least a week, but Kiira knew he preferred to take his time packing to ensure he had all that he might need. "I do not like it anymore than you, but I told you in the Shade Realm that I need to plan my actions with care, and if it means being obedient to Grayten for the time being then so be it."

"I know!" Kiira slumped into a nearby chair, defeated.

Terren squatted by her arm. "I will be as quick as I can for this assignment, you have my promise. I'm going with Kamaria and

Tempest only as it will be easier to hunt the Wapiti without a company of men."

"That's what I'm afraid of, Terren! There is a reason the Great Elk is feared. It is ruthless, and not to mention elusive. You could be gone for months!" Tears pricked at Kiira's eyes. She was trying to be strong for Terren's sake, but he had only just returned and was already being sent out once again. She didn't want to be alone in a place she barely knew without him. Living in Klynotia was taking a toll on her mentally. "Why does Grayten want a Great Elk anyway? It will not improve his reputation. People will know he was not the one to hunt the beast."

"I am not sure why he has a sudden fixation on having a Wapiti. It feels as if he is testing me to see if I will return," Terren admitted.

Kiira nodded her agreement.

"He does not know me anymore. I am not the child that left this kingdom, so I will return no matter how long it takes. Make sure he does not declare me dead."

"You are joking."

Terren tried to keep a somber face, but he could not help the half smile.

Kiira smiled, but there was no humor. "Now is not the time to joke. It is difficult without you here."

"I know, love." Terren kissed her fingers. "I need you to be strong without me for a bit longer."

Kiira nodded, tears gathering on her lashes.

Terren pulled her to her feet. "Grayten may take the credit for having the Wapiti, however, it will only serve to bring respect to my name. I return alive and it shows the peerage and the people I am a knight capable of leading with strength and resolve. I seem to have unwittingly earned the hearts of the soldiers on my last venture, and certainly the rumors of my fighting are already traveling through the ranks."

"I suppose," Kiira replied, her nose pressed into his chest.

"Is that all that is bothering you?" Terren asked gently.

Kiira shook her head. He seemed to know when something deeper was coloring her emotions, though. Terren had learned to read her well during their Lundemai. She thanked Windrah that their bond would only grow the longer they were together.

"Come," he said, leading her to the cushioned bench at the foot of his bed. He pulled her to his side as she turned to put her legs across his knees and rest her head on his shoulder. "Now, tell me what is on your mind."

"It's Grayten. Something is off about him, and I think this quest is proof enough that he is trying to keep us separated."

"Why do you think that?"

"I crossed paths with him one day coming out of the kitchens and after our conversation I saw him take the hallway into the lower parts of the castle. Since then, I've seen him go down there multiple times, and it is concerning me. I have not gone down there yet myself out of caution and, if I'm honest, fear, but it seems odd for him to go down there when he has rooms far superior in the royal wing. Plus, Grayten gives me the oddest looks when he believes I am not looking. It feels like contempt, which I ignored the first time, but I have seen the looks often enough to question it."

"You're sure it is the lower part of the castle and not the dungeon? The dungeon can be accessed from that hallway as well," Terren said.

Kiira shrugged. "Maybe, but I have not heard of any prisoner down there worthy of Grayten's interest, nor has the kitchen mentioned taking food down to anyone. If there is someone, why would he care about a prisoner that much?"

Terren looked thoughtful for a moment. "I think this is worth looking into when I return. Grayten has been eccentric since my mother's death so I do not necessarily see this as overly odd, but I trust your instincts, Kiira. That and something has not felt right about Grayten since our return to Klynotia. I want to be careful with our actions, if our plan is discovered—"

"I know, and whatever is down there is important enough for no one to know about it. He is careful about who sees him, but the kitchen workers are more observant than he thinks. There is not even a guard, never has been."

"How do you know?"

"I listened to the gossip mill in the kitchen. I think the servants forget I am there when I help with the prep work," Kiira admitted.

Terren nodded, thinking through the information. Kiira waited comfortably in his embrace while he considered it. He was leaving soon, so she would cling to him as much as possible.

He pulled her into a hug and said, "What you told me has merit. It is concerning, but it can be put on-hold until I return. You do not need to put yourself in unnecessary danger if it can be avoided."

She nodded even though she did not agree, but at least Terren wasn't outright dismissing her thoughts. That was not in his nature, but it had been a concern when she considered telling him about Grayten's movements. This topic was too vague to discuss further, so she asked, "Where will you start your search?"

"I'll ride to Fellos and begin there. I need to seek out the Veripoi if I am to have any luck finding the Wapiti. Sometimes a member will go to Fellos for trade. It'll be better than wandering aimlessly."

"I thought the Veripoi did not venture near the mountains."

"In the Yielding and Renewing Seasons, yes, which is why I will make my camps in places where they might see my fire," Terren said. "In the Dead Season, they like to camp in the mountains. Why, I do not know, it's cold, but they do. The Wapiti is sacred to them and they will be able to help me so my search is not in vain."

"How will going to Fellos help you?"

"It will just be a base as I search."

"I wish I could accompany you," Kiira sulked. "I have always wanted to meet the Veripoi."

"They are elusive for a reason. I only met them by chance. The chieftain's son 'found me intriguing' apparently. I never did learn what exactly he meant by that," Terren said with humor.

"How long do you think you'll be gone?"

"Three months, if I am lucky. Kamaria's sensitive nose will be a considerable help in tracking the Wapiti."

"Three months!" Kiira wailed, tears coming far easier than she wished.

"This is not the best time of year to find it, which is exactly why Grayten gave me this task, but let us not talk about this now. I leave in a week, so we still have some time together," Terren said, kissing the side of her head. "Things will look differently in the morning."

Kiira nodded even though she knew nothing would look different in the morning. Her emotions were darker than ever. He was trying to be positive for her sake, but this was not something to be positive about. How could she even try? One thing was for certain—she would not be waiting three months to discover what had Grayten's attention buried deep beneath the castle. By then, a discovery might be too late.

CHAPTER 36

CUPUN

TERREN

'*How long are we going to look for the Veripoi? I do not smell anything,*' Kamaria said from her place amongst the deepest trees.

The sun was below the tops of the trees, but still shone well enough through the trunks at his back to prevent her from exiting the Shade Realm altogether. At least she could hold a door open indefinitely and cross over soon. Terren poked at the low fire, stirring the coals to warmth before adding another set of damp logs to encourage the flames to smoke. A column of white billowing into the air was an obvious signal, and one he'd been maintaining in different locations for a few weeks. Between this and the message he left with the Veripoi's trading partners in Fellos, it had to get their attention at some point. Terren pulled his wool cloak tighter about him to stave off the chill. The fire cracked, causing Tempest to jump and nicker. She threw her head a couple of times before returning to the grasses at her hooves.

'*I told you what to expect,*' Terren chided his Bear.

'*Yes, but this excursion has been unusually boring. I need more action.*'

'*You say that, but you will immediately regret it.*'

'I will not. I like when things are interesting,' Kamaria countered.

Terren stilled as a sharp point dug into the middle of his shoulder blades. Immediately, the crash of branches from Kamaria's hasty entrance broke whatever camouflage she had. Terren was still sitting in the last few rays of sunlight, so she couldn't get close to him without severe pain. A growl of frustration bounced between the trees as she found herself cut off from him. He hadn't considered how he was going to explain his Bear to the Veripoi. He hadn't planned their meeting in the first place.

The knife disappeared from his back. "SIKUK! Is that a Great Spirit?"

Terren stood and turned to catch his old friend Kallik with rounded eyes and dropped jaw. He rubbed the back of his neck with a wry smile. "Ah, yes. I've experienced a lot since I saw you last."

"That, Cupun, is an understatement," Kallik responded. "How have you come to have a Great Spirit watch over you?"

"That is a lengthy tale."

Kallik, still the easy-going friend he remembered, sat himself on the log Terren was using. "How many times have I said you cannot surprise me, Cupun?" Kallik asked.

"I've lost count."

"Well, you surprised me."

Terren laughed, joining him on the makeshift bench. *'Peace, Kamaria,'* Terren relayed to her mentally. She calmed and faded into the shadows, but tension still pulled at his thoughts. "I did not think to live and see such a day," Terren said jovially, but also haltingly in the language of the Veripoi. It had been many years since he had needed to recall the strange words and sentence structure. Even after living with them for two years, it still wasn't a language that rolled naturally from his tongue.

Kallik, dressed in thick fur-lined leathers, grinned mischievously at him. Terren couldn't help but grin in return. His friend's long hair, braided with wooden beads, feathers, and bones, clacked lightly as he shifted to poke the fire with a stick. An elaborate necklace decorated his chest and shoulders. How Terren missed his entrance with all the noisy objects on his person he didn't know, but then the Veripoi were stealthy. "It is good to see you, Kallik," Terren said.

"You need to practice! Your accent is terrible!"

"What did you expect? I have not needed to use it for many years."

"I am not to blame for such a separation," Kallik reprimanded.

"No indeed. I see you are chieftain now."

Kallik's smile faded. "Yes, my father was sent on his Kannelner to the Spires last Mountain Season."

"I am sorry to hear it, my friend," Terren said, leaning forward to take Kallik's forearm. "May you have the strength of heart to follow his footprints and be a beacon for your people."

"Nahkahkurmehk." Leaning back, Kallik continued, "What brings you to us, Cupun? Other than to thoroughly shock me."

Terren turned solemn. Switching to Sunarian to better explain, he said, "I need to hunt a Wapiti, and I need your help finding one." In the two years he lived with the Veripoi, it was the one hunt in which he could never take part. Terren never let it offend him since the Great Elk was held in such reverence by the Veripoi. It would be the equivalent of letting a stranger into the royal vaults of Klynotia; thus, he never expected involvement in the annual hunt.

Kallik frowned before also replying in Sunarian. "You know the Wapiti is sacred to us. We hunt only one a year to help support our people."

"I know, but it is a task set before me by Grayten. You know of my desire to rid Klynotia of a tyrant king, but I need to bide my time. Regicide will not win me the favor of the kingdom."

"And hunting the Wapiti will not keep the favor of my people," Kallik said.

Terren groaned, rubbing his head. "Kallik, I know. I do not wish to offend or lose the friendship of the Veripoi, it is why I sought you first before hunting. You and your people treated me with such kindness for the years I was with you."

They listened to the birds of the Forest for a time, each contemplating the situation. Terren didn't want to push the subject and utterly silence his friend, so he was content with being still, waiting as the sun lost the battle of light amongst the ancient grove. There had to be a way to appease Grayten and not offend the Veripoi. He much preferred the friendship of these nomadic people to the favor of an unbalanced king, but he needed to complete this task to keep his true intentions secret.

Ny, please let there be a just solution, Terren prayed.

"You have shown strong reverence in coming to us first, Cupun. Tonight we feast and offer sacrifices to the spirits for atonement and perhaps they will hear our plea to grant favor in hunting a second of the sacred animal," Kallik said.

"I thank you for that much help, my friend."

"Then, come! The people will be happy to see you and you will regale us with the tale of how you came to be in the friendship of a Great Spirit. Plus, you will meet my sons, Aput and Panuk."

"You married Myna?"

"Yes, and the same year she gave me two boys that will give me gray hair early."

Grinning, Terren said, "Sounds like they took after their father."

TERREN SAT in the place of honor with Kallik. The large central fire lit the faces of the people he'd shared so many fires with in the past. It had been nearly nine years since he'd last sat around the campfire to digest the animated conversation, and the act warmed him more than any heat from the flames. He missed this way of life, the simplicity of eating excellent food with people who knew how to enjoy it. Tonight's dinner consisted of root quail stewed with copper berries. It was a standard dish for this time of year since the quail was abundant in the Forest and easy to hunt even as cold came down the mountain. The feast would last until the coals burned dim, and the stars shone bright. This moment could only be made better if Kiira were here to enjoy it with him. Maybe Kallik would be willing to let her visit one day.

As much as he enjoyed himself, thinking of Kiira embedded a

granule of impatience in his mind. He preferred to be at home with her, but would first have to sit through this meeting of the people. This was no ordinary feast, since any matter presented tonight would be taken seriously, with prayers and sacrifices to the spirits for guidance. The courtesy of coming to them first was the least he could do for the people who had sheltered him at one of the worst times in his life. Terren knew he could have eventually found the Great Elk on his own, but the guilt of skirting around the Veripoi would have been a burden he didn't want to carry for the rest of his life. He just needed to have patience. The people would listen, and they could come to an agreement. Even if it did not go his way, at least he'd remembered their language, and his conversations were not so clumsy.

When the people's faces were little more than general shapes dimly illuminated by the orange coals, Kallik raised his arms and said, "My people! The spirits have seen to bless us with a reminder of the past. Cupun has joined us again after many seasons away." He looked at Terren. "We are grateful you have come to us once again."

Terren acknowledged the recognition with a nod.

"My people, Cupun has come to us with an inquiry. We must seek the spirits' guidance on a hunt for Wapiti."

"But we have already hunted the Wapiti. We must wait until the next Mountain Season," Qimmiq said.

"Yes, however, Cupun has come seeking our permission to hunt another," Kallik answered.

"We cannot do this!" several people cried.

"It would anger the spirits," another voiced.

"Why should we let an outsider destroy our sacred animal?" A third asked.

Kallik raised his hands for silence. "He honored us by seeking our permission first. Most of you here know this man, he is not our enemy. Think of those who do not honor us in this way."

"Chief Kallik, may I speak?" Terren asked.

Kallik gestured to the people, allowing him to make his plea.

"People, I seek not the Wapiti for amusement. I seek the Great Elk to pave a path for me to help the citizens of Klynotia. If I could leave the beast alone I would. If it makes any difference at all, I need only the antlers."

"Chief, we still have the nagruk of the Wapiti from this last hunt. It has yet to be made into other things. Are our knives not still sharp and our clothes still in a good state? Could we spare the nagruk this one year and be sustained on what we have? It would prevent us from hunting another, and it would help Cupun in his quest," Myna said.

"That is a solution, Myna." Kallik turned to the people. "What say you, my people? Can we not spare the nagruk of the Wapiti this one year to help Cupun?"

"We need the nagruk for our tools and clothes," cried a member.

Myna replied, "Yes, but we have a store from past years. It would not be such a burden to part with the nagruk this one year. If we help Cupun then we are helping our way of life. The man sitting on the throne of Klynotia now does not respect us, but the man before you will give us consideration. If losing the nagruk this one year secures a promise of future peace, then it is an easy price to pay and one I support."

Terren threw a grateful glance at Myna as whispers moved around the fire. He took a deep breath to keep his composure. The Veripoi would not be swayed by baleful looks on his part, and they would not be swayed by beseeching words.

Grayten said he wanted the whole beast brought before him as proof. It was an impossible task unless he traveled via the Shade Realm with Kamaria; otherwise, the Great Elk would decay over the distance he needed to travel. The king's oddly specific request to see the whole animal made Terren lean toward what Kiira mentioned before he left and her gut instincts about the king. The *only* thing Grayten should know is that transporting an animal of that size across a formidable landscape and distance was near impossible. Even deer from the Aria Bells couldn't be transported intact without a thorough field dress and proper storage. The mere size of the Great Elk made his assignment even harder. No single person could haul an animal that size, and as soon as the king uttered the words of his next task, Terren decided he would only return with the antlers even though it would incur the wrath of Grayten. Plus, the king did not deserve to see such an amazing animal in its entirety merely for a display of posturing.

Terren had never seen one alive because he'd not been allowed to join that specific hunt each year, but he had seen the fruits of it, and the Great Elk was a beautiful animal to be sure. The Veripoi legend surrounding the Wapiti was that a Spirit Wapiti—what they referred to as Shade Beasts—had mated with a Wapiti from the Sun Realm, therefore making the animal here in this realm vastly larger. Its frosted blue-tipped antlers faded to a deep brown and often spanned four to five meters. The entirety of the animal was about half the size of Kamaria's head, which was sizable. Terren used to believe in the Veripoi legend until he learned Shade Beasts were only predatory animals. Now, he assumed the Great Elk to be just one of the many fantastic creatures the gods wanted to make.

"So, then it is agreed?" Kallik asked above the chatter. Affirmative nods followed the question, though some seemed a little reluctant to give it. Turning to Terren, he said, "As a friend of our people, we have agreed to give you the nagruk of the Wapiti."

Terren bowed his head. "I am humbled and grateful to you all for this gift."

Thank you, Ny, for the favor you have shown me here today.

As others left for their tents, Terren said to Kallik, "I will leave early in the morning before others are awake to lessen the agitation."

Kallik studied him for a moment. "Cupun, we all agreed to give you the nagruk, there will be no resentment from my people."

"It was not difficult to read expressions," Terren said, giving him a knowing look.

"We cannot please everyone in this life. Myna is correct, we have plenty of stores to see us through until next year. It will not be a burden to part with the nagruk this time." With an ornery grin, he added, "Besides, the naysayers from tonight have always disliked you."

Terren chuckled. "I suppose that is true." He stared for a moment at the fire. "You have my promise Kallik, that once I am king, your people will be openly welcome in Klynotia."

"That is kind of you, Cupun, but we like our seclusion."

"I know, but the offer is there regardless."

"Perhaps, when you are king, I will come sneak up on you in your big castle, " Kallik said, grinning.

Terren smiled at his friend. "I would like that very much."

CHAPTER 37

PUPPETS & MASTER

ZERREC

He stopped before the door to his secret chamber—the one he'd found while filtering through Grayten's memories—with one hand on the false stone allowing him entrance. A twist in his stomach made him turn to peer into the darkness. No one was there, and he would feel any active magic, but that didn't mean an amulet wasn't in use, which is why Zerrec never liked to trust his eyes when his gut told him a different story. Paranoia got the best of him. He swept a hand through the cool, damp air for a few feet but felt nothing. He narrowed his eyes, scrupulously scanning everything within the light of the torch. Zerrec saw no distortions in the air, and for the moment he trusted the facts. The only person near him that could use magic was Kiira, and so far her actions did not suggest she knew something was amiss. To his surprise, the princess had been mild-mannered and compliant, the very opposite of what he'd expected. Plus, he'd been extra cautious with his own magic use since her arrival, so she shouldn't be suspicious, but it would do him no favors to become lax now. Everything would crumble if he blindly charged forward.

With one more pass of his eyes to confirm his gut feeling was unwarranted, he pushed the false rock and waited as the groaning scrape of stone against stone revealed the chamber where he contacted those in his service and cast any minor spells he needed. He gave one last scrutinizing look before proceeding into the crystal room. Waving a hand, several candelabra came to life about the room. It tired him when he used magic outside of his school, but with this many candles he didn't have the patience to light them all. Zerrec looked behind him one last time to confirm nothing was there, and pushed the lever to close the door.

Stepping up to the Night Crystal, he skimmed the sharp planes of the jagged surface, and in the deepest part of the crystal a distorted image of Aaliyah, Terren's cousin, appeared. She was completing her task as instructed. Currently, she was following the wild Beasts around and tracking them through their doorways if they came into the Sun Realm at night to mark the high traffic places so Zerrec could map the patterns. As of right now, he didn't plan to use the Beasts, since summoning them was tiring, but like a hunter following a deer trail, he wanted to know where Beasts passed so he could more easily pull them into this realm if he needed. Aaliyah had been reluctant to harm the Beasts, but her lust for revenge was easy to tease into something useful. He didn't care if the Isokanii worshipped the creatures.

Now, it was time to contact the leaders of the mercenaries. They served their purpose at Woodlands Deep, but from the initial brief report he received, they were sore at the loss. Not surprising for Janissairian men, who thrived on conquering others, especially since they'd been certain of their prowess against the prince and a small group of soldiers. At least he'd paid them enough for their trouble. Total control of a mine's profits for their service was far more than they deserved. He'd received a tally after the battle from Duke Aubin approximating how much they'd taken in the few weeks they had control, and the mercenaries had not wasted his generosity. In fact, the Janissairians needed another assignment to make the cost worth it.

Again he swiped his palm over the crystal, and this time an image of the mercenary leader glowed in the middle.

"This is a waste of time," Amol said, more a grumble than coherent words.

"I will decide what is a waste of time." Zerrec squeezed his fist, and the amulet gifted to the mercenary glowed. When he gave the amulet to the Janissairian leader, he embedded an additional casting that would allow him to collapse the man's lungs. The gasps of air were pleasing to Zerrec's ears. "Speak like that again to me and you will be passing leadership to the man beneath you. That's not what you want is it?"

"No, Sire."

Amol's reply was more respectful, but Zerrec held no illusions of it lasting. "I want him dead, no holding back this time," he said. "Make your way toward the capital as quickly as possible so you can be ready at my command."

A smirk stole the scowl from the man's face. "My men and I will need some place to store our treasures so our haste is not burdened."

Zerrec stared at the man for a long moment and very seriously considered choking him again. Maybe next time he should add a casting to boil his blood.

I suppose a parcel of land in my kingdom is a small price to keep the mercenary loyalties.

'MY KINGDOM!'

Zerrec did his best to hide a wince. The old king's *voice* was getting stronger. Never in his nearly 800 years had the voices of the past souls he'd taken been so persistent. He remembered some men whose bodies he'd stolen to have been more lively than others and took longer to subdue, but he always won in the end. Grayten's soul, however, was by far the most unruly. No matter how much of his magic he stored to suppress the king's soul, it wouldn't stay away. He needed to study the effects happening to him, but would it cause him to lose control? Did he have time? If he rushed his study and lost the grip he did have over Grayten's soul—it would kill him.

"Fine, you can have some land in the most northern part of my kingdom. It is barren and uninhabited. I will write you a note with my seal detailing the parameters of the gift. It will be ready when you arrive," Zerrec said. "Drop your treasure and come without any other delays."

A pleased grin filched the mercenary's smirk. "Then my men and I are at your service, Your Majesty."

The image faded, leaving behind an opaque center once more. Zerrec sneered at the obsidian crystal.

These hired mercenaries might be more trouble than they are worth, but I still need them.

He took a deep breath, knowing that ideal underlings were always hard to find. The pirates he'd hired to help him capture Kiira were proof enough. The people of this age did not have the same work ethic that existed when he was a much younger man. If only magic allowed him to go back in time.

I would change so much, make so many different decisions. Save Loralyn. Dear younger me … He mused, giving a rueful shake of his head.

For now, Zerrec was pleased that his plans were coming together. He strode to the door and flipped the lever to open his way to the passage. Fisting his hands, he snuffed the lights, pitching the room into darkness.

CHAPTER 38

DISCOVERED

KIIRA

Standing in the deepest shadow of the hall, she spied Grayten as he paraded past, his firm strides confident in a torch-less path. When he was far enough for the assertiveness of his boots to cover her own soft steps, Kiira followed. The amulet around her neck would protect her from sight, but nothing more. He could still hear her presence if she wasn't careful. At least she'd spent years learning to walk the Forest and not disturb the tranquility. Never had she been more grateful to know a hunter's step.

This had been her first opportunity to follow Grayten down into the lower parts of the castle. After her initial discovery, she first needed to learn his schedule, which she accomplished by being in the kitchens. Hiding in plain sight was better than exhausting herself with magic. Amazing what a simple dress, a head wrap to hide her curls, and a dusting of flour could do for her appearance. She had thanked the goddess when the servants agreed to help her learn his schedule without repeating a word. Not that Kiira believed the servants would tell the king of her escapades, but she was nevertheless thankful they noticed something different about the king and also wanted answers.

Grayten never entered the kitchen, but his march past the door could always be heard, and the servants knew when he approached.

All conversation ceased, lest they give the impression of reveling. Only the sound of knives on boards and the slap of dough on counters escaped the confines of the claggy-aired kitchen. After two weeks of daily work in the kitchen, she decided it was time to take a bold step.

Then Terren returned from his first assignment, and even though he agreed with her gut instincts needing to be investigated, Kiira didn't want to wait until after he returned from hunting the Great Elk. Her husband would not approve, but the itch to know why Grayten visited the lower depths of the castle on a near daily basis wouldn't go away. Something was down here for him to seek the privacy of such a place so frequently. So, she had planned a way to spy on the king and ascertain his secrets, and knew his routine down to the minute. The king visited his sanctuary between the hours of four and six bells past midday, and the only way she could prove to Terren that something treacherous was happening was to see the proof for herself.

Kiira had promised to be careful. Terren's grave warning that the people in Klynotia did not take kindly to magic still rang in her ears. Amulets were the only way someone could use magic without the gift or detection from other magicians. She and Liem theorized it had something to do with it being stored magic versus active magic, but of course no magician unquestionably knew what made amulets undetectable. Night Crystals were the best, but regular gems could be just as useful. She had made a hasty decision on the picnic to use the opal necklace for a simple invisibility casting. Terren would have been vexed if he'd known, but because she thought it might be her only chance to be outside the walls without question, she used the necklace. It wasn't much, but it provided a way. The casting was outside of her school of magic, and the effort drained her to the point of dehydration. A savage headache had made her temples throb, and she hadn't wanted to even look at any sort of light. The ride back to the castle from the picnic had been awful, and she'd almost given herself away during an excruciating dinner with Grayten that evening. But it was all worth it to be where she was now, finally getting proper answers.

Kiira slipped out of her shadowed corner to follow the king. She used her fingers to trail lightly along the wall so she didn't run into another. The last thing she needed was to give herself away by smacking into an unknown sharp corner.

It didn't take long for Grayten to reach his destination. When he turned, she froze like a deer when the wind changed directions on a hunt. Kiira kept her breath. After a moment he pressed a false stone, and she recognized an opportunity to move. With feathered steps, she moved to the door and slipped inside just behind Grayten. The doorway once again scraped across the stone as it closed. Unfortunately, the pitch black room was now a problem. A flood of light from torches all the way around the room made her wince. She hastily backed into the nearest shadow. Flickering light would give away her presence for sure.

Magic? But Grayten is not a magician.

And the sudden light was definitely magic; there was no mistaking the act. The worst part was that it felt familiar.

Zerrec is dead. Liem and Terren said he was dead.

The king walked over to the square table with a nice chunk of Night Crystal perched in the center. A piece that big was either stolen or paid for at a hefty price. He waved a hand across the surface, and magic tingled her skin as an image formed in the ragged edges of the obsidian mineral. There was no dismissing where the casting came from this time; it had definitely been Grayten.

Kiira took a few slow, careful steps to get a better look at the king's wrists. Surely, if Grayten was a magician, Terren would have known. Had the king really been able to hide his gift for this long? It didn't seem likely, especially with his known hatred of magicians because of Terren's mother. His wrists were covered, but she could see the barest hint of a red glow coming from beneath the leather bracers. She bit her lip—hard—to keep from making a sound.

"Have you accomplished your task yet?" Grayten asked.

Kiira turned eyes to the crystal.

Aaliyah?

"Not fully, but I have made progress. I've marked another four points since we last spoke," Aaliyah said.

"Good. Report again to me in another five days."

"Of course, Sire."

The image faded from the crystal, and Grayten leaned back before summoning the next contact. She kept her eyes glued to the crystal as the king conversed with the mercenary leader. The Janissairian man—she could tell by his thick beard and accent—was the leader of war band here to kill Terren. They were to attack him on his way back into the kingdom from hunting the Great Elk. She would need to find a way to contact Terren as soon as possible to warn him. Was Grayten really so evil that he would kill his own son? She scrunched her brow. From what Terren told her, the king was power hungry and a tyrant, but also obsessed with keeping his bloodline on the throne, especially a male. If that were no longer true, what changed? The king's voice interrupted her thoughts.

"Once I am rid of the prince, then I can announce he tragically died defending the kingdom. I shall make sure the court knows he gave a valiant effort, and after a brief time of mourning, I can easily establish myself on Klynotia's throne to usher in a new age of a mage king."

The pleased look on his face and twisted curl of his lips rent her stomach. Kiira, in an instant, knew Grayten was not the man she met in Lorea for her wedding. But who was he? She watched the king leave the room, and to be extra sure she was alone, counted slowly to fifty. A dimly glowing lily in her palm barely defined the space, but as her eyes adjusted, it was enough for her to navigate to the exit without stumbling.

Kiira tiptoed into her room and released the casting on the amulet. The familiarity of plants and flowers allowed her to breathe deeply. Skehtra stretched from her curled spot by the fire and came over to nose her. The soft click from the Wolfcat's nose while she scented the air was the only sound in the room. Kiira rubbed along the cat's jaw–who was almost eye level with her–while she mentally ticked off the evidence.

What did following the king reveal? He was a magician; that was new. If Grayten had been a magician when first coming to Lorea, she'd have known since all mages, no matter their strength, were flagged by the kingdom's border protections. So, the king's ability to use magic could have only come from one source. Kiira stopped rubbing Skehtra as the realization hit her.

The glow on his wrist was crimson. The magic was familiar. There was only one school of magic that could use the forbidden casting and corrupt another. And he wanted Terren dead.

Zerrec is alive … and he's taken the king's body.

Flashes of memories from her time with her mentor only months ago slammed into the forefront of her mind. Visions of death caused her hands to shake and turned her breathing ragged. How could she have lived in the presence of her torturer for so many months without noticing? She felt nauseous. All the evidence seemed to make it conclusive. Her old mentor had set himself not only in a position of power, but in a position to be above reproach. Who would challenge the king other than Terren? She couldn't expect her father and brother to march Lorea into a war, and once Grayten—Zerrec—revealed he had magic, no one in Klynotia would stand against him because too many years of cowardice and eschewing ran deep in the hearts of the nobility and people.

Kiira collapsed to the floor. What were they going to do? How could she act normal around Zerrec with the truth revealed? From this point forward, she walked on a knife's edge.

Windrah, give me wisdom and courage to do what is necessary. Keep us safe. And send Terren home quickly.

CHAPTER 39

SEPARATED, AGAIN

TERREN

"You were supposed to bring back the entire Azure Elk!" Grayten bellowed. "*That* was my command to you."

The menace saturating each word had the gathered people recoiling. Terren had anticipated the anger. He'd returned far sooner than expected and without the entire animal as directed, but from the beginning he assumed the entire thing was a test, and one he was intended to fail. Of course, Grayten would be angry that he had succeeded, even if only in part.

Still, being shamed in front of the court reminded him of his childhood. To counteract it, Terren held his shoulders back and lifted his chin, but he didn't make direct eye contact with the king. "Forgive me, Sire, it was not possible to bring back the entire animal without it spoiling, even with a field dressing. The animal is far too large." He kept his words low and even.

A loud hollow clang jumped from stone to stone, dissipating at the back of the hall as Grayten's mug made contact with the floor. The wooden vessel lay cracked and useless at Terren's feet, ale seeping through the velvet runner and his trousers.

"I *know* you could have gotten it back on time. That is why I gave you the task. You are deliberately trying to disobey me!"

How exactly do you know I could return on time?

Terren tightened his teeth in order to keep his face neutral. This is what had bothered him from the beginning; the timeline for this task was far too specific. He glanced at Kiira, but she kept her eyes studiously on the king as he paced. What he gathered in that brief glance told him she had portentous information. His wife was far too focused on the situation not to have something. He needed a safe space to discuss it with her. "My deepest apologies, Sire. I will go and retrieve another if you wish," Terren said, though he had no intention of doing so. At the very least, the statement would pacify the king until he could garner a better excuse.

Grayten sneered at him. Terren bit his tongue. That was a look he hadn't seen in a long time and definitely didn't miss.

"No. I have other tasks for you. Report to me in the morning," Grayten barked. He stormed from the throne room, his new advisor and young valet on his heels.

Terren bowed with the rest of the room upon the king's hasty exit. Escorting Kiira and his sister from the room, he breathed normally in the hall where the gathered tension surrounding the throne no longer oppressed him. The murmur of courtiers' gossip dispersed as everyone followed them.

"Father seemed excessively angry," Sairah said after a few moments of silence. "The antlers are proof enough that you found and killed one."

"His command had been specific. I was to bring back the whole animal, but it's not possible. You can't get them from where they live to the capital in one piece. Even a head for mounting would have started to rot," Terren replied. A small measure of guilt pricked his conscience at giving half truths to his sister. She was as much Isokanii as he, but she knew so little of her heritage that Shadow Walkers and enormous Beasts were mere stories to her. One day he would show her more, but right now he was navigating too many other things to be an effective teacher.

"That is exactly what I mean. Father has hunted enough to know distance matters."

Terren nodded. "I found the request odd." Stopping in front of Sairah's door, he asked, "Will you join us for the evening meal?"

Sairah glanced at Kiira before declining. After she closed her door, Terren moved toward his suite. "You seem contemplative," he said.

"Take a ride with me?" Kiira asked. "It is such a nice day for winter and Starfire could use the exercise."

"Tempest still needs to rest."

"Surely the prince of Klynotia has more than one horse?"

"Yes, but she's my favorite."

"I just need to get outside these walls for a bit."

TERREN INHALED as much of the salty air as possible; hints of damp beach grass mellowed the tang that usually came with it. "Kiira, what is the real reason you brought me out here?"

"Is Kamaria able to listen? I think this is important for her to hear as well," Kiira said.

He raised a brow at her. The relationship between his wife and his Bear had so far been tumultuous at best, and it intrigued him how she now included Kamaria in the conversation. The thought was sobering because it probably meant he wouldn't like what she had to say. His Bear effortlessly slipped into his mind when he called. "She can hear you through me."

"If I create a shield of magic will that cut you off from her?"

He looked at where they stopped. The small dune overlooked the castle grounds hidden behind the dual-toned siege wall, one side more battered than the other thanks to the salty sea breeze. To the west, the sea glittered despite the clouded sun, and the grasses bent beneath the cool breeze. "We should be far enough away from anyone that you don't have to use magic," he said.

"I know we are, but I prefer it all the same. Will it cut you off from Kamaria?"

Terren lowered his brow. "It did not the last time you created a shield. When I told you about being a Shadow Walker."

Kiira nodded and set about creating a dome of glittery pale green that faded and reappeared intermittently. The feel of the magic was the same as it had been on their Lundemai. Now he knew for sure why she strapped extra water skins to her saddle. A shield was outside her school; it would parch her. Terren frowned at all the extra precautions. This was not the greeting he wanted or expected after returning from the hunt. He definitely wasn't going to like what she had to say.

"Can she still hear?"

"Yes."

"Alright." Kiira drank deeply before settling comfortably in her saddle. "Zerrec is not dead, he's taken over Grayten's body."

Kamaria roared in his mind, and Terren had to take a moment to calm her with his thoughts.

"Are you sure?"

"Yes. I followed him to the—"

"I told you not to follow him, Kiira!" His horse, a chestnut named Luna, danced beneath him. Terren counted to five.

Why does she never seem to listen? Now I understand Liem's constant irritation with her better.

"I was careful! He did not catch me." She frowned.

Maybe he had reacted a little too hastily. Terren relaxed some after she described the precautions taken, but he still didn't like it. He was learning to pick his battles with her. "Fine." He scrubbed a hand over his face. "Tell me what you saw to make you think Zerrec is still alive."

With each new point Kiira made, Terren became more and more tense. He even had to calm his horse because his grip on the reins upset the otherwise mild-mannered mare he chose for this outing. Terren finally just dropped the leather straps, letting them hang from the saddle horn. He flexed his hands and used the measured breathing he had learned from the priests to relax his mind.

Ny, guide me on what to do. I had a feeling we were not that lucky back in the cave.

Terren kept watch over the land all the way to the sea. He could just make out the outskirts of the port that never seemed to sleep.

Ships bobbed with the tide, as unsettled as his thoughts. Several things crossed his mind, but the most important thing was the safety of those he loved. "You should take my sister, Lucien, and Jemma, and go back to Lorea. I need to stay here and do what I can to protect the people."

"I am not leaving you, Terren," Kiira said. The spark lighting her emerald eyes would not be easy to put out.

"And I am not letting you remain in proximity to the man who almost killed you less than six months ago," he retorted.

"Then you need to leave too and come with us to Lorea," Kiira said, raising her voice.

"Kiira," he lowered his tone to keep her calm, "I left my people because I was a coward, and almost turned my back on them completely. If I abandon them now, it could give leeway for Zerrec to take complete control of the kingdom." Terren shook his head. "I have to protect them, and if I go to Lorea, the distance will hinder my efforts. The nobles are too afraid to fight back. And realistically? I have the most immunity to magic without also using magic."

Kiira pressed her lips into the tightest line he'd seen in a while. Her next words came out more frustrated than angry. "What are you even going to accomplish by remaining behind?"

"I can be hope for my people. If their prince does not abandon them, hope will not abandon them."

"I think you are romanticizing the situation." Kiira made a face. "The people barely know you. No one knows the man you are because they've had no opportunity to get to know you."

"Maybe, but my influence has started. The men I went with to the mines respect me. I will not leave my kingdom to chaos when I can be the leader they need, not to mention a thorn in Grayten's—Zerrec's— side." He paused for a moment before giving his final argument. "You agreed to help me with this endeavor, and you knew some sacrifices would need to be made in order for me to take the throne."

"This is *not* what I envisioned when you mentioned sacrifices," she countered. Kiira glared at the ground. Starfire was restless beneath her. Terren could see the strain in her body as she thought. "I will leave Klynotia on one condition."

Terren nodded.

"You *will* travel by the Shade Realm at least once each week to come to Lorea. I will not have you be a ghost while we are separated. You were lucky to have avoided that mercenary trap he laid for you. If I have to endure another torment of not knowing where you are or what is happening—"

"It is the least that I can do," Terren agreed before her words became too tight with pain.

Kiira, taking a resigned breath, asked, "When do we leave?"

CHAPTER 40

BLACK MASS

KIIRA

Three nights later, Kiira stood in the shadows of the dimly lit barn, frozen with Starfire's reins in her hand. Everything around her was muted or silent, and for the moment it felt safe. Terren planned everything carefully, but as soon as she stepped from the shelter of the barn, her world would be turned upside down, and she wasn't ready to accept the terms of her agreement with her husband. She understood his reasonings, reluctantly agreed with them, but the whole situation rubbed her the wrong way. She would take these few minutes for herself before fleeing Klynotia, a home she'd barely known. Terren was still speaking with Sairah as he tightened the straps of the saddle around Luna, the mare she was to ride. His movements were not jerky, but Kiira could still see the conversation between them was getting more heated with each word spoken, and with each thing he said, the princess' looks descended from annoyance into displeasure. Several angry glances were thrown her way when Terren wasn't looking. Outside, the other horses stamped and shifted as the wind blew Skehtra's musky smell across the stable yard.

Kiira sidled up to the Wolfcat to give her a hug and a proper scratch behind the ears. Pulling the smallest amount of magic to impress the meaning of her words, she said to the cat, *'follow behind so horses more ease.'*

Skehtra pushed into her chest with a pitiful whine. Because of her gift, Kiira could feel the pain and displeasure at the command given. "I know." She showed Skehtra the feelings she had by asking her to follow behind. The cat wouldn't understand her next words, but it made her feel better to say them out loud. "See, I do not like it either, but we need this journey to be as swift and easy as possible. The horses out there do not trust you like Starfire, and I need to save my magic for our safety." She hugged the large feline. "You can be in the open once we cross into Lorea where we're safe. Okay?"

Skehtra flicked her tail, giving Kiira one long stare with her glowing violet eyes before turning away and jumping into Starfire's empty stall.

Standing, Kiira sighed. It hurt to make her beloved Wolfcat travel alone in the back, but it was for the best. She'd have to make up for it somehow once they reached Lorea. Kiira brushed the long strands of fur clinging to her travel clothes before slinging her bow around her shoulders and buckling the quiver to her side. She checked the two other quivers attached to Starfire's saddle for security and touched the staff tucked into her bedroll. Her favorite bone handle knives rested at her lower back in her favorite pliable corset. It was all the defenses she had at her disposal that didn't require magic. Maybe it was overkill, but if for any reason flight from danger would not save them, she chose to be as prepared as possible for a fight. Leaving things to chance, especially with Zerrec involved, would make her the worst sort of idiot.

She ushered Starfire out of the barn and over to her lady's maid, Jemma. The older woman needed help to get into the saddle of the gentle Palomino she'd been assigned. Kiira whispered to her faithful lady's maid more to keep from breaking the tension of the moment rather than for fear of discovery. "Jemma, we will take it as easy as possible, but you should be prepared for some galloping."

"Don't you worry about me child, these old bones still remember how to handle a horse," she said, her smile a welcome bit of sunshine in an otherwise dark moment.

Kiira returned the affection and turned to give her attention to Lucen. She gave one last half-hearted attempt to persuade him to come, but she already knew the answer.

The manservant shook his head. "I'm staying with my prince."

Kiira glanced at Terren, but he was still deep in the throes of a muffled argument with his sister. She gave the valet an understanding smile, but it didn't reach her eyes. She would miss the steadfast man. Despite Terren's displeasure at Lucen's insistence on staying, it was for the best that he remained at her husband's side. Terren was capable, but it never hurt to have an ally.

She turned to Sairah, who was now holding Luna's reins and wearing a fierce scowl. Kiira knew she shouldn't tease her sister-in-law, but the temptation became too strong to ignore. "I suppose you're unable to ignore me now."

Sairah's frown melted into a grimace before she turned to glare at the horse's neck.

"Sairah," Terren said, frustration evident, "this trip will be more pleasant if you do not isolate yourself."

The princess refused to acknowledge either of them, instead choosing to struggle her way into the saddle. Kiira almost moved to help, but thank the gods Lucen stepped in to do it. She only had so much patience for Sairah's sour attitude. Instead, Kiira turned to her sister-in-law's soft-spoken maid.

"I do not know how to ride," Orella said, shaking her head, her face blanched.

Kiira smiled. "I know, but we will go easy and Jemma can give you pointers. The plan is to take our time for as long as possible and only rush when necessary."

Orella nodded, but looked no more pleased than her mistress.

"You will be fine," Kiira assured, walking her over to the last of the horses. "To go forward, give him a gentle kick, and to slow or stop, pull back gently on the reins. To turn, pull one side of the rein or the other. For the most part, these horses will follow Starfire, so you should not have to do much unless it's more than a walk or trot. I will coach you through that once we are away from here."

"Yes, princess."

"You will call me Kessa while we are traveling," Kiira corrected, scrunching her nose at having to respond to the same name as one of her brother's dogs, but glancing at Sairah to make sure she heard as well. Orella nodded and put a hand to the pommel of the saddle as Kiira walked her through how to mount up. Once the maid was seated with reins in hand, Kiira turned back to Terren.

"Lucen, make sure everything is secure one last time," Terren said before pulling Kiira away from the others and into the shadows. He pressed his forehead to hers. "I will keep Zerrec distracted for as long as possible. Kamaria will be following your trail the entire time. She will intervene if you need any help. Remember, go as far as you can and only travel at night after the first day. Once you are in Lorea, I will come visit."

He kissed her. Kiira did her best to keep her composure, but tears slid down her cheeks. She pulled away.

This is unfair.

The goddess warned her on the ship things would be difficult, but why did it feel like peace would never find her? If not for Zerrec, she wouldn't need to leave Terren this way. The black plume of hatred, seeded in her heart a few days ago, filled her mind. She buried her face in his chest. He pulled her as close as possible, and she didn't care that it smashed her nose, because the hitch in his breath told her this separation was just as painful for him as it was for her. Terren was only doing what he thought best to keep those he loved safe, but she wished for another way.

Looking up at him, she said, "Promise me that at the first sign of danger you will go into hiding."

"I will."

"I am serious, Terren. Because of Grayten's body Zerrec's magic will be stronger." She was repeating herself. She'd said the same thing countless times over the past three days, but maybe if she said it one more time it would delay the inevitable.

He played with a loose curl for a moment before laying his hand along her jaw and making her look at him. "I know. I haven't taken any of your warnings lightly."

Words no longer described her feelings. Kiira's vision blurred as more tears fell. She could barely breathe. Terren held her through it. He gave her one last kiss and stepped away, moisture in his own eyes. Numbly, she pulled herself onto Starfire. Lucen took up a place next to her husband.

Clearing his throat, Terren said, "Be safe, all of you."

Kiira swiped at her tears and nudged the horse forward. With one last look behind, she took a deep breath and nudged Starfire into a fast walk. Kiira looked to the sky to prevent any more droplets from rolling down her cheeks.

Windrah, please, I beg you, keep my husband safe.

CHAPTER 41
DOUBT
TERREN

Taking a deep breath, he chanted the Nyuten prayers for peace. An attempt to convince himself of normalcy.

Why should I be separated from those I love? Have I not had a hard enough life? You gave me someone to love, cherish, and feel safe with only to rip her from me because she isn't physically safe? Why?

Terren's hand stung. He opened his eyes to his fists pressed against the balustrade of the balcony. Hopefully, he hadn't punched hard enough to summon a bruise. Walking the fine line as he was with Grayten—Zerrec—he didn't need something small like a bruise to fuel the fires of the man's suspicion. As it stood, he needed to be as unassuming as possible to give those he cared for as much time as possible to escape over the Lorean border. Taking an unknown path through the Aria Bells was not the fastest, but he and Kiira agreed it would be safer than the main roads. If the four of them could at least traverse the plains before their absence was missed, the mist and ancient trees of the Bells would go a long way in protecting their trail.

Looking to the sea, Terren watched the barely visible specks of lanterns from the port define a hazy horizon. A nearly moonless night made them more visible than usual, but his bond with Kamaria gave him even greater clarity. They were still only insignificant points of light, but they gave him hope. It reminded him of the paean from the Book of Ny.

The unfolding of Your words gives light;
It gives understanding to the simple.

Right now he needed the unfolding of Ny's words. Since returning to Klynotia, his faith in the gods had seemed dimmer than the lights beyond. He knew the gods could help. He believed it because he'd seen their help in his life before, but right now his frustration and hopelessness roared above his faith. If Ny's words gave understanding to the simple, he must be far too complex at the moment to gain wisdom. Yet, something inside told him that wisdom wasn't the answer he sought.

Last night had been more difficult than he had expected. He thought the three days prior had prepared him enough to watch Kiira ride away, but the vice of pain around his chest had not relented. Concern scored his brow, and any attempts to smooth the lines only lasted moments. Terren had every confidence in his wife's abilities to guide the group safely to Lorea, and Kamaria would always be near, but the fact he could not be there himself made the separation harder. He squeezed his fist to control the tumult of feelings racing through him.

Now I just need to convince the king nothing is amiss.

"Terren, the bell for the evening table will ring soon," Lucen said as he stepped onto the balcony.

"Thank you, Lucen."

"Do you know what you will say to the king?"

"At this very moment, no, but I have some ideas. I take comfort in knowing they've traveled since midnight, but I want to give them as much time as I can."

As he made his way to the dining hall, he assembled his posture and features into that of the meek prince he wanted to portray. If he could give Kiira three days of safe travel, that would please him. Terren stopped for a moment before the entrance, making sure he was actually prepared to confront the king. With a nod to himself, he stepped through. Grayten was yet to arrive, but as soon as he did, the expected questions were not long in coming.

"Where are your wife and your sister? They should always accompany you, as I commanded," Grayten said.

Keeping his gaze averted, attempting to retain the act of a timid prince, Terren replied, "Kiira ate a late meal after an earlier ride and was not hungry. Sairah apologizes for her absence for she is not feeling well. I assumed it was okay to let them be." He slumped his shoulders to emphasize his supposed insecurity about the answer. Terren felt the air change as the king's suspicion was roused.

The king narrowed his eyes. "I do not care for assumptions nor excuses."

"I was not trying to make—"

"I said, I care not. Kiira and Sairah are expected to attend the evening table so we may dine as a family. They will be here tomorrow regardless of their feelings or appetite."

"Yes, Your Majesty," Terren said, averting his eyes and dipping his head.

***

Sleep circumvented him that night. Eventually, he forfeited any attempts at sleep and went out to the balcony wrapped in his obsidian wool cloak, the gift from Tereyssa. The night was bitter and stabbed away at any pieces of sleep he might have still had. Pre-dawn fog whirled in moonlit arcs as Terren paced between his room and the balcony, his anxious energy refusing to wane. The light creak of a door told him Lucen had slipped into the room. Terren winced when he heard a muffled grunt as his valet tripped over a discarded shirt.

Item in hand, Lucen scolded, "For all the things that have changed about you, it's comforting to know you still randomly discard your clothing."

"Sorry, Lucen."

Terren could feel his friends' eyes tracking him.

"You really do love the shadows like the Silver Coyote."

"The shadows are soothing. Having an easy connection to the Shade Realm calms me," Terren replied.

Lucen stacked wood in the fireplace. "Did you not sleep?"

"No. I'm worried, Lucen."

"I would say that it is normal," he said, fanning a flame.

Terren fell into the nearby chair. "I know Kiira is traveling as fast as she can to reach the Lorean border, but what if it is not enough of a head start?"

"All you can do is pray the gods are watching over their journey."

Terren used his thumb to twist the ring Kiira had made him for their wedding. An ache looped around his chest. "I hate being separated from her, Lucen. Kiira helps me to not … think so much. The missions Grayten sent me on were not so bad because they were minor interruptions to me being with her. I knew I would be coming back to her, but this situation feels so much more permanent. I've come to rely on her more than I thought possible."

"Not to belittle your feelings, but you made the right decision, Your Highness. The people need you here, you were right not to abandon them again," Lucen said, taking the chair across from him.

"But what will they think when rumors spread that Kiira left Klynotia? Will it send them into despair because it looks as if she's given up hope for this kingdom? Will it emphasize how inhospitable and bleak it feels?"

"That is your role as future king, to show them hope is not lost despite what may come in the near future."

"Okay, but what if I cannot hold onto hope when my thoughts are so divided?" Terren asked.

"That's a valid question. I think it is in times like these that we need to remember the promises of Ny because it his promised hope that anchors our soul. It's what held me together when I was at the mercy of the king's wrath after you left."

Terren winced. Would being reminded of what he endured ever not affect him? Lucen's statement was logical, but he needed more time for it to feel true. He stared at a glowing log. "If only there were two of me," he said sentimentally, tapping the arm of his chair. "Then I could be with Kiira and be here for my people."

"I believe one of you is enough, Your Highness."

Terren looked at the servant. With a small smile he said, "That was rather cheeky of you, Lucen."

His friend answered by rising to fold clothes into a travel bag, knowing it would soon be needed. Terren chuckled before returning his gaze to the fire. He supposed one of him would have to be enough.

CHAPTER 42
SLIPPING
ZERREC

'*Peace should be kept at all costs!*'
'*You stole my kingdom!*'
'*No, express your anger!*'
'*We need more power!*'
'*Fool!*'

"Quiet!" Zerrec demanded.

"Your Majesty?" A disembodied voice asked.

He grasped at his hair, pulling the scalp to rip the voices from his mind. He didn't know if it was the pressures of running a kingdom or his insatiable thirst for revenge that brought the voices to the forefront.

'*Anger!*'

'*Stolen!*'

'*Peace!*'

'*Fool!*'

Zerrec shook his head. The voices in his mind, ones he'd worked so hard to suppress over the years, took more and more effort from him. "Kreshkt!" He halted the swing of his fist an inch before hitting the obsidian crystal. Good thing too, because it would have split his knuckles open and shattered the one means of controlling what went on outside the walls of the castle. He needed this crystal, and, limited as he was to this room for castings, a broken crystal was not a problem he needed to have right now. Zerrec pivoted and gave a solid punch to the stone wall. The vibration rattled the bones in his hand and sent it up his arm.

"Your Majesty?"

He turned to see the distorted image of the mercenary leader attempting to peer into the gloom of the room. Flexing the stiffness from his fingers, he allowed his magic to heal the stippled skin welling with points of oxygenated blood. At least the voices had quieted enough so he could focus on the task that needed assigning.

"Amol." Zerrec was fairly certain that was the man's name, but needed to say it to be sure. He'd talked to the man enough times that he ought to have remembered it by now, but more and more things had become scattered in his mind since taking Grayten's body. He hated to admit it because he did not want to be beholden to someone else, but more and more he needed the help of his young valet, Zulen, to manage the kingdom.

"Your Majesty," Amol answered, with a slight bow.

"I have a task for you. Four people have escaped the kingdom and I need them brought back to me alive. It is of the utmost importance they are alive. I will not tolerate anything less, am I understood?"

"Yes, Sire."

"Excellent. They are heading east from the capital. You'll need to ride hard to catch up to them," Zerrec said.

"That will be quite the strain on my men, Sire."

'Ingrate!'

'People should be well cared for so that they are loyal.'

'Disrespect!'

Zerrec snarled to silence the voices. Out of the corner of his eye, he saw Amol flinch, but he didn't care; right now he just wanted the voices to stop. The band of Janissairians were being paid more than fair for the jobs he'd given them. "Take whatever supplies you need, I'll pay recompense to whatever villages or towns you raid," he said, rubbing his forehead.

"That is a generous offer for the task at hand, Sire, but what about the actual reward for completing the task?"

"You're trying my patience," Zerrec managed through gritted teeth.

"I'm not tryin' to be any sort of trouble, Your Majesty. I'm just looking to make sure my men and I are paid fairly," Amol noted.

Zerrec narrowed his eyes. Closing his fist, he slowly increased the strength of the casting hidden inside the gifted amulet around the mercenary's neck. "You already have gems and a parcel of land, what more do you want?" He snarled.

"Mighty generous of you, Sire." Amol smiled. "My men—"

Amol's eyes bulged as his air supply lessened.

"Remember what I told you about displeasing me, Amol," Zerrec said.

The mercenary nodded, now very red-faced. With a desperate gasp he said, "My men and I will start on the trail immediately."

Zerrec cut the flow of magic. He was annoyed that the mercenary continued to force him to act so stringently, but he supposed some people just needed more discipline than others. If the Janissairians thought they could gain wealth and prestige for themselves or their Uman, they chose the wrong man to test the waters with. He could easily afford to pay Amol and his men, thanks to Grayten's greed, but he preferred to control them, which was sadly limited in its effectiveness.

'Fop!'

'Why?'

'Stolen!'

Zerrec butted the heel of his hand to his forehead. At least with the growing number of things to do, Kiira's escape was handled. He didn't put all his faith in the mercenaries, but they were all he had, so he used them. Now, he needed to find Terren. The prince had disappeared, and finding him was top priority. If the Klynotian people knew their prince was still out there, escaping his grasp, it would make him look like a fool.

He probably used his Shadow Walker abilities to escape. If he's in the Shade

Realm, I'll never find him, but I need him dead. If he's alive, the people have hope, and I cannot use that.

Hope was such a vile emotion. It had never served him.

'Failure!'

'Fiend!'

'Brute!'

Zerrec thinned his lips. Yes, he was a failure for letting so many escape his grasp. The only things he could rely upon were his persistence, observance, and patience.

'Strength.'

'Man of caliber.'

'Fearsome.'

Yes, that was true. He had strength, and it had always served him well. Especially now inside Grayten's body.

Zerrec shook his head, destroying the tangent thoughts. He needed to track down Terren. Sending magic once again into the crystal, he barked, "Aaliyah." The outline of her form jumped at his command. She'd been staying in the Forest Wilds still mapping Beast trails, but now he needed her for a job only she could complete.

"Yes, Your Majesty?"

"Terren has gone into hiding, likely in the Shade Realm. I need you to find him, and kill him."

"You are sure? It was supposed to be your kill," she responded.

Zerrec thought for a moment. "Yes. As long as he's dead, I'll be satisfied."

"It will take me some time to sneak through a Beast doorway and find him."

"I do not care *how* long it takes, *what* you have to do, or *who* you have to use. Just see that it's done," Zerrec barked.

Aaliyah bowed her head. "As you wish."

Zerrec waited for the voices to pester him, but he must have suppressed them again. Dousing the lights, he stomped from the room. His scheduled timeline of steps had just been catapulted weeks ahead, and now he needed to rearrange and modify. Why did everyone always ruin his perfect plans?

CHAPTER 43

MIDNIGHT CONCLAVE

KIIRA

Skehtra stopped, flicking her tail with unease, ears swiveling to catch all the forest sounds. Kiira had told the cat to stay behind the horses, but that only lasted until they entered the Aria Bells five days after leaving the capital and decided it prudent to keep her in front. It took a bit of magic to convince the horses they would be unharmed by the Wolfcat's presence, and she could sense their mounts were still tense, but at least they didn't bolt. Now, Kiira was glad she'd done so, for the cat had far better senses than even the horses.

Kiira pulled Starfire's reins to halt him, and the other horses followed her gelding's lead. Trusting her cat's nose, especially in the thick trees of these mountains, was important. They had pushed hard to make it across the plains in two days to have better protection in the forest of the Aria Bells. Here they could lose followers much easier, and they'd avoided any entanglements thus far, but Terren could only keep the king occupied for so long before their absence was discovered. Kiira hoped the plan of going directly east into the mountains would keep them safe since it led them over steeper terrain more easily navigated by a smaller party.

She kept her eyes on the dark forest and her ears open to any unnatural sounds. Her face stung from the high altitude air in the fleeting winter, and clouds of white vapor filled her every exhale. Kiira twisted to see obvious tracks behind them and prayed it would snow soon. Maybe she could devise a way to cover the tracks while they continued. She lightly snapped her fingers and used a casting to allow her to see in low light. She wouldn't use it long; exhausting herself for something so mundane would be foolish when the protection of the women behind her was more important. Still, she felt relief at being able to see her surrounding. She saw nothing to cause alarm, but Skehtra had yet to move, and Kiira trusted the Wolfcat to know if something was not as it should be. It could be nothing more than a clumsy fox or frightened rodent, but safe was absolutely better than not.

Kiira turned to look at her companions. Various degrees of fear marked each of their faces, with a fraction of annoyance from Sairah. She shook her head and turned forward. Most of her frustration so far lay with Sairah and her maid. Neither knew how to live without certain comforts, and the princess was quick to voice her complaints. Orella, at least, kept quiet and followed her directions, seeming to mostly be thankful to be alive and leaving Klynotia. Kiira hoped Sairah was thankful to be heading toward safety, even if she didn't say it, and prayed for patience to endure the princess' acerbic countenance. If Sairah only knew the lengths to which Kiira had gone to keep this trip from being desolately miserable.

"Skehtra," Kiira quietly whispered, hoping to spur the cat into action. They couldn't stay here much longer; they needed to make camp for at least a few hours to rest.

The cat regarded her and blinked before turning back to the forest. A few more minutes passed until the Wolfcat moved again as if everything was fine. Relieved, Kiira eased the horses forward. As they inched through a narrow grouping of aspens, she touched a nearby tree and used her gift to find the closest source of fresh water. Since entering the forest, they had followed a deer path, making their progress easier, but watering places could still be few and far between. Luckily, there seemed to be something nearby and, even better, through the scant light, Kiira spotted a small clearing perfect for sheltering all of them.

She dismounted. "You know what to do everyone. I'll be back as soon as possible." Unslinging her bow, Kiira strung it and strode into the woods with Skehtra on her heels. She shoved the head of the Wolfcat. "No. You go hunt your own food so you don't scare off mine."

Skehtra gave a sound of protest before trotting off in another direction. Kiira shook her head at her pet and smiled. She loved her so much and could not have asked for a better companion, and it made this arduous journey easier.

Readying an arrow, she shifted her walk into a silent stride the further she moved from their camp. Hopefully, she wouldn't need to travel too far before finding game to eat. Jemma wouldn't find much if there was anything to forage, not this time of year. Thank the goddess she had a maid who'd been around her whole life, learning to identify plants the same as Kiira. She would have to find an extravagant way to thank her for her help once they got to Lorea.

With the moon still well in the sky, she might get lucky with some brave rabbits. At this time of year the rabbits would be skinny, but food was food. All of them were hungry, and the faint orange dot in the distance meant she would soon get to rest before a warm fire.

"Kiira."

She whipped around with an arrow strung to find Terren just stepping out of the shadows.

Dropping her bow, she ran into his arms. "I'm so happy to see you!" Kiira couldn't help it; tears of joy spilled from her eyes. "I thought you were not coming to see me until we reached Lorea?"

"I was going to wait, but I wanted to see you"—he pulled her tighter—"to hold you again, and to warn you that Zerrec knows you're missing."

Kiira nodded. "Did he suspect you like we thought?"

"Not only did he suspect me, he revealed his hand. If I had still thought he was Grayten, I definitely would not be thinking that now."

"What did he do?"

"When you and my sister didn't attend dinner the next night despite his command, he didn't accept my excuses as valid. Apparently, you and my sister were never allowed to be ill."

Kiira smirked at the levity.

"He left the table to demand that both of you come. I followed at a distance, and when he found your rooms empty, he became so enraged he blasted fire outward from him. It caught the tapestries on fire. I don't think he knew he'd done it at first. He spun and seeing me demanded where you were; I told him I sent you to Lorea for safety, and as he processed the betrayal, his eyes caught on the hungry flames, and when he looked back at me, I could see the pieces fall into place as he realized I knew the truth of who he was. He didn't attack. Zerrec just snarled and strode away. After that, I disappeared with Lucen."

"Wow," Kiira said with an exhale. "I'm glad you're okay and you escaped. Where will you hide?"

"I'm not sure at the moment. The Shade Realm is the safest until Lucen can reach one of his contacts. Can you believe the man created a network of people while we were on our Lundemai that want to overthrow the king?"

"Really?"

"I was as shocked as you. We will move from place to place so we cannot be tracked to any one location," Terren said.

"I hate this," Kiira pouted.

Terren kissed her temple. "I do, too. Have you contacted Liem yet?"

"No. We are still a bit too far to make it not strenuous and I wasn't sure if your sister could sense the use of my magic. Honestly, she's been difficult this entire journey, I didn't wish to add one more reason for her to hate me."

"She cannot sense it unless you are touching her or she visibly sees something. I am slightly more sensitive because of Kamaria."

"Could you not go to him? Please? I can reach him when we are closer, but it would help keep me from becoming too tired if you were to give him the message of whereabout we'll be along the border. Just in case we cannot cross before someone comes after us."

Terren thought for a moment. "Since I need to stay hidden in the Shade Realm until Lucen comes through with his contacts, I believe I can. You are at least another five days' ride from the Lorean border from here, so if I can get to him later this morning while you sleep, that should give him enough time to travel to you at a fast enough pace."

"Thank you."

Terren gave her another tight squeeze. "I need to go. Kamaria will keep watch through the shadows so you can fully rest."

Kiira released him and backed away, though it was not what her arms longed to do. She watched him melt into the shadows, and her heart cracked just a little to see him disappear. This separation wasn't permanent, she knew it, but it certainly felt more so with each passing day. Before she could let her emotions get the best of her, Kiira gathered her bow and hurried to find food.

She returned to the fireside half an hour later with a raccoon dangling from her hand. A bubbling pot waited over the fire, simmering.

"What took you so long," Sairah complained. "I am hungry."

"I was disoriented in the dark, lost my way for a bit," Kiira said. She glanced at Jemma, who just raised a brow at her statement. Jemma knew Kiira couldn't get lost in the woods thanks to her magic. The exception had been the one time before her wedding, and that had been the goddess. "I got us a raccoon. It's a small thing, but it was close."

Sairah made a face.

"My lady," Orella softly reprimanded.

"Yes, raccoon. Be grateful I found anything at all and you can eat a warm soup on a frosty night instead of choking down cold cheese and stale bread," Kiira snapped.

Sairah glared at the ground but remained silent.

Jemma took the animal from her hand. "Well, I can now officially say that I've skinned a raccoon."

Kiira sagged with relief. "Thank you, Jemma."

She moved away from the fire toward the horses. Scanning the trees, she stroked Starfire's muzzle and noticed the faint glow of two large obsidian eyes. Kiira smiled just a little toward the Shade Bear. At least in a small way, she had a connection to Terren even if she couldn't talk to the Beast.

CHAPTER 44

FLIGHT & FIGHT

KIIRA

Windrah, please just let us make it to the border. Let us make it to Lorea.

Kiira hoped her plea to the goddess did not fall on deaf ears as she hunched over Starfire, leading the gallop toward safety. She peered under her arm to check and make sure the others were with her, and grimaced as she glanced at Jemma. Her lady's maid was going to be sore after this, hopefully Liem brought a Blood Mage to soothe the damage being done by this hard ride.

For most of the journey, their little group had stayed ahead of the men Grayten sent to capture them. Before dawn this morning, though, Kamaria, through a series of grunts, alerted her to a group's approach. It would have given them a vast advantage if she had immediately roused her companions, but Kiira opted for some intelligence. What she discovered dropped her spirits. Zerrec's men had caught up with them so quickly. They must have stolen horses because with a two day start and the pace she kept, their small party of four should have gotten them to Lorea with no encounters.

Keeping a safe distance this morning, she attempted to count the number of men in pursuit, but was unable and, since she was the only one with any real fighting skill, she opted for flight over fight. Bravery wasn't always about confronting one's enemies. Kiira raced back and wasted no time in saddling the horses and getting the women from their bedrolls. Leaving everything else behind, the four of them made for the Lorean border.

Kiira glanced again under arm. The mercenaries were gaining on them, and she wished they could go faster, but this downhill could be a deathtrap for the horses if she were reckless. It was little comfort, but at least the mercenaries were in the same position. Kiira had communicated the urgency to Starfire before leaving camp, so she trusted him to pick the most appropriate pace. She prayed her twin was close to the signal she sent into the air, because the horses were rapidly nearing exhaustion. The last thing she needed was for them to drop. As soon as they were on flatter ground, Kiira would get behind the others and use her magic to slow their pursuers down and ease the burden on the horses. She wished Kamaria could help, and she probably would, but the sun was well above the horizon, unfortunately. If the Bear was smart, she was already on her way back to notify Terren of what was happening.

Starfire's gait changed to long even strides as the land smoothed to flatter ground and he picked up pace. She gave a mental whoop of joy. Even if she could get another five minutes of a solid run from the horses, it would give them a distance advantage. Glancing ahead, she saw a group of soldiers waiting along the Lorean border.

Liem! Thank you, Windrah!

Slowing Starfire, she pulled up next to Jemma. The older woman had a deep grimace on her face, both in concentration and pain; she deserved an award.

"Jemma! I need you to lead them to the border. Cross and you'll be safe," Kiira shouted over the thunder of hooves.

"What about you?"

"I am going to slow them down!"

Jemma flashed her a look, which Kiira ignored. This was not the time nor the place to be worried about her. She slowed Starfire and let the horse trot to cool himself, and as she turned she saw their pursuers coming off the decline.

'Kreshkt! Kiira, what are you doing?' Liem shouted in her head.

'I need to do some kind of damage!'

'Well do it closer, don't be so reckless.'

Kiira ignored her brother and leapt off Starfire's back with a painful jar to her knees. The horse pranced irritably, but didn't leave her side. Laying her palm flat on the ground, she used her gift to seek the grasses and roots covering the foothills. Much of it was dry and brittle because of the time of year, making the casting more difficult, but she had little choice. Kiira had the strength to cast something this big, but there was still a chance it could drain her. She just needed enough energy to escape, yet just thinking about it made it seem as if black dots danced in her vision.

Get it together!

She shook her head once to dispel the negative thoughts and, taking a deep breath, Kiira released the built casting into the ground, coaxing the dry grasses to weave together. She didn't need to build the woven grasses tall; she just needed them to change the terrain. An element of surprise. Each second, Kiira felt the drain on her magic. When the grasses were woven together in thick, uneven blocks, she released it and dashed for Starfire. She didn't want to watch the effects of what she had created; the screams from the pursuers' horses would be enough. Kiira fought back tears and rising bile as the dreaded squeals of horses filled the air, trying to focus on the necessity of her actions.

She pulled herself into the saddle, and Starfire immediately bolted for Lorea, Kiira clinging to his mane as he flew across the ground. A heavy rumble started, making Starfire falter.

Connecting mentally to the horse, she said, *'fast as you can.'*

Starfire picked up his speed.

The vibrations in the ground grew stronger as she neared the border. Kiira looked up to see Liem crouched as she had just been. He was using his magic to move the finite pieces of metal ore in the dirt so he could destabilize the ground. Their eyes connected, and a flash of annoyance went through her.

He's going to make me jump!

He should know how exhausted Starfire would be after a hellish flight, and yet he was going to open the ground right before she crossed to make her horse jump! Kiira would have to gripe at him later. Readying herself, she kept focused on the point she wanted to reach and waited until the last possible moment to signal Starfire to take a mighty leap. Out of the corner of her eye, Kiira could see the earth yawn open. No sooner had Starfire touched the ground did she hear the wrench and sudden split as the dirt and rock sheared away from one another.

Safe over the border, she turned to look at the damage the two of them had caused. It looked like a quarter of the men were lost to her uneven grass trick, and they wouldn't be caught by Liem's mini gorge, but it would slow them down, giving the archers a chance to do some damage. At least forty men were still making their way to the border. From this vantage point, she could see what Liem had done. Twin gouges in the earth funneled the men into a narrow area, giving the Lorean soldiers a tremendous advantage.

Her body suddenly registered how her throat felt as dry as brittle bone, but she remained awake. Liem strode toward her, anger squishing his face. She slipped from the saddle and fell limply into his arms. Did his arms feel smaller, or had time and distance altered her memory of his strength?

"I need water!" He shouted to no one in particular. To her he said, "You are the grandest of idiots."

Kiira nodded weakly, too thirsty to care about his scolding. Water sloshed across her hand as he shoved a skin into it. After draining the pouch, she had enough rejuvenation to stand without falling over.

"Will you be fine?"

"Yes, I will drink the rest of my water from the saddle."

"I am going back to the front, you—"

"I will join you in a minute," she said, cutting him off.

"No, you will stay here," Liem commanded.

Kiira narrowed her eyes at him. "We have the same military rank, Liem. I am not some fresh recruit you can order around."

"Do not be so narrow-minded, Kiira," he said with annoyance.

"You need to stay back here with archers where you'll do the most damage." He didn't wait for a response before running back to the main group of men and women.

I will stay in the back for as long as I have arrows, she thought.

Draining another waterskin, Kiira glanced at the group of archers, spotting Leo among them. No doubt he'd seen her fly across the border, and she briefly wondered what he was thinking. Studying the formation, Kiira directed Starfire near the lineup, but not so close as to disrupt what Leo was doing. Instead, she directed her gelding to stay still as she balanced on his back. Her horse deserved pounds of milk oats after this. Now, all Kiira needed to do was wait for a target.

TIME SEEMED to slow as the enemies drew ever closer, a cloud of dust rising in their wake. Kiira took a deep breath and took aim at the first man charging into the gaps Liem created.

She timed it late, and her arrow missed, but it drove deep into the shoulder of a rider three back from the leader. His startled movement made his horse rear in protest, causing a blockage to the others behind him. That was enough encouragement for Leo to command the rest of the archers to fire arrows with her. By the time the mercenaries reached Liem, their ranks were thinned, and many who continued forward were wounded.

The grate of metal on metal reached her ears as the enemy plowed into her brother and his men, and the archers had to cease firing. Kiira scanned the fight looking for Liem. His sword glowed a brilliant orange as the heated metal sliced through armor and weapons, followed by very short screams of pain. She hated that casting because of its decisiveness, yet it was effective, and a favorite for Liem. He'd ruined many swords perfecting his control over the magic in the blade.

As the confrontation between the mercenaries and the Lorean soldiers continued, smaller groups formed, and Kiira focused her firing on the straggling mercenaries coming into the melee, keeping a steady stream until she reached to find the last arrow in her quiver.

Well, I better make it count.

The leader of the men would be her best target if she could find him in the battle. It took a few minutes, but finally Kiira spotted a man with a dark oily beard and scarred features. The giveaway was a blue glow surrounding him.

He has a shield. She growled in disgust. *Zerrec.*

Her arrow would be useless. Hopping off Starfire's back, she danced through the pockets of battle toward the leader, slicing her knives against enemies as needed. The mercenary leader was doing damage to the Lorean soldiers, and only someone with magic had a chance to kill him. How Liem saw her she didn't know, but the reprimand that seared across her mind made her wince.

'Kiira, I told you to stay back!'

'I'm out of arrows! Little good it does for me to sit there and watch,' she chided.

'You're exhausted, you don't need to be fighting!'

'The leader has a shield on him. I refuse to sit there and watch Lorean soldiers be cut down!'

There was a brief pause. *'Kreshkt. Folen, Merkus, and I will be right there.'*

The connection with her twin severed as she reached the leader. The soldier who had been fighting him was holding on valiantly, but Kiira could see visible fatigue gaining traction in every part of her limbs.

Kiira stepped into the fight, swinging her long knives at the enemy.

The man stopped his assault to sneer at her. "You are the one the king wants."

Without removing her eyes, she told the woman next to her, "Soldier, three back."

The grateful woman nodded, stepping away from the fight. It was a phrase Liem typically used in training to tell the soldiers to take three swigs of water before returning to the training field. She hoped the woman recognized the misused phrase for what it was—a chance to escape, but likely she'd wind up engaging another mercenary before getting too far. At least she wasn't against an opponent who had magic defending him.

Kiira and the mercenary leader circled each other for a brief moment.

The mercenary attacked first. Kiira crossed her knives, bracing for the impact, and the pulse from his swing radiated up her arms. She would be forever grateful to Liem for using his magic to make knives that could resist such an impact. When he stopped pushing, she broke her knives to take a slash at his arm, but the blade glanced from the shield. She expected that since her knives could not penetrate magic, metal was finicky and magicians could only weave one casting into the steel with reliability, but her action did reveal the pendant as the power source for his shield. The large sapphire glowed brighter when she hit him. Definitely the handy work of Zerrec, and if she had to guess, it was keyed to deflecting sharp objects. That was the most common shield casting, and hopefully her old mentor was not thinking extravagantly. Kiira just needed to hold the man off until her brother and his friends arrived. Merkus and Folen would have the weapons to get through the mercenaries' protection.

"You are the chit the king has been on about," he said through curled lips and a heavy, stilted accent. "Making me sick all the things he said about you. What makes you so special?"

"How could you work for a man like him? The money good?" Kiira countered.

"I get a nice patch of land when all this is over. And servants. And gems. I will tolerate anything for that kind of payment, sweetheart."

Kiira wretched in disgust. "There is only one person I tolerate atrocious endearments from"—she lunged at the mercenary, her knives singing against his sword—"and I do not like it when he does it!"

She started a series of attacks, swinging from the left and then right, forcing her opponent back. Her advantage was his retreat.

"Passion flower, you should not allow this man to get to you," Folen said as he stepped next to her, adding his own sword for the man to defend against.

Liem and Merkus joined the action on her left. The mercenary surged with a few offensive swings before putting distance between the four of them, wary of the fresh additions. There was no fear in his eyes at being surrounded by four fighters. Terren had told her of the skill of Janissairian swordsmen, and she had to agree his descriptions seemed to be accurate. At least she knew why Zerrec had hired these men as mercenaries.

Kiira gestured casually. "This, gentlemen, is the leader of the mercenaries and he has a nice little protection amulet dangling about his neck preventing anyone from getting in a hit." The leader briefly showed his surprise before schooling his features. "That is a generous gift the king gave you"—she smiled darkly—"too bad it will not be of any use."

At that, Merkus lunged at the man. He was the one who wore the armor with the same type of shielding as the mercenary's pendant. Stepping back, Kiira allowed her brother and his two friends to take on most of the fight while she casually circled around to reach the back side of her opponent. Maybe she could snatch the shield from his neck, and if that did not work, maybe tangling the grass around his feet would gain them the advantage.

She was nearly at his back when the mercenary suddenly broke from Merkus and the others to swing at her. She leaned far enough away to keep the blade from slicing deep, but a stinging line of red did well across her stomach. Unfortunately, the momentum worked against her, and she fell to the ground.

"Kiira!" All three men shouted.

It was Folen who stepped in front of the mercenary in time to protect her. Her friend blocked a few swings, but his movement to shield her put him in an unbalanced position. The sickening sound of metal to metal and then into flesh roared in her ears. His body jerked at the unexpected hit.

"No!" Kiira screamed.

She grabbed a fistful of grass. Sending her magic into the ground, thick stalks climbed up the mercenary's legs, locking him into place. Surprise took the place of his triumph as he pulled his sword free. Folen, dazed, fell to his knees before falling on his side at her feet.

Kiira blocked everything else as she casted a shield around her and Folen. She wouldn't be able to hold it for long, but abandoning her friend was not an option. Kiira settled his head onto her crossed shins. Holding a hand to his temple, she tried to determine the extent of his injuries, but she was so exhausted. She couldn't maintain the shield and see what was killing her friend. Tears dripped down her cheeks and onto his face. She dropped the shield, but she was too exhausted to do anything else outside her school of magic.

"Do not cry, Poppy," Folen whispered.

Kiira strangled a laugh. "Don't you dare leave me, Folen." She hiccuped in a breath. "You can call me all the stupid endearments you want for the rest of our lives, but you must live. You must! I do not have enough magic. You stay alive long enough for the Blood Mage to arrive. That's an order."

He coughed a wet laugh. "That is not going to happen, Daffodil."

Kiira looked up to keep more tears from falling onto his face. Through the blur, she noticed Liem and Merkus coming to kneel at their friend's side.

"It was an honor to serve with both of you, my prince and my friend," Folen said, his weak arm bobbing in the air before it was grabbed by the two of them.

"Kreshkt, Folen, just hold on, we will get a Blood Mage here to heal you," Merkus said.

Liem looked at her, begging for her to heal Folen like she had healed him after the Oranta fight. Kiira shook her head. Her throat was beyond parched, and she was feeling dizzy. In her desperation to stop the mercenaries, she had sent more magic than necessary into the grasses.

Goddess, please restore my magic. He does not deserve to die.

"Merkus, find the mage. Kiira, walk me through what to do, maybe we can do enough to keep him alive," Liem ordered.

Merkus stood looking for the mage, reluctant to leave his friend in search of vain hope, but she felt his presence disappear.

"Liem, no," Folen managed, "I am not worth the drain. You have lost too much strength as it is with your earlier attack."

Emotion gathered at the back of Liem's throat. "You are worth everything I have. You are my best friend!"

Folen weakly squeezed his hand. He focused first on Kiira and then on Liem. "We will see each other again and feast in Apelgo's halls, eh?" He gave a feeble smile. Looking at Kiira, he added, "I do not regret dying to protect you, Kiira."

Folen closed his eyes.

"No!" Liem shouted. Bowing over his chest, he said, "Gods, please, not like this. Use my magic, anything!" he begged, beating the ground with a fist.

Merkus came running back up with the Blood Mage directly behind. When he saw everything, he immediately fell to his knees next to Liem.

Kiira held Folen's head and let the tears fall.

CHAPTER 45

NOMAD

TERREN

Tempest meandered among the enormous trees in the Shade Realm. The brown flakey trunks held a hint of red in them. Above, the pines rocked in the wind, the creak of branches loud in the otherwise tranquil forest. Terren enjoyed the deep woods with no people around. He was on his way back to the Klynotian capital to meet up with Lucen, hoping his valet had made a plan of movement to evade the king and talk with the people. As much as he wanted to deny it, the fight for his kingdom had begun.

He'd left Lorea and his note for Prince Liem two days ago. With the prince on his way to meet Kiira and Kamaria watching over his wife, he felt good. Not great, definitely not that. A part of him would never be settled until he could be with the woman he loved again, but this separation was required of them, and he could deal with it for now.

Ny let all of this pass swiftly. I would love just to have some normalcy.

A branch breaking caught his attention. Suddenly, Tempest hopped nimbly to the side. He twisted when a loud thunk came from the tree behind him. A short-bladed knife, buried to the hilt, poked from the tree. Terren scanned the trees for who sought to attack him. Surprise took him as his cousin stepped out from behind a tree. Terren jumped from the saddle and unsheathed his sword. In Isokanii, he said, "My wife beating you wasn't enough, you needed to come after me too?"

Aaliyah snarled. "I didn't come here to talk." She pulled long dueling knives from her sides.

"Clearly." He looked her over. "You can walk away."

She smirked. "King Grayten gave me the honor of killing you."

Terren sighed. "Let's get this over with then."

CHAPTER 46

POWER SUPPLY

ZERREC

The *tump, tump, tump,* of his fingers against the chair was the only sound besides the flicker of a candle. Zerrec relaxed in the plush chair while he pondered his next steps. When he checked the crystal earlier, he saw nothing but deep obsidian, which told him the mercenary leader was dead, and it came as little surprise. Kiira and Liem were excellent magicians and fighters, even he could admit that. His teaching had made them into the talented mages they were.

The list of problems was growing, and every setback irritated him. He needed more mercenaries, Kiira escaped capture for him to use against the prince, and Terren had yet to be found. Hopefully, the Uman was in a forbearing mood. Amol had likely left twenty or so men on the lands bequeathed to him, but Zerrec was counting on their numbers to assist him. He might have to give up the total profit from one of the mines as payment, but it would be worth it when he won his campaign against Lorea and absorbed its riches. *Tump, tump, tump.*

Kiira, what am I going to do about Kiira?

Zerrec hated to admit it, even taking a moment to be sour about the acceptance of it, but Kiira was now out of his grasp. Lorea's borders protected her now. After giving it some thought, he reasoned she'd somehow discovered he was still alive, pinpointing it to the time he suspected being followed. He had no conclusive evidence, obviously, but he should have listened to his instincts a little more. His slothfulness worked against him, and now he would have to settle for taking his revenge on her when he confronted Lorea with his army. Not the direct reprisal he dreamed of, but as long as she was out of his life he could accept it. *Tump, tump, tump.*

By far the biggest thorn in his side was Terren. The whelp fooled him for two days before he discovered four people had fled his kingdom, and now … now he was in the wind. Aaliyah still hadn't found him, but whispers of his presence echoed across Klynotia. Zerrec knew the prince was working to undermine his authority as king. If he wasn't quick and merciless, he would lose everything. He'd lived enough lives to know.

'*Stupid!*'

'*Who's really the whelp?*'

Zerrec jerked his head. Maybe all those other things were not the problem.

I need to get rid of these voices.

His magic was as strong as ever, but still they crept through, and it hindered his thinking.

Maybe what I need is more power. To augment gems and crystals.

After a few minutes of stewing, an idea came to him. Zerrec shifted in his chair. It had been a long time since he had thought about the power flashing between the realms in the Glazefire Canyon.

'*My studies!*'

Right. The memory was grainy as it had been many lives ago, at least a couple of centuries, but if he remembered correctly, only verified scholars were allowed in the Letra Mera library. The scholar had been studying any information about … Demons from the Mage War. What he had discovered instead was an even older scholar trying to harness the power of the canyon inside gems.

I could have a power I never even dreamed of.

Tump, tump, tump. The problem was that the memory was too vague to recall anything clearly. He needed to go to the library. At least this time he had the means to buy his way inside.

If I could find those records again and discover the secret to harnessing the power of the canyon, I could lay claim not only to Klynotia, but to the entire Sun Realm.

He sat up. The candle danced violently with his sudden movement.

Everything. Everyone. Under my influence.

A satisfied smile pulled at his lips.

The entire Sun Realm would be my empire. I would have the recognition and respect I have long deserved.

Zerrec pushed from the chair and strode to rip open the door. The guard posted outside jumped. "Zulen!"

Within seconds his valet appeared. "Yes, sire."

Zerrec circled back into the room, lighting more candles with his magic as he did. There was no need to hide the truth any longer, and he reveled in the bit of a surprise on Zulen's face. "I need to investigate something. Pack and prepare a horse, I journey alone." He gave the young man a serious eye, stepping to his desk to pull a quill. "You have proven yourself loyal, so I am giving you a temporary promotion. In my absence, you will have the control to direct most things as you see fit. You will be one step below me. This missive with my seal will give you that power. Do you have questions?"

"No, Your Majesty. I thank you for this generosity," Zulen said while bowing, and he quit the room to do as bid.

Impatience coursed through Zerrec as he scrawled words on the parchment. A sense of renewal urged him to write fast so he could leave. The Sun Realm was now a world of possibilities, and with the power from the canyon, none could stop him.

REVIEW

 I know this is the last thing you want to do after reading a good book. Personally, I would already be on the hunt for my next adventure, but reviews for Indie Authors are important. It is the lifeblood to our success. It doesn't have to take long. One sentence with an honest star rating will do. Can you give me less than five minutes of your time? It's so easy. All you need to do is scan the QR code (psst, for digital you can click on it), and it will take you directly to the review page. If I could say thank in person I would. Instead, I'll leave it here. "Thank you, thank you, THANK YOU for bolstering your bookshelf!"

REFERENCE & PRONUNCIATION

- **Aaliyah — EH-Luh:** Terren's cousin and the woman that challenges Kiira to the d'Khebezii.
- **Albea — AL-Bey-uh:** The city at the Eastern base of the Klaroni Cordillera. This is the first city that Kiira and Terren are in after leaving the Temple of Ny.
- **Knight Aldus — AL-dUS:** The knight Terren served as a squire when a youth. He was the father figure he always wanted.
- **Amol — Ah-Mole:** The leaders of the mercenary group that Zerrec uses as a proxy to his actions when testing Terren.
- **Apelgo — Ah-pell-Go:** Considered the third god of the trinity and the messenger of the gods. A chain of islands is named after the god and is credited with having a feasting hall for those that have died.
- **Aradyll — Are-uh-dill:** The capital of Klynotia.
- **The Aria Bells:** The lower mountains running north to south and semi-dividing the kingdoms of Lorea and Klynotia.
- **Ariella — Are-EE-ella:** The lady Liem marries upon his return to Lorea after assisting in rescuing his sister.

- **Asimesta — Ah-sEYE-Mess-Ta:** The tools and weapons makers for the Isokanii people. They produce everything from farming tools to the weapons of the Royal Guard and Shadow Walkers.
- **Duke Aubin — OW-bin:** The duke over the lands in which Gem River resides. He is related to Terren as an uncle. He despises King Grayten, but is smart enough to not outright say anything. He pledges his loyalty to Terren when he understands the prince wants to change Klynotia for the better.
- **Bahtii — bAH-tEE:** The given name of the Mafayyba of the Isokanii.
- **Barikkaa — Bare-eye-Kay:** The judges of the Isokanii people. They are the law regulators and settle disputes between individual tribe members and the tribes. Often used in business dealings to make sure that all parties present are honest and abiding by the law.
- **Bayyan — Bah-Yan:** One of Terren's many uncles and the Gariisurii to the region of the Shade Realm nearest the Glaze Fire Canyon and Kilunys Bridge. He was the closest in age to Terren's mother.
- **Bremert — BreM-erT:** King Grayten's personal valet and servant of many years. Zerrec gets rid of him after taking control of Grayten's body so that he does not compromise his position as the new king of Klynotia.
- **Biiko, chejiira ke! — (bEE-Koh) (CHeh-jEEr-AH) (Keh):** Translated means, "Please, be careful!"
- **The Burnished Plains:** Kiira and Terren cross a portion of these plains when making the journey to Fellos and again toward Letra Mera or Forchid.
- **Byloraan — By-Lore-An:** Also known as the Ristern Mera. The city is in the Shade Realm and is enormous. Considered one of the sister cities.
- **Captain Abiimola — Ah-bEE-moh-lah:** He is the captain of the ship Kiira and Terren use to sail back to the Sun

Realm after their visit in the Shade Realm during the tail end of the Lundemai.

- **Ceress — Sare-Ess:** An established identity of Terren's from the time he was traveling to keep people from learning of his true identity and creating a trail for his father to follow.
- **The Charlarae River — S-Har-lu-Ray:** The river running from the splitting point of the Rustean River, eventually flowing to the sea.
- **Chausekkii — Chow-sek-Kee:** The royal family of the Isokanii people. They are also the only family within the tribes that can become Shadow Walkers.
- **Chekeluu — Ch-eh-Keh-LOO:** The leader of the Isokanii merchant caravan that travels to and from Lorea. He has been the leader for a long time, almost seeming ageless.
- **Coran — Cor-AN:** An experienced archer under Kiira's command, who she will miss after her marriage.
- **Corsair Cay:** The rough skerry where pirates live and Zerrec finds his mercenaries.
- **Cupun — Koo-Poon:** Terren's name among the Veripoi. It's a shortened meaning for 'one who is easily snuck up on'.
- **Curavailed — Cure-ah-Veiled:** The term for the excommunication from the Nyuten Priesthood.
- **Dain — Day-N:** The old beggar Terren speaks with to gain clues about Kiira's disappearance. He is a Pheneojek, so most people see him as addled, even though he is very intelligent.
- **Danel — Dan-EL:** The Cook Master for Lorea.
- **Daswadii — Das-wad-ee:** The leading tribe over the Isokanii people. The tribe is a part of the royal line, but they can not become Shadow Walkers.
- **d'Kehbezii — d-Kay-BeZ-ee:** The fighting challenge of Isokanii women. It was traditionally a test to ensure that the strongest woman was chosen for marriage into the royal line. Women in the Isokanii culture are protectors of the

home and their husbands, similar to the idea of a last line of defense. A woman who wins is allowed to turn down the suitor, but it is not common to do so.

- **Drenton's Ascent — Drenn-Tun:** Named after the first priest to discover Klaron Point. It is the steep incline that you must ascend in order to gain access to the point and exit the caverns.
- **Drymera — Dry-Mare-uh:** A painting done with magic. The magician must picture the image they want to put on paper and the paints or inks will transfer from their pots to the paper to create the image.
- **The Dueling Bells Inn:** The inn in the Forchid, also known as Letra Mera. It is a well-kept popular inn in the heart of the maze-like city. Terren knows the owner, but under a false name.
- **The Ebony Spires:** The strange tall rock columns of the northwest coast of the Sun Realm.
- Ewiidu soup, definitely a must try. The Eebaa
- **Eebaa — EE-bAY:** This is a Mandalltii tribe specialty presented at Terren and Kiira's wedding feast in the Shade Realm. It is a fermented tuber that's been dried and rehydrated into an edible past.
- **Ermyjek — Err-meh-Jzsh-ek:** The ceremony that takes place for a Shadow Seeker to become a Shadow Walker. It is a painful process and extremely taxing on the body, especially the mind. The process can go wrong and have some serious side effects.
- **Ermii — Air-mEE:** The title/position of the person who has been trained to go through the Ermyjek ceremony. Only members of the royal family are able to bond with Shade Beast.
- **Eshalahee — Esh-ah-La-hE:** The merchant tribe of the Isokanii people. They deal in every manner of trade, buying, and selling. This is both in the Shade Realm between the tribes and the Sun Realm.

- **Ewiidu — Eh-wE-duh:** A specialty soup made by the Iamloruu tribe. It is one of the main dishes presented at the wedding feast for Terren and Kiira while in the Shade Realm.
- **Fellos — Fell-Ohs:** The town at the Western base of the Klaroni Cordillera. This is where Terren and Kiira stop and rest after the wind storm before ascending the path up the mountain to the temple.
- **The Fire Falls:** The location on the beach Kiira takes Terren on their first required outing. These falls are very colorful when the light hits the water a certain way.
- **Folen — Foal-En:** Prince Liem's best friend. He is a laid back and easy-going guy and a terrible flirt with all the women, especially Kiira because he has known her for so long.
- **Forchid — Fore-Ked:** Also known as Letra Mera of the sister cities. It is a massive maze-like city on the Western side of the Kilunys Bridge. Though it is so close to the Shade Realm, Shade Born are rarely seen walking the streets. If any Shade Dwellers are seen, they are usually merchants or traders. The city is described as always being covered in a layer of soot because of the proximity to the canyon.
- **Gahijett — G-ah-ee-Jet:** One of the two tribes that trains warriors and guards for Isokanii people. The people from these tribes serve in every capacity of protection, from guarding the royal family to helping the merchants guard their goods.
- **Garisurii — Gar-ih-sur-ee:** The title of magistrate among the Isokanii. Terren's uncle, Bayyan, is the Garisurii for the plains closest to the bridge. His Sunarian is the best because he lives so close to the Sun Realm and has business with many different Sun Realm merchants.
- **Gettii — GeT-Tee:** The traveling merchant both Kiira and Terren have met.

- **Ghabaamitsu — G-hab-AY-my-tsu:** The area or region of the Forest to the Isokanii.
- **Gimetii — Gi-Meh-Tee:** The god of the Isokanii responsible for creating the massive trees of the forest for the Shade Beast to roam.
- **Gioll — GEE-ohL:** The name for someone who was born without magic during a time everyone in the Sun Realm was born with magic.
- **Glazefire Canyon:** A deep and wide canyon separating the Shade Realm and Sun Realm; it was created during the Mage War and it is the rift that exists between the two realms. It is the unbalance of the Shade Realm and the Sun Realm being forced to exist side by side, producing spectacular and dangerous flames within the canyon.
- **Glazen Tavern:** The tavern that the old beggar Dain takes Terren to for the offered meal. It is considered one of the best taverns in Forchid because of its excellent ales and delicious food.
- **Grayten — Grey-Ten:** The king of Klynotia and Terren's father. He is a hard man and rules his people with intimidation and fear. He is especially brutal towards his children, expecting perfect results when it is sometimes not possible, and harbors an extreme dislike for magic and magicians.
- **Gresher — Gresh-Er:** The Master Priest of the gods for the kingdom of Lorea and the officiate for the royal wedding.
- **Harmend — HAR-mend:** a guard assigned to Terren.
- **Hayla — Hay-Luh:** One of the newer archers that Kiira plucks a drink from her hand during The Yielding Festival.
- **Herretus — Hair-eT-Us:** The king of Lorea and the father to Kiira and Liem. He is a kind man the people love and respect. He cares for others, but also expects to be obeyed when he has given the final say in a situation.
- **Hira — hEYE-rAH:** The Isokanii word for Lord. Example: Hira Terren

- **Hiraa — hEYE-RAY:** The Isokanii word for My Lord. Example: "Hiraa, may I pour you more wine?"
- **Hiira — hEAR-rAH:** The Isokanii word for Lady. Example Hiira Kiira
- **Hiiraa — hEAR-RAY:** The Isokanii word for My Lord. Example: Hiiraa, may I pour you more wine?"
- **Iamloruu — Eye-am-lore-U:** The tribe dedicated to the making and coloring of cloth. They also create and design all the clothing that is sold by the merchants.
- **Injiir Maala — In-jzheer May-la:** Roughly translates to "pale valueless woman" in Sunarian.
- **Isikolrii — Eye-siKohl-rEE:** It is an honorary title like sir or ma'am when referring to Isokanii royalty.
- **Isokanii — Eye-so-Kahn-EE:** The name of the people that dwell in the Shade Realm. The people group is built upon twelve tribes that all have a specific function that helps protect and advance the culture. Everyone of pure Isokanii blood is very dark-skinned and they all have the same eye coloring that is unique to their people. The eye color allows them to see vividly in the Shade Realm.
- **Ishaiio — Eye-SH-ee-oh:** The name given to a beloved among the Isokanii. It roughly translates to "the missing half of my heart".
- **Jaburshelee — Jaw-bor-Shell-ee:** One of the two tribes that trains warriors and guards for Isokanii people. The people from these tribes serve in every capacity of protection, from guarding the royal family to helping the merchants guard their goods.
- **Jahiim — Jah-Heem:** The second oldest son of the Mafelbno of the Isokanii, a prince.
- **Janissair — JAN-i-S-air:** The kingdom across the sea known for its mercenaries and constant infighting. The Uman encourages this making life there turbulent and unstable.

- **Jayan — J-eye-Ann:** An established identity of Terren's from the time he was traveling to keep people from learning of his true identity and creating a trail for his father to follow.
- **Jearut Oasis — Jay-rooT:** The capital of the Isokanii people.
- **Jemma — Gym-uh:** Kiira's lady's maid and one of her dearest friends. She is quiet and does not say much, but fusses over Kiira and is almost constantly worried about her whereabouts and the way she looks.
- **Jiirus — JEEr-us:** The Horse Master for Lorea.
- **Johsh — Joe-sh:** The priest greets Terren and Kiira when they first arrive at the temple. He is the second attendant to the Master Librarian. He is a stickler for protocol and is very proud of his position within the temple.
- **Jurica — Jzhur-EES-Uh:** The queen of Lorea who died while trying to calm Zerrec. Kiira cherished her mother. It was a hard loss for their family, but her death affected the princess the most.
- **Juston — Joos-Tun:** The deactivating word used on the invisibility necklace that Terren gives to Liem to borrow.
- **Kallik — Kah-Leek:** The chief of the Veripoi and Terren's friend. Kallik discovered Terren in the woods not long after Terren fled Klynotia as a young man.
- **Kamaria — Kah-Marr-ee-ah:** The Shade Beast that Terren is bonded to via the Ermyjek. As Shade Beast, she is massive and Kamaria, raised to her full height, towers another fifteen meters above Terren's own almost six-foot stature while still on four paws. She is a Beast, both material and immaterial, and grants Terren a range of abilities.
- **Kannelner — KAN-Nell-Nair:** The name for the traditional burial right of the Veripoi. When an old member of the tribe is ready to die, they journey to the rough waters in the Ebony Spires to allow the sea to take them from the world.
- **Kessa — Kess-Uh:** The name that Terren picks for Kiira while staying in Fellos. It is one of her cover identities to

keep anyone from knowing that she is the princess of Lorea, since many of the people they meet in their travels do not know of Terren's true identity.

- **Kiira — Keer-uh:** The princess of the Lorea and is the twin to Liem. She marries Terren through an arranged marriage, but has a secret love for Leo an Earl and her second in command of the archers. She loves her family and the people of the kingdom, but she is also incredibly stubborn, which often gets her into trouble. Kiira is often compared in likeness to her mother.
- **Kiiroth — Keer-Oth:** The large town on the northern edge of the Forest Wilds near the Glazefire Canyon. It is where Terren and Liem travel to while waiting for Kiira's injuries to heal.
- **Kilunys Bridge — K-eye-loon-iss:** The massive bridge that expands the Glazefire Canyon connecting the Shade Realm and the Sun Realm. It takes an hour to cross the bridge.
- **Kiivulii — KEE-vul-EE:** The actual name of those among the Isokanii that bond with Beast and can travel the realms. It is a lost name from before the realms were broken, but a few still remember the term. Most, however, refer to them as Stieti Tetsaa (Shadow Walker).
- **Klaron Point — Klair-On:** A flat landing on a tall peak in the Klaroni Cordillera. It can only be accessed via the temple and was discovered by the priest Drenton.
- **Klaroni Cordillera — Klair-Oh-N-eye:** The mountain range that stretches across most of the northern edge of the Sun Realm. The peaks are tall, soaring to heights above an estimated 10,000 kilometers. This is also where the Nyan Temple is located and the Nyuten Priest dwell.
- **Klynotia — Kleh-Noht-sha:** The neighboring kingdom to Lorea. It is known for its gem exports, as much of the kingdom is bordered by mountains. It has some beaches, but a vast majority of the kingdom is rocky and barely fertile

soil. A lot of goods are imported into the kingdom and it is afforded because of the gem exports.

- **The Knobby Seas Pub:** The pub where Zerrec waits to find mercenaries to hire. It is a disgusting place and sadly the best pub on Corsair Island.
- **Kreden — Kray-Den:** The activating word used on the invisibility necklace that Terren gives to Liem to borrow.
- **Kreshkt — Kresh-Kt:** An expletive that various characters used to convey great anger. It is a word not used often, so when it is spoken, one understands the upset of the speaker.
- **Lady Liane — Lee-Ain:** The wife of Marko, sister-in-law to Herretus, and aunt to Kiira and Liem.
- **Lenden — Len-Den:** A guard assigned to Terren.
- **Leo Moredell:** The second in command of the archers after Kiira. He is an Earl of Wirlen and the princess' secret love. The two courted each other without the king's knowledge for several months.
- **Letra Mera — Let-Ruh Mare-Uh:** Also known as Forchid and one of the sister cities. It is a massive maze-like city on the Western side of the Kilunys Bridge. The city is described as always being covered in a layer of soot because of the proximity to the canyon.
- **Liioh — lee-Oh:** The twin god to Gimetii and the creator of the Shade Beast, according to the Isokanii.
- **Liem — Lee-em:** The prince of Lorea and Kiira's twin brother. He is bulky and stands at five foot eight. His size is because of his school of magic. If he ever depletes his core magic, fuel is then pulled from his muscles. He loves his family fiercely and will do anything necessary to protect them, even if it means bending the rules. He looks more like his father in build and demeanor.
- **The Lieta Springs — Ly-eh-Ta:** The Lieta Springs, or more commonly known as The Springs of Windrah. This is the clearing that Kiira stumbles into after running into the Forest Wilds and meets the goddess.

- **Loracia — Lore-ay-see-uh:** The capital of Lorea
- **Loralyn — Lore-uh-lin:** Zerrec's first wife. The mage considers Kiira the reincarnation of her and, therefore, destined to be his.
- **Lorea — Lore-ay-uh:** The neighboring kingdom to Klynotia. It is a prosperous and fertile kingdom that exports many goods. Produce, woodwork, clothing, and glass are just a few examples. Most of the land is covered by the Forest Wilds and it is known to have beautiful black sand beaches. The people of the kingdom are generally happy and loyal to the crown.
- **Lorestan — Lore-Ess-Tan:** The surname of the royal family of Lorea.
- **Lorestan Lake:** An immense lake located almost in the center of the Lorean kingdom. It is home to a variety of fish and almost always has calm waters because of the surrounding forest and mountains that block much of the wind. The water is relatively clear and one can see rather deep into the lake.
- **Lunedemai — Loon-Deh-My:** The yearlong trip that newly married couples take. It was a tradition started before the Mage War and it is meant to act as a way for the newly married to get to know one another. There are no restrictions on the Lundemai on what a couple can do during the year, but it is frowned upon to have contact with anything familiar.
- **Lucen — Loose-en:** Terren's personal servant. He is loyal to the prince even though he was abused by the king after the prince fled Klynotia.
- **Mafelbno — Mah-Fell-B-no:** The title of emperor within the Isokanii people.
- **Mafayyba — Mah-FAY-bah:** The title of empress within the Isokanii people.
- **The Magician's Cloister:** The smallest island of The Tears of Apelgo and is a refuge and sanctuary for magicians.

- **The Mage War:** The devastating war that brought the Shade Realm into alignment with the Sun Realm and created the Glazefire Canyon. The war started because of a young mage that believed that those with more powerful magic should be in leadership and many disagreed. It was a civil war that pitted children against parents and friends against friends. The conflict lasted a century until a last act by hundreds of Elder Mages misaligned the two realms that sent a shockwave killing almost everyone.
- **Maireen — My-Ree-N:** The wife of Tanan and the cook for the Starbryt Inn and Tavern in the town of Fellos near the base of the Klaroni Cordillera.
- **Mag jou tafii ke ya nagligte gaan — (Mag) (jzhou) (tah-fee) (kay) (ya) (nah-glee-G-tay) (gay-an):** Translated means "May your journeys go by the lights of night." Kiira says this to Dain the beggar as she leaves after giving him a loaf of honey bread.
- **Mandalltii — M-ahn-doll-tee:** The tribe responsible for mining the Night Crystals. They are also the smallest of all the tribes.
- **Marko — Marr-Ko:** The younger brother to Herretus and uncle to Kiira and Liem.
- **The Meladaai River — Mel-uh-day:** The river running from Loel Lake to Lorestan Lake.
- **Merkus — Merr-Kuss:** One of Liem's closest friends next to Folen. He helps with searching the royal quarters because Liem feels magic being used.
- **Morokuumdhozii — Moro-kOOm-dOH-ee:** An honorary title among the Isokanii, meaning Virgin Warrior. It is an exalted status that Terren's cousin Aaliyah wears with pride. She's won many d'Kehbezi but refuses to take a husband.
- **Mythieres — Mith-Ear-es:** The surname for the royal family of Klynotia.
- **Myna — ME-nah:** Killik's wife of the Veripoi.

- **Nagruk — NAHG-rooK:** The Veripoi name for the antlers of the great elk that they hunt once per year to sustain the people.
- **Nahkahkurmehk — NahK-ah-KURrr-mehK:** A thank you in the language of the Veripoi. It is said to Terren after he blesses his friend Kallik upon learning he is now the chieftain after his father's passing.
- **Ndatenda — N-Dah-Ten-dah:** Thank you in Isokanii.
- **Ngozee — Nuh-go-Zee:** The tribe specializes in the jewelry that all the Isokanii people wear. It is even highly prized and traded within the Sun Realm.
- **Niell — Kneel:** The soldier that Terren calls upon to protect Berro in Woodlands Deep.
- **Night Crystal Quarries:** Rocky cliffs where the Mandalltii Tribe harvest the Night Crystals used in jewelry and sold to magicians.
- **Ny — N-eye:** Considered the head god of the trinity. He is the god of both light and dark and the creator of the realms.
- **Nyuten Priesthood — N-eye-you-ten:** The priests that have dedicated their lives to serving and worshiping the god Ny. They live in seclusion, high in the Klaroni Cordillera, and are known for their fighting skills with a bo staff. Their ways are only taught to those who are a part of the order, but all are welcome to the temple as long as they are pure of heart. Both men and women are welcome to join the priesthood.
- **Omii — Oh-Me:** The name of the camel Kiira is given to ride across the desert. The name means water in Isokanii.
- **Oranta — Ore-anT-uh:** A sleek wolf-like animal that attacked the citadel in Lorea. The beast is as large as a manor house and black as midnight.
- **Ojeda — Oh-Jay-Duh:** Kiira's playmate as a child, the daughter of the caravan leader for the Isokanii merchants that would pass through Lorea.

- **Pheneojek — P-heno-Jzsh-ek:** A Shadow Seeker that failed the Ermyjek or the bonding process with a Shade Beast. They are often considered insane because of the mindless babble. These Shade Born are not anchored to the Shade Realm or to a Shade Beast, so it has serious repercussions on the mind.
- **Piirdstutsii — Peer-D-sTuTzEE:** The area or region of the cordillera to the Isokanii.
- **Ramilkretna — Ram-ill-Kreet-Na:** The spiritual guides for the Isokanii people. The specific beliefs of the people are unknown in this novel.
- **Reberak Peninsula — Reb-AIR-aK:** The most common place for fishermen to go in the Kingdom of Lorea.
- **Ristern Mera — Res-Tern Mare-uh:** Also known as Byloraan and one of the sister cities. It is a massive maze-like city on the Eastern side of the Kilunys Bridge in the Shade Realm. The description of this city is unknown.
- **Rustean River — Rus-TeeN:** The river is fed from Loel Lake and surrounds the capital of Klynotia before going to the sea.
- **Sael — Say-El:** The hunter that brings Zerrec food and news from Lorea.
- **Sairah — Say-Ruh:** The princess of Klynotia and Terren's younger sister. She is seven years younger, so she was only ten when the prince disappeared. She is considered pretty, but has a difficult life, so most of the time she pushes people away. Her relationship with Terren is strained, but is on the mend.
- **Sartenn — Sar-Ten:** The Horse Master in the Nyan Temple that Terren makes a deal with for practicing. This is also the same man that gave him Tempest.
- **The Seas of Reana — Ray-ana:** The seas bordering the western edge of the Sun Realm. They are a darker blue and can seem like a deep purple in the right light.

- **Senuresko — Sin-Yur-es-Ko:** The tribe responsible for building and assisting with any transportation needs for the Isokanii people.
- **The Shadow Desert:** The dark, massive sand dunes that make up where the main gathering of Isokanii live.
- **Shadow Walkers:** The ultimate protectors of the culture, people, and the Shade Realm; since The Mage War, their job is even more important.
- **Siiko — sEE-kOH:** The youngest sister to the Mafayyba.
- **Sikuk! — s-IH-KooK:** Not so much a word, but an expression of surprise, similar to the modern English EEP!
- **The Skefii — Sk-eh-Fee:** The long slide built into the side of the cliffs by the Isokanii in the Shade Realm.
- **Skehtra — Sk-Eh-T-Rah:** Kiira's Wolfcat cub she rescued from a sprung rabbit trap. The cub refused to leave her side even with encouragement and was kept as a pet.
- **The Slate Cliffs:** Dark cliffs rising from the sandy beach and are the conduit for the Fire Falls.
- **Staesi Storja — Stay-See Store-Jha:** The star stories that the Veripoi tell. They are a history of their culture and existence, giving the listener life lessons.
- **Starbryt Inn — Star-Brite:** An inn in Fellos. This is where Terren and Kiira stay after dealing with the Windstorm.
- **Starfire:** A uniquely colored gelding that Kiira absolutely adores. He has a playful and stubborn personality and does not warm up to others quickly.
- **Stietii Tetsa — Sty-ET-ee TET-sah:** Shadow Walker in Isokanii.
- **Storm Gulf:** The end of the whispering river coming out of the canyon so forcefully it makes a loud thunderclap sound.
- **Surveysor — Sir-vey-Sore:** The name of the pirate ship Terren sailed with for a time during his travels.
- **Taam — Tay-Am:** The other hunter that will sometimes bring meat to Zerrec.

- **Tanan — Tan-ann:** The owner of the Starbryt Inn in Fellos. He is a portly man that is always in a jolly mood and thinks of Terren as a son.
- **The Tears of Apelgo:** The chain of three islands south of the Shade Realm. These islands were not pulled into the Sun Realm at the conclusion of the Mage War, however, they were formed after and are part of the Sun Realm.
- **Tendii — ten-dEE:** The middle sister to the Mafayyba.
- **Tereyssa — Tare-Ess-Uh:** The older priestess Kiira becomes very close to in the months she is there. The old woman is wise, a little mysterious, and has a witty sense of humor.
- **Terren — Tare-En:** The prince of Klynotia. He marries Kiira through an arranged marriage. He is a mysterious character, not a lot is known about him. It is known that he traveled and he obviously has some skill in fighting and being sneaky, but not much else is known to others. The truth of him emerges through Kiira's eyes, but he still has a lot to hide.
- **Trinesteo — Trin-Es-Tayo:** A casting that is used to show you are telling the truth. It is a binding spell that will hurt the person with physical pain should they lie.
- **The Shade Realm:** A shadow of the Sun Realm physically, but has unique animals and people.
- **The Sun Realm:** A wild and beautiful land that has dangers, but many adventures for those willing to take the chance. It has extreme landscapes, with mountains and seas being very close to each other.
- **The Tayros River:** The river running from Lorestan Lake to the Reberak Peninsula.
- **Tilkt Point — Till-Kt:** The cliffs on the southern end of the Shade Realm riddled with caves; created by the high waves of the sea.
- **Torrel — Tore-ell:** The owner of the Dueling Bells in Forchid.

- **Uman — Ooh-Mahn:** The king of the Janissair kingdom. He is a ruthless man that encourages fighting and war.
- **The Velpani River — Vell-pah-Nee:** The river that runs from the Klaroni Cordillera down the base of the Aria Bells and feeds Loel Lake and Lorestan Lake.
- **Veripoi — Ver-eh-Poy:** Nomadic people group that live in both the northern tip of the Forest Wilds and the tall grasses of the plains.
- **The Whispering River:** The river used to run between the two halves of the Sun Realm before the Mage War and fell into the canyon upon the splitting of the realms.
- **Windrah — When-druh:** The goddess of the story and physical representation of the gods. She appears to Kiira multiple times in the book. This is due to the princess's strong devotion and worship of the goddess that she appears before her. Normally, messages from the gods are sent through Apelgo.
- **Wolfcat:** A large cat that is vicious in its attacks and weighs up to 1,000 pounds. It has a silvery grey fluffy fur, lilac/violet eyes, and lives in the Forest Wilds and prefers to hunt at night, but will also sometimes roam during the day.
- **Yven — Yeh-Ven:** A guard assigned to Terren.
- **Zainabdee — Z-ain-uh-B-dee:** The tribe responsible for farming and fishing among the Isokanii people.
- **Zahjerra — Zah-Jair-ah:** The second eldest sister to the Mafayyba.
- **Zergoni — zAIR-jOHn-EE:** A particular tribe within the Janissairian people that live across the Seas of Reana.
- **Zkinne — zKin-nEH:** A paste substance made from a Shade Realm plant that will stain the skin temporarily. It is drawn onto the skin in intricate patterns for beauty and to tell a story of the bride and groom.
- **Zerrec — Zehr-eK:** An evil magician and incredibly powerful. He is an Elder Mage and used to be Kiira and Liem's teacher. He was also an advisor to King Herretus

before turning on the royal family and killing the queen. Banished from the kingdom and disappeared for ten years, he has resurfaced after hearing news of Kiira's arranged marriage. He is also centuries old, having kept himself alive with his healing magic.

TRIBES & BELIEFS
OF THE ISOKANII

The Isokanii consisting of twelve tribes, each with a designated specialty to fully support the people. The trades of each tribe are concrete, but children learn the trade of their home tribe, but are not bound to stay and can leave to learn the ways of other tribes. Most, however, are content with their lot.

- **Barikkaa** are judges and settle disputes among the tribes.
- **Asimesta** are tools and weapons makers
- **Ramilkretna** are the spiritual guides
- **Gahijett** and **Jaburshelee** are warriors and guards.
- **Iamloruu** are clothing makers
- **Mandalltii** mine the night crystals
- **Zainabdee** are farmers and fishermen
- **Ngozee** tribe are excellent jewelry makers
- **Senuresko** build and assist in transportation needs
- **Daswadii** tribe is the largest and rulers over the others
- **Eshalahee** are merchants and deal in every manner of trade, buying, and selling.

Kiilee Maker Earth–Was the father and king of the gods. He created the earth with mountains, rolling sands, and crystal hills. He fell in love with the sky goddess.

Lehlo Sky Queen–She is the mother and queen of the gods. She would watch from her place above the earth as Kiilee designed the land. She fell in love with Kiilee and went to earth to convince him to love her. Together, they had several children.

Giiha Child Wind–Firstborn of Maker Earth and the Sky Queen. His favorite things to do was play with soft grains of the earth, using his winds to shift and shape the land into something different each day. After his younger brother grew the trees, he liked to play with the winds to make the trees sway and the leaves rattle.

Ostiimii Child Water–She was the second born. She asked her father if he would give away some of his land so that she could break up the monotony of the earth. Kiilee said no and in her outrage, she flooded the lands. Her tears formed the seas. After, her father gave her the space she desired, and she cried happy tears forming the lakes and rivers.

Jurana Child Sun–She was the most beautiful of the king's and queen's children. Lehlo loved her the most and so cradled her in the sky. Jurana loved her mother, but she wanted to be with her brothers and sister. She cried and her tears dotted mother with thousands of her sparkling teardrops.

Liioh Child Beast–He was the twin of Giimeti. He saw that the earth could sustain life. Leeoh created the beasts that roamed. There was much space, so he gave the beasts enormous proportions. However, it was not all the beasts. He only gave big proportions to the fiercest.

Gimetii Child Nature–He was the twin of Leeoh. He thought the Beasts should not be given as much freedom. Gimetii created soaring trees to coral the beasts. This made Leeoh angry, so to appease, Gimetii created beautiful flowers and this made his twin happy.

Kiiholii Child Moon–The last child to be born the opposite of the sun. He did not have her beauty and Maker Earth and Lover Sky were going to destroy him. Jurana, though, protected her younger brother and spirited him away. This made her father and mother angry, but then Jurana shined her brightest and her light reflected off Kiiholee and his parents could finally see his beauty. They set him in the sky to always be the opposite of his sister.

ISOKANII LANGUAGE RULES

Double letters are the long form of the vowel.

(ii) is (ee)

(aa) is (ay)

(uu) is (ooh)

(ou) us (ooh)

(ee) is (ee)

Single letters are the short form of the vowel.

(i) is (eye)

(a) is (ah)

(o) is (oh)

(e) is (eh)

(u) is (uh)

Of course, as with all languages, there are exceptions to these rules.
You may see one or two examples of this in the
Reference & Pronunciation Guide.

Acknowledgments

This book has been a long time coming. Seriously. I kept promising book two and then had the audacity to rewrite book one.

For those of you who have stuck with me from the very beginning, thank you.

I owe it to my Father for the gift to see entire worlds when I close my eyes, or as I wander down the street. I wouldn't be an author without the stories You've put inside me. Thank you for being the spark of my inspiration.

To my chosen partner in shenanigans. I'll never regret the night I said yes to your proposal. I cried happy tears, and then we stumbled through the dark back to the car without a flashlight. We've been on an adventure from the very beginning.

Addressing my editor and friend. Your challenge honed me into a better writer, and I am thankful for that. Even though sometimes we disagree about how the story should go, I still appreciate your edits. You have my fealty.

Finally, to the loyal readers who have clamored for another book since 2018. I promised when releasing Magic's Daughter that I would have book two to you soon. Considering I moved halfway across the United States while in the middle of edits for this book, I'm glad I could still get this book to you. With as long as it took me to finish this book, I hope you think I did Kiira and Terren's story justice. I'm looking forward to the ending as much as you! Again, thank you to those who have stuck around since the beginning; it means the world.

ABOUT THE AUTHOR

T.J. Fisher is the author of *The Broken Realms Chronicle*. As a former mermaid, T.J. is a lover of all things fantastical and magical. After decades of watching humans write stories about her kind; she joined the fray and added her knowledge of magic to give characters a 'breath' of fresh air—so to speak. Lured to land by the love of a halfling and his endless supply of delicious culinary creations; T.J. now dines on the delicacies of enchiladas, breakfast tacos, milkshakes, and chocolate chip cookies. She may have lost her fins, but she still loves water in all forms.

ALSO BY T.J. FISHER

Divided - A Broken Realms Novella

Magic's Daughter

<u>Coming Soon</u>

Mage's Legacy - 2026

PRAISE FOR
MAGIC'S DAUGHTER

5 Stars

"I was privileged to be an advanced reader for this book, and I'm so glad. It was really great and full of adventure and entertainment — with just enough romance. A villain you want to like but just can't. A strong female heroine who is also soft and kind. A gentle and protective hero you want to cheer for."
-Amazon Review

5 Stars

"Fantasy isn't the usual genre I pick but I'm glad I stuck with it. Magic's Daughter exceeded my expectations! T.J. Fisher has a way of describing her characters that make them relatable while also creating a big picture. The tale of Kira and Terren is complex and thought provoking. I honestly couldn't predict what was coming next and I really liked that. I was left with a few questions, I can't wait to read the rest of the series and find out what happens next!"
-Amazon Review

4 Stars

"This is a great book to read if you are just starting fantasy or trying to get into fantasy stories! I really enjoyed the story outline and really grabbed my attention the more I kept reading. There were some parts that were a little hard to understand, but eventually got explained later on in the book. Overall, it definitely kept me on my toes and I can't wait to see what's next!"
-Amazon Review

SNEAK PEEK

DIVIDED: A BROKEN
REALMS PREQUEL NOVELLA

To save himself from a horrible fate, Irigiim chooses a path he never thought he would, but will his bond to the wild-natured Rayle be worth the choice?

Sun Glimmer is not so much a haven as perdition for Castell and the itch to fight keeps him restless, but he has choices to make. Now he needs to decide on the right one.

Irigiim is part of a dwindling species, noble Beasts that roam the raw lands of the Shade Realm. His majestic form, however, is no salvation against the aberrant magicians in the Sun Realm who are using his kind to control others. To keep his kind alive, Irigiim bonds with a young Isokanii royal to prevent suffering the same fate as his sire. Rayle keeps him safe from the Sun Dwellers, but their tumultuous relationship does little to provide the peace and stability he craves. Rayle's rambunctious and adventurous spirit is so much like that of a pup, he is hesitant to fully trust his new human partner. All he desires is to avoid a caustic death, but the anxiety created by monitoring his bond partner might be more than he bargained for.

Castell has pacifist parents to thank for his peaceful and worry-free life. It is also thanks to them he is eager to leave. Every day spent mining Sun Crystals is another day he wishes to be elsewhere. Gifted with weather magic, he knows he could be more helpful at the front lines of the war, rather than living a banal life chiseling rock and stone. The problem? Leaving would break his parent's hearts, but he knows he can no longer remain a neutral party to the war. Armed with his conviction, Castell leaves the only home he's ever known to face a turmoil he's never known.

Will Irigiim find the peace he craves or be forced to live in disquiet?

Will Castell finally do something worthwhile with his magic?

Break into the Broken Realms with this prequel novella! Discover magic, adventure, and the power of choice.

IRIGIIM

My pup slashes at the air. A squall of legs and arms as she twists, pretending to sever or maybe stab a supposed enemy, a tight grip on the knives in her hands. I can never tell the difference between the many fighting forms, the human shape is still relatively unknown to me, even though Rayle took the time to explain the katas. She is dedicated, as she should be for a Stieti Tetsaa. It is one of the many attributes I admire and why I chose her to be my partner, but honestly, it makes little sense to me to attack something that is not there. As a wolf, all my actions have purpose. Why humans determine it necessary to keep practicing with their sharp objects is beyond me. Once my play sessions from puppyhood turned into real hunts with teeth and claws, everything I did from then on was instinctual. I do not understand why it is not the same for the Isokanii people. In my brief time bonded to Rayle, I recognize that, for her, the fighting sequences are a means to help her focus a bundle of energy. My partner reminds me so much of myself as a puppy exploring outside the safety of the den for the first time. She is not timid and shy, but she seems fascinated by the smallest things. I should not be so harsh in my critiques. I, too, was a pup once, discovering the whipping quiddity of new branches, but that was many years ago.

Rayle does a pretty flip and twists through the air to give a hard chop toward her imagined enemy. The stone and wooden beads in her hair clatter as the long, thin braids settle into stillness across her back and over her shoulder. The riot of colors in the filtered light interests me. Purple opals intertwined with copper and silver wire around the crown of her head impress her status as royalty among the Isokanii, but the addition of blue, yellow, and red wooden beads is uniquely Rayle. Her final pose gives her a very cat-like quality as she spreads her legs low and wide. I wonder at the difficulty of keeping her head aloft with the extra weight from the beads, but then again, I wonder at how any human moves at all with only two thin legs to propel them.

I tilt my head, twitching an ear forward as I listen to the steadying of her breath. Rayle told me a few days ago that the long pause at the end of her practice is so she can pray to the gods. I do not believe in her gods, but I suppose our bonding—on the dark moon a few days ago—would now allow me to find out more, but the connection between us is still more ghostly than tangible, and I often forget it is there. Perhaps more so due to hesitation in the face of the unknown than any true obstacle.

I unblock the mental link between us and, sure enough; she is praying to Jurana, the goddess of the sun. I should ask later why she chooses that goddess in particular to venerate with her prayers. My pup's thoughts differ vastly from my own, they are wild and untamable. She will think of one thing and then be on to the next before the first is finished, never committing to one idea or thought for long. The only thing that seems to focus her attention are the sword and dagger practices, and these she does with unbridled determination and concentration. So far, my conclusions about humans have settled between complicated and messy. Still, I look upon her with fondness.

My world—at least before the pup—consisted of eating, sleeping, wandering beneath soaring trees while socializing with my brethren, and hunting. It was a simple life, and I liked it. Though the generalities of my life before mirrored that of the lowly insipid creatures that resemble my kind but have the mental complexity of a frightened rabbit; I was capable of more than living a life of basic urges. We Beast are intelligent and thoughtful creatures, able to communicate on a higher level than any other animals in existence. It is why we have the ability to choose partnership with the royal family of the Isokanii, like I did with Rayle. It is a position of power I relish.

Bonding, however, limits me in some aspects, but I do not regret my choice. The advantages I gain in spite of this uncomfortable transition period—my skin still spasms and itches—are worth the price. I now understand human speech, and with it, a seemingly endless list of words to describe the complexity of an object or situation. Something I find to be a pleasant challenge as I translate my native Beast communication to new descriptors, even if I stumble over an apt word or phrase from time to time. I have learned the Isokanii language quickly because of my bond, but sometimes when I try to use the appropriate words to speak with Rayle, they stick in my mind like an old dried piece of game between my teeth. My pup always has a laugh at my expense in those moments, which frustrates me, but Rayle assures me that with time I will taste the marrow of words' usefulness.

Bonding also ensures my survival. The Sun Dwellers, for the past twenty-some-odd years for unknown reasons, have hunting fever, like the lesser animals who lust to bite something with their white-foam mouths. The selfish mages covet the abilities of my kin. Since our discovery, I have seen several of my brethren murdered. I cannot recall how many Beast have been ripped from this realm into the other, sentenced to a life of abasement and horror. It both angers and frightens me to know they are used merely for mindless killing. I bonded so I would not be one of them. My sire never liked the idea of bonding with a human and always discouraged the pack from doing so. He often compared it to being alone and cornered for the rest of existence. What my sire did not foresee was his demise because of his staunch position on freedom. If he was still alive, I like to think he would understand the advantages of bonding, but antecedently, I would have followed his lead and remained wild. Our numbers dwindle every day because of the Sun-Dwelling mages, and other than siring more Pups, this is the only way to preserve my kind. Sure, my lifespan reduces to that of my partner's, and I will only live for another sixty or seventy years, but I keep my sanity, and I remain, mostly, my own master, since a bonded Beast cannot become a puppet to the defilers in the other realm.

So far, my bond with Rayle feels nothing like being cornered. Granted, it has only been a few days, but she thus far treats me with respect and kindness, and I foresee a camaraderie between us that will deepen our tender friendship. She is a handful. I hear many attribute this description to her nature, but I picked her during the Ermyjek Ceremony because she is strong both in spirit and body. If I am going to attach my life to a human, I want one that will not dart from danger like my meals.

Rayle's movement pulls me from my thoughts as she rises from her deep position and turns to give me a big grin. I snort my approval at her regimen. I may not understand the incessant practicing, but she *is* one of the best fighters amongst the Chausekki family. My choice of partner is a good one.

"Irigiim," Rayle says, "I was thinking we should explore the other realm when it is full night. Now that we are bonded, I can finally open pathways to explore!"

'No.'

"Irigiim, do not be like that. The full night there is when all the Sun Dwellers are sleeping and you are a big, strong male and can protect me."

I bare my teeth at the taunt. *'My answer is still no. Why should either of us put ourselves in harm's way when those mages are acting like nothing more than selfish pups, all trying to share the same teat? They need to act more like a pack.'*

Rayle lets out a huff. "Fine."

I flatten my ears and give her a small growl. I do not know Rayle well enough yet to know if she will keep her word, but I figure a minor threat does not hurt.

She is nonplussed.

"Well, if you will not go to the other realm, at least venture with me to the quarries after the wedding. I have always wanted to see them."

Unease trickles through me, but the link I share with my wild brethren indicates no lurking, foul smells or sounds in that area. I see no harm in visiting the quarries as long as we remain in the Shade Realm. If we keep closer to the Eastern edge, we will be away from the primary conflict along the river. I obviously do not worry about being pulled, but it is better to be safe than sorry. Rayle seems to have a propensity to find her way into sticky situations, that is what my gut tells me. I snap my teeth at my pup, still somewhat irritated by her request, but she can feel my intentions. A smile blooms across her face. I like this display of happiness. The energy pleases me, making my acquiescence worth her happiness.

CASTELL

Several more hours of this drudgery, he thought, after peeking at the position of the sun; and he didn't even have the midday break to look forward to because it already passed.

Castell sank onto his heels from his hunched position with a burdened sigh. Using a small burst of wind, he cleared away the dust from the rock he'd been chiseling. Could he have used the brush sitting next to him? Yes, but that didn't provide a refreshing breeze to give him a respite from the blazing sun. Castell squinted at the burning orb as he removed his large scrub grass hat and wiped away the sweat threatening to drip into his eyes. Why couldn't he have been an Amber mage like his brother? They had it so much easier here at the mines, being able to sense the metals and minerals in the ground. They could shift the earth to soften it and simply pull the Sun Crystal formations from the rock. Those workers, by far, had the highest collection count of anyone else and were paid the most. It was useless to complain, though; no one chose their gift from the gods. At least he could summon light breezes to keep himself cool while the brutal sun lashed at his back. That was infinitely preferable to constantly sucking in the arid radiant heat intent on slowly baking everything.

The hard stone of the quarries, with its ever-present dusting of dirt, was not his choice for a living location, but Castell had lived here his entire life with his parents and siblings; he knew nothing else. More than once he'd daydreamed about living under the cool canopy of a forest with soft loam under his feet, like from the stories his father told. The longer he was a resident of the quarries, the more he questioned his reasons for staying.

Of course, it was the thought of his family that usually subdued the itch to leave. What would he do without family dinners on the sixth moon each week where he played hide-and-seek with his youngest sister, or threw good-natured punches at his brother? His family and friends were content with the life they'd made here, but for years now Castell felt his life would be better lived somewhere else. Which again begged the question: why did he continue to stay?

What good was a weather mage to a quarry? Sure, he could provide cloud cover or create breezes to make workers more comfortable, but he certainly didn't provide any useful contributions of Sun Crystal to the foreman each evening.

Did he stay because of his reliance on familiarity?

The only thing in his entire life he counted as useful was work with the other Weathers to summon showers so crops grew in excess in this desert highland. He supposed creating storms and rain wasn't entirely useless, but that work only happened for a portion of the year and their small settlement didn't need eight Weathers to complete the tasks needed for growing crops. His presence and talents were in excess. What really was stopping him?

Castell looked around him. To his right his father chiseled at a crystal, and he could hear the faint hum of *Beneath the Canopy*. It was a song Castell heard often over the years, and his father once admitted he sang it because it reminded him of his childhood home. On a higher rocky outcropping, his brother too chiseled at a crystal, but his movements were aggressive, as if he could simply coerce the stone to give up its prize instead of gently removing the layers. His father and brother were far enough away that he couldn't talk to them, but at least they were there, always in range for a shout or breezed message. Would it be their presence he missed if he left?

If I found a life somewhere else, I would be completely alone.

Leaving here would come with a huge amount of loss. Could he actually handle that kind of breakaway? Tucking an errant strand of his sun-lightened brown hair behind his ear—he really needed another trimming—Castell replaced his hat and set his chisel to the stone once more. Light taps flaked the bleached shale around the base of the Sun Crystal.

But should my fear prevent me from living a life I might enjoy? I would hate staying here for the rest of my life, that is certain. If I join the war I could put my gift to better use. Yes?

Leaving was a question he'd contemplated for months. He'd hesitated between staying and going. Life in Sun Glimmer was familiar and comfortable, but he also wasn't happy. He needed to decide. Stay or go? A simple question with a complicated answer.

He could be an asset to the war effort. Spending hours at a time maintaining breezes for himself and others had made him a strong mage. Those with exceptional gifts were always wanted, right? Maybe that was his own justification, since he had no formal schooling thanks to his parents' beliefs, but Castell felt he could hold his own against at least a Prime Mage, a Cleric classification. It was his estimate. The majority of the castings he knew now were niche, designed specifically to benefit Sun Glimmer. Maybe, given the proper knowledge, he could work castings better suited to war. But what would his parents think of him leaving to join a decades long conflict?

His parents would hate his decision.

Every resident of the quarry kept discussion of the war hush, and his parents were no exception. Questions or comments that could start even a flicker of a debate were snuffed. Out here, no one wanted to be involved with the fighting, even though they still craved the latest news of the conflict. What was it with people who wouldn't fight but still opined on something? That alone made leaving to join the war more appealing. At least his magic could be used for something more than mundane tasks. What Castell didn't know—because no one would tell him—was which side he should support. That was the problem of living with pacifists.

He agreed that the fighting should stop. It was doing nothing for their society or the land, but he wanted to know which faction would bring about the best changes.

If there was such a thing as winning in war.

The most recent merchant caravan brought news that the battles along the great river had become worse. Each side gathered more and more followers, making the war a constant tug of back and forth between sides. The news of a once lush area now barely clinging to survival had saddened his father.

The most hated side from overheard conversations in the tavern, and the one often blamed to have started the war, were The Clerics; and those allegedly justified in their retaliation were The Purists. The Clerics believed a centralized system of government should be in place where the strongest mages filled the more prominent ranks. The Purists believed that the way life had been for hundreds of years—groups of people living as they wished with their own government structures—should remain untouched. In Purist living, information passed from older mages to the younger, and every once in a while, a new spell was discovered. The information was then given to traders and passed around to other settlements. Clerics wanted people to always push the limits of their understanding, studying to gain mastery with ruthless zeal. Castell did question the Clerics' ideologies when the ways of Purists had worked for so many generations. What really did they gain from their system? No one he knew had an answer nor wanted to answer his question.

Right now, not knowing which side to support was the major reason preventing him from leaving his small community. It was a tough decision to make. On the one hand, there was something redeemable in a planned, standardized structure of government that had balance, but he did question why the most *powerful* mages should be the ones in charge and decide things. Just because he was a strong Weather Mage didn't mean he should be the quarry's foreman. Here in Sun Glimmer, no one cared about your magical strength. Everything of importance was debated by those who had seen at least twenty summers or more, which was most of the settlement. Decisions often took weeks, if not months, to make collectively. He'd been a part of every one of the Fire Talks for six summers now and he hated them, even if they were necessary. There seemed to be a constant lack of keenness to move through the agenda. It frustrated him.

Despite his lack of enthusiasm for the meetings, Castell recognized the value of multiple voices being heard. His father was an Indigo Mage, using his gift to tell complex stories with detailed illusions. But that didn't mean he should be automatically overruled by someone just because they were more powerful.

Castell scrunched his face. Why couldn't there be some type of compromise? Designing a hierarchical rating system could help magic-users know where they could put their skills to use more efficiently, but that system did not have to come with dogmatic rules. Did it? From what his parents had told him, sharing all knowledge had been the basis of society until the Clerics, born out of a group who created the Magic School System, sought control.

Frustration surged in Castell and he huffed out a breath. All of his knowledge still brought him back to the question of what he should do about it. Should he follow the path of his parents and remain an uncertain pacifist? Should he join the Purists? The Clerics? Which choice would bring back some semblance of normalcy? What was normal? If the Fire Talks taught him anything, it was that 'normal' meant something different to each person.

Castell threw his tools to the ground in front of him, which made Olke perk her large ears. He reached over and scratched the small fox. The attention had her crawling into his lap with a flick of her black-tipped tail. Castell smiled at the little fox, no bigger than the length of his forearm. He'd found Olke as a kit abandoned and terrified in one of the many tunnels of the quarry, her sandy fur mud-caked. She'd cried in fear with her warbling chirp each time she saw him before he'd given her enough food to show that he was trustworthy. Now Olke was an inseparable companion. Many didn't understand why he kept company with one of the many predators roaming the quarries, but Castell couldn't let her starve. He knew the way of things in the wild. Animals died all the time without the intervention of mages. He had just chosen for it to not be this one.

Olke's affection made him feel better, but it didn't distract him. The manual labor of the quarry did nothing to improve his thoughts, and right now, anything looked more appealing than the work in front of him, even the war. He, of course, needed to finish chiseling this Sun Crystal before he could retire for the day. Castell retrieved his chisel and hammer. Striking the rock, he concluded he needed information. He would only get it by confronting his parents. In the past, they'd scarcely mentioned the war and their reasons for fleeing. Now their silence wasn't a good enough answer. If he was going to make a proper decision, he needed his parents to talk about the war, and he would do it tonight. The topic would pain them because it had uprooted their lives, but Castell no longer wanted to live in ignorance or passivity. He might agree with some of his parents' ideals, but living noncommittally would not cut it for him anymore.